Praise for Stuart MacBride

'A magnetic mix of creepy places, dark humour,
horror and violence'
Sun

'Dark and brilliantly written'
Linwood Barclay

'MacBride is a damned fine writer'
Peter James

'MacBride's thrillers just keep getting better'
Express

www.penguin.co.uk

By Stuart MacBride

STANDALONE
The Dead of Winter

THE OLDCASTLE NOVELS
Birthdays for the Dead
A Song for the Dying
A Dark So Deadly
The Coffinmaker's Garden
No Less the Devil

THE LOGAN MCRAE NOVELS
Cold Granite
Dying Light
Broken Skin
Flesh House
Blind Eye
Dark Blood
Shatter the Bones
Close to the Bone
22 Dead Little Bodies
The Missing and the Dead
In the Cold Dark Ground
Now We Are Dead
The Blood Road
All That's Dead

OTHER WORKS
Sawbones (a novella)
12 Days of Winter (a short-story collection)
Partners in Crime (two Logan and Steel short stories)
The 45% Hangover (a Logan and Steel novella)
The Completely Wholesome Adventures of Skeleton Bob
(a picture book)

WRITING AS STUART B. MACBRIDE
Halfhead

THE DEAD OF WINTER

STUART MACBRIDE

PENGUIN BOOKS

TRANSWORLD PUBLISHERS
Penguin Random House, One Embassy Gardens,
8 Viaduct Gardens, London SW11 7BW
www.penguin.co.uk

Transworld is part of the Penguin Random House group of companies
whose addresses can be found at global.penguinrandomhouse.com

First published in Great Britain in 2023 by Bantam
an imprint of Transworld Publishers
Penguin paperback edition published 2023

A CIP catalogue record for this book
is available from the British Library.

ISBN
9780552178327

Typeset in Stone Serif ITC Pro 9.25/13pt by Jouve (UK), Milton Keynes.
Printed and bound in Great Britain by Clays Ltd, Elcograf S.p.A.

The authorized representative in the EEA is Penguin Random House Ireland,
Morrison Chambers, 32 Nassau Street, Dublin D02 YH68.

Penguin Random House is committed to a sustainable
future for our business, our readers and our planet. This book
is made from Forest Stewardship Council® certified paper.

For Victoria Wood

master of the non sequitur, maestro of the absurd;
an alchemist who could turn mundane life into absolute gold

who's probably had more of an influence
on my writing than anyone else

1953–2016

—trust no one—

(unless you *want* stabbed in the back)

O

I never really wanted to be a police officer.

Thick flakes of white drift down from a low, grey sky, adding their weight to the drooping branches of beech trees. Making the gorse and broom slump in surrender.

A burn gurgles, just out of sight behind knotted clumps of barbed-wire brambles.

A duvet of white smothers the forest clearing, snow robbing the shapes and colour from everything, leaving only the frozen ghosts of what lies buried beneath.

I wanted to be an astronaut, or a football player, or a rock star . . .

Everything is calm and still and crisp, marred only by a line of deep footprints and a smooth-edged scar where something heavy has been dragged through the drifts.

Then there's the noise: the *ping and clang* of a pickaxe, chipping away at the frozen ground – a regular, methodical sound, an industrial metronome, marking out the time of death. Every blow accompanied by a grunt of exertion.

My big brother, Dave, he was the one meant to follow the family tradition and join up, but a drunk driver blew straight through the Holburn Street junction, and that was that.

*

The person swinging that pickaxe is tall, broad-shouldered, powerful. Hair pulled back from her flushed face. Mid-forties, give or take a year or two.

Her high-vis padded jacket hangs from the branch of a twisted Scots pine, like a flayed skin – one of the sleeves blackened with blood, more smears on the front. A second jacket, dark as coal, and a petrol-blue shirt are draped over another branch.

Steam rises from the shoulders of her burgundy T-shirt. You'd think she'd be wearing something a bit more ... *death-metal*-like. You know: a skull and crossbones, or a snake with a dagger in its teeth, but her T-shirt features a cartoon black cat in a bow-tie and eye patch, posing with a gun like it's from a James Bond movie.

The hole's already waist-deep, a pile of dark earth slumping beside it. A wooden-handled shovel poking out of the heap, like a skeletal flag.

Dave swapped his police dreams for a wheelchair, and I swapped mine for a warrant card. Cos that's what you do when your dad's a cop, and his dad before him, and his dad before that.

A body lies off to one side, partly covered by a stained sheet, curled against the Scots pine's hungry roots.

The body's high-vis jacket is the twin of the one hanging from the branch, only there's a *lot* more blood. Deep scarlet stains the jacket's fluorescent-yellow back; it's soaked into the grubby-grey suit underneath too. The jacket's owner doesn't look a day over twenty-four, but he does look very, *very* dead. His skin's got that waxy, translucent, mortuary colour to it, where it isn't smeared in dark red. More blood on his shirt, and on the cheeks of his sharp-featured face. Bags under his closed eyes. Short brown hair and a matching Vandyke ...

Strange the way things turn out, isn't it?

The muscled woman in the cartoon-cat T-shirt stops swinging the pickaxe and stands there for a moment, head back, breath fogging above her as the snow falls. Face pink and shiny.

*

Sorry – where are my manners? The lady doing the digging is one Detective Inspector Victoria Elizabeth Montgomery-Porter, North East Division.

Some people call her 'Bigtoria', but never to her face.

She tosses the pickaxe out of the hole and grabs the shovel instead. Muscles bunch and writhe in her thick arms as she digs, the shovel's blade biting into the loosened soil, before flinging it onto the pile.

She's not the worst boss I've ever had. And yeah, given what's happened, that's pretty hard to believe. Sometimes events just get away from you and before you know it: there you are, in the middle of a remote, snowy glen, digging a shallow grave.

The shovel growls as Bigtoria stabs it into the ground, stones and dirt adding their mouldy-bread scent to the peppery ozone tang of falling snow.

I, on the other hand, am Detective Constable Edward Reekie. And I guess you could say I'm having a very bad day.

One last shovelful gets added to the pile before Bigtoria scrambles out of her pit, then stomps over to the body, scoops her hands in under its armpits and drags it back to the hole.

It's weird. I know I should be angry about it – furious even – you know, being the dead body and everything? But mostly I'm just cold.

Bigtoria tumbles Edward into the pit. Stands there, staring down at him for a moment, head on one side. Shovel held like an executioner's axe. Then she grunts. Grabs her high-vis from the branch.

You'd think she could manage a few words, wouldn't you? Express a bit of sorrow and guilt. Maybe beg my forgiveness? A sodding apology wouldn't hurt.

But Bigtoria doesn't say a thing. Instead, she pulls a mobile phone and a child's walkie-talkie from her jacket pockets. The walkie-talkie's shaped like a clown's head, complete with jaunty red nose and big beaming smile, and it's dwarfed in her huge hand.

Have to admit, this isn't exactly the funeral I thought I'd end up with. I'd kinda hoped for more mourners, maybe a few tears, some inspiring speeches about what a great guy I was. Distraught wife, two-point-four inconsolable children, and a heartbroken golden retriever.

She chucks her emptied jacket into the shallow grave. It lands on Edward's body, hiding his bloodied, dirty face. Followed by the bloodstained sheet he was wrapped in.

And it's not like I wanted a massive mausoleum – a nice headstone would've done.

A shovelful of dirt and gravel patters down on the jacket. Then another one. And another.

After all, it's not like any of this was my fault.

An electronic twiddling noise bursts into life somewhere nearby. It's a cheap one-note-at-a-time rendition of that olde-worlde circus theme tune: *Yata, yadda yadda, yata yaaaaaa da.*

There's a pause, some swearing, then a bleep as Bigtoria presses the clown's nose. She barks into it, hard and sharp as the pickaxe's blade: *'What?'*

A distorted voice crackles out of the walkie-talkie. It's an old man, sounding every bit as cold and sharp as Bigtoria, but where her accent is posh-girl Scottish, his is gravelly Glaswegian. Redolent with tenements, whisky, and putting the boot in. *'Is it done?'*

'God's sake. I'd get through this quicker' – she's getting louder with every word – *'if you didn't keep checking up on me'* – till she's roaring it out – *'EVERY BLOODY MINUTE!'*

Silence falls with the snow, settling into the landscape. Now the only sounds are the babbling burn, the jagged cawing of a distant crow, and Bigtoria's breathing. In and out like angry bellows.

The man's voice sounds again. *'Just get it done.'*

There's a snarl. A sigh. And another shovelful of dirt clatters down on Edward's body.

Bigtoria keeps filling in the shallow grave. *'Should* never *have agreed to this.'*

Like she's *the one lying at the bottom of a shallow grave.*

On and on the earth rattles down, till there's nothing left but muffled death.

But I'm getting ahead of myself. Probably better if we start at the beginning . . .

—the beginning—

(AKA: before it all went horribly wrong)

I

'. . . *so stay tuned for that.*' The cheery DJ's voice crackled out of the pool car's speakers, turned down till it was barely audible. *'You're listening to* Carole's Cavalcade, *it's ten forty-five on a lovely Tuesday morning, and we've got some excellent tunes coming up . . .'*

That weird creaking squeak was back – getting louder every time Edward tapped the brakes. Which wasn't exactly reassuring.

The Vauxhall's dashboard was as filthy as the rest of it: a grey fur of dust, streaked by the occasional finger. That was the trouble with pool cars: no one ever cleaned the bloody things, did they? Just added to the mess and left it for the next poor sod to deal with. Only the next poor sod never did. And on and on and on it went.

A parade of never-ending grubbiness and passing the buck.

That was a metaphor for your modern Police Scotland right there.

Bigtoria filled the passenger seat like a grumpy bear, squinting out through the windscreen, phone clamped to her ear. 'Yes, uh-huh . . . No . . . Not a chance.'

Which was nearly as many words as she'd said to him on the journey from Aberdeen. Because why speak to the lowly Detective Constable when you were a lofty DI?

'*So, let's get this party back on track with Stereoface and their brand-new single, "Dancemonkey!"*' Cheerful music burbled out of the car's stereo. Not bad. Not *great*. But not bad.

Gave him something to hum along to, anyway. Tapping his fingers on the steering wheel as a bland slice of the north-east slid by. With only the chimney sticking out the top of Peterhead Power

Station to break the monotony – trailing a line of bright white steam across the sapphire sky.

A sneaky peek to the left.

Bigtoria was still at it. Squinting and scowling. Radiating brooding menace. Because detective inspectors loved that kind of thing, didn't they: like they'd seen one too many crime dramas on TV and decided that was the look for them. 'I don't care what he says, the man's an idiot . . . Yes . . . As *mince*, that's how thick he is.'

Hadn't even cracked a smile when Edward pointed out they were twinnies today: both in machine-washable grey suits with matching white shirts. Yup, no doubt about it: going to be a *long* day.

'. . . Uh-huh . . . Hold on, I'll check.' She transferred her glower from the landscape to Edward. 'We were supposed to be there an *hour* ago.'

He shrugged. 'All due respect, Guv, I wasn't the one who jack-knifed an artic lorry full of tatties all over the A90.'

'Still got a *five-hour* drive ahead of us, and if I'm late for rehearsal tonight, it's you I'm blaming. Now' – spelling it out, like he was thick as mince too – 'when – will – we – get – there?'

Edward checked his phone, sitting in its little plastic mount fixed to the air vent, with the satnav app running. 'Five minutes? Give or take. Going as fast as I can.'

She harrumphed at him. Then back to her phone: 'You hear that? . . . Yes . . . OK. I'll let you know if we get anything.'

The outskirts of Peterhead loomed in the middle distance – all warehouses and business parks, with a smattering of beige and brown housing estates in the background.

Edward took a right at the roundabout – a circular hump of weeds, wedged in between a garage, a McDonald's, and the loneliest-looking KFC in the world – then a sharp left, following the signs to Her Majesty's Prison and Young Offender Institution, Grampian '←Visitors'. Into a quiet rural street fringed with trees and acned with potholes.

Bigtoria hung up and turned the brooding scowl up a notch. 'They want us to grill him about the Abercrombie shooting as well.'

'Never heard of it. Who's—'

'So far that's the Mintlaw Post Office raid' – counting them off on her fingers – 'the Fraserburgh bank job, the Huntly arson attacks, the Gerald Freebairn murder, the disappearance of Emily Lawrie, and now Wayne sodding Abercrombie.'

The trees gave way to a bland housing estate – all service-station-coffee bungalows with brown pantile roofs.

'Yeah.' He slowed past the forbidding pink-granite mass of Burnhaven School. 'No idea who any of those are.'

'Hmph ... Before your time.' A frown creased her forehead. 'Before *my* time, to be honest. But unlike *some* people, I did my homework.'

Oh come on!

He tried for a smile. 'Lowly DC, remember? We're "not paid to think" till we make sergeant. And even then the jury's out.'

Nothing. Not so much as a smirk. She just sat there, face like a skelped arse as four rows of quaint old-fashioned houses appeared, with glimpses of the North Sea shining between their grey granite ranks.

'OK . . .' Try again. 'And how am I supposed to do homework when no one told me I'd be sidekicking you till ninety minutes ago?' He took a hard right at the 'HMP & YOI GRAMPIAN' signs, down the hill, towards the half-empty car park. The North Sea lurked past the last row of parking spots, glittering in the sunshine and dotted with the jolly coloured blobs of offshore supply vessels.

Most of the original Victorian and no-longer-used-as-a-prison prison was hidden away behind a high granite wall on the left of the road, but there was no hiding the newer bulky lumps that made up HMP Grampian. Its boundary wall was probably even taller than the old prison's but the buildings were much, *much* bigger. More like a collection of airport Travelodge hotels than a correctional facility.

Edward followed the arrows on the tarmac towards the ugly Co-op-on-an-industrial-estate-style Family Centre and Help Hub. 'I was *meant* to be having a cushy Tuesday: checking CCTV and drinking tea. Not my fault DC Guthrie got bladdered and fell down the stairs like he was some sort of half-arsed stuntman.' Adding a wee humorous image at the end there, to dial back the petulant whine a bit.

She sniffed. 'As if.'

Well, it wasn't a smile, but it was a start.

'Totally: who'd hire Guthrie to be a stuntman? Guy's got the coordination of a—'

'I meant it's "as if", not "like".' Glowering across the car at him. '"Fell down the stairs *as if* he *were* some sort of stuntman." Didn't they teach grammar at your school?'

Why? Why did he bother?

Detective inspectors were all the sodding same.

He pulled in round the back, parking sideways across the long bay marked 'MOTORBIKES', and climbed out into the crisp sunshine. Ears nipping in the wind, the razor-sharp chill turning his breath into a thin pale fog.

No sign of his resident grammatical pedant, DI Victoria 'As If' Montgomery-Porter. So he opened his door again and peered in at her. 'Guv?'

She looked back at him, face like concrete. 'You're the one who made us late, you're the one who goes to check.'

He straightened up and clunked the door shut.

Then rolled his eyes and bared his teeth.

Flicked the Vs at the car roof, turned on his heel, and stomped off towards the main entrance. Which, let's be honest, had all the architectural charm of a shopping centre crossed with an airport departures lounge. But it was a thousand percent nicer than Detective Inspector Victoria Montgomery-Porter.

Edward eventually found him down the far end of the car park, basking in the arctic sunshine, leaning against an old Volvo estate and staring out to sea.

Mr Bishop had to be eighty-something if he was a day, bent under the weight of a curved spine. His suit probably went out of fashion long before Edward was even born – a sort of blue herringbone tweed thing, with a grey tweed waistcoat. White shirt, blue tie. A luxurious camel-hair coat on over the top. Only none of it seemed to fit, like it'd been made for a bigger, younger man, not this little, white-haired OAP with a hunched back and arthritic fingers.

'Mr Bishop?'

A cigarette dangled from the wrinkled corner of his mouth. Which probably wasn't that great an idea, given the oxygen mask in his left hand. The mask was connected to a knee-high brown gas cylinder, strapped into a wheeled trolley thing. One of those old-fashioned suitcases sat beside it – the kind that didn't even have *wheels* – and a cheap, metal NHS walking stick rounded off the outfit.

'Mr Bishop? Mr Mark Bishop?'

The crooked man swung his watery grey eyes away from the sea and the boats. Voice like honeyed gravel. 'Depends who's asking, son.'

'DC Reekie. Edward. Me and DI Montgomery-Porter are here to take you to Glenfarach?'

Back to the boats again. 'Is that so?' A smile spread its slow way across Mr Bishop's face, then he sooked on his cigarette – the fag cupped in his right hand, hidden away, in case someone stole it. '"Edward Reekie"? Let me guess: the other kids at school were cruel, weren't they? Name like that.'

Cheeky bugger.

Edward stuck his chest out. 'You want a lift or not?' He pointed at the tank. 'And you shouldn't be smoking around one of those.'

'Don't listen to them, son. Kids are vicious little bastards. Especially when they smell weakness.'

'Seriously, oxygen and naked flames don't mix.'

Mr Bishop took another drag, then a tote of oxygen. 'Least I'll go out with a bang.' He gazed at his cigarette like it was a kitten, or a puppy. 'Besides, this is the only vice I've got left.' A sigh. A nod. He abandoned the Volvo and leaned on his NHS walking stick instead, the rubber tip *skiff-thunk*ing against the tarmac, the wheels on his oxygen tank squeaking as he shuffled off, leaving his suitcase behind. He didn't look back. 'Be a good lad and bring that, would you?'

Lazy old git.

But Edward grabbed the suitcase anyway, grunting as the thing barely left the ground. What the hell did he have in here: breeze blocks? Had to use both hands to carry it, leaning sideways to counterbalance the weight as he waddled after Mr Bishop.

Even going at auld-mannie pace, Edward didn't manage to catch up till they reached the manky Vauxhall, where Bigtoria had her bum perched on the bonnet, her back to them. She was hunched over, massaging her temples with one hand and clamping her phone to her ear with the other.

Sounding pained. 'I'm not *saying* that, I'm saying— . . . Of course I'm not going to abandon the operation. We've come too far for that . . . Uh-huh . . . Yes.'

Edward clattered that horrible, heavy suitcase down by the boot. 'Guv?'

No response. 'Well, I know it's not ideal, but we'll just have to improvise, won't we . . . Uh-huh: make the best of it . . . *Exactly*. That's what I thought.'

He tried a singsong voice instead. 'Gu-uv?'

Still nothing. 'We can salvage this; but it's going to take a bit of—'

A shrill whistle sliced through the air, then Mr Bishop lowered his fingers from his mouth. 'HOY, BIGTORIA! You still into all that am-dram crap?'

She froze for a moment. Then sat up straight. 'I'll phone you back.' Bigtoria hung up, but didn't turn around. Voice flat and cold as a mortuary slab. '*What* did you call me?'

A grin split Mr Bishop's face. 'Well, well, if it isn't Police Constable Victoria Montgomery-Porter, all growed up and in plainclothes.'

She turned, bringing an industrial-strength glare with her.

Didn't seem to bother him, though. He took one last drag on his cigarette and pinged the smouldering butt away into the bushes.

'Littering is an *offence*, Mr Bishop.'

'Aye, what you going to do: arrest me? And you're late.' He scuffed his way to the pool car's rear passenger door, dumped the oxygen tank in the footwell, and creaked himself inside. 'Get a shift on. I don't have all day.'

Bigtoria's face was heading towards an unhealthy shade of puce. Edward tried a smile. 'Found him.'

'Lucky me.'

Edward popped the boot, hefted that heavy-arsed suitcase ... and stopped. Some idiot had left a dented metal toolbox in there – chickenpoxed with stickers advertising various shows: *Sweeney Todd*, *Dracula Reborn*, *Les Misérables*, *The Crucible* ... But the biggest sticker of all had 'V.E.M.P.' printed on it in big black letters.

Ah, OK. Victoria Elizabeth Montgomery-Porter. It was the DI's.

He shoved it to the side and squeezed Mr Bishop's suitcase in beside it.

Quick look left and right, to make sure no one was watching, then Edward had a wee nosy in the toolbox. The different levels cantilevered out as he opened it, exposing row after row of pots and sticks of stage make-up. Letting free the stodgy, waxy scent of past-their-sell-by-date candles.

Urgh.

He closed the thing again.

Well, she did *say* she had a rehearsal tonight.

By the time he'd clunked the boot shut and climbed in behind the wheel, she was scowling at him from the passenger seat, tapping her watch like somehow this was all his fault.

'When you're ready, *Constable*.'

Mr Bishop sat in the back seat, looking up at the grey prison boundary wall. Eyes misty and damp, like he was seeing through it to something inside.

'Hmph ...' Bigtoria hauled on her seatbelt. 'Homesick for your cell already?'

His rattling sigh wheezed out into the car. 'It's not the place, it's the *people* you miss. Got friends in there who won't get out till long after I'm dead and buried.' There was a pause. And a nod. 'Makes a man think.'

Edward started the engine, doing his best to sound bright and positive. 'You can always come back and visit, Mr Bishop. Your friends would like that.'

'Sod off, son. I'm never setting foot in that place ever again.'

2

Something soothing and classical burbled from the car's speakers as Edward took them south, towards Ellon. The countryside was painted in sparse tones of burnt toast, and cheap margarine, no green left in the grass or hedgerows. The trees and bushes reduced to jagged skeletal ink blots.

Bigtoria and Mr Bishop weren't exactly the most exciting of travelling companions. She was head down, fiddling on her phone; he was in the back, staring out the window with his wrinkles drooping – like he was remembering unhappy times, filling the rear-view mirror with misery. He'd filled the car with something else, too: the gritty-brown scent of stale cigarettes and the sharp, chemical tang of an aftershave that probably went out of fashion round about the same time as his suit. You could taste them both with every inhale – sour and burnt.

'So . . . Marky.' Bigtoria turned the radio down. 'You were quite the lad in your day, weren't you?'

A grunt from the back, and the old man checked his watch. 'Twelve minutes. Got to be something of a record, that.'

'Only making conversation, Marky. We've got a long drive ahead of us.'

'They give you a list of things to grill me about? See if you can't get me to rat someone out, or cop to a cheeky murder or two on the way? Help clean up your backlog?'

She pursed her lips, gave a theatrical shrug. 'Like I say, it's going to be a long drive.'

The car grumbled on down the road.

A taxi went past, the other way.

A Ford Focus driven by some spotty wee Herbert overtook them, even though Edward was definitely doing sixty.

And still the silence grew.

Edward cleared his throat. 'You follow the football, Mr Bishop? How do you fancy the Dons' chances tomorrow? Hibs are looking a bit spicy this season.'

Another grunt. 'Nice try, son.' He thumped the handle of his walking stick against the back of Bigtoria's seat. 'Come on then: they give you a list or not?'

'Of course they did.'

Mr Bishop sat forward. 'See, son, this isn't the first time me and your DI have crossed paths. Or swords. When *was* the first time, Bigtoria? Twenty-six, twenty-seven years ago?'

She stiffened. 'My name isn't bloody "Bigtoria"!'

'Aye. Could be worse, could be "Stinky Ted", right, son?'

Edward tightened his grip on the steering wheel, jaw clamped shut.

The old scumbag smiled. 'No offence.'

'. . . which of course brings us to 1838 and Chopin's intense love affair with the French author, George Sand, which was the pen name of Amantine Lucile Aurore Dupin . . .'

The world had opened out on either side of the road into a bland, flat plain. Carved into squares of dead grass or frost-paled ranks of ploughed earth. Here and there, sheep stood, focused on the task of cramming neeps down their gullets, between bright-orange strands of temporary electric fencing.

Fun, fun, fun.

'. . . but they had to leave Majorca when Chopin contracted tuberculosis, travelling to Marseille to rest and recover . . .'

Edward cleared his throat again.

Mr Bishop sighed.

Bigtoria poked away at yet another text message. *Tick-tick, tick-tick-tick-tick-tick, tick-tick . . .*

Yup, laugh a minute.

'But it was there that Chopin composed his magnificent Piano Sonata Number Three in B Minor, played here by the wonderful Ray Ushikubo.'

As the opening notes rang out through the car, Mr Bishop shifted in his seat. 'You'd think more would've changed, wouldn't you? But this place is every bit as sharny and dreich as it was a quarter-century ago.' He glowered out at a lake of mud. 'Twenty-five years gives you a lot of time to think, son. See, there was a time when I would've given anything to get your DI here in a soundproofed room with a pair of pliers and blowtorch.' He hit the back of her seat again. 'Ain't that right, Bigtoria?'

She kept on texting. *Tick-tick-tick, tick-tick, tick-tick-tick-tick-tick . . .*

'Course you were just a wee PC at the time, weren't you? Or was it still "policewoman" in those days? Before you lot went all politically correct. A wee PC with a big nose and a weird ability to get certain of my business associates to tell you things they really, *really* shouldn't.'

She didn't look up, but she did smile. 'They were surprisingly helpful.'

Mr Bishop's voice darkened. 'Life sentence with a minimum term of thirty-two years doesn't sound very helpful to me.'

'And yet here you are, only twenty-five years later, having a nice day out in the countryside.'

Edward tensed, waiting for the shouting to start, but instead Mr Bishop let loose a rattling laugh, that ended in coughing and wheezing. Shuddering, gasping, trying to haul in some air, before collapsing back in his seat and scrambling for the oxygen mask.

Then deep hissing breaths, eyes closed, till the trembling faded. 'God's sake . . .' Sounding every one of his eighty-plus years, voice echoing inside the mask like a dying Darth Vader. 'Go on . . . go on then . . . give us . . . your list.'

She put her phone down. 'Wayne Abercrombie.'

'Doesn't ring . . . a bell.'

'Property developer. Someone doorstepped him at home in Stonehaven – with a sawn-off shotgun.'

Mr Bishop lowered the mask. 'I knew men who'd name their shooters. Treat them better than they'd treat their women.' A note of nostalgia crept in. 'You ever meet Bulldog Riley? Ran protection for Wee Hamish Mowat's crew? Had this beautiful side-by-side Winchester twelve gauge – all engraved stock and fancy fretwork. Called it "Maggie", after his dear old mum. Used her to take the kneecaps off bastards who shirked their financial obligations.'

'You're saying this "Bulldog Riley" killed Wayne Abercrombie?'

A dismissive hand. 'Nah, course I'm not. I'm just reminiscing. I could never see the point naming a shooter. Shooter's a tool, like a spanner or a hammer; you don't name your screwdrivers, do you?'

True.

Edward nodded. 'Maybe they do it because they think it makes them sound scary?'

'You turn up on some bugger's doorstep at seven in the morning and stick a sawn-off in his face, he's going to be plenty scared enough, son.' Bigtoria's seat got another thump. 'Who else you got?'

'Gerald Freebairn.'

A frown in the rear-view mirror. 'He that nonce from Glasgow, got himself peeled like an onion and dumped in the Loch of Skene?' Sounding more and more tired. 'Oh, I remember him *fine*. Word is he was scouting for the Morrison Brothers – thought they could muscle in on the drug scene. Seems Freebairn trod on the wrong toes.'

'*Your* toes?'

'Nah . . .' It went quiet for a moment, like Mr Bishop was trying to work up the energy to say anything else. 'I was never into peeling folk . . . Not my style. Too . . . fiddly. Who's got time for that?'

She turned in her seat. 'Would you tell us, even if you had?'

The wrinkles deepened across his forehead. 'You remembering . . . why they let me . . . out seven years early?' Every breath a whistling gasp. 'Got . . . got no reason . . . to lie . . . I'd be long gone . . . before anything came . . . to trial.' Mr Bishop clamped the oxygen mask into place, muffling his voice again. 'Tired . . . Think I'll . . . I'll just shut . . . my eyes for . . . for a bit.'

The sonata rattled on, but there was nothing else from Mr Bishop.

More miserable fields passed by. More miserable farmhouses. More miserable sheep.

The poor old sod in the rear-view mirror did *not* look well. Slumped there, with his head sagging back, making scuba-diver sounds.

Edward lowered his voice. 'Think he's going to croak before we get there?'

Bigtoria snorted, sticking to full volume. 'We should be so lucky.'

The blue sky that had followed them all the way from Peterhead had darkened and lost its shine, turning to a layer of murky clay by the time they reached Bridge of Alford. Now tiny flakes of white settled against the windscreen, melting as they hit the warm glass.

Mr Bishop had his thinking frown on again. 'A bank heist in Peterhead? Naw . . .'

'*Fraserburgh*.' Bigtoria narrowed her eyes at the rear view. 'The bank was in Fraserburgh. And it wasn't a heist, it was a tiger kidnap. Grabbed the bank manager's wife and daughter, threatened to rape and kill them both if he didn't unlock the safe and help empty it.'

'Oh aye?' Hard to tell if Mr Bishop could've sounded more bored by that if he'd tried. 'They get away with much?'

'Two-point-five *million* in cash and God knows how much in safety-deposit boxes. Money's never been recovered. And they raped his family anyway.' She swivelled around, till she was staring over her shoulder. 'Six months later, the bank manager's wife kills herself and her daughter. Sleeping pills. Couldn't cope any more. He has a breakdown and chucks himself off the cliffs at Kinnaird Head Lighthouse.'

Mr Bishop's chin came up, bringing with it a dangle of pale wrinkly wattle. 'You really think I'd have anything to do with raping a *kid*? Hope the bastards burn in hell.' This time his NHS walking stick tapped Edward on the shoulder. 'We there yet?'

Edward checked the map on his phone. 'Hour and twenty minutes.'

'Gah . . .' He bared smoker's-yellow teeth at the village. 'When did houses get to be so bloody ugly? Everything's prefab these days.'

Bigtoria had another go. 'What about Emily Lawrie, then? She disappeared.'

'You got anything to eat?'

'Does this *look* like meals on wheels? Now answer the question: Emily Lawrie. We know you knew her. What happened?'

Mr Bishop shoogled in his seat. 'I've got to eat at regular times, or I'll end up with a hypoglycaemic episode. That what you want?' Pulling out his cigarettes. 'I'm on twenty different types of pills.'

Her finger jabbed at him. 'No you don't. No smoking in the car, it's against the law.'

'Then pull over and let me have a damn fag.'

Edward slowed as they turned the corner into what should probably have been the middle of the village, but they must've passed through it already without noticing. They were on the outskirts again. But there *was* a pub, on the left, just before the bridge. He pointed. 'Could see if they'll do us a couple of sandwiches?'

Bigtoria shook her head. 'Keep going.'

OK . . .

He took a right at the junction, following the signs for the A97, spurning the heady delights promised by the A944 – Alford, Aberdeen, and Banchory – and heading towards the Cairngorms National Park instead.

Five more granite houses and he was accelerating out through the limits. Past yet more trees and fields.

Mr Bishop had another shoogle. 'I need a piss too.'

Bigtoria faced front again. 'Tie a knot in it.'

'You try being eighty-two: see how "robust" your bladder is.'

'We're *not* stopping.'

'When you're hosing out the back of the car, don't say I didn't warn you!'

Edward winced. 'Guv?'

'Oh, for God's sake.' She growled for a moment, then: 'Fine.' Glared at Edward. 'Pull over.'

'Where?' It was all just fields and trees, no sign of a public toilet anywhere.

'The nearest sodding bush.'

'Urgh . . .' Edward stamped his feet, then huffed a breath into his cupped hands, getting a faceful of steam for his troubles. Which was better than the steam rising off what Mr Bishop was doing.

It wasn't what you'd call 'private' – a clump of woodland by the side of a track, just far enough from the road to mean passing vehicles couldn't cop a look at an old man struggling to pee.

At least their rusty Vauxhall was only barely visible through the bushes and trees.

The oxygen tank's wheelie trolley thing threatened to tip over, so Edward stopped warming his hands and grabbed the handle again.

Mr Bishop rocked back and forwards, cigarette poking out the side of his mouth, as he tried to anoint a sycamore tree trunk with a sputtering dribble of stewed-tea urine. Which stank, by the way.

Edward grimaced as another waft of bitter green slithered in his direction. 'Did you have *asparagus* for breakfast?'

'*I* can't smell anything.' He gave himself a jiggle, getting nothing but a trickle in return. 'This would go easier without you bloody watching me.'

Yeah, because this was how Edward wanted to spend his Tuesday lunchtime.

'Sorry, my DI says I have to. Think she's worried you'll do a runner.'

'Hmmph. She always was a bitch.' He grunted out another feeble stream. 'Never get old, son, your prostate'll hate you.'

'She showed me the charge sheet, from when you got sent down?' A glance back towards the car. No sign of Bigtoria. Which was just as well. 'Did you *really* kill Nigel McLean with a circular saw?'

'Naw. Killed him with a crowbar. Took my time too. The circular saw was for chopping him up. Christ, what a mess that made. See, there's a wee hole where the saw spits out sawdust and skelfs and that, only when you're doing a body it's bone and blood and *bits* everywhere . . .' Straining to get a tiny spattering of festering brown. 'Judge said it was "A particularly vicious and brutal slaying, devoid of mercy or pity." Was quite proud of that.'

What a *lovely* old man.

Still, this was a chance to earn some brownie points with the DI while Mr Bishop was in the mood to chat. 'What about this Emily Lawrie woman?'

'That wasn't me, son, it was Black Joe Ivanson. And that's not me ratting him out, cos he popped his clogs in the first wave. Mind you, from what I heard he was in a home with dementia at the time, so maybe getting the Covid was a blessing?' One more rocking, straining, fruitless grimace. Then Mr Bishop hauled in a deep breath and bellowed it out at his own genitals: 'IN THE NAME OF CHRIST, WILL YOU JUST PISS!'

Edward slid back in behind the wheel.

As his door clunked shut, Bigtoria *actually* looked up from her phone for a change. Frowned. Suspicious. 'Where's Marky Bishop?'

Edward hooked a thumb over his shoulder. 'Says it was some "Black Joe Ivanson" bloke who killed Emily Lawrie, but the guy's dead, so—'

Bigtoria's eyes bugged. 'Why on earth did you leave him unsupervised?' She scrambled out of the car. 'If he's done a runner, I'll bloody kill you!'

Sod.

Edward hurried out after her. 'How's he going to do a runner? He's eighty-two; he's on oxygen; he can barely walk!'

That got him a full-strength glare.

'With . . . all due respect. Guv.' Edward pointed up the track. 'Look.'

Mr Bishop hobbled out of the woods, leaning on his walking stick like it was the only thing holding him up, dragging his oxygen tank behind him.

'See? No harm done.'

Bigtoria turned on Edward, face a mass of angry lines and teeth.

'When I tell you to watch a suspect, *Constable*, you bloody well watch them!' Spittle flying.

He shrunk away from the car. 'I was . . . It wasn't . . .'

Mr Bishop struggled his way to the rear passenger-side door, and fumbled it open. Stood there puffing and panting for a moment, then held up his hands, like a surgeon. 'Got any . . . any wet wipes?'

Bigtoria narrowed her eyes, grinding out every word. 'Get – in – the – car!'

He glowered back at her, then sniffed, shrugged like he didn't care, and folded himself into his seat. 'More hygienic in sodding prison.'

Soon as his door shut, Bigtoria jabbed a finger across the car roof, giving Edward her *full* attention. 'Don't you *ever* do that again. You go against a direct order and I swear on my mother's life: I will *end* you!' She stayed there, glaring at him. Then jabbed her finger once more. And got into the car.

Soon as she was out of sight, he rolled his eyes and sagged. Kept his voice so low even he could barely hear it. 'Mr Bishop was right, you are a complete—'

Her voice boomed out from inside. *'Now, Constable!'*

Some days it was great being a police officer.

This was *not* one of those days.

3

Icy specks of white drifted down from gunmetal clouds as the pool car coasted to a halt in front of the padlocked, eight-foot-tall chain-link gates blocking the single-track road. More chain-link stretched off into the distance on either side of the greying tarmac – swallowed by the trees that reached away up the hill. Rising in angry ranks.

Mountains glowered down at the car: left, right, and dead ahead. Dark silhouettes, lurking against the snow-laden sky. More *Deliverance* than *Sound of Music*.

A trio of signs added a cheery air to the fence – which, on closer examination, had razor wire looped around the top of it. 'THE GLENFARACH ESTATE ~ Emergency Vehicles Only Beyond This Point' went perfectly with: 'No Unauthorized Vehicles Allowed Beyond This Point', and, to make sure everyone got the point: 'FOOT AND MOUTH WARNING – NO ACCESS!'

A tall concrete pole sat off to the side, just inside the gates, with three security cameras mounted on it – two facing this way, one watching the road as it slithered away into the forest.

'Forbidding' wasn't a bad word for it.

Edward undid his seatbelt, took a deep breath, and climbed out of the pool car.

Holy crap. It was like jumping into an ice bath; the cold wrapped itself around his chest and *squeezed*. He hurried over to the gates, dug the set of keys from his pocket, and unlocked a thick brass padlock – the metal frigid enough to stick to his fingers. Rattled the chain holding the gate's two sides together, and hauled them open on squealing rusty hinges.

Shivered his way back to the car and threw himself in behind the wheel. 'Dear hairy *Jesus*, it's cold out there.'

Bigtoria just grunted, hunched over her phone, as per sodding usual. Mr Bishop was sparked out in his seat, head back, mouth hanging open like a glistening cave, showing off his dentures.

Edward put the car in gear and drove through the gates. Took a deep breath. Girded his bits. And ventured out into the Arctic Circle again.

They were easier to open than they were to close – fighting him every inch, hinges screaming like pigs in a slaughterhouse as he put his shoulder into it. He used his sleeves as makeshift gloves to get the chain on again, then padlocked it.

Buggering hell: why did everything have to be so *cold*?

Back to the car, ASAP. Thumping into his seat. Slamming the door shut. Curling into himself and shivering. Huffing wobbly breaths into the trembling pink claws pretending to be his hands. 'Gahhhh . . .'

Bigtoria didn't look up from her phone. 'In your own time, Constable Reekie.'

Easy for her to say, sat on her arse in the nice warm car.

Soon as he'd worked a bit of life into his poor, abused fingers, Edward drove off into the falling snow. Getting heavier now. Windscreen wipers thunking back and forth, barely able to clear the glass before it whitened over again. Road was beginning to disappear too, going from frosted grey to dirty white as the flakes built up.

The pool car grumbled its way up a small rise, then down the other side – the single-track tarmac snaking through dense dark woodland. The clawed branches of Forestry pines reaching for the car as it passed, hungry. Searching.

Only thing missing was a sodding gingerbread cottage, a cannibal old wifie, and a talking wolf. On the upside, the trees offered a *little* shelter from the snow, but given the rate it was coming down now, that probably wouldn't last.

Edward checked their passenger in the rear-view mirror. Still fast asleep and showing off that set of twenty-eight artificial teeth. 'So how come we got lumbered playing taxi?'

Bigtoria *tick-tick, tick-tick-tick-tick*ed away at her phone. 'Mark "Marky" Bishop requested us specially.' She raised her head for a moment. 'Well, he requested *me*. You're more of a buy-one-get-one-free.'

The flakes were growing bigger. 'But he blames *you* for getting his mates to clype on him. Why would you want to spend two and a half hours stuck in a car with someone who got you sent down for thirty-plus years?'

No reply.

The road twisted its way further down the hill, windscreen wipers going full pelt now. *Thunk, squonk, thunk, squonk.* Edward clicked on the headlights. Not that they illuminated all that much. Nothing beyond a small cone of light immediately in front of the car, quickly devoured by the swirling snow.

Trees bristled up the valley's sides, disappearing into the low cloud, leaving the pool car trapped at the bottom. Thousands and thousands of ancient pines, looming above them.

Watching.

Waiting.

And instead of doing the sensible thing – turning around and getting the hell out of here – they were heading deeper and deeper into the woods.

Still nothing from Bigtoria.

'Guv?'

She kept her eyes on her phone. 'Suppose Marky Bishop wants to get past deeds off his guilty chest. Like he said: even if he confesses to something, what are we going to do about it? Vicious old sod's already got early release on compassionate grounds; Crown Office won't charge him if he'll be dead before it can go to trial. Waste of time and money.'

In the back, Marky gave a twitch and a snork . . . then settled into soft, wet, rhythmic snores.

Bigtoria frowned. 'Well, it's that or he just felt like screwing with us.'

The pool car broke free of the deep, dark forest, emerging into a long clearing with a little shortbread-tin village at the far end – twinkling frostily in the snow. Slivers of sickly sunlight slashed down through the lid of grey, more in warning than welcome.

No new-build sprawl here, it was all old-fashioned Scottish houses: plain granite walls, black slate roofs, dormer windows for anyone swanky enough to merit an attic extension. Most of it seemed to be arranged around the main road, with maybe a couple of streets on either side. Place was tiny, though. Doubt there could be more than two hundred and fifty people living there. Three hundred tops.

Mounds of dirty snow flanked the road, the tarmac between them visible in sandy patches, like the gritter and snowplough had been through recently. They'd done the pavements too, but the fresh snow was filling it all in again.

Trees surrounded the village, the ordered ranks of Forestry Commission pines giving way to something much older. Maybe even ancient woodland. Twisted and sharp toothed and unwelcoming.

Bigtoria frowned at her phone, holding it up, moving it about. Up. Down. Left. Right. 'Still no bloody signal.'

A big sign with 'WELCOME TO GLENFARACH' sat next to the road, its greeting undermined by the ones clustered around it like angry protesters: 'NO OVERNIGHT PARKING!', 'AUTHORIZED VEHICLES ONLY', 'ALL VISITORS MUST REPORT TO POLICE STATION!'

Edward reached back between the seats and gave Mr Bishop's bony knee a shake. 'Mr Bishop? We're here.'

'Mmmmph?' The deep-sea-diver snoring came to an abrupt halt and Mr Bishop sat bolt upright, letting out a startled fart. Blinking and smacking his lips, peering blearily around him, like he was surprised to be waking up in a car instead of a cell. 'Whmmmt?'

'Glenfarach. We're . . .' Oh no. Oh no, oh no, oh no. The stench of a burning landfill site, laced with a million eggs and four tons of rotting cabbage, whumped through the car.

'Urgh . . .' Bigtoria recoiled, one hand wafting the rancid gas in front of her face.

Coughing and spluttering, Edward wound his window down, letting in a slump of cold *fresh* air. 'Flipping heck. What've they been *feeding* you?'

The stinky old sod scowled in the rear-view mirror. 'Don't be so bloody childish. I can't smell anything.'

'Course not: you smoke four million cigarettes a day.' Cranking the blowers up to full. 'Gah . . . It's stripping the plastic off the dashboard! Your—'

Bigtoria hit him. 'All right, Constable, that's enough. We can do without the toilet humour, thank you very much.'

Spoilsport.

But he left his window open and the blowers on, because, let's face it, that was bloody *rank*.

Lampposts lined the road from here on in. Lots of them. About twice or three times as many as you'd expect in even a busy city centre. Edward sat forward and peered up as they passed one – the thing had two CCTV cameras mounted on top of it. So did the next lamppost. And the one after that. And the ones on the other side of the street too.

That was a bit . . . wasn't it?

Who on earth needed *that* many CCTV cameras? What the hell did they get up to here that required so much surveillance?

Bigtoria shoogled around as far as her seatbelt would let her. 'Our time's nearly up, Mr Bishop. There anything you want to get off your chest? Anything not on our list?'

A big yawn showed off those perfect plastic dentures again, then Mr Bishop had a stretch, cricking his wrinkly neck to one side and then the other. 'Absolutely sodding starving . . .'

Something else that wasn't exactly *right* about the place – all those quaint granite buildings, with their snow-crested slate roofs and gaily coloured front doors, and none of them had a satellite dish.

Weird.

A handful of people were out and about, bundled up against the weather, crunching their way along the pavements. And they all stopped to stare as the pool car rumbled past. A couple even gave Edward a cheery wave. Smiling.

Should've been nice, welcoming, but there was something about it that crawled up his spine with slimy little paws.

'OK . . .' He waved back, doing his best not to look completely creeped out by the freaky sods.

'Hmph.' Bigtoria turned to face front again. 'Thought as much.'

Some of the houses had been converted into shops, with colourful displays in their mullioned windows: an art gallery, a craft shop, a second-hand bookshop, a café with only one person in it.

Then, towering above all the others: a country pub, three whole storeys high, with a gold and red sign on the gable wall where it reared above a plumber's: 'GLENFARACH HOUSE HOTEL ~ LUNCH & DINNER SERVED DAILY ~ BOOKING REQUIRED'.

In the rear-view mirror, Mr Bishop took a hit of oxygen, and frowned out at the bustling metropolis. 'Could go another pee as well.'

Bigtoria bristled. 'Thanks for wasting a whole day of my time, Marky. Very kind of you. What was this: some sort of petty revenge?'

A sigh. 'Not everything's about you.'

That hotel sat on the edge of a largish village square, bordered by its own mini ring road and rows of bare-branched trees. The shape of park benches softening beneath the snow. A smattering of bins for dog waste. No play area, or swings, or even rocking-horse-mounted-on-an-industrial-spring, but a clock tower/monument thing sat in the middle of the square. It was a good twenty or thirty feet tall, with bronze plaques around the bottom; helmets and rifles and swords and flags carved into the pink granite bulk above them; and then the tower itself, crowned by an illuminated clock-face. The hands marked four minutes after two, but two other lines radiated out from the centre – a red one at twenty past four, and a green one at half eight.

Oh, and a whole heap more lampposts.

Because who didn't need loads of those.

Edward pointed at the opposite side of the square. 'This is us.'

It might have been a village hall in a former life, but looked like it'd been 'modernized' sometime in the architecturally murky mid-seventies. Now the imposing granite lump, with its pillars and portico, was topped with an extra storey of concrete and glass. An extension jutted out the side too – *brick*, concrete, and glass this time. Layers of dark-blue cladding between the rows of windows, giving it the striped appearance of an angry zombie bee. Someone had tried to blend the whole thing into the surrounding buildings by hanging one of those twee blue lamps over the main doors, but the backlit sign gave the game away: 'GLENFARACH POLICE STATION'. It was way, *way* bigger than somewhere this small and sleepy should ever need.

As Edward parked outside, a lone figure stepped out of a side door in the new extension bit. She pulled a peaked cap on over her curly auburn hair, rounding off the Police-Scotland-black-and-padded-high-vis-jacket ensemble. Not the tallest of officers, with slightly elfin features, piercing green eyes, and sergeant's stripes on her epaulettes. A bright shade of pink tinged her ears and nose as she hit the cold air. She marched into the road, right in front of the pool car, and held up a hand – like she wanted them to stop, even though they already had.

Bigtoria nodded. 'Constable.'

Sigh. 'Yes, Guv.' And he climbed out into the freezing afternoon. Again. Shoulders hunched, hands buried in his pockets, he crumped his way through the ankle-deep snow. 'Sarge?' Giving her his best professional smile. 'Got a new resident for you: Mr Mark Bishop?'

Those elfin eyes narrowed. 'You're late.'

'I get that a lot.' He worked a hand free of its cosy pocket and held it out. 'Detective Constable Reekie, by the way. Edward.'

Her handshake was firm as a vice. 'Louise Farrow, Glenfarach Duty Sergeant.'

'Cool.' He tipped a nod towards the rusty Vauxhall. 'Where do you want him, Sarge?'

Sergeant Farrow marched across the road to a long-wheelbase Land Rover Defender. 'Follow the Big Car.' It wasn't one of the modern ones either: a proper boxy, old-fashioned, drive-through-everything Defender, kitted out with winter tyres, bull bar, front winch, spotlights, and a massive roof rack. She climbed inside and the engine rumbled into life like a smoker's first cough of the morning. Only instead of tumour-brown sputum, blue-grey fumes sputtered out of the exhaust.

'Lovely.' Edward hurried back to the car. 'Thanks for the warm welcome.' Throwing himself into the driver's seat. Shivering . . .

Hang on a minute.

The binbag smell had dissipated, but something else had clearly happened while he was out talking to Sergeant Not-So-Friendly, because a heavy silence filled the car. The kind of atmosphere you could carve with a spoon. Bigtoria staring out the passenger window; Mr Bishop sitting there with his arms folded and his face blank.

OK . . .

Edward pulled the Vauxhall around. 'Not long now.'

If anything, the silence thickened.

Not his problem, though. Whatever it was, the DI could worry about it.

He followed the Land Rover, up one side of the square, then into a small street, past more twee little granite houses. Another tea shop. Somewhere selling art supplies. Then right, onto a narrow road with bungalows down one side and trees down the other. 'Looks like a nice place, Mr Bishop. I'm sure you'll be very happy here.'

'Hmmph. Going to die here, son. How happy do you think that makes me?'

Fair enough.

'Much nicer than doing it in HMP Grampian, though.'

The road opened up on the left as trees gave way to a chest-high wall and great-big elaborate wrought-iron gates. The church that lurked behind them wasn't huge, but it had a decent spire on it and an extensive graveyard. Not all of them were crumbling lichen-eaten stone either: some were clearly new – the marble still shiny, all topped with a little hat of snow.

A rusty yellow mini-digger was at work, excavating a fresh hole, and the driver stopped what he was doing to smile and wave at Edward and the Land Rover as they pulled up opposite the church gates.

Yeah, that was definitely getting creepier.

Sergeant Farrow climbed out of the Big Car and marched up the snowy ramp that led to a two-storey detached house at least twice the size of everything around it. Even the front door was oversized. She leaned on the bell.

Inside the Vauxhall, Bigtoria undid her seatbelt. 'One last chance, Marky.'

Mr Bishop patted Edward on the shoulder. 'A wee bit of advice from a dying man, son. In this life, you catch more flies with honey than vinegar. But it's much easier with shite.' He fumbled his door open and groaned his way into the snow. 'Grab the luggage for us, there's a good lad.' Then hauled his oxygen cylinder out after him, bumping the door shut again.

Bigtoria watched him shuffle away. 'Stinky old bastard.'

Definitely.

Edward grabbed the hernia-heavy suitcase from the boot and followed Mr Bishop up the ramp. No path and no steps, so probably designed for wheelchair access – would explain the extra-wide door too.

A wrought-iron sign poked out from the snow: 'JENKINS HOUSE', the words gently disappearing in the never-ending fall.

Mr Bishop stopped halfway up the ramp and turned to squint across the road at the graveyard as that yellow digger made room for one more. 'If that's meant to be foreshadowing, it's not funny.' He spat, then scuffed his way towards the front door, struggling with his NHS cane, the wheelie trolley for his oxygen tank leaving twin gouges through the snow.

Sergeant Farrow tried the bell again. Then looked over her shoulder at Mr Bishop. 'Given your . . . condition, we've assigned you a live-in carer: Paul Richards. Don't worry, he's been fully trained. Very experienced.'

Finally, the big door swung open and a hatchet-faced wee man blinked out at them. Mid-fifties, early sixties? Bespectacled and balding, in a flannel shirt, brown cords, white smock, and red Crocs. A web of scar tissue twisted his left cheek, pulling his mouth into a lopsided, sarcastic sneer. Proper Belisha-beacon nose too – like he'd been blowing it for days. On sandpaper. His voice couldn't have been more bunged-up or Glaswegian if he'd tried. You could've clubbed seals with it. 'Aye? This the new boy, is . . .' Then his eyes opened wide. 'Marky? Holy shite, man, it is. Marky Bishop!'

A sad smile slipped its way across Mr Bishop's face. 'Razors. What you doing here?'

'Lookin' after dying folk and fusty auld buggers. You?'

He tapped the oxygen tank with his walking stick. 'Dying fusty auld bugger.'

'Aw, man . . . That sucks balls.'

Sergeant Farrow stiffened. 'You two *know* each other?' Frowning at Mr Richards. 'Why didn't you tell me you knew him?'

There was a raised eyebrow, a sniff; then Mr Richards blew his nose on a tatty-looking off-brown hanky. 'Didn't know he was coming, did I. You should've said.'

Mr Bishop looked back at Edward. 'Me and Razors were on the same wing at Shotts for a while, son.'

That brought a lopsided grin to Mr Richards' scarred face. 'We was there when Owen Morrison transitioned. Wasnae his idea, mind, but that's what happens when you get on Big Paul Paterson's tits.' He mimed a pair of scissors with his fingers.

Mr Bishop turned his sad smile on Sergeant Farrow. 'To be honest, I've probably done time with half the folk in Glenfarach. Not the *nonces*, the decent folk.'

'Urgh . . .' A shudder curled its way through Mr Richards. 'Couldn't look at sausages for a *month*, man, gave us the total dry boak. Lying there, on the Rec Room floor, like a—'

'All right, we get the picture.' Sergeant Farrow stuck her chin out. 'It's against official policy, but there's no one else free. So . . .' A shrug. 'Inside.'

4

The hallway featured a rickety-looking stairlift and decidedly old-fashioned decor. On the plus side, though, at least the living room was warm, thanks to the stoic efforts of an electric fire, pinging and glowing away beneath an ornament-free mantelpiece. Sad, dusty rectangles marked the wallpaper where pictures had been removed – now the only decoration came from a pair of wall sconces, topped with tartan lampshades. A wheelchair lurked in one corner, below a winch-and-sling contraption for lifting people in and out of it. A stack of cardboard boxes, with 'CHARITY' or 'RECYCLING' printed on them in wobbly black Sharpie, piled up by the door. A ceiling the same browny-yellow as Mr Bishop's teeth. The carpet: an abattoir of stains.

And the entire room reeked of stale cigarette smoke, cut with the aggressive, toilet-cleaner stench of old-lady perfume.

Edward shuffled closer to the fire. 'Lovely place you've got here.'

Mr Richards helped Mr Bishop into a fusty brown sofa, fussing over him as he suckled at his oxygen mask. Bigtoria fiddled with her phone, eyebrows drawn in and down.

Sergeant Farrow pulled a large Ziploc bag from her high-vis pocket. Opened it, and produced an ankle tag. Not a sleek modern one, though, this was a thick grey band with a cigarette-packet-sized lump attached to it. Thing belonged in a museum. 'Mr Bishop, you know the conditions of your residency.' Not a question.

He answered anyway, voice muffled and echoing inside the

oxygen mask. 'Aye . . .' Sounding like he'd never manage another decent breath in his life.

'You are to stay within the posted limits of Glenfarach. You are to cooperate with the Social Work Team at all times. You will follow all instructions from any officer and may be searched at their discretion.'

Mr Bishop worked up a bit of steel. 'I said . . . "I know!"'

So did Sergeant Farrow. 'You are not to consort with anyone placed on your no-contact list under *any* circumstances. You will not participate in abusive or violent behaviour. You will *not* indulge in threats. You *will* obey the curfew.'

The old man's eyes narrowed. 'Telling me . . . who I can . . . and can't . . . can't talk to . . . I'm not a *child*!'

'Same as it is when you get released from prison, Mr Bishop, you should know that. You're on licence: you follow the conditions of your licence or you're out of here.'

Mr Richards adjusted Mr Bishop's mask. 'Come on, Marky, don't upset yourself. Breathe.'

She pointed. 'Roll up your trouser leg.'

'God's sake, hen, can you no' see the man's unwell? Here . . .' He pulled up Marky's left trouser leg, exposing six inches of pale hairy skin.

'Good enough.' Sergeant Farrow fastened the ankle tag in place, fiddled with it – until a red light started blinking on the bulky transmitter – then took out her Airwave handset and pressed a couple of buttons. 'Golf Foxtrot Four to Control. Safe to talk?'

A young man's voice crackled out of the speaker. *'Go ahead, Golf Foxtrot Four.'*

'Run a check on Mr Bishop's new tag.' She loomed over the old man. 'Don't even *think* about trying to remove it – your foot'll come off first. And you can't block its signal either.'

'GPS location shows Jenkins House; battery and transmission status are green.'

He struggled out a small, wheezing laugh. 'Where . . . where am I going . . . to go? . . . Dundee? Paris? . . . San Francisco? . . . Mars?'

'Residency in Glenfarach is a *privilege*, not a right, Mr Bishop.'

She pointed with her Airwave – through the living-room window and the lazy haze of snow beyond, across the road. Where that mini-digger was just visible on the other side of the churchyard wall, its hydraulic arm rising and falling. 'If it wasn't for Mrs Jenkins' unfortunate demise, freeing up a space, you wouldn't be here.'

Mr Richards sighed. 'Poor old bag fell down the stairs.' A sad shake of the head. 'Shame, she was nice, too. You know, for a chain-smoking paedo.'

'Breach *any* of our rules and you *will* be cast out.'

Mr Bishop grumbled at that, but then his shoulders sagged and he nodded.

'Good.' Sergeant Farrow put her Airwave away, then turned to Edward. 'DC . . . Sorry, I've forgotten your name?'

'Reekie. Edward.' For some weird reason heat rushed up to the tips of his ears. 'Er . . . I mean: Detective Constable Edward Reekie.'

'DC Reekie, I need you to search Mr Bishop while I go through his luggage. Make sure nothing's been smuggled in.'

Eh?

'But he's just come from prison. How could he smuggle—'

Her answer came out cold and hard: 'Glenfarach's policies and procedures exist for a *reason*, DC Reekie.'

'Right. Yes . . . OK.' Why did everyone have to be such a dick?

He abandoned the fire and hunkered down in front of Mr Bishop. 'Sorry.' Then did a full stop-and-search job: going through every pocket and cuff, checking the belt and shoes, inside the shirt collar, feeling his way through the camel-hair coat's lining and the tweed suit too. Finding nothing more than a pack of cigarettes, a lighter, and a leather wallet that crackled when he opened it. It contained four expired credit cards and about three hundred quid in banknotes that weren't even legal tender any more. 'He's clean.'

Sergeant Farrow had a final rummage through that heavy old-fashioned suitcase, then stood – holding a double handful of pill boxes. One eyebrow raised. ''Ello, 'ello, 'ello, what's all this then?'

Mr Bishop's breath hissed and whistled in his throat, mouth open wide to drag in as much air as possible, eyes closed, hands trembling, fighting to rasp the words out, 'Prescrip . . . prescription.'

'You can get them back from Dr Griffiths.' She pulled a tote bag from her pocket with 'GLENFARACH LIBRARY ~ READING ROCKS!' on it and tipped the pill boxes inside. 'Welcome to Glenfarach, Mr Bishop.' A sharp nod at Mr Richards. 'Make sure he knows the rules.' And with that, Sergeant Farrow swept from the room.

Bigtoria was hot on her heels. 'Hold on.'

The pair of them disappeared into the hall; then the front door creaked open . . . and whumped shut. Leaving nothing but the electric fire's pings and clicks, and Marky's tortured wheezy breaths, to break the hush.

Edward hunkered down again. 'Are you OK?'

'He'll be fine.' Mr Richards clapped a hand on Mr Bishop's shoulder. 'Toughest old bastard you'll ever meet. Right, Marky?'

No response.

In the silence, Mr Richards let loose a huge sneeze, then blew his nose like it was the most painful thing ever.

'Erm . . .' Edward looked at the open living-room door. 'Your boss is a bit . . . you know?'

'She's no' *my* sodding boss. I'm here on a strictly volunteer basis. Well, that and it gets me extra community credit. Wee privileges, here and there, but.'

Mr Bishop surfaced from his oxygen mask, twisted the valve on top of the cylinder, then slumped forward – holding himself up with his hands on his knees as he scowled at his new ankle tag, every breath whistling and rasping in his throat. 'Sodding . . .'

'Ach, it's no' as bad as it looks, Marky. Bit itchy to start with, but. You'll soon get used to it.' Mr Richards hauled up his own trouser leg, showing off an identical ankle tag, complete with winking red light.

Interesting.

Edward angled himself back in front of the fire. 'You're on licence too?'

That produced a nasal laugh. 'They didn't tell you shite, did they, Wee Man? Every bugger *here* is on licence. That's what Glenfarach's for – somewhere safe for us to hide out, far from the glaring eye of Tommy Tabloid and his Angry Mob of Bastards.' Mr Richards checked Mr Bishop's oxygen tank. 'Running a bit low, there. How we doing?'

A grimace. 'Could really do with a piss.'

'Come on then, let's get you seen to. And we'll swap yer tank for a fresh one. The boy here can see himsel' out.'

Edward emerged from Jenkins House into a flurry of swirling white. If it kept up like this, they'd need that snowplough to escape Glenfarach. Even worse – what if they got snowed in? Trapped here, with the misery-faced lump that was Detective Inspector Victoria Montgomery-Porter? Didn't bear thinking about.

She was standing by the pool car, fiddling about with her mobile phone again.

Sergeant Farrow was on her Airwave. '. . . not ideal, but we'll just have to live with it. Get Social Work to pop past, and he'll need to see Doc Griffiths too. ASAP on that one.'

The same voice as before crackled out into the snow. *'Will do, Sarge.'*

'Thanks, Shammy.'

Bigtoria swung her phone about. 'Is there nowhere in this godforsaken place with a decent signal?'

'Nope: no masts.' Sergeant Farrow pointed at the misty boundary between the surrounding forest and the low clouds. 'And nothing gets in over the hills. We're a little dead spot.' She smiled. 'Means we don't have to worry about them smuggling mobile phones in to chat with their dodgy mates.'

Edward joined them, hooking a thumb towards Jenkins House. 'He's not looking too great.'

'That's lung cancer for you.' Sergeant Farrow stuck her hand out. 'Sorry about that in there; new residents cause less of a fuss if they think I'm some kind of hard-arse bitch. At least for the first couple of weeks.'

'Oh, right.' Well, that kinda explained things. He accepted the handshake. 'Sarge.' Then wrinkled his nose. 'Seriously, I've seen post mortems where the cadaver looked healthier.'

She turned to Bigtoria. 'Sure you won't stop for a cuppa? The hotel does a good dirty-chilli burger for lunch, Tuesdays?'

The DI finally put her phone away. 'Got rehearsal tonight, don't want to be late.'

'Can't say we didn't offer.' She unlocked her ancient Land Rover. 'If something comes up – you know, if he coughs to anything – we'll give you a call.'

'We should be so lucky. Marky Bishop's a slippery bastard, always has been.' Bigtoria thumped herself into the pool car.

'Fair enough.'

Edward nodded at Sergeant Farrow. 'Sarge.'

She smiled and nodded back. 'Edward.' Then climbed inside her Land Rover, started up the clattering diesel engine, and pulled away.

Shame he wasn't going with her, instead of Bigtoria.

Would be nice to work with someone who wasn't a grumpy egotistical monster for a—

'Constable!' The DI had her door open, tapping her watch with an angry finger.

Ah well . . .

Edward got behind the wheel. Did his best to sound positive: 'Back to the ranch?' Fiddling his phone into the holder and setting it calculating the fastest route to Aberdeen. Clearing his throat as it chugged away. 'Guv – and I say this with all due respect, et cetera – but could you not have been a bit more . . . you know . . . *nice* to Mr Bishop? Flies and honey and shite and all that?'

'Nice? To Mark "Marky" Bishop?' She turned a withering stare in Edward's direction. 'Have you got any idea what that man did?'

Edward set the windscreen wipers going – full speed and they still struggled to keep the glass clear of snow – then headed towards the end of the narrow road. 'I'm not saying he's a saint, or anything, but—'

'Murder, extortion' – counting them off on her fingers – 'punishment beatings, drugs, prostitution . . . Once, he gouged a rival dealer's eyes out and made him *eat* them. Marky Bishop got thirty-two years, and we barely scratched the surface.' A snort. 'Don't let the doddery-old-fart act fool you: Marky Bishop is a violent, vicious, dangerous bastard.'

He took a right, at the end of the road, past another row of quaint little cottages, all of which, according to Mr Richards, were full of dodgy prisoners out on licence.

Three of them stood in their respective, snow-smothered gardens, watching the pool car go by. All three smiled and waved.

Only this time Edward didn't wave back. 'OK, so he's dangerous. That means it's even more important we pretend like we're on his side. Make him trust us, so he'll tell us what we want to know.' Edward risked a sideways glance. 'Thought you were into all that am-dram stuff?'

Left, at the T-junction, and they were heading out of town again.

Wouldn't have believed it possible, but the clouds had crept even lower, devouring most of the trees to either side. Narrowing the world to one icy monochrome slice.

Bigtoria stuck her chin out. 'I work on *professional* shows, thank you very much. Am-dram! We've been on tour all over the country; five-star reviews in the *Guardian*.'

'OK, OK, I'm sorry, I'm sorry.' Jesus, talk about touchy.

The pool car drifted past the village limits, with its collection of unwelcoming signs. Would be nice to put his foot down, but no way he was risking that in all this snow.

He checked the map on his phone – the GPS had finally worked out their route. Two-and-a-bit hours. There wasn't a chance in *hell* they'd make it home that quickly. Not in this.

Whatever shelter the forest had offered on the way down to Glenfarach, it wasn't offering it on the way back. Maybe the wind had changed direction? Whatever the reason, snow *pelted* down. Barely mattered how fast the wipers went, even with a clear windscreen the visibility was down to fifteen feet. If that.

Forty minutes of this and Edward's hands ached, gripping the steering wheel tight enough to drain all colour from his knuckles.

Face pulled into a jaw-grinding grimace. Doing his best to keep their rusty Vauxhall from slithering into the drainage channels that ran either side of the winding road.

A double bleep sounded in his jacket pocket, followed by a distorted voice. Just audible over the hissing static, pops, and electronic *squonk*s. *'Golf Foxtrot Four to DC Reekie, safe to talk?'*

He turned an apologetic smile on Bigtoria. 'That's my Airwave.'

'I know what an Airwave sounds like, Constable.'

'Well, I'm *kinda* busy keeping us out of the ditch, so . . . ?'

She pulled a face. 'Where is it?'

'Inside jacket pocket. Sorry.'

Bigtoria reached across the car and dug for the handset. Dragging it out and pressing the button. 'DI Montgomery-Porter, go ahead.'

'Inspector?' Difficult to tell if what followed was Sergeant Farrow clearing her throat, or just more static, but either way, she sounded seriously worried. *'We need you back here, ASAP.'*

Bigtoria sat up straight. 'Has something happened to Marky Bishop?'

'We've . . .' Deep breath. *'We've got a dead body.'*

No points for guessing where *this* was going. Edward took his foot off the accelerator and let the car drift to a halt. 'Sod.'

'We've not had a murder here for over thirty years. It's a bit . . .' Another breath. *'How soon can you get back?'*

'What happened to your Duty Inspector?'

'Coming in from Ballater, Guv. Procurator Fiscal wants you to hold the fort till he gets here.'

Bigtoria sucked on her teeth for a moment, then nodded. 'OK. Secure the scene, we're on our way.' She passed the handset to Edward. 'Well, don't just sit there: turn this car around!'

Thought as much.

Looked like his luck was for shite, today.

Not to mention how hard it was going to be, making their crappy old Vauxhall face the other way without ending up in one of those drainage channels.

'Soon as you like, Constable.'

Urgh.

'Yes, Guv.'

Time for a *very* careful eight-point turn . . .

Ten past four and the sun had vanished. It *should* have been low in the sky by now, perhaps skimming the tips of the trees at the top of the valley; instead, there was no evidence it had ever existed. Nothing but dark and grey as Edward drove them down one of Glenfarach's little side streets.

And then one by one the streetlights flickered on. Only they weren't your standard off-yellow sodium jobs, these were high-intensity LED units. *Blazing* out their surgical-white glare, catching the snow as it fell, making it shine.

A right turn took the pool car onto Gallows Row – a line of four cottages with nothing but a narrow strip of white between the last house and the gloomy depths of the forest beyond.

A patrol car was parked at the end of the road, lights off, nobody home.

Edward pulled in behind it, but when he hit the brakes the pool car just kept on going, ABS juddering as the Vauxhall slid and slid and slid, rear wheels kicking out as the bloody thing started to spin.

Oh God, they were going to bash right into the patrol car and there wasn't a sodding thing he could do about it.

He yanked the steering wheel in the other direction, foot jabbing up and down on the brakes, lips pulled back from gritted teeth, sphincter clenching, ready for the buckling *crump* of metal-on-metal . . .

But the manky Vauxhall came to a slithering halt just shy of the patrol car's rear bumper.

'Oh God.' Edward sagged forwards, still clutching the steering wheel. 'That was a close one.'

Bigtoria looked at him like he was a complete and utter idiot, then climbed into the snow.

'You're very welcome.' Edward huffed out a shuddery breath. Shut his eyes for a count of five while the thudding in his chest settled to a less urgent tempo, then followed her.

A wrought-iron sign, like the one outside Mr Bishop's new home, sat beside the garden gate: 'NEWMAN COTTAGE'. Another tourist-brochure, tartan-and-haggis, granite house with a slate roof and dormer windows. The lights inside cast their cheery golden glow across the blanketed garden. Not that the LED lampposts needed any help.

Bigtoria peered into the patrol car, then followed a line of foot-prints through the snow to the front door. Deep. Like no one had shovelled the path since the weather turned.

Edward caught up as she rang the doorbell.

Bigtoria didn't wait for an answer, though, just barged her way inside. 'Hello?' She wiped her feet on the welcome mat and disap-peared into the hall.

He stopped on the threshold. 'Guv, are you sure we should be doing this? Guv?' But she didn't even pause. 'Great.' Because why should anyone follow crime-scene protocol? Not like they'd been told there was a dead body in there or anything, was it?

OK. Well, she was the senior officer: if she wanted to piss all over correct procedure, and compromise the—

'Constable!'

'Yes, Guv.' Edward stepped onto the welcome mat.

Newman Cottage was . . . homely. In a slightly antiseptic kind of way. If anything, it was actually colder inside than out, turning each breath into a cloud of fog. A weird *funky* smell filled the place – sweaty and meaty and stale.

Bigtoria kept going, glancing into each open-doored room as she passed.

He did the same. Living room: chintz sofa, dark carpet, small TV. Bathroom: *ugly* salmon-pink suite, daffodil shower curtain, blue vinyl floor tiles. Bedroom: double bed, black silk sheets, and flat-pack furniture. And, finally, the kitchen.

It was a medium-sized, Shaker-style room with some shonky DIY cabinets. Crappy landscape paintings on the walls. Everything else was hidden from view by the pair of uniformed PCs – in padded high-vis jackets – blocking the doorway. They weren't guarding it, they were standing with their backs to the hall, peaked caps clutched in both hands, mouths hanging open as they stared inside.

One was about two inches shorter than Edward, with a sensible haircut and serious face. Squinting, like everything was permanently too bright. His companion was a bit of a bruiser: shaved head covered in blue-grey stubble, and a jaw you could break rocks on.

The big one let out a low whistle. 'Jesus . . .'

The short one blinked. 'How would . . . I mean . . .'

Neither of them seemed to have any idea that they had company.

Bigtoria put a hard, sharp end to that. 'Who's in charge here?'

The big one flinched, but his mate jumped a good six inches, letting out a startled squeak. They both turned, thumping into one another on the way. Like they were in some sort of slapstick comedy, written by, and for, morons.

The big one regained his composure first: chest out, shoulders back, putting on his official police-officer voice. 'What the hell do you think you're doing? You can't be in here!'

That seemed to embolden the short one. 'This is a crime scene!' He stuck a hand up, barring the way. 'Out. Now!'

Bigtoria snapped her warrant card at them. 'DI Montgomery-Porter.' Her official police-officer voice was a *lot* scarier than either of these twits'. 'So I'll ask you again: who's in charge here?'

The short one licked his lips. 'Er . . . You are?'

'No, you idiot, who's Crime-Scene Manager?'

The big one cleared his throat. 'We haven't got that far . . .'

An uncomfortable silence saturated the corridor as Bigtoria screwed up her face. Followed by a muttered 'God help us.' She put her warrant card away. 'Where's Sergeant Farrow?'

The short one seemed to be trying to blend into the wallpaper, flattening himself against it and pointing down the hall, past Edward, towards the front door. 'She's gone back to the station, needed to make some phone calls. Guv. I mean, Inspector. Ma'am?'

'Where's the body?'

'Ah . . .' The big one backed out of the way, revealing the rest of the kitchen.

Edward sucked a breath in through clenched teeth.

No wonder Sergeant Farrow sounded worried when she'd called.

'Sodding hell . . .'

5

A man's body lay on its back, draped over a pine kitchen table. Stripped down to his underpants. Wrists and ankles tied to the table's legs. Head hanging off the edge to stare at the hob and oven. Or at least he would've been if whoever did this hadn't gouged out his eyes.

The rest of him hadn't fared much better – bare skin covered in slash marks and small circular bruises, and far bigger bruises, and large raw patches. Blood colouring the butter-pale skin in scarlet smears. Drips pooling on the linoleum. A thick line of purple around his neck . . .

And the *smell*. Like a septic tank crossed with a butcher's shop.

Edward clapped a hand over his nose and mouth.

The body was still wearing its ankle tag, the red light winking away. Bigtoria shuddered, lips pinched as she stared at it. Then, calm as anything: 'Everyone out.' Like they hadn't just walked into a horror film.

The big officer shuffled his feet. 'Look, Guv, we weren't—'

'OUT!' She turned, shoving both of them. 'THIS IS A MURDER SCENE, YOU PAIR OF IDIOTS! GET YOUR BACKSIDES OUTSIDE NOW!' Driving them before her.

They scurried out into the snow, with Bigtoria hot on their heels, and Edward bringing up the rear. Soon as he was outside, he thumped the door shut behind him. Took a deep breath of blessed clean cold air.

Bigtoria jabbed a finger into the big one's high-vis jacket, hard

48

enough to make him stagger backwards. 'What were you thinking, contaminating the crime scene? You're supposed to be police officers!' Another concrete-fingered jab. 'This is *not* some sort of bloody playground where you can do whatever the hell you like; there are policies and procedures!' Throwing her other hand towards Newman Cottage. 'Do you have *any* idea what'll happen if we can't lift fingerprints or DNA from the scene because you *bloody clowns* have TRAMPED ALL OVER IT?'

He lowered his head, ears colouring. 'Yes, Guv. Sorry, Guv. It was just . . . Well, you don't normally see something as horrible—'

'I'll be having words with your superiors.' She snapped her fingers. 'Names!'

A flinch. He stared at his shoes. 'Phil Samson. This is Dave Harlaw.'

The wee one sounded like he was about to soil himself. 'I'm only new!'

Edward, not being an idiot, kept his mouth shut, making sure he was far enough behind Bigtoria not to catch any of the shrapnel.

She glared at the pair of them. 'Who discovered the body?'

PC Samson had a bash at sounding helpful. 'Agatha Reynolds: one of the Social Work Team. Found him when she did her daily check.'

'Where is she?'

'We . . .' PC Harlaw shrank back, like he was regretting saying anything, but it was too late now. 'We sent Aggie home. She wasn't doing that great.'

His fellow idiot nodded. 'Well, you saw: the body's not exactly—'

'Victim?'

'Geoff Newman, Guv.' Samson tried an ingratiating smile. It didn't help. 'Bit of a troublemaker, but never quite enough to get him kicked out. Ex-Metropolitan Police, did twenty years for money laundering, corruption, and extortion.'

Harlaw grimaced. 'Had a kinda . . . kiddy-porn habit too.'

'You know what the Met's like, Guv. Any cocking disaster and they're in about it like flies on a dead dog's arsehole.'

Hello Pot, this is Kettle calling. Are you receiving me? Over.

She stared at him till he lowered his eyes again.

'Sorry, Guv.'

'We any idea how long he's been dead?'

Samson had another go being helpful. 'He was definitely still alive yesterday afternoon; social worker check-ups are seven days a week.'

Bigtoria pulled her chin up. 'And I take it, given the shameful display of unprofessionalism I just witnessed, that neither of you have done the crime-scene management training?'

'Erm . . . ?' Harlaw looked at Samson, then at the house, then at Bigtoria, then at the snow around his boots. 'No, Guv. Inspector . . . Sorry.'

'Of course you sodding haven't. You' – pointing at Samson – 'until someone *competent* turns up, you're Crime-Scene Manager. I want a common approach path, scene logbook, and the place taped off. No one enters or leaves without my say-so.'

Harlaw put his hand up, like he needed the toilet. 'Want me to search the gardens, Inspector? Whoever did it must've got in and out somehow – maybe they left a clue?'

She turned on him, nice and slow, giving the terror time to build. Her voice a dangerous purr. 'Why, of course, Constable, what an *excellent* idea. Why don't you go rummaging about, mucking up whatever evidence is out there *before* the Forensic Services Team arrive? I'm sure the Procurator Fiscal will be *delighted* when he gets here. He'll probably give you a SODDING MEDAL!'

He shrank away from her, eyes wide. 'Eek . . .'

Bigtoria poked her finger into Samson's chest again. 'What are you still standing there for? I want this scene secured *now*!'

'Yes, Guv!' And he was off – hurrying to the patrol car and searching through the boot.

'Constable Harlaw: you get started on the door to doors. I want anything out of the ordinary in the last thirty-six hours. And try not to make a sodding mess of that too.'

Harlaw snapped to attention. 'Yes, Inspector!' Then legged it, skittering through the snow to the next house on the street.

She didn't bother keeping her voice down. 'Pair of bloody amateurs.'

OK, couldn't hide in the shadows any longer. It was time to be useful.

'Guv?' Edward made a show of looking up at the nearest lamp-post. 'Think all these CCTV cameras are real? I mean, they're *probably* not just for decoration, right?'

There was a pause; then she nodded. 'One way to find out.'

Edward rattled the handles on the station's front doors. Locked. The portico and pillars offered a bit of shelter from the snow, and the old-fashioned blue lamp glowed, but other than that: useless.

He backed away down the stairs, looking up at the ugly glass-and-concrete extension. The lights were on; surely *someone* had to be home?

Maybe the side door – the one Sergeant Farrow had emerged from when they'd arrived with Mr Bishop?

But when he tried the handle, it was the same result. And pressing the intercom button didn't even generate a grating buzzing noise, so probably knackered. The Big Car, AKA: Sergeant Farrow's Land Rover, was parked at the kerb, wearing a three-inch toupee of snow, so she couldn't have gone far; not like she was going to knock off early with a tortured-to-death resident on the go.

But there was no sign of life anywhere.

Bigtoria hadn't moved from her comfy, *warm* seat in their manky Vauxhall, but she did him the courtesy of winding down her window and scowling up at him. 'Call her on your Airwave.'

Bloody detective inspectors.

But he pulled his handset out and poked at the keypad anyway. It bleeped at him. 'DC Reekie to . . .' He bent over and looked in through the passenger window. 'What was her call sign again?'

'It doesn't matter, you idiot.'

Thanks a heap.

He straightened up. 'DC Reekie to Sergeant Farrow, safe to talk?'

More snow drifted down from the burnt-orange sky.

Edward stomped his feet, trying to keep the circulation going.

Bigtoria did her brooding-menace thing.

Finally, his Airwave registered an incoming transmission, swiftly followed by a horrible squawking noise. Sergeant Farrow's voice popped, fizzed, and crackled – sounding like she was a million miles away, surrounded by angry robot wasps. '. . . *ello? Who is . . . Hello?*'

'Sarge? We're outside, can you let us in? It's freezing.'

'Tell her to get her finger out!'

'*Can barely . . . you. Where . . .*'

'God's sake.' Bigtoria wound her window back up, climbed out of the car, lumbered over to the side door, and hammered the palm of her hand against it, setting the whole thing booming. 'LET US IN!'

The hissing and crackling disappeared.

Edward gave the Airwave a shake, but nothing doing. They'd been disconnected. 'Think she heard that?'

She must have, because a rattling clunk came from the other side; then the door swung open and Sergeant Farrow stuck her head out. Face like a wet weekend in Lossiemouth. Eyebrows pinched, mouth too. 'Sorry, Guv, we've been trying to get the Airwaves sorted for months. Every time the weather's bad, it's like tin cans and damp string.' She stepped back to let them inside.

Had to admit, of all the rural police stations he'd been in, this was the biggest. And grubbiest.

They'd emerged into a sort of low-key reception area, with a desk that seriously needed a coat of paint, the bulletproof screen all scratched and fustered with cobwebs. Stairs leading to the floors above and down into the earth.

Sergeant Farrow locked the doors behind them. 'But will they send a repair team out to fix it? No, I have to use a resident to patch the fudging system up with duct tape and bogies. It's—'

'CCTV?'

'First floor, Guv.'

'Good.' Bigtoria marched for the stairs. 'We've got a major murder inquiry to run, we need those Airwaves.'

'I'll get Jenna in first thing.' Hurrying after the DI, Edward bringing up the rear. Again. 'Inspector Draper called: he's stuck on the A939 near Torbeg – gritter lorry hit a minibus. So . . .' A shrug. 'Where do you want to start, Guv?'

Round the landing and onto the next flight.

Bigtoria kept going. 'How about with that pair of idiots you've got masquerading as police officers? They hadn't even sealed the scene; they were in the room with the murder victim!' Thumping out onto the first floor.

'Oh, for . . .' Sergeant Farrow paused for a moment, fists clenched. 'I'll fudging *kill* them.' Then she led the way through a set of double doors into a corridor where a faded smattering of Police Scotland 'motivational' posters curled away from the corkboards they'd been pinned to. Stains on the ceiling tiles. A path scuffed down the middle of the floor where the blue terrazzo had worn through to the concrete.

'And we're going to need more bodies. Competent ones. How many officers you got here?'

'Three per shift. But no one lives locally, for obvious reasons.'

OK, *what?*

'Three?' Edward stopped where he was. 'You've got *three* people watching *four hundred* sex offenders?'

Sergeant Farrow kept going. 'It's *two* hundred, total, and only a hundred and eighteen of them are sex offenders. I have to work with what I'm given: I don't set the budgets.' She threw an apologetic look over her shoulder. 'Sorry, Guv.'

'Call everyone in. What about the Procurator Fiscal, pathologist, Forensic Services?'

'PF's at a drive-by shooting in Govan: he'll be a while. Pathologist's on her way from Aberdeen. Forensic team have made it as far as Kincardine O'Neil, so, in this weather? Two, maybe three hours?' A frown. 'Assuming the pass stays open. How was it when you were out there?'

Edward grimaced. 'Bloody horrible.'

'It was *fine.*' Bigtoria followed Sergeant Farrow through a door marked 'CCTV SUITE ~ AUTHORIZED PERSONNEL ONLY', leaving Edward alone in the corridor.

He waited till the door swung shut, before sticking two fingers up at it. Keeping his voice down to a bitter muttering. 'What would you know about it? *You* spent the whole thing sat on your backside, playing with your phone, while *I* did all the sodding driving.'

Her voice boomed out, barely muffled by the closed door: *'CONSTABLE!'*

At least she couldn't see him rolling his eyes. 'Yes, Guv. Coming, Guv.'

The CCTV room was far too big for such a teeny village, easily four times the size of the one back home in Aberdeen. And *that* was for over two *hundred* thousand residents. All this for two hundred?

Dozens and dozens of TVs – not flat-screen ones, but old-fashioned cathode-ray jobs – completely filled three of the walls. Bathing the windowless space with their flickering glow. Each one showed a different bit of Glenfarach, lit up like high noon by those LED streetlights.

An island unit sat in the middle of the room, with one office chair and a trio of monitors – proper modern ones this time – mounted on arms. A map of the village took up a good chunk of the fourth wall, marked out on some sort of oversized whiteboard in coloured vinyl strips and blocks.

Sergeant Farrow settled into the room's only seat and fiddled about with a mouse, pausing every now and then to poke a key on what looked like a professional video-editing set-up. 'Can't believe someone killed Geoff; I just spoke to him yesterday. Well, told him off for littering, but still . . .'

One by one, the views of Glenfarach disappeared, replaced by four large composite images. Screen 1: the end of Gallows Row, with Newman Cottage slap bang in the centre, woods lurking in the background. Screen 2: the next-door cottage, and a bit of Newman Cottage. Screen 3: another cottage. Screen 4: the first cottage on the street, with a view along the other three.

Her fingers hovered over the keyboard. 'When do you want to start?'

Bigtoria folded her arms. 'Thirty-six hours ago.'

'Thirty – six – hours – ago . . .' Sergeant Farrow fiddled with the controls and each one of the four composite images flickered, their timestamps jumping back to seven o'clock yesterday morning. Darkness reigned beyond the harsh white LED streetlights.

She twisted a big volume-knob-style thing and the picture spooled forwards at many times normal speed – the timestamps flickering away an hour and a half in a couple of minutes, until the steel-coloured sun crept above the trees, only to disappear into a veil of low cloud.

The footage kept going until round about ten-ish, when some fat bloke lumbered his way out of the house next door to Newman Cottage.

Sergeant Farrow slowed everything down to normal and pointed. 'Leonard Walker. Did eighteen years for the rape and murder of a sixty-three-year-old man.'

Mr Walker lurched towards the camera: a chunky, florid bloke, bundled up in a padded jacket, with a woolly hat and the kind of moustache that *screamed* 'sex offender'. He cast a shifty gaze up and down the street, then hurried on his way, clutching a pair of bulging tote bags.

He bustled across screens three and four, then disappeared.

Sergeant Farrow rewound to just before he'd left the picture, zooming in until his face filled the composite screen. 'We think Leonard's responsible for at least another half-dozen sexual assaults, but he's keeping his mouth shut.' And the footage leapt into fast forward again. 'To be honest, the cameras are about the only things that still work properly around here. Well, most of the time. Fudging government thinks this is some sort of luxury holiday camp, not a place to keep gangsters and sex offenders away from the general public.' A sour expression curdled her features. 'Every year: budget cuts.'

There followed a fast-forward view of absolutely nothing happening on Gallows Row. The highlight came just after eleven o'clock, when a chubby tuxedo cat waddled its way down the pavement. Then yet more nothing happening.

Sergeant Farrow shook her head. 'Victims of our own success, I suppose. Thirty-odd years we've been keeping a lid on this place: worst crime we've had to deal with is the occasional bit of shoplifting. Yes, it *seems* safe, because the residents are all terrified of getting kicked out of Glenfarach, but scratch the surface and . . .' She slowed the footage down again. 'Here we go.'

According to the timestamps, it was nearly midday when Geoff Newman stepped out of his cottage. A tall, thin, angular man, wearing a dark-green parka jacket and carrying a red holdall. They didn't get a good close-up of his face, though, because instead of turning right and heading towards town, he went left at his garden gate – marching to the end of the road, across the small section of scrubland, and vanishing into the woods.

Bigtoria sniffed. 'That him?'

A sad sigh. 'Yes, that's him.' It looked like she was going to say something else, till she clocked the slightly outraged look on the DI's face. 'Residents are allowed within a two-mile radius of the village limits.'

'So where's he off to?'

'No idea.'

Edward pointed at the mass of brown and green at the end of Gallows Row. 'No cameras in the woods?'

'With *our* budget?' Sergeant Farrow put the footage into fast forward again.

The composite screens dimmed as the cloud thickened, then the snow swept in. Little flakes at first, building in intensity, turning the scene monochrome as it settled on road and gardens alike.

Then bang on ten past four, Geoff Newman and Leonard Walker scurried back to their cottages. Both were carrying tote bags, but you could tell by the way he was struggling that Walker's were heavier than Newman's.

Sergeant Farrow let the footage run. 'Curfew is sunset, so everyone has to be in their homes by twenty past.'

Before darkness could settle, though, those LED streetlights bloomed into life, turning the falling snow into glittering, swirling petals. Lights flickered on inside the houses too. And, finally, a set of headlights swept across the scene and a car pulled up outside the first house on the street.

A woman climbed out of the driver's side, clutching a clipboard. She looked pretty large, but that might have been because of the shapeless puffa jacket she had on. Shoulder-length auburn hair.

Sergeant Farrow slowed the footage.

'That's Aggie. Agatha Reynolds. Has about forty residents to see every day.'

Edward raised an eyebrow at that. '*Forty?*'

'Like I said: budget cuts. We're supposed to have a team of ten, we've only got five.'

Onscreen, Agatha Reynolds marched up the path to house number one and rang the doorbell.

'OK.' He did a quick calculation. Say it was an eight-hour day – times sixty, equals four hundred and eighty minutes – less sixty for lunch, and maybe two statutory fifteen-minute breaks – so three hundred and ninety, divided by forty sex offenders . . . 'That's just under ten minutes per visit?'

'Including travelling time.'

Right on cue, Aggie bustled out of the first house and round to the next one on the street. Knocked, and went inside.

She did the same thing with the remaining two cottages.

When she emerged from Geoff Newman's place she checked her watch and scurried back to her car. The headlights snapped on, she made a three-point turn, and was gone.

Bigtoria leaned forward. 'And she didn't spot anything out of the ordinary?'

'Not that I know of.' Sergeant Farrow sped the footage up again, but the only sign of movement between then and dawn the next day was a solitary fox, loping across the street, before veering off into the woods.

The sun struggled its way above the treeline. One of the residents headed out for a jog. Leonard Walker lumbered off into town. A handful of people came and went. A battered snowplough cleared the road, leaving a ridge of snow heaped up on the opposite side to the houses. And then it was quarter to three and Mr Walker hurried home again carrying another pair of bulging tote bags – staggering under their combined weight.

The only house that had remained completely still was Newman Cottage. No one in, no one out.

Edward puffed out his cheeks. 'Not exactly a thrill a minute, is it?'

A little snort from Sergeant Farrow. 'Believe me, the *last* thing you want in a village populated by organized criminals and sex offenders is "excitement".'

'Fair enough. Would he normally go out every day?'

Agatha Reynolds' car appeared again – driving much slower this time, probably because of the snow. She visited the first cottage in the row, same as last time.

'*Some* do, but it's fairly common for residents to not leave the house for three or four days. As long as they obey the curfew and cooperate with their social worker?' Shrug. 'They'll surface again when they're hungry.'

Reynolds worked her way down to Newman Cottage, knocked, and waited. And knocked a second time. Then tried the bell. Then checked her watch. And finally let herself in.

Sergeant Farrow slowed the recording to normal, and fifteen seconds later Aggie was bursting out through the door, staggering into the garden, and hurling her lunch all over what might've been a snow-covered rose bush. Clutching her knees as she retched.

Edward tried not to watch. 'So, if no one visited him, maybe someone was already there? You know, staying, like a guest?'

'Residents aren't allowed house guests. If you even want a friend over for tea you need to book it twenty-four hours in advance and spend community credits.' The footage sped up again, but it didn't take long before PCs Harlaw and Samson arrived, ready to trample all over the crime scene.

'Hmph.' Bigtoria pointed at the screen. 'What about back doors: you got CCTV covering those?'

Another sad sigh. 'Maybe fifteen years ago; they were the first thing slashed out of the budget. Now we're supposed to rely on everyone wearing an ankle tag. But at least it all gets logged.' She scooted her chair over to a console, mounted on the rear wall, with a handful of flat-screen monitors of its own. Rattled her fingers across the keyboard until a map of Glenfarach appeared on the screens, populated with a lot of little red dots. 'Our residents.' She attacked the keyboard again. '*This* is Geoff Newman.' The map zoomed in on Gallows Row, and there was Newman's red light blinking away inside his house.

Bigtoria curled her lip. 'Shame you don't have tags on those two idiots, Harlaw and Samson.'

'Don't be too hard on Dave and Shammy.' Sergeant Farrow held up a hand. 'Look, I'm not trying to excuse their *utter* fudge-up at the crime scene, but this kind of stuff never happens here.'

'You're right: that's no excuse.' A big, unforgiving finger pointed at the screen. 'Rewind it.'

She did, setting the timestamp birling backwards. Geoff Newman's little red dot stayed where it was, isolated, dead, and alone. Then, when the countdown reached yesterday afternoon, it came to life, leaving the house to reverse around town.

It stopped, briefly, in three locations, then left Glenfarach entirely to hang about at the same spot in the woods for about two hours – going by the timestamp. Then the light was on the move again, heading for Gallows Row and home.

Edward leaned in closer. 'Stick it back half an hour or so, please, Sarge.'

She did, and Geoff Newman's ankle tag winked away, just inside the two-mile safe-to-wander zone.

'What's he up to?' Bigtoria squinted at the screen.

A shrug from the sergeant. 'Many of our residents like to "commune with nature". Some paint, some sketch, some read books, some . . . well, let's say they take the opportunity to *pleasure* themselves, al fresco.'

Now there was an image.

The DI curled her lip. 'And Geoff Newman?'

'He liked to build things out of wood. But I wouldn't be surprised if he was also . . . pleasuring himself.' The tips of Sergeant Farrow's ears glowed a delicate shade of pink. 'Geoff was that kind of person. Doc Griffiths says it's a compulsion. Like being an alcoholic.'

A two-hour wank in the woods, in the cold? That was dedication for you.

Sergeant Farrow pressed the buttons and Geoff Newman's GPS marker returned home again.

'Hmmm . . .' Bigtoria poked the screen. 'Go back to his last social-work visit, then zoom out a bit. I want to see everyone who went anywhere near the place.'

But other than Geoff Newman, the only GPS tracker that traversed Gallows Row was Leonard Walker's. Newman's other neighbours, Laura Dundry and Jane Miller, didn't set foot outside all day.

Edward nodded. 'OK, so it can't have been a resident who killed him, right? Otherwise they'd have shown up. How many of you *don't* wear an ankle tag, Sarge?'

'None of the police officers, or the social workers, or the Duty Doctor.' Eyes narrowed, lips moving as she counted. 'Nine, including me.' Then her face fell. 'But that's . . . I mean, I *trust* these people. I work with them *every* day.'

Bigtoria didn't look impressed. 'Better do a headcount: make sure everyone's where they're meant to be. Staff *and* residents.'

Sergeant Farrow suppressed a groan. 'Yes, Guv.'

At least now *someone* else knew the joys of working for Detective Inspector Montgomery-Porter.

'Dig out a couple of high-vis jackets too. One for me, one for DC Reekie.' The DI marched for the door. 'And I want to speak to this Abbie social-work person too.'

'Actually, it's *Aggie*. Short for . . .'

But Bigtoria was already gone.

Sergeant Farrow pulled a face – mouth turned down, showing off gritted teeth, nose wrinkled, eyebrows pinched. 'Constable, is she always this . . . ?' A tortured grimace.

'Oh yeah.' Edward patted her on the shoulder. 'Welcome to the club.'

6

Edward scrunched across the road, zipping up his brand-new, shiny high-vis jacket, on his way to their horrible, manky, rust speckled Vauxhall. The jacket glowed nuclear-yellow as those LED streetlights caught it, mirroring the one Bigtoria was wearing as she folded herself into the passenger seat.

They'd only been in the station, what, an hour? But the pool car was already crusted with an inch of fresh snow. He gave the wind-screen a quick wipe, then hurled himself in behind the wheel and cranked the engine into life.

'Are you *sure* we can't borrow the Big Car, Guv? This thing's like driving a tea tray on a skating rink.'

'Would you rather be checking up on two hundred thugs and sex offenders? Sergeant Farrow needs it more than we do.'

'Suppose.' But it still sucked.

He pulled away from the kerb, heading across Market Square, keeping it at a nice, safe ten miles an hour. Watching out for the slippery bits.

Bigtoria's hand came out, palm up. 'Printouts.'

'Back of the car.'

'God's sake . . .'

Because he didn't have anything important to do right now, did he? Not like he was driving through a winter horror show, was it?

She shoogled around in her seat and reached, stretched, and

pawed for them. Grumbling and grunting. Then sat back, clutching the document wallet Sergeant Farrow had given them. 'You know what worries me?'

'Yup.' Edward turned the blowers up full to counteract the fogging windscreen. 'Geoff Newman was tortured, right? And you only do that if someone has a secret you want to know. And *you'd* have to know that *he* knew something worth torturing him for.' Right, onto Thistle Lane, past back gardens and an old Scots pine already bowed under the weight of snow. '*And* it'd have to be something valuable enough to risk torturing him in a place peppered with CCTV cameras where nearly everyone's movements are recorded.'

She opened her mouth. Then closed it and frowned for a bit. 'Actually, I was going to say we should've switched off the central heating in Newman's house – it won't do the body any favours. But that's an *excellent* point.'

'We could always give PC Harlaw or Samson a shout: ask them to turn the heating down?'

Bigtoria snorted. 'And trust them not to rampage through the crime scene again like drunken wildebeests?' She pulled a handful of printouts from the document wallet, all clearly readable in the streetlights' glare. 'We'll do it ourselves, right after we've spoken to this Agatha Reynolds.' A nasty smile slithered into place. 'They can troop off into the woods and find out what Geoff Newman was doing out there for two hours.'

'What, other than being a wankaholic?'

She didn't return Edward's grin.

'Yeah, but, Guv, don't you think that's a bit cruel? I mean, I know they screwed up and everything, but it's dark and it's snowing and it's gotta be *way* below zero out there.'

'They should've thought of that before they compromised my crime scene.'

Hell hath no fury like a detective inspector with an axe to grind.

Still, on the plus side, if Harlaw and Samson had to do it, that meant Edward *didn't*. Made a nice change for someone else to get the crappy jobs.

He took a left at the end of Thistle Lane and—

The car's backside kicked out, tyres slithering and *vwipping* on the snow and ice, heading into a slow-motion spin.

'Aaaaaaargh . . .' Fighting with the wheel, trying to put some opposite lock on, like you were supposed to, but it didn't make any sodding difference, and then they were facing the other way, and still going around and *oh God* here came a lamppost – heading straight for the bonnet!

Only the front wheels must've hit the buried kerb, or something, because the Vauxhall lurched to a halt inches away from it.

Edward let go of the wheel and slumped in his seat, head back, breathing hard. Thank Christ there weren't any other cars out here. If this had been Aberdeen he'd have written off at least half a dozen four-by-fours with personalized number plates by now.

Instead, it was just them; a row of three houses on the left – lights glimmering in the windows; a snowy slope leading down and away into the darkness; and two cottages that looked like they died sometime in the last century. Sagging roofs, boarded-up openings, crumbling chimney stacks, and overgrown gardens. All being eaten by the snow.

Bigtoria didn't even look up from her files. 'Will you drive like a normal person?'

Like a . . . ?

Deep breath. 'Doing my best.' He reversed, gently, *oh* so carefully, until the pool car was pointing the right way along South Street. 'We need snow chains or something. Or the Big Car.'

'Hmmph,' she turned the page. 'Says here that Newman was a sergeant in the Metropolitan Police for seven years, before they caught up with him.'

'Shock, horror. PC Samson said that when—'

'Wonder if he had prior dealings with anyone living here? Either in his official capacity, or his dodgy side business.'

'Maybe we could ask the Met to send us up his records? Who knows, they might even have a copy here already, if they're keeping proper tabs on everyone.'

She pulled one shoulder up. 'Worth a try. Now, can we actually get going, here? Could've walked there quicker than this.'

Edward did his best not to roll his eyes, he really did. 'Yes, Guv.' But he kept the car at a crawling pace.

Sanctuary House was a sprawling complex of interconnected bungalows – arranged around what looked like a central courtyard – not far outside Glenfarach, screened from the village by a palisade of lonicera and Douglas fir.

Edward pulled up, just short of the car park, because the snow was at least six inches deep in there. And he wasn't an idiot. Five hatchbacks were stranded in their parking spaces, and they weren't going anywhere soon. Not unless someone dug them out.

Bigtoria crumped her way towards the less-than-welcoming reception area, with its barred windows and grille-covered door. Edward locked up and scuffed after her, using her footprints as a path, because, you know: not an idiot.

If anything it was getting even colder, the air a stinging weight against his skin, pressing down on his head, turning his breath nearly solid beneath the harsh LED lights.

The intercom mounted by the entrance didn't have individual names and buzzers on it, just the one button marked 'EMERGEN-CIES ONLY!'

He jabbed it with his thumb. 'Think this counts?' Stamping his feet, huffing warmth into his cupped palms as they waited.

'Soon as we get back to the station, I want you out helping with the door to doors. I'm not trusting that idiot Harlaw further than I can hurl him.'

Urgh.

'Guv.' Sounding about as enthusiastic as he felt.

'And while you're at it, we need to set up a murder board and an incident room. We have to be up and running the minute reinforcements—'

A hatch in the door slid back and a suspicious pair of eyes peered through the toughened safety glass. A strangled *bleep*ing noise crackled from a hidden speaker somewhere above them, followed by a voice. Female, mid-forties-ish, and very, very tired. *'Hello? It's after curfew, so you shouldn't be—'*

Bigtoria thunked her warrant card against the peep hole window. 'DI Montgomery-Porter, this is DC Reekie. We want to speak to one Agatha Reynolds.'

Silence.

'Did you hear me? I need you to open up: it's the police.'

A hissing electronic sigh. *'Hold on.'* Then a bit of muffled clunking, and finally the door swung open, leaving a lip of snow – like a frozen wave – waiting to crash in on the tiled flooring.

A short, plump woman peered out at them: heavy bags under her eyes and a brown bob that had a good inch-wide strip of grey roots on show. Big round glasses. 'Aggie's not feeling very well. The Doc gave her some pills for her nerves.'

Bigtoria stepped over the threshold, forcing the doorkeeper to retreat out of the way. 'We'll only be a minute.'

Edward followed her inside. 'Hi. Sorry about this.'

There wasn't a reception desk or anything, just a large hallway with a bunch of doors leading off it: 'SUPERVISOR', 'BREAKOUT ROOM 1', 'BREAKOUT ROOM 2', and 'OCCUPATIONAL HEALTH'. Another door sat at the far end, with a key-code lock, barring the way into those interlinked bungalows. Not exactly cosy, but they'd made a bit of an effort with pot plants and paintings on the calm magnolia walls.

Bigtoria pointed. 'Name?'

The woman blinked. 'What?'

'Your name. What is it?'

'Oh . . .' Pink rushed up her cheeks. Chin tilting up in a wee show of defiance 'Helen Sneddon. Team Lead. I'm *in charge* here.'

'Are you now.' Not even vaguely impressed. 'Where's Agatha Reynolds?'

Ms Sneddon opened one of the breakout-room doors and ushered them into a windowless space with a circular grey table plonked in the middle. Four matching grey plastic seats. A grey office sideboard with pads of paper and a jar of pre-chewed pens. The only thing with any colour to it was the framed print of Van Gogh's sunflowers. 'Wait here.'

Bigtoria moved closer, loomed over her. 'It's very *important* we speak to Ms Reynolds.'

'Just . . . wait here, OK?'

She shut the door on them, did some muffled swearing, and then she was gone.

Bigtoria did another lap of the room, checking her watch. 'How long does it take to fetch one stupid social worker?'

Edward turned over the next sheet in the document wallet – a mugshot of Geoff Newman. 'Only been fifteen minutes, Guv. Give them a chance.'

Going by the date, it was probably taken the day they arrested Newman for being a bent cop. He was staring at the camera, face set somewhere between fear and defiance. He looked younger, and a lot less dead. A tall man with a proud nose and weak chin. More forehead than hair. His eyes were bloodshot and blue, but at least they were still in his head . . .

The next photo showed him much older, with deep-gouged crow's feet, heavy creases down either side of his mouth, and rows of wrinkles across his temples. A greying beard hiding that feeble chin of his.

Bigtoria did another lap. 'Wasting time in here. Got a bloody killer to catch.'

After the photos came some sort of yearly assessment, carried out by the Social Work Team.

'Says here he was a member of the woodworking club, and he'd started taking painting lessons at the library.' Which explained the DIY cabinets and amateur landscapes in his kitchen. 'Think we should round the students and club members up? Grill them about Newman's past: see if anyone knew he had a secret?'

She cracked her knuckles. 'Right, that's it. I've had enough of—'

A knock at the door, and Helen Sneddon stuck her head into the room. Face still and serious. 'OK, she'll talk to you, but you have to *promise* you won't stir things up. OK?' A nod, agreeing with herself. 'OK.'

Then the door opened fully and in walked the social worker from the CCTV footage. Even without the padded jacket, Agatha Reynolds was large. A lumpen woman in a shapeless white smock top, jeans, utilitarian glasses, and a lanyard. The bags under her eyes were deeper and darker than Ms Sneddon's. She was clearly knackered, and – going by the big dark pupils – possibly a little stoned.

She slumped inside and collapsed into an empty chair. Ms Sneddon sat next to her, leaving the last vacant seat for Bigtoria. Who didn't look very pleased that they had an extra body in the room.

Ms Sneddon made herself comfortable. 'Either I'm supporting my colleague, or I'm helping her back to her rooms. You decide.'

An icy silence was followed by a bit of bristling. Then a scowl. 'Fine. You can stay.' Bigtoria snatched the printouts out of Edward's hand and rifled through them – slapping the photo of Geoff Newman down in front of Agatha Reynolds. 'I want to know about this man.'

Edward pulled out his notebook and pen – ready to take it all down.

Ms Reynolds smacked her lips a couple of times, creases deepening between her eyebrows like she was trying to get the picture in focus. 'God, it was . . . *horrible*. All this blood and . . . and . . . it . . . They took his *eyes*. His eyes! Who does that?'

'Did Newman seem different in any way, last time you saw him?'

'Different?' It seemed to take a moment for Ms Reynolds to realize Bigtoria meant while he was still alive. 'He was . . . Geoff was upset about something, but he wouldn't talk about it.' She drew a circle in the air with one wobbly hand. 'Sometimes he gets a bit . . . depressed. But this was more like . . . paranoia? Maybe? Kept kept muttering about someone out to get him.' A small pause as the implications of that sank in, and Ms Reynolds dissolved into juddering sobs. 'Oh God, he was *right*!'

Ms Sneddon put her arm around those quivering shoulders. 'Shhh . . . Shhh . . .'

Edward lowered his pen, making his voice as gentle as possible. 'It's OK. Take your time.'

It took a minute or so for her to get herself together, but eventually Ms Reynolds sniffed, wiped her eyes, and nodded. 'I think he'd been . . . drinking. He's not meant to drink. It makes him . . . *sexual*. Towards children.'

Bigtoria's top lip curled. 'Did he say who was "out to get him"?'

'Everyone. The police, support staff, the neighbours, even Doc Griffiths.'

Edward wrote them all down. 'Not exactly narrowing the list of suspects, then.'

'No, you . . .' Another big damp sniff. 'You have to understand: Geoff was a Venn diagram of everything wrong.'

Ms Sneddon poked the tabletop with a bitten fingernail. 'The organized criminals look down on the sex offenders. The sex offenders look down on the paedophiles. And they *all* hate bent coppers.'

Couldn't exactly blame them.

'And Geoff ticked all three boxes: ex-cop-turned-gangster child molester.'

Bigtoria had another go: 'But was there anyone in particular? Anyone he seemed especially upset about?' When that only produced a shrug, she changed tack. 'Did he say what he was doing in the woods yesterday?'

Ms Reynolds sat back, eyes narrowing. 'In the woods?'

'Constable.' Bigtoria snapped her fingers, because why behave like a civilized human being and ask nicely when you could be a dick about it?

'Right.' Edward checked his notes. 'Eleven fifty-six: Mr Newman exits his property carrying a red holdall and disappears into the woods at the end of Gallows Row. Reappears at ten past four, coming from the opposite direction.'

The frown deepened. 'He never said anything to me about it. Are you sure?'

'It's on camera.'

'In the woods? Why would he go in the—'

The breakout-room door banged open and in charged a wild-haired young man, hauling a padded jacket on over his long-sleeved T-shirt and rainbow braces – peppered with little metal badges. All he needed was an American accent to shout, 'MORK CALLING ORSON, COME IN, ORSON!' Instead, his voice was private-school-central-belt posh. 'Hels, Aggie: sorry to intrude.' He pulled a face at

Helen. 'Have you seen Caroline, Hels? She's not in her rooms and I've *really* got to go.'

'I don't—'

'If you find her, tell her to get her arse over to the firehouse quick as a quick thing, OK? Sergeant Farrow's been on the blower.' He zipped himself up and nodded at Bigtoria. 'You're the police, right?' Patted himself on the chest. 'Ian Casey. Sergeant Farrow says it's urgent – someone's battered Shammy Samson over the head and set fire to Geoff Newman's house.'

A pause, while everyone stared.

Then Bigtoria scrambled out of her seat. 'Constable: move it!' And she was gone.

Edward scooped up the printouts and his notebook. Gave Helen and Agatha a quick smile. 'Thanks. Sorry.' Then charged out of the room after her.

Ian Casey followed them.

Bigtoria strode for the door. 'It's all right, sir, we can see ourselves out.'

'I'm head of the volunteer firefighters. Got to get the engine stoked up. Besides, you'll need someone to unlock the front door.' He punched numbers into the key-code lock and hauled the door open, standing back to let them lurch out into the snow.

If anything, it was even heavier than before, but the sky it fell from had taken on an angry orange glow. Like the gates of hell had opened wide.

Ian pulled the door shut behind him then stopped. Stared at the snowed-in car park. 'Buggering wank.' He gave Bigtoria a pained smile. 'Any chance of a lift?'

She hooked a thumb at the pool car. 'In.'

They dropped him off at a red-brick garage, not far from the only road out of Glenfarach, then Edward hauled the Vauxhall around and headed for Gallows Row – fighting the thing along the slippery roads, muscles clenching at every corner. Holding on tight to stop the car from doing another three-sixty pirouette.

The closer they got, the more the hellfire glow grew.

Edward turned off West Main Street, nice and slow, keeping it under control. 'You know what this means, don't you?'

'Of course I bloody do.'

One last slithery junction and they were on Gallows Row.

'Holy crap . . .'

Searing orange and yellow flames leapt and roared from the body of Newman Cottage, lighting up the thick pall of churning black smoke, the throat-catching stench of burning plastics and smoky wood belting out of the car's air vents.

Someone had moved the patrol car two houses down, out of the way, and Sergeant Farrow's Big Car sat right behind it. Both had their blue-and-whites on, strobing through the flickering snow.

A cluster of three high-vis figures were gathered around the Land Rover's open back door.

Edward pulled up to the kerb, leaving plenty of space after last time, and clambered out. Stood there for a moment as the sheer volume of the blaze washed over him in hot, crackling waves. The pops and bangs of things exploding deep in the inferno. Fire roaring like a furious animal. Shadows dancing on the crisp white snow in shades of blood and gold.

Bigtoria lumbered towards the Big Car, shouting over the noise. 'WHAT ON EARTH HAPPENED?'

PC Samson was sitting on the floor of the Land Rover's boot, legs dangling, one hand clutching a pad of gauze to the back of his head as he wobbled there. Pale and shaky, even in the fire's glow.

Sergeant Farrow glanced up from rummaging in a first-aid kit. 'SOMEONE TRIED TO CAVE HIS SKULL IN.'

Samson gave her a weak thumbs up.

'IT'S JUST . . .' PC Harlaw shuddered. 'I MEAN . . . I FINISHED INTERVIEWING JANE MILLER, STEPPED OUTSIDE, AND THERE WAS SHAMMY: LYING IN THE ROAD!'

Bigtoria squatted in front of Samson. 'DID YOU SEE WHO HIT YOU?'

It came out as a barely audible mumble: 'Behind me . . .'

Edward took a step back, away from the heat, as bright-orange sparks swirled and danced their way into the sky like a flock of starlings. 'SO MUCH FOR TURNING THE CENTRAL HEATING DOWN.'

Bigtoria stood. Trembling. Fists clenched as she dragged in a deep breath, then bellowed it out again. 'AAAAAAAAAAAAAAARGH!' She aimed a boot at the snow, kicking up a flurry of white that turned blood red as the firelight caught it. 'HOW AM I SUPPOSED TO CATCH A KILLER WITH NO CRIME SCENE AND NO *SODDING* PHYSICAL EVIDENCE?'

Harlaw stuck his nose in the air. 'SAID WE SHOULD'VE SEARCHED THE GARDEN.'

Ooooooh . . . That *wasn't* good.

Bigtoria snarled, sending Harlaw scurrying behind Sergeant Farrow with a terrified squeak.

Sergeant Farrow thumped him. 'WHAT IS *WRONG* WITH YOU?'

Off in the distance came the plaintive wail of a siren. That would be the fire engine, then.

OK, maybe this wasn't as bad as it looked?

Edward put on his reassuring voice, the one you were supposed to use when someone's kid had gone missing. The one that was meant to make them believe little Jack or Lucy wasn't already dead in a ditch. 'WELL . . . THEY'LL PUT IT OUT, RIGHT? THE VOLUN-TEER FIREFIGHTERS WILL PUT THE FIRE OUT AND WE'LL BE ABLE TO SALVAGE SOMETHING THAT WE CAN USE TO—'

A chunk of the roof collapsed with a groan and a boom – flames blasted out of the windows, bringing with them a shimmering hail of broken glass. Sending everyone ducking for cover, shielding their heads with their arms, hiding behind the Big Car as debris rained down. Pinging and clanging off the Land Rover's metalwork.

And when they straightened up, the fire was bellowing like a wounded beast. Even brighter and hotter than before.

'Ah . . .' No way in hell *anyone* was putting this out anytime soon. Edward licked his lips, all traces of that reassuring voice devoured by the blaze. 'WE'RE BUGGERED, AREN'T WE?'

Bigtoria just stared. 'Bastard . . .'

7

Edward pulled the curtains back a little.

The fire engine was parked outside, in front of Newman Cottage, hoses reeled out from the side as Ian Casey and PC Harlaw sprayed water on the inferno. It wasn't a modern, flashy, state-of-the-art fire engine, it was old and boxy, its bright-red paint faded to a grimy pink, with rust around the wheel arches and patches of grey filler. And while Casey and Harlaw weren't having much success putting out the actual *blaze*, you had to give them points for trying.

'Constable! You're meant to be taking notes.'

'Sorry, Guv.' He let the curtains fall into place, shutting out the flickering light. Turned to face the room again. 'Just checking how they're getting on.'

Dusty stuffed animal heads dominated the crowded space. Boar, wolf, cheetah, badger, fox, and tiger, mounted on the walls, snarling out at them with glittering glass eyes. Lurking in the gloom of a single standard lamp.

The rest of the living room was full of books. Thousands of them. Books in bookshelves – packed higgledy-piggledy with hardbacks, paperbacks, coffee-table books, fiction, non-fiction; books piled up in the corners; books on the mantelpiece; books on the sideboard, in the sideboard, *under* the sideboard; and all of them tatty, used, their spines creased, their dust jackets battered and torn.

Like a serial killer had opened a second-hand bookshop, but couldn't be arsed organizing the stock.

Bigtoria occupied a small clearing in the book forest, arms folded, radiating menace, doing her usual *stellar* job of putting the public at their ease when being questioned.

More books surrounded the room's only seat: a wing-backed buttoned-leather armchair whose ancient green skin was patched with grey duct tape. And the chair's occupant/owner wasn't exactly an oil painting.

Leonard Walker – every bit as chunky and florid as he'd looked on the CCTV footage. Not a single hair remained on top of his head, but enough clung around the edges to make a ratty ponytail – a fashion statement not helped by the dark, baggy cardigan, worn over a pair of tartan pyjamas. Throw in a voice so slithery it'd give porridge the creeps, and Mr Walker ticked every box on the sex-offender bingo card. 'And I know we're not supposed to talk ill of the dead, but there you go.'

Bigtoria loomed. 'Did you see who did it?'

'Burned the house down, or killed him?'

'*Either.*'

'Oh, I already spoke to your little friend, David, about the former.' A slimy, simpering smile. 'That would be Police Constable *Harlaw*, for the uninitiated. And as for the latter . . .' Walker plucked a cloth-covered hardback of *Nicholas Nickleby* from the pile by his chair. Stroking the cover like a Bond villain's cat. 'Are you sure we're safe here and the fire isn't going to spread?' Looking out at his collection. 'I would so hate for something to happen to my babies.'

'Did you see someone or not?'

'I came home from the library with my usual haul.' Pointing at two bulging tote bags, over by the window. 'Can you imagine thinking books should be *thrown out* at the end of their working lives? It's barbaric.'

'Mr Walker!' Getting a bit red in the face, now.

He sighed – a soft wet sound that made the hairs squirm on the back of Edward's neck.

'I came home from the library, prepared a cup of tea, closed the curtains, and spent time with my children, Inspector. Same as I do every day. I didn't see anyone. I didn't hear anything. And I'm not in the least bit sorry that *Newman* is dead.' He gave the book in his hands a cold, slippery smile. 'And now that his house has burned down, we shan't be getting a new neighbour anytime soon, making noise at all hours of the day and night.' A satisfied hum. 'Perhaps it would be nice if that Miller woman's house burned down too? Then we might get some peace and quiet to *read*.'

The snow hadn't let up any. Its thick falling flakes circled the hot air rising from the blaze, like a slow-motion tornado.

Edward and Bigtoria stood on the forest side of the fire engine, where the diesel drone of the pumps wasn't *completely* deafening, their breath making a cloud of solid white in the headlights. You'd think a massive inferno like that would warm things up a bit, but there you go.

Sergeant Farrow crumped her way through the snow towards them, nose glowing pink in the firelight.

Bigtoria nodded at the other cottages on Gallows Row. 'Any joy?'

'Jane Miller says she was having a bath. Didn't know about the fire till she heard sirens.' Sergeant Farrow pointed further along the line of cottages. 'Laura Dundry says she's been working on her book all day. Some sort of horror novel set in the trenches of World War One. Didn't see or hear anything.'

Edward gave the sergeant a little wave. 'Same as Mr Walker. Only he was reading, not writing.'

'Urgh . . .' Bigtoria scrunched up her face and rubbed at her eyes. 'So someone just waltzed in, tortured Geoff Newman to death, sodded off, then waltzed *back* in, set fire to the cottage, and sodded off again.' She gave her eyes a break and scowled at the CCTV cameras instead. 'In the most heavily surveilled and closely monitored town in the whole bloody country? AND NOBODY SAW ANYTHING!'

Edward shared a look with Sergeant Farrow. Because who didn't love unstable, angry, shouting superior officers?

'Unbelievable!' Bigtoria jammed her hands into her pockets and stomped off towards the pool car.

'Guv?' Edward hurried after her. 'Where are we—'

'Back to the station: I want that incident room set up *now*. Murder board, the victim's file, known contacts, movements, everything. We're finding whoever did this!'

—a better class of criminal—

(still can't be trusted)

8

Edward juggled the mug and tinfoil-covered plate into his left hand, freeing the right up to knock on the cell door.

Smothered a shuddering yawn.

Burped.

Blinked.

Gave his head a wee shake.

Far too early in the morning for *this* crap.

Quiet reigned in the cellblock – well, except for the buzzing strip lights, but they didn't count. They gave the windowless room a subterranean-twilight feel. It wasn't exactly small – plenty of space for a custody desk; several noticeboards covered in tatty old notices and instructional posters; three interview rooms; a row of stainless-steel sinks; a shower block; and a dozen cells, arranged six to a side along a drab corridor – each one hidden behind a heavy, blue metal door.

Edward knocked again. Cleared his throat. 'Guv?'

Still nothing.

Another yawn.

The shower had helped, a bit, but then you've got to put dirty clothes on over a clean body and that's not good for the soul, is it? Course it isn't. And everything stank of smoke too.

You know what? Sod this.

He slid up the tab on the peep screen, and . . . peeped.

The cell was smothered in gloom.

Great.

He turned the handle and hauled the huge, heavy door open. Artificial light spilled over the threshold, illuminating the contents: one scuffed grey floor; one chromed metal dome, fixed to the ceiling, acting as a fisheye mirror; one jaunty blue go-faster stripe on the magnolia walls; and one raised concrete platform with a blue plastic mattress on it. On top of *that* lay a large rounded lump, slightly smaller than a bear, covered by a mound of scratchy blankets, letting out the occasional *snork* to break up the monotony of low-key snoring.

That dented metal toolbox of hers sat on the floor by the mattress, with its rash of show stickers and fusty odour of funky greasepaint.

Edward sneaked inside. 'Guv?' Once more, with a singsong lilt. 'Gu-uv?'

And still Bigtoria snored on.

'Guv, it's seven o'clock.'

That, at least, got him a grunt.

'Wakey, wakey.'

Indistinct mumbling.

Right, enough pussyfooting about. 'GUV!'

She scrambled awake, fighting her way up through the blankets, letting free the occasional flash of thrashing limbs, a vest, and a *massive* pair of off-grey pants.

Bigtoria squinted at him, her face pasty and blotchy. Packed blue bags hanging beneath her eyes. Her voice was squashed and gritty. 'Time is it?'

'Seven. You wanted to do morning prayers at half past, remember?'

She slumped onto her back. 'Urgh . . .'

'Don't blame me: *I* said we should postpone till nine. Up working till three in the sodding morning, how's that supposed to help?'

'Go – away.'

He put the coffee and the plate on the floor. 'Did you a bacon roll.' Showing top organizational, foraging, and culinary skills, thank you very much.

'Ketchup?'

'None left; have to make do with HP Fruity.'

'Oh, for God's sake.' She covered her face with her hands. 'Could today *get* any worse . . .'

'You're *welcome*.' He backed out and walloped the cell door closed far harder than was necessary, but sod her.

He gave it the benefit of a two-fingered salute.

Another door opened, down at the far end of the corridor, and out slouched PC Dave Harlaw, tucking his black Police Scotland T-shirt into his black Police Scotland trousers. Yawning as he went. Looking like a drunken teenager had used him for a sleeping bag.

Soot smudged his cheeks, and his hair had that wiry, slightly crispy-dry look to it from last night's blaze. He stopped for a full-body stretch and some more yawning. Then sagged. 'Pfff . . .'

'Morning prayers at half seven.'

'Feel like I've been run over by a fire truck.' Harlaw rubbed at his face. 'Any word on Shammy?'

Edward just looked at him.

'Shammy? Phil. PC *Samson*.'

'Oh. No, not yet. Better get yourself cleaned up. Going to be a long day.'

Harlaw closed his eyes and moaned.

Upstairs. Scuffing along the corridor. Sipping at a mug of instant with a dollop of UHT and two sugars in it. Edward paused to take in the glory of Police Scotland's idea of motivational posters. A beardy bloke on a street somewhere with 'RESPECT!' above him in big bold letters, and some madey-uppy story about how he never calls members of the public 'wankers', even when they're clearly being wanking wankers who wank a wanky wank.

Who came up with this crap?

The door to the CCTV room opened and Sergeant Farrow slumped out. The luggage under her eyes was larger and darker than Bigtoria's. Her yawn was bigger than Constable Harlaw's too – a proper jaw-stretcher that showed off all her molars. She had a mug of something pressed to her chest and some papers stuffed under her arm.

Edward toasted her with his coffee. 'That's the DI up and doing, Sarge. Morning prayers in ten.'

She blinked at him with bloodshot eyes. 'How was your cell?'

'Horrible. And everything I own stinks of smoke.' A grumph. 'Still don't see why we couldn't stay in the hotel.'

'Because no one's stayed at the hotel for twenty years – well, except for Andy and Charlie, who, you know, live there . . .' Another massive yawn displayed two decades of Scottish NHS fillings, followed by a slump. 'It's all storerooms and cupboards now. Somewhere to dump stuff we'll probably never need again.' She ground one eye into her head with the heel of her free hand. 'Ungh . . .'

It wouldn't be chivalrous to say anything, but she really *did* look terrible.

'You OK, Sarge?'

'Couldn't sleep.' She jerked her thumb at the closed door. 'Trying to see if somebody was out and about last night, when Shammy got attacked.'

Hello . . . That was worth standing up straight for.

Sergeant Farrow rubbed at the other eye. 'No sign of anyone on the CCTV, and every ankle tag stayed where it was meant to be. All night.' She pulled one of the printouts from under her arm. 'Here.'

It was a computer-generated map of Glenfarach with a red line marking out a lopsided circuit of the village. 'Er, thanks?'

'It's a plot of everywhere Geoff Newman went on Monday. Before he died.' Another yawn, even bigger this time. Like she was trying to unhinge the top of her head. 'Going to be a long day . . .'

'And on that happy note.' He headed down the corridor. 'Better make tracks. The guvnor gets a bit vindictive if you're late for her briefings.'

The sun hadn't risen yet, but the cold-white glow of Glenfarach's streetlights shone through the briefing-room windows. It was easily big enough for about sixty people in here, with rows of those Formica-and-metal seats that had a little built-in table for an arm. The fixtures and fittings had probably been state of the art at some point, but now they just looked dated and shabby.

A chunky projector was mounted on the ceiling, clarted in dust. Whiteboards and corkboards all around the walls – covered in the comments, observations, logs, printouts, and photos they'd spent half the night putting together. Geoff Newman's mugshot staring out at them in disapproval, surrounded by Post-it notes and hand-written actions.

Bigtoria had installed herself at the front of the room, resting her bum against a proper desk, mug of coffee sitting next to her as she pointed at the scrawled-up network of boxes and lines she'd just finished drawing.

She looked nothing like the tired and grumpy lump Edward had woken up. She looked alive, alert, and healthy. Almost glowing. It really wasn't natural . . .

She must've *really* gone to town with the contents of her toolbox.

Had to admit, she'd done a bloody good job of it.

Her audience looked like crap, though: Edward, Sergeant Farrow, and PC Harlaw. Squeezed into those stupid table-armrest chairs, yawning, blinking, taking notes, and pretending not to be one-hundred-percent zombified.

Bigtoria put the cap back on her dry marker. 'Any questions?'

Edward nodded. 'If there's no sign of anyone on the CCTV, and all the residents' ankle tags show they didn't go out last night, shouldn't we be focusing on the staff?'

'We are. But we're not discounting the possibility that one or more of the residents are involved.' She pointed. 'Yes: Sergeant Farrow.'

'Is this *actually* going to be possible with only the four of us?'

Good question.

'Just about. How long till the cavalry arrive?'

'Ah . . .' Sergeant Farrow pulled a face. 'You want the bad news or the worse news?'

A pause while Bigtoria glowered at the ceiling tiles. 'Because why should *anything* be sodding easy?'

'Last update I have: the A939's completely blocked, Cock Bridge to Tomintoul. The forensic team made it as far as Tarland and had to hole up for the night. Inspector Draper got stuck at Gairnshiel and didn't make it back to Ballater till five this morning. The pathologist had to sleep in her car. And the Procurator Fiscal says he's staying in Glasgow till the roads are safe.'

Lazy sod.

'And the forecast is heavy snow and high winds from now to Friday lunchtime.'

Bigtoria kept her eyes on the ceiling. 'Of *course* it is.' Then stood, chin up, shoulders back. 'OK, so we've got no choice. We keep going until we get reinforcements.'

'Yes, but, and I say this from experience, policing Glenfarach is unlike any other place you've ever worked. Geoff Newman's murder will be all round the village fifteen minutes after curfew's lifted.'

'Surprised it takes that long.'

Sergeant Farrow shrugged. 'They've no internet. No mobile phones. And the only places with landline access are here, Sanctuary House, and the doctor's. I mean, can you *imagine* what would happen if we let our residents have free rein online? Or if they could coordinate with people on the outside? Doesn't bear thinking about.' She puffed out her cheeks, like she was running the scenarios in her head and not coming up with anything pretty. 'Point is: even if they saw the firelight in the sky, they won't know what caused it till they're allowed to leave their homes in . . .' – checking her watch – 'sixteen minutes.'

Harlaw nodded. 'Then it'll be all over Glenfarach like greased Marmite.'

A low growl rumbled out of Bigtoria. 'This place is a nightmare.'

'Oh, definitely.' Sergeant Farrow wriggled out of her desk-seat. 'I know what'll help.' She bustled from the room, leaving Bigtoria blinking at this sacrilegious affront to the sanctity of morning prayers.

Time to put some sort of positive spin on this crapshow, before they all reached wrist-slitting levels of motivation. Edward tried on his most optimistic voice. 'OK, so we can't do fingerprints or DNA, but we *can* still run PNC checks, right? And we could go through the records as well: see if anyone had a connection to Geoff Newman before he was sent down.'

Bigtoria's face softened. 'Worth a try.' She jabbed a finger at Harlaw. 'Can you do that?'

'Er . . . Think so.'

That was more like it.

Edward turned in his seat. 'You're looking for anybody who was in London when Newman worked for the Met. Maybe he arrested one of them? Or did a dodgy deal for them. And include the Social Work Team, Duty Doctor, and every police officer that works here too – not just this shift, all of them.'

A pinched expression crabbed its way onto Harlaw's face. 'OK . . .'

'You sure?'

'Yes.' Deep breath. 'No, I was good at this stuff at school. I can *definitely* do it.'

Bigtoria gave him an actual, honest-to-God, seen-only-once-in-a-lifetime smile. 'Fair enough. I want a map of Glenfarach too, and a list of every single resident: names, addresses, what they did, how long they've lived here.'

Might as well make the poor sod work for his living. Edward added another lump to Harlaw's pile. 'And we'll need everything the Metropolitan Police have on Geoff Newman: case files, suspects, interviews, who he sent down, who he let get away. The whole bag of wingwangs.'

'Er . . .'

'Good idea.' Bigtoria rolled her shoulders, getting into it. 'Now, we're going to—'

The door thumped open again and in came Sergeant Farrow, carrying a laptop. She plonked it down beside Bigtoria. 'Every new officer gets an orientation, because of it being so different here.' A cluster of cables were Velcroed together at the back of the desk. Sergeant Farrow picked one and fiddled it into a port on the laptop. Pressed a couple of keys. A view of the desktop appeared across the whiteboard as the ceiling-mounted projector flickered into life.

She pulled over a chair and climbed up on it, reaching her full length to grab a metal handle and pull a projection screen down from its casing, giving a much clearer picture. 'Here we go . . .' Another couple of key clicks and a video appeared, joined by a weird electronic theme tune that was clearly trying too hard.

The caption 'A JOB LIKE NO OTHER' appeared, superimposed over a bustling control room. Quite a while ago, judging by the haircuts and porn moustaches. Over a dozen desks filled the space, each one featuring a bulky computer monitor and blocky keyboard; a switch panel with flashing lights; at least two phones; a microphone on a stick; and a PC in white shirt, black tie, black epaulettes, and antique haircut. Doing efficient things and looking busy as a chisel-jawed individual marched into the front of shot. She was done up in the full old-style Grampian Police kit – black jacket, white shirt, checked cravat, checked rim around the bowler hat she had tucked under one arm. Three pips on her shoulders.

Another caption: 'CHIEF INSPECTOR JESSICA SMITH'.

Her voice was a clipped RP, with hints of Glaswegian lurking underneath. *'So, you've decided to join our policing family here at Glenfarach. Welcome.'* Smith gestured at her fellow officers. *'You'll be helping us run a state-of-the-art operation, designed to handle one of the country's most challenging offender-management environments.'*

The control room disappeared, replaced by a shot of the police station's grand entrance, where Chief Inspector Smith marched out the door and down the stairs, into the glare of summer sunshine.

She walked towards the camera and it panned around as she did, taking in Market Square with its trees and their glowing-emerald leaves, the manicured grass, and the clock tower/monument. The red curfew bar was set at ten o'clock, but the green one still pointed at eight thirty. A couple of posed residents were sitting on separate benches, not interacting with each other.

And the camera was back on Smith again. *'As you've no doubt heard, Glenfarach is a community unlike any other. Purpose built in the mid-nineteenth century to service the Glenfarach Estate, it's been repurposed to house offenders who have been released from prison, but can't be returned to the general population because of the danger posed to them by members of the press and public.'* She nodded at one of the residents. *'Keeping your nose clean, Charlie?'*

Charlie was like something off those horrible *What We Did in the Eighties!* TV shows: dressed in stonewashed jeans, high-tops, and a billowy scarlet shirt. He even had a curly mullet and a hoop earring. Where Smith was clipped and RP, Charlie was unwholesomely cheery. *'I am indeed, Chief Inspector Smith. Lovely day!'* Throwing in a wave for good measure.

Smith didn't wave back, just kept on walking, talking to the camera. *'It's important to remember that while these people have paid their debt to society, that doesn't mean they can simply be allowed to do as they please.'*

In the background, Charlie was still waving and grinning, milking his part for all it was worth.

She marched along one of the paths, crossing the grass. *'Many will have licence conditions that restrict their association with other residents – those who've been convicted of sexual offences, for example. That's why communications are kept* strictly *off limits to residents.'*

Chief Inspector Smith stopped beside an old-fashioned Rover SD1 patrol car with the Grampian Police logo on the driver's door. She opened it. *'Let's take a look around the village and talk about the various categories of offender we house here.'*

Bigtoria stepped in front of the projector, partially blocking the screen as Smith went for a drive. 'All right, enough of the pre-flight safety video bollocks.' She mashed her thumb down on the space bar, freezing the image, then pointed at Sergeant Farrow. 'Give me the highlights.'

Sergeant Farrow's shoulders dipped at that. 'OK. Potted version.' She took control of the laptop again, fiddling with it until a map of Glenfarach appeared on Bigtoria and the projector screen. It looked a lot like the one she'd given Edward, only there was no wriggly red line and each of the houses was colour-coded.

She waited for Bigtoria to step out of the way, then unfurled a three-foot-long extendable pointer. 'We've currently got one hundred and eighteen sex offenders' – tapping the screen – 'that's the yellow, orange, and red houses. Sixty what you'd call organized criminals – green is drugs, blue is violence' – *tap, tap, tap* – 'and twenty-two miscellaneous offenders – purple, pink, brown, and turquoise, depending on the category.' *Tap, tap, tap, tap.* 'That puts us at full capacity: two hundred residents.' Pained smile. 'Which is why we had to sleep in the cells last night.'

Harlaw stretched his neck, acting the martyr. 'There's a few abandoned properties about the place, but you wouldn't keep a dog in them. Holes in the ceilings, mice-infested, pigeons, cat piss, that kinda thing.'

'Sex offenders aren't allowed to socialize with anyone who's got the same offending profile. So a paedophile can be friends with a rapist, but not another paedophile. Which is why two reds can't live next door to each other.'

Edward stared at the map. 'You got many serial killers?'

'Of course we don't.' Looking at him like a dafty. 'They end up in secure psychiatric facilities, like that big one outside Montrose.'

'Oh.' Shame.

'We don't *want* "excitement", remember? We've got quite enough on our plate as it is.' She tapped the screen again. 'Glenfarach is kind of a safe house cum halfway house, cum care home, cum hospice. Take Geoff Newman: before he came here, he'd been hounded out of five different cities. Same pattern every time: someone recognizes him, calls the tabloids. Next thing you know he's all over the front pages and mobs are throwing bricks and bags of burning dog poo through his windows.' A sigh. 'Very few communities want sex offenders housed in their midst.'

Shock horror.

Harlaw curled his top lip. 'Even the organized crime guys are lying low here. Only it's not so much the paps they have to worry about, it's rival gangs settling the score.'

'Apparently, it's cheaper to dump everyone here than look after them all, individually, out in the real world. They get daily visits from a dedicated social worker, and a police assessment once a week. And the powers that be cut our budget every year.' She clacked her pointer back down to pen-sized and closed the laptop. 'Anything else you need to know?'

Bigtoria stared off into the middle distance for a bit, then nodded. 'Where are the phones? I have to make a call.'

The control room was the same one from the orientation film, only much, *much* scruffier. Those old-fashioned, boxy computers and keyboards were gone, but they hadn't been replaced with top-of-the-range modern models. Instead, everything had a neglected layer-of-dust feel to it. Doubt most of the kit had been used for years. Assuming it still worked.

A big map of Glenfarach dominated one wall, the outlines fading. Each house was colour-coded to show which kind of resident lived there, but they'd been erased and filled in so many times that they'd all ended up a vague sludgy brown.

Gloomy in here, even with the lights on.

Edward opened the blinds – coughing as clouds of dust broke free – letting in a thin watery light that somehow made the place look *more* miserable. The lampposts must've hit their tripping point to turn off, leaving Glenfarach to the miserly scowl of a Scottish January sun. And still the snow fell . . .

Sergeant Farrow pointed at the nearest desk. 'Nine for an outside line.'

Bigtoria sank into an office chair, pulled the phone towards her and dialled. Sat there with the handset to her ear, frowning. Then hung up and had another go. More frowning. This time, instead of returning the handset to the cradle, she clicked the button-thing up and down a few times.

Edward wandered over. 'Problem, Guv?'

'Nine for an outside line?' She poked the button again. 'Not even getting a dialling tone.'

Sergeant Farrow tried a different phone. 'Fudge.'

Edward joined in, but the receiver just hissed in his ear. 'This one's buggered too.'

'Honestly!' Sergeant Farrow picked up another handset, jaw

working on something tough as she listened. '*How* are we supposed to work like this? "State-of-the-art operation, designed to handle one of the country's most challenging offender-management environments" my . . . bottom.' Slamming the handset down.

'OK . . .' Edward raised his eyebrows at Bigtoria. 'So we've no mobile signal, the Airwaves are shagged, and the landlines are down. We're completely cut off, aren't we.' In a village populated with sex offenders, murderers, and the general dregs of the criminal justice system.

'Bastard.'

And then some . . .

9

A knock on the door, and in popped PC Harlaw. 'Sarge? That's Jenna Kirkdale turned up.' Jerking his head towards the corridor. 'You want me to . . . ?'

Sergeant Farrow tried another phone. 'Can't get an outside line.'

'What, *again*?'

Edward hunkered down under one of the desks. 'Maybe if we unplug them and plug them in again?' Following the wires to a small plastic trapdoor in the carpet tiles.

Back up in the real world, Sergeant Farrow sounded like she was *this* close to having a proper whinge. '*See? I said they had to overhaul the comms. "It's a fudge-up waiting to happen," I said. Might as well piddle into the wind.*'

Edward levered the trapdoor open, exposing a couple of power points with plugs in them, a phone jack, and a network point. He unplugged the lot.

'*Bloody . . .*' You could almost *hear* Bigtoria grinding her teeth. '*There has to be some other way to contact the outside world!*'

'*Oh God, I wish there was, Guv, but right now the only option is wading eight miles through the snow, through the pass, and out to where there's a mobile signal.*'

Edward counted to ten and plugged everything back in again.

Up above, something bleeped.

'*This place is a sodding nightmare!*'

'*Welcome to our world.*'

He closed the trapdoor and crawled out from under the desk, peering over the edge. 'Try that.'

Only no one was looking at him: they were watching Harlaw ushering a short woman into the room. *Properly* short too. Like, four foot six. Broad in the hips, but not fat. Little upturned nose. Freckled cheeks. Huge smile. Fluorescent-orange jacket, greying black hair in a ponytail that emerged from beneath a spotted beanie hat.

She carried a big metal-and-plastic toolbox, heavy enough to leave her tilted over to one side. A full-on upper-middle, Home-Counties, jolly-hockey-sticks accent, belting out: 'Morning, Lulu, how's your bum for lovebites? Hear your Airwaves are borked.'

Sergeant Farrow held up a handset. 'And now the phones are down.'

'What, again? Have you guys been . . .' She stared as Edward got to his feet and brushed the dust from his trousers. Then dumped her toolbox and strode towards him, hand out. 'Morning, handsome. Jenna Kirkdale, at your *service*.' When he didn't take her hand she winked. 'Don't worry, I'm not one of the nonces.'

'Er . . .' Heat seeped up from the collar of his smoke-stained shirt. Come on, be professional. He gave her a firm-gripped handshake. 'Detective Constable Edward Reekie.'

Sergeant Farrow gestured at the graveyard of dead phones. 'Jenna, I really need these working.'

Ms Kirkdale didn't let go. She stepped in closer, staring up at Edward. 'It's OK, Lulu: just making friends with Eddie here. Have you tried the local network? Might be a fault on the external line.'

'They're all dead.'

Edward cleared his throat. Nodded towards the phone that sat on the desk he'd been under. 'I unplugged it and plugged it back in again.'

'Ah, every IT Department's best friend – the "power cycle", good man.' A wink. 'Knew you weren't just a pretty face.'

It was definitely getting warmer in here.

Ms Kirkdale let go of his hand; plucked the handset from its cradle and pressed nine, one, two, and three. Stood there, listening. Then hung up. 'OK, *not* getting an outside line. Let's try Sanctuary House . . .' Poking at the keypad. 'That's more like it: ringing now.'

Sergeant Farrow marched over and liberated the handset. 'At least that's something, I suppose. We— Helen? . . . Hels, it's Louise, how's Aggie? . . . Uh-huh . . . Uh-huh . . . No, it must've been quite a shock . . . Tell her we were asking for her, OK? . . . Listen, are your phones working today? . . . Uh-huh . . . No, same here . . .' She went still as a corpse. 'What?' There was something wrong in her voice. Something off. Something that made everyone turn to look at her. 'Are you sure, Hels? You checked the— . . . OK . . . OK. No. I understand. We'll be right there . . . OK, thanks, Hels. Bye. Bye.' She replaced the handset and stood there, frowning at it.

Ms Kirkdale closed the gap till her chest pressed against Edward's, looking up at him with doe eyes. Not quite fluttering her eyelashes, but close. 'I love a man who's good with his *hands*.'

Sergeant Farrow harrumphed. 'I hate to interrupt your love life, Jenna, but we need these phones working.'

The big smile brightened. 'I bet the snow's brought the line down somewhere, but I can have a crack at what's here, if you like? And perchance, in exchange, you might do me a *teensy* favour?' She gave Edward a loaded wink. Then turned to face the sergeant. 'My dear old nan's getting buried in Edinburgh next week, and I should *probably* be there for it. You know, for Mother's sake? Don't want her to think I'm a *complete* monster.'

Sergeant Farrow's expression wasn't exactly enthusiastic.

'*Please*, Lulu: I absolutely *promise* I'll be a good girl. No disappearing for days, no going out on the razzle-dazzle: just down, funeral, sandwiches back at Nan's, then home in time for tea. Hand on heart.'

'Maybe.' Sergeant Farrow stared at the phone again. 'We'll talk about it. *If* you fix the Airwaves.'

'Abso-posi-lutely! Get right on it.' She shot Edward another wink. 'Later, handsome.' And with that she grabbed her heavy toolkit and swagger-staggered out of the room.

Well, she was . . . interesting.

Bigtoria sat in front of one of the less dusty computers. 'Can I at least send an email?' Flexing her fingers.

Edward shook his head. 'If the phones are shagged? Doubt it.'

'Urgh . . .' She huffed out a breath. Then pulled her chin up. 'Changes nothing. We keep going till the cavalry gets here.' Stood. 'I want to know where Geoff Newman went the day he died. Reconstruct his movements. Who was the last person to see him alive? Where was . . .' Bigtoria rapped her knuckles on the nearest desk. 'Are you *listening* to me, Sergeant?'

Obviously not, because Sergeant Farrow came back to earth with a little jolt. Blinking at them. 'Hels . . . I mean Helen Sneddon, she says one of the Social Work Team's gone AWOL: Caroline Manson. Her bed's not been slept in . . .'

'Great.' Edward slumped his bum against a dusty windowsill. 'So we've got a missing social worker, who doesn't have an ankle tag, and a dead ex-cop sex offender who was killed by someone who doesn't have an ankle tag. Not to mention a battered police officer and burned-down crime scene.' A grimace. 'That sound like a coincidence to anyone?'

Sergeant Farrow took a detour past a desk in the corner – picking up a binbag-wrapped parcel about the size of a cricket bat, but rectangular – then marched from the room. *'I'll get the Big Car.'*

Helen Sneddon opened the door to Sanctuary House, setting free a distinct whiff of oven-cleaner gin; a wobble to her step as she backed out of the way to let Bigtoria, Sergeant Farrow, and Edward in.

The three of them stamped their feet on the mat, shaking the snow off their matching high-vis jackets.

Ms Sneddon closed the door again, then dug her hands into the pockets of her shapeless, pastel-blue cardigan. 'She's never . . . I mean no one has. I'm worried something might've happened?'

Sergeant Farrow patted her on the shoulder. 'It's OK, Hels, I'm sure she's OK. Caroline's not daft, is she?'

'Her rooms are this way.'

They followed her through the internal key-code door into a circular corridor with floor-to-ceiling windows, wrapped around a large central courtyard. A thick blanket of snow smothered the patio furniture, trees, benches, and brick barbeque area, leaving only the occasional hint of what lay below to break free and gasp for air.

Doors led off the corridor, marked with things like 'KITCHEN', 'GYM', 'COMMON ROOM', and 'THE GLENFARACH ARMS'. That one had a sign-up sheet pinned to the wall beside it: 'KICKING KARAOKE FRIDAY FUNFEST!'

Helen went left, wobbling her way along, one hand out to steady herself against the glass.

Bigtoria marched after her. 'Who was the last person to see Caroline Manson?'

'We don't know.'

'*What?*' Bigtoria grabbed her arm, pulling her up. 'How can you not know?'

'Because I can't *remember*.' Bottom lip trembling, eyes glittering as the tears started. 'Every day's the same, OK? You go out, you visit your twenty-four sex offenders, twelve thugs, one bent cop, and three miscellaneous *bastards*, then you come back, try to shower the filth off you, and spend the rest of the night in the Glenny. Doing your best to blot it all out with cheap gin and own-brand tonic.'

Edward cracked the door marked 'THE GLENFARACH ARMS' and peered into a shabby, medium-sized room decorated to look like an old-fashioned, traditional Scottish pub – complete with bar, optics, beer taps, and red vinyl seating. A mirrorball hung above a postage-stump dance floor, exuding all the joy and charm of a sequined tumour.

He let the door swing shut again.

Helen looked away, one hand coming up to gesture at the outside world. 'You wade through that . . . horror, trying to treat them like normal people, when you know the vile things they did. When you've seen the photos and read the victim reports. And the impact statements.' Wiping the tears from her wet cheeks. 'Some days it's . . . I'm not religious, I'm really not, but some days it's as if we've all died and *this*, this is hell.'

'Hey, it's OK.' Sergeant Farrow stroked Helen's back. 'It'll all be OK.'

Bigtoria snapped her fingers. 'They got CCTV here?'

Sergeant Farrow took a moment, like she was suppressing a less-than-polite reply. Then: 'Main entrance?'

'Check it.' The DI transferred the full weight of her questionable people skills to Helen. 'I need to speak to everyone on the team. And I want Caroline Manson's personnel file. *Now*.'

Flies, honey, and shite had nothing on her.

Breakout Room 1 was the same as Breakout Room 2, only with a different framed print on the wall.

Bigtoria and Edward sat on one side of the round grey table, with Ian Casey on the other – slumped over a mug of coffee. He'd swapped his *Mork & Mindy* costume for jeans and a *Timmy & the Timeonauts* T-shirt. Blinking at them with bleary eyes, blue stubble coating his chin, the bitter tang of smoke oozing out of him like an infected wound.

He stifled another yawn and squinted. 'Sorry, do I think Caroline could *kill* a man?'

Bigtoria was bolt upright in her chair. Even sitting down she loomed. 'Perfectly straightforward question, Mr Casey. Is she capable of killing someone?'

'Caroline?' Rubbing at his eyes. 'Caroline's gone *missing*. Shouldn't you be out there finding her? What if something's happened?'

Edward put down his pen. 'I know it seems a bit harsh, but we have to cover all the bases, Mr Casey. Did Ms Manson ever talk about Geoff Newman? Ever have to work with him, for example?'

'Probably.' A swig of coffee. 'It's sort of an unwritten rule that if, say, maybe you've got the squits, or it's your day off, then everyone else pitches in and shares out your caseload. We're a tight team here.'

More looming from Bigtoria. 'So, she never mentioned having a problem with Geoff Newman? Given what he did. What he was sent down for?'

'Urgh . . . You can't. Honestly, you just *can't* take that kind of stuff home at night. We've got two hundred residents, and they're only here because they've done some seriously screwed-up shite. You take that personally, you'd go insane.'

Which was kinda the worry.

Agatha Reynolds looked a bit less groggy than she had yesterday, not quite bushy-tailed, but her eyes didn't look like massive black buttons any more. She'd pulled on a cheerful blue smock top with daisies on it; her hair was neatly set, her lanyard squint. Filling the breakout room with the syrupy, throat-catching reek of patchouli oil.

She frowned at Bigtoria over the rim of her glasses. 'Well, yes: I suppose Caroline *did* like the occasional tipple. What has that got to do with anything?'

'Had she been drinking last night?'

'How would I know? I was zonked on happy pills, remember? After what happened to . . .' A shudder set her lanyard swaying. 'Aren't you worried that whoever did *that* to Geoff Newman might've done the same to Caroline? What if she's lying dead in a snowbank somewhere? Or, or she's lost in the woods? Or maybe one of the residents has . . . I don't know, got her locked in the basement?'

Edward dragged out his soothing voice, yet again. Because apparently Detective Inspector Victoria Montgomery-Porter didn't own one. 'It's OK, Ms Reynolds, we're only trying to get an idea of how this all fits together.'

That earned him an outraged stare. 'I resent the suggestion that Caroline deserved whatever's happened to her because she was drunk. You're sitting there, victim-shaming her, when she could be injured or dying!'

With a name like Clive Fox-Johnson, you'd expect a gammon-faced middle-aged bloke in tweeds and polished brogues. Short back and sides. A Labradoodle. Resentful wife. And children called 'Zeus' or 'Monty' or 'Ophelia'.

Instead, the social worker had long greying-blond hair, tucked behind ears with at least three piercings in each. Round wire-framed glasses, buckskin waistcoat, denim shirt. A completely unplaceable accent, like he didn't really come from anywhere. His fingertips had more than a hint of smoker's yellow to them, but all ten of them were kept busy – creating a never-ending series of roll-up fags that got placed one at a time in a small metal tin. Shrouded, thin, little bodies in a mass grave.

Mr Fox-Johnson's tongue slipped its way along the edge of a Rizla. 'Now you're asking.' He twiddled the paper and tobacco into a perfect, filter-free cylinder. 'I think Caroline's been having problems, you know? I mean, it's not exactly the easiest place to work at the best of times, but these last thirteen, fourteen months? Nightmare.'

Edward wrote that down. 'In what way, Mr Fox-Johnson?'

'Call me "Clive", Edward. Much easier to build a rapport when you use someone's first name. Surnames only really come out when you're in some sort of trouble.'

Bigtoria tilted her head on one side, staring. 'You didn't answer the question.'

'Very well observed.' Those nimble fingers plucked another paper from the Rizla packet. 'Things have been getting . . .' A see-saw gesture with his free hand. 'You know, with the residents. Not everyone, of course, but some of them? You can *feel* the tension building. Like there's going to be a reckoning.'

She sniffed. 'A "reckoning"?'

'Sex offenders and organized criminals. Mods and Rockers. The Sharks and the Jets. Pie and a Paris bun.'

'And Ms Manson was on the side of the organized criminals?'

He made a straight line of tobacco down the middle of the paper. 'No. Caroline was letting it get to her. Letting the stress eat her up inside.' A strange, lopsided smile. 'Letting it *fester.*'

'Enough that she'd snap and kill Geoff Newman?'

One shoulder came up, then Mr Fox-Johnson's tongue marked the join of another roll-up. His fingers twiddled the cigarette into shape, and it went in the tin with its dead brothers. 'You know, you should have a word with Dr Singh. Used to be a forensic psychologist, before the ... incident; he's one of Caroline's. Wouldn't surprise me if the good doctor might have an idea what she's capable of and where she's gone.'

The disco ball rotated slowly, sending its chips of cold white light sweeping around the Glenfarach Arms, glinting in the optics, glowing in the brass fittings of the pumps and handrail, shining back from the mirror above the bar – like little creatures' eyes staring out at them from the gloom. A stereo in the corner played an Adele CD, adding to the general ambience of despair.

Helen Sneddon sat at the bar, back hunched, elbows out, head wobbling over a large tumbler of what looked like gin and tonic.

She didn't look up as Bigtoria marched across the tiny dance floor. 'We've spoken to everyone.'

Nothing but a grunt in reply.

'Isn't it a bit early to be hammering the booze?'

'My day off.' The words were mushy around the edges, delivered with care. 'My *one* day off a week; I can drink if I want.'

'Ms Sneddon, we—'

'*You* try living here. Dealing with these ... these *animals*!' She rotated her bar stool till she was facing them. 'Think I'm happy Geoff Newman got himself killed? Cos I'm not.' She took a big swig. 'I'm *ecstatic*.'

Edward perched himself on the next stool over. 'Come on, Ms Sneddon, you don't mean that.'

'Six years I've been here. Six. Years.' Raising her glass in toast. 'You can burn the lot of them, far as I'm concerned.'

Dear God, and she was the *head* of the Social Work Team? No wonder this place was struggling.

The door swung open and in came Sergeant Farrow. 'Guv? Got Caroline on the CCTV, heading out yesterday morning, coming back here for lunch, heading out again at half one. She never returned.'

Bigtoria nodded. 'Get onto the station: I want that idiot Harlaw going through every bit of footage there is. *Find* her.'

'Guv.'

'As for *you*' – Bigtoria loomed over Ms Sneddon – 'I want a list of Caroline Manson's clients. And I need to search her rooms.'

A small laugh, then Ms Sneddon folded over her gin again. 'Knock yourself out.'

The sign on the door read 'Maison Du Manson', but inside it was more like a hotel suite. Not a cheap hotel, but not a boutique one either. A three-star-chain kind of hotel, all painted in a bland shade of magnolia. Had to hand it to Caroline Manson, though – she'd tried to make it look homely with photos and paintings and ornaments. A knock-off Fender sat in the corner, next to an amp and a music stand with a copy of *Heavy Metal Guitar Riffs for Dummies* on it.

So maybe not the *best* of neighbours.

Three doors led off the main living area.

Bigtoria rummaged through the sideboard while Edward snapped on a pair of blue nitrile gloves and headed for the nearest door.

It opened on a clean and tidy bathroom – just big enough to not feel claustrophobic. OK, so the salmon-pink tiles were revolting, but at least they were clean. And they went with the salmon-coloured bath, toilet, and matching sink.

Wicker laundry basket on the floor next to the bath, a bathroom cabinet mounted above the sink.

Edward opened the mirrored door – it had a whole shelf devoted to pill boxes, bottles, and tubs. He worked his way through them, raising his voice enough to carry through to the living room. Hopefully. 'Painkillers, anti-inflammatories, sleeping pills, and I'm pretty sure three of these are for depression.'

Bigtoria's reply boomed out: *'Not surprised.'*

He closed the cabinet and took the lid off the laundry basket instead, picking through the contents – checking the pockets and cuffs of anything with pockets and/or cuffs – then dumping the searched items in the bath. Out of the way. 'Ms Sneddon's a bit . . . "tired and emotional" for ten on a Wednesday morning, isn't she?

Wonder what the burnout rate is for social workers? Got to be massive.'

'*Nothing here. You?*'

'Not yet. I mean, can you imagine doing this for a living and only getting *one* day off a week? That Ian Casey bloke's right: drive you mental.'

Edward dropped the last pair of dirty pants into the bath, and all he had to show for it were a few scrunched-up tissues and a couple of elastic hair ties.

He levered the lid off the cistern and peered inside. No suspicious packages wrapped in binbags and duct tape. No guns, drugs, or money. Just manky water.

Ah well, worth a try.

Lid back on the cistern. Then he stepped through into the living area again.

No sign of Bigtoria.

One of the other two doors was open, though – revealing a small craft room, with a desk, stereo, and art materials.

'I'll do the bedroom, then?'

No reply.

Why did he even bother?

Edward let himself into a nice-sized double with a neatly made divan and tidy bedside cabinet. Chest of drawers. Mirrored wardrobes.

Let's start with the classics.

He squatted in front of the bedside cabinet, working his way down through the drawers, methodically searching and then placing the contents on the duvet cover. 'You think you could do it? Torture someone like that?'

Still nothing.

'I mean, I know Geoff Newman was an absolute scumbag, but he was a human being. Doesn't matter how awful the things he'd done were, nobody deserves *that*.'

Maybe she'd nodded off?

'Not that I'm saying he didn't deserve a stiff kicking.' Easy enough to say that, wasn't it? Sticking out your chest and playing the hardman. 'Mind you, don't think I could actually *give* someone a stiff kicking. You know, leather into them, not in self-defence or anything. I mean: what's the point of having a criminal justice system if you just batter the crap out of people every time they do something wrong?'

He'd searched everything but the bottom drawer, and found nothing more exciting than cheap jewellery, hankies, assorted gewgaws, greying bras, and saggy pants. The last drawer revealed ordered rows of multicoloured socks.

'Guv?'

Still no reply.

Might as well be talking to his sodding self, here.

Edward worked his way through the colourful cotton bundles, separating each pair and checking inside every sock. Finding nothing more exciting than lint. Until . . . 'Well, well, well, what do we have here?' A black leatherette zip case hid at the bottom of the drawer, tucked away at the back, about the size of a hardback book.

That didn't look suspicious *at all*.

'GUV? FOUND SOMETHING!'

He plonked the case on the bed and unzipped it as Bigtoria hurried into the room.

'What? What have you got?'

'Let's find out.' He opened the lid, and there, nestled in black foam-rubber compartments, were a glass bong; a lighter; two small, clear-plastic baggies of white powder; a slightly larger one containing a dozen red pills; another with maybe twenty small yellow ones; and a thumb-sized lump of brown resin, wrapped in clingfilm, in a Ziploc bag. Everything fitted into its own special slot. Like the whole lot had come in a presentation case.

Bigtoria smiled. 'Looks as if our missing social worker isn't the paragon of virtue after all . . .'

IO

The Big Car crumped its way along the snowy street, blowers up to full roar, Sergeant Farrow behind the wheel, Bigtoria in the passenger seat – flipping through Caroline Manson's file – and muggins relegated to the metaphorical child's seat in the back.

Snow fought a losing war with the windscreen wipers. But, going by the coal-scuttle sky, plenty of reinforcements were on the way.

Sergeant Farrow stared at Edward in the rear-view mirror, when she really should've been watching the slippery road. 'Drugs?'

He held up the evidence bag containing Ms Manson's pills, hash, and powder. 'Probably coke – have to do a presumptive test to find out. No idea what the pills are, though.'

'Caroline was on *drugs*?'

They took a left onto East Main Street. A couple of residents were out window shopping in their heavy coats. Someone was clearing the opposite pavement with a self-propelled snowblower – it sent an arc of juddering white spraying out into the road. As soon as they saw the Big Car, all three of them stopped what they were doing to give it a happy smile and a cheery wave.

Edward shrank back into his seat. 'Does that not creep you out?'

'How could Caroline be on drugs? How'd she even get them into Glenfarach? We search *everyone*.'

Bigtoria didn't look up from her paperwork. 'You didn't search us.'

'Creeps *me* out.' He watched the residents go by. 'I mean, they're all so *nice* and *well behaved*. Sort of *Stepford Wives* meets *Village of the Damned*. Only with, you know, sex offenders.'

'Yes, Guv, but . . .' Sergeant Farrow bit her top lip, like she was trying not to say something she'd regret. 'There wasn't *time*. You were gone soon as you'd arrived and the only thing you dropped off was Marky Bishop and I searched *him*.'

Edward turned in his seat, watching the grinning residents drift by. 'Does it not creep you out?'

'Hmmm . . .' Bigtoria put the printouts down. 'Is there somewhere the social workers go to let off steam? Somewhere Caroline Manson could be lying low?'

'That's why they've got the Glenny.' Sergeant Farrow pointed through the windscreen at the Glenfarach House Hotel's dour bulk. 'It's not like they'd want to party at the hotel with all the residents, is it. And it shuts at curfew, anyway.' She took a right, cutting across Market Square, heading north.

Bigtoria frowned. 'We're meant to be going to—'

'I know, Guv, but I need to do a quick check on Marky Bishop first. See how he's settling in.' A shrug. 'Procedure.'

'God's sake.' Returning to her paperwork. 'Did we not see enough of the old git yesterday?'

'All residents get a follow-up visit from a supervising officer. Should be the Duty Inspector, but we're stuck on that one, so it's down to me.' She cast a sly look across the car. 'Unless you want to do it, Guv? You outrank me, so . . . ?'

Silence from the passenger seat. Followed by some low-level swearing.

Edward stood at the window of Jenkins House, looking out through the curtains of snow. Bigtoria hadn't moved her arse from the Big Car, just sat there – scowling her way through printouts and whatnots. Radiating all the charm and warmth and goodwill of a chainsaw in a nursery school.

Sergeant Farrow was going through yet another checklist with Mr Bishop, while Mr Richards rolled his eyes and chipped in every now and then with an 'I already *told* him that, hen!'

Yesterday's pile of cardboard boxes had disappeared, replaced by some decorating gear: ladders, wallpaper table, some pots of paint, rollers, and paintbrushes. They'd even made a start peeling the ugly, cigarette-stained paper from around the fireplace, giving the room an abandoned look.

Still, at least that three-bar electric fire kept it nice and warm, glowing and pinging away for all it was worth.

'He knows, hen, he knows!'

'I'm just making sure, OK, Razors? It's my job.'

Mr Bishop's wheezy voice sounded weaker than it had on the drive over from HMP Grampian. Like something had drained out of him. Like he'd shrunk overnight. Like there was just that teeny bit less of him there today. 'I understand . . . the conditions . . . of my tenure here.'

But that was cancer for you.

'Then we're all done.' Sergeant Farrow held out her clipboard and a pen. 'You sign here, on the dotted line, and you're officially inducted.'

Mr Bishop did as instructed, signature jittering in his shaky hand, then took a good scoof on his oxygen.

'Excellent.' She returned the pen to her pocket, tucked the clipboard under her arm. 'Someone will pop in from time to time – make sure you're settling in OK – but in the meantime, we try to be one big happy family here in Glenfarach, so if you have any concerns, you know where to find me.' A pause. A smile. 'Oh, and before I forget: we have a present for you.' She handed him that binbag-wrapped parcel, nodded, and then she was gone.

Mr Richards commandeered the package from Mr Bishop, before scuffing out after her, their low voices barely audible in the hall as Mr Bishop levered himself up out of the wheelchair and, leaning heavily on his cane, joined Edward at the window.

Took a while, though.

By the time he arrived, Sergeant Farrow was striding down the path towards the Big Car. Which meant it was probably time for Edward to get moving too.

'How you doing, Mr Bishop?'

'Shite.' The old man looked up at him, that hunch in his back making it difficult to raise his head much at all. 'You got any . . . idea . . . how it feels to know . . . you're going to die here, son?' Whacking the tip of his walking stick against the nasty carpet. 'Right here.' His grey-ringed eyes slid past the Big Car and over to the graveyard on the other side of the road. 'Life's a funny bastard . . . and no mistake.'

Edward nodded. 'Mr Bishop? I was wondering, I mean, did you hear someone died yesterday?'

'Oh aye. Razors told me.'

'His name was Geoff Newman. Used to be a sergeant in the Metropolitan Police. Into money laundering, extortion, and child pornography.'

Mr Bishop took a couple of shaky breaths on the oxygen, then, 'And some bugger murdered him?'

'Yes.'

One word rasped out of him. 'Good.'

In the Big Car, Bigtoria and Sergeant Farrow were talking about something. Pointing at the paperwork, then pointing out into the snowy landscape.

'I was wondering if you had any thoughts about that, Mr Bishop. I mean, it's kind of a weird coincidence, right? You turn up and all of a sudden, Glenfarach has its first murder in thirty years?' He held up a hand. 'I'm not accusing you of anything, by the way – I know you were with us – but do you not think the timing's a bit suspect?'

'Hmmm . . .' The old man's reflection creased in the window. 'I wondered if maybe it was . . . a warning, or a threat . . . or maybe even a gift? . . . A *welcoming* present.' Pointing vaguely back into the room. 'Like whatever the hell that was . . . "Here's a dead nonce to brighten up . . . your stay."' He gave a little snort. 'I'd've preferred . . . a poke of liquorice allsorts, mind.' Then a shrug. 'Trouble is, I know no bugger here, other than Razors . . . So who's gonna treat me to . . . a dead paedo?'

'Thought you'd done time with most of the people here?'

'Oh aye, to talk to . . . maybe. But not *know*, know . . . Not like . . . I'd help them bury . . . a body, or anything.'

Interesting.

Edward turned his back on the window before Bigtoria and the sergeant started making get-your-arse-in-gear gestures. 'So how come you moved here, then?'

A sad smile. 'Where else . . . am I going to go, son? . . . My Irene died thirty years ago . . . I was doing five in Barlinnie . . . and Leo "Big Boy" McQue . . . firebombed the house . . . His way of saying thank you . . . for me crippling his dad.' Mr Bishop abandoned the window and shuffled back to the wheelchair. 'All brave . . . and bold . . . when a man's in prison, eh?' His voice softened. 'They had to identify . . . her from her . . . dental records.' He lowered himself onto the padded seat.

'I'm sorry to hear that.'

'Aye, so was I, son.' He blinked away at the middle distance. 'So was I.' The silence stretched for a count of ten, before Mr Bishop returned from wherever he'd gone. 'My eldest, Neil . . . he's doing fifteen in some . . . Australian jail . . . for drugs . . . Tina married . . . this investment banker . . . arsehole . . . popping out kids . . . like she's a springer . . . spaniel . . . Think they want . . . an old fart . . . dying in their . . . spare room?' He clamped the mask to his face and dragged in wheezing breath after wheezing breath, till the tremble in his arms and legs subsided.

'Do you need me to call the Duty Doctor?'

He waved the offer away with a liver spotted hand. 'So, I looked about . . . did some research in the prison library . . . and this was the best option.'

'I should probably go. Let you rest.'

'Wasn't always called Glenfarach . . . Back in the sixteenth . . . century it was . . . Gleann na Fola – the Valley of Blood . . . Because of a wee disagreement . . . that ended up with every male . . . over the age of six . . . getting their throats cut at a waterfall . . . up in the hills there.' A skeletal finger pointed through the window. 'And all the streams ran red . . . Legend has it, on a quiet night . . . you can still hear their ghosts screaming . . .'

An awkward silence filled the Big Car as Edward climbed into the back, but at least nobody shouted at him for being late. Instead, Sergeant Farrow and Bigtoria sat there, not talking to each other, all the way to Market Square. Like they'd had a falling out, or something.

Then the sergeant's Airwave gave three bleeps and PC Harlaw's voice echoed out of the car's speakers, loud and clear, breaking the stalemate:

'*Golf Foxtrot Six to Golf Foxtrot Four, safe to talk?*'

'Thank goodness for that.' Sergeant Farrow crowbarred a bit of jollity into her voice. 'Sounds like Jenna's fixed the Airwaves.' Then pressed a button on the steering wheel. 'Go ahead, Dave.'

'*Er . . . Sarge? I . . . Erm . . .*'

'Come on, Dave, spit it out.'

'*OK . . .*' Deep breath. '*Sarge, you know how you asked me to look at all the CCTV footage? See if I could find Caroline Manson? Well . . . Erm . . . There isn't any.*'

Nobody moved.

The windscreen wipers grunted and whined.

The snow fell.

The car slowed to a halt.

And the colour darkened on Bigtoria's cheeks. 'What?'

Yeah, that wasn't good.

Edward shrank back into his seat, keeping out of her eyeline, because the last thing you wanted when a DI had their blood pressure up was to make yourself an easy target.

Sergeant Farrow's voice was surprisingly calm and flat. 'What do you mean, "There isn't any"?'

'*I've checked all the disks and the backups*' – getting faster and faster – '*and it's all just static and I can see everything from Monday night and earlier but there's nothing for yesterday or today and I don't know what to—*'

Bigtoria slammed her fist down on the dashboard. 'WHAT DID YOU DO?'

'*I didn't do anything! . . . I don't know. I've only ever used the CCTV suite a couple of times and . . . maybe I—*'

'OH, FOR *GOD'S* SAKE!' Spittle hit the windscreen.

'OK, OK.' Sergeant Farrow held up a hand. 'Nice calm breaths.' She turned her reasonable voice in the DI's direction. 'The systems are all fudged, remember? This happens from time to time; it'll be a glitch in the wiring or something.' She faced front again. 'It's all right, Dave, don't worry. Just get Jenna to take a look when she's finished with the phones.'

Two miserable words slumped out of the speakers. '*Yes, Sarge.*' Then the Airwave bleeped, and he was gone.

'*Wonderful.*' Bigtoria gave the dashboard another thump. 'So we've got *no* DNA, *no* fingerprint services, *no* forensics of any kind, and *no* CCTV! How on *earth* am I supposed to—'

'I know, Guv, I know.' Sergeant Farrow gave her a sad smile. 'Told you Glenfarach wasn't like anywhere you've ever worked.'

Bigtoria sagged in her seat, both hands covering her face. 'So help me . . .'

OK, now the main stormfront had passed, it was probably safe to become visible again.

Edward sat forward. 'What are we going to do about Caroline Manson?'

Bigtoria rubbed at her eyes. 'Normally, I wouldn't jump to conclusions: treat them as separate cases until we had something to corroborate her involvement in Newman's death. But I don't have the manpower to run a missing person's and a murder inquiry.'

'We can't just leave her out there, Guv!' Sergeant Farrow stuck the car in gear again. 'Caroline's part of the team. What if she's hurt? What if—'

'Or dead.' Edward shrugged. 'Sorry, but no one's seen her since yesterday lunchtime – in this weather?'

Bigtoria looked out the passenger window.

Sergeant Farrow's jaw tightened as she took a right at Market Square.

Edward shifted in his seat.

Watched another resident, with a tartan tote bag, smile and wave at the Big Car.

Cleared his throat.

'Sarge? Your two hundred residents: how many of them do you trust?'

'Depends.' Suspicion dripping from her voice. 'Why?'

'Like the DI says, we haven't got the bodies to run *both* investigations, but we *could* draft in civilians to search the village, couldn't we? See if they can find Ms Manson.'

Her brow furrowed. 'You'd have to exclude some of the sex offenders . . . but maybe?' She glanced across the car at Bigtoria. 'Above my paygrade, though.'

A nod. 'Do it.' Then Bigtoria took a sheet of paper from the document wallet and handed it over. 'And get your idiot, Harlaw, to work his way through Manson's client list. Find out who she saw last. If we're lucky he won't manage to screw *that* up.'

Edward watched another creepy, waving resident go by. 'What about us, Guv?'

'We've got a forensic psychologist to visit.'

Singh House was a nice little two-storey detached in the north-east corner of Glenfarach. The street was full of them, each a little different from its neighbour, in an understated, but stylish fashion. One of those areas that probably belonged to people with money, back before the village became a haven for thugs and sex offenders.

Edward climbed down into the snow and locked the Big Car, before following Bigtoria up the path to the front door. 'Guv? Are you not worried we're asking a bit much of Constable Harlaw? I mean he's—'

'A moron.' She pressed the doorbell.

True.

Still . . .

'He's *young*. Looks like he's barely out of probation.' Pulling on a half-judgemental, half-pitying look. 'It's just we're sticking a *lot* on his shoulders and I worry he's . . .'

The door to Singh Cottage opened, revealing an old man in an ill-fitting rugby shirt and turban: arms folded, scowl on his lined face. His beard was grey and lustrous, reaching halfway down his chest. Large square glasses. A diamond stud in one ear. His accent caught somewhere between a Dundee primary-school drawl and a St Andrews University sneer. 'Can I *help* you?'

Bigtoria flashed her warrant card. 'Mr Singh? Helen Sneddon tells me you were a criminal psychologist.'

His chin came up, bringing that spade of a beard with it. '*Forensic* psychologist. Yes, I am.' A pained pause. 'Well, I *was* until the unfortunate misunderstanding. Twenty years consulting for Tayside Police.'

She looked him up and down. 'You any good?'

DI Montgomery-Porter's legendary people skills strike again.

'Any good? Any *good*?' His eyes widened, cheeks trembling as his mouth pinched and his voice went all clipped. 'Remember the Stobswell Strangler and the Perthshire Ripper? I wanted to call him "Desperate Dan", but the force lawyers wouldn't let us for copyright reasons. But it was *my* behavioural evidence analysis that caught both of them.' A haughty sniff. 'And *many* others besides.'

Edward stepped forward, laying it on a bit thick. 'Ms Sneddon says you're probably the smartest person in Glenfarach, and we should *definitely* talk to you. You know, in your professional capacity?'

His face softened. 'Are you, the police, asking Dr Kuwarjeet William Singh – DSc, FBPsS, FAcSS – for help apprehending a suspect?' Eyes going all misty and hopeful. 'After all these years?'

'Sort of. Absolutely. If you *could* help, that would be great.'

Those misty eyes were tearing up, now. 'You don't know how long I've waited to hear someone say that.'

Mr Bishop was right – honey and shite caught more flies every time.

Edward ladled it on with a trowel. 'It'd be *massively* useful, wouldn't it, Guv?'

Bigtoria just stood there, silent. Couldn't even be bothered joining in. Know what? Bugger her; time she saw how a real police officer worked a witness.

'Don't think we could do it without you, Dr Singh.'

A beatific smile parted the beard. 'Well, in *that* case . . . fuck right off.'

He slammed the door in Edward's face.

'Ah . . .'

Bigtoria gave Edward a slow round of applause. 'Oh yes, very good. I was *so* impressed with your shite-and-honey routine. Clearly, I can learn *much* from you.' A snort. 'Idiot.'

'Come on, that wasn't my—'

The door swung open again, and there was Dr Singh: chest out, chin up, peering down his nose at them. 'One condition: you speak to someone about quashing this ridiculous conviction of mine – which was a complete miscarriage of justice, by the way – and I get three weeks' worth of social credits for my services.'

Bigtoria stepped forward. 'We'll think about it. *If* whatever you tell us pans out.'

He performed an elaborate bow. 'Then you may step inside.'

Dr Singh's 'study' was huge, with bay windows overlooking an enormous back garden suffocated by snow. Bookshelves lined two walls, but a row of four filing cabinets and an enormous oak desk dominated the rest of the space. A random collection of corkboards covered nearly all the available wallpaper, but an oversized map of Glenfarach had pride of place – the houses all coloured in with felt-tip.

He settled himself into a black-leather swivel chair. Smiling like someone's proud dad as they took it all in. 'One likes to keep one's hand in.' He pointed at the line of cabinets. 'I have files on all of Glenfarach's residents, support staff, and police officers.'

A pair of folders sat on his desk. The first was phone-book thick and marked 'GEOFF NEWMAN'. The other looked nearly empty: 'MARK "MARKY" BISHOP'.

Bigtoria helped herself to Newman's file, flicking through it. 'And your social worker's OK with this, are they?'

'Caroline thinks it's nice to have a hobby.' He scooted his chair over to the filing cabinet and had a rummage. 'Now, you wanted to know *all* about her. Manson, Manson . . . Ah, here we are.' He scooted back again, clutching another folder. Opened it on the desk and arranged the contents into piles. 'Joined our happy little family six years ago.'

He selected a glossy eight-by-ten photo and presented it with a flourish.

According to a handwritten sticker on the bottom corner, this was Caroline Manson: a handsome woman; long, straight nose, dark-brown wavy hair – sun-bleached at the ends; mid-twenties. Slightly uncomfortable smile, like she wasn't *really* sure she wanted to be photographed.

Dr Singh removed his glasses and tucked them into a pleat at the top of his turban. Replacing them with a small round pair from a drawer. Peering through them as he dug into one of the paper piles. 'Aha.' Coming out with a few sheets of handwritten notes in a dense, indecipherable hand. 'Caroline Rosemary Manson, twenty-nine' – so older than she looked – 'graduated from Glasgow Caledonian University with an MSc in Social Work. Her first job was in the City of Edinburgh Council's North East District Criminal Justice Team, as a Domestic Abuse Service Women's Worker. Caroline's caseload often involved—'

Bigtoria poked the desk. 'All right, we don't need to go back to the sodding Big Bang. Relevant details only.'

He stiffened. 'I see.' Another haughty sniff. 'It would help me know what *is* and *isn't* relevant if you told me why you're asking about her.'

A pause, then a nod. 'Geoff Newman was murdered.'

'Was he, indeed?' The doctor's eyes sparkled. 'Of course I'll need to see the crime-scene photographs, your initial pathologist's report, and I always find visiting the locus to be enormously . . . Ah.' His smile grew. 'Only we can't, because whoever killed him burned the house down. Oh, very good.' Rubbing his hands together. 'I've not worked an active case for a long, long time.'

He looked from Bigtoria to Edward and back again. 'Well?' Holding his hand out, palm up. 'Photographs?'

The DI developed a sudden interest in the carpet. 'We don't

have any. We sealed the scene to preserve it till the forensic team turned up.'

'Yes, but *first* you took a few snaps on your phone, didn't you?' He did the looking-at-them thing again. Then raised an eyebrow as he finally twigged. 'Oh dear.'

Edward shrugged. 'Not really allowed to do that any more. If it helps, he was tortured to death. Eyes gouged right out of his head. Lots of bruises. Stab wounds. Hell of a lot of blood. And he was tied to a table.'

'Tied to a *table*?'

'On his back, wrists and ankles tied to the table legs, head hanging over the edge. Stripped down to his pants.'

Dr Singh took his reading glasses off again, chewing on one arm as he frowned. 'I see. I see. Like he was a sacrificial offering . . . They didn't carve his heart out, did they?'

Now *there* was a way to make the image even worse.

'*No.* Just the eyes.'

'Pity. And you have some reason to suspect that Caroline Manson was responsible?'

Bigtoria perched on the edge of the desk, leafing through Dr Singh's notes. 'Whoever killed him, they weren't fitted with an ankle tag. Manson doesn't have one, and she's missing.'

'I see . . . Yes.' He pinched the bridge of his nose. 'You know, photographs really would make this a *lot* easier.' A long slow exhale. 'But let's see what we can do with what's available.' Glasses back on again. All business. 'Who found the body?'

'Agatha Reynolds, yesterday at . . . ?'

Edward checked his notes. 'Sixteen minutes past three.'

'First attending officer?'

He took that one, too. 'Constables Harlaw and Samson.'

'Interesting. And I take it there's nothing on CCTV – or at least nothing *identifiable* – otherwise you wouldn't be here talking to me.' Steepling his fingers. 'It won't be easy, working up a profile with so little to go on, but I may have a couple of ideas about that.'

Bigtoria dumped his notes back on the desk. 'Cut to the chase: could she do that to Newman?'

He didn't move.

Outside, snow fell silent and slow, like feathers from a dying bird. A cat picked its way along the garden fence.

Then, 'Caroline had a troubled relationship with her mother, no doubt caused by—'

'Relevant – details – *only*.'

Going by his voice, you'd think Dr Singh was addressing a small child: 'I'm talking about Caroline's psychological make-up, Detective Inspector. You want to know if she's capable of torturing a man to death. This *is* relevant.' Dr Singh paused, head on one side like he was awaiting permission to proceed. And when Bigtoria rolled her eyes: 'Caroline's father was an abusive drunk. Her mother suffered terribly at his hands, and so did Caroline. Possibly not just emotional and physical abuse; my impression is there was a sexual element to it as well.'

Edward pulled his chin in. 'How on earth do you know that?'

'She's been here six years; people like talking to me.' Waving at the filing cabinets. 'If you listen carefully enough, for *long* enough, it's amazing what you can piece together.'

'So she goes into social work because of what happened with her dad. And that's why her first job's in domestic abuse.'

Dr Singh turned to Bigtoria and smiled. 'You see? Relevant.' Back to the file. 'But, sadly, as is often the case, history is doomed to repeat itself. Caroline got into a series of abusive relationships, with wholly unpleasant men, until six years ago, when she decided she needed a fresh start and came here.'

Bigtoria checked her watch. 'Still waiting.'

A sigh. 'Caroline was quite possibly abused by her father, and now here she is, in Glenfarach, working with child molesters and violent thugs every day. It took its toll.'

'So, what, one morning she just snaps, ties Newman to a table and tortures him to death? As a sort of proxy revenge?'

'She's been complaining about her stress levels for months. If she decided to do something about the *causes* of her stress? Then yes.' Dr Singh nodded. 'Caroline could've been capable of some very terrible things indeed.'

11

Edward eased the car onto West Main Street again. At least it was a promotion from sitting in the back. 'Did you buy any of that?'

Bigtoria had assumed her usual throne, squinting away at the notes she'd commandeered from Dr Singh, lips moving as she traced a finger across the rabid scrawl. 'What is it with doctors and their handwriting?'

'Ms Manson wakes up one morning and decides torturing paedophiles to death is her new hobby?'

'Hmmm . . .'

Oh, for God's sake.

'You're not listening, are you.'

Bigtoria let loose a big whumping breath. 'Why does nothing here ever go according to plan?'

'Because it didn't look like an amateur job to me. Whoever did *that* to Geoff Newman knew exactly what they were doing.'

She shut the file and frowned out the window for a while, mouth moving behind closed lips. Like she was chewing something over.

She was still at it when Edward parked the car.

'Guv?' Pointing. 'That's us. Last place our victim visited before he died.'

The Glenfarach General Store was the kind of picturesque olde shoppe you'd find on a supermarket Christmas card. A Dickensian two-storey building with a mullioned bay window, perfect for carol-singing urchins to gather outside. The snow dusting the woodwork only added to the effect, lights casting a welcoming golden glow out into the wintry morning.

Bigtoria undid her seatbelt. 'We have to find Caroline Manson ASAP.'

'We're doing everything we can, Guv. You know, with what we've got.'

'Urgh.' She rubbed at her face for a moment. Then let her shoulders sag. 'I need ten times as many officers, *plus* a HOLMES unit, Forensics, pathologist, Procurator Fiscal, budget and resource managers, senior oversight . . . But what do I have? A sergeant and two idiots.'

She better be talking about Police Constables Harlaw and Samson there.

He drummed his hands on the steering wheel. 'Maybe Sergeant Farrow's search teams will find something?'

'The way *my* week's going it'll be another dead body.' Bigtoria levered herself out of the Big Car. 'In the meantime: we carry on as planned.'

Fair enough.

He joined her on the snowy pavement. Checked the printout. 'According to this, Glenfarach General Store's run by one Kevin Clarke. Sixty-two, used to be a drug dealer in Stirling before killing three people and going on the lam. Put one police officer in a wheelchair and another in a coma for eight months.' Sounded like a right charmer. 'Been here for twenty years.' Edward turned the page. 'Second in command's a Wendy Hamilton. Embezzled all her mother's money, then did the same with two charities raising cash for malnourished children in Africa. Three point six million in total. Living the high life in Monaco when they caught her.'

'Was she now.' Bigtoria shoved through the shop door, setting an old-fashioned bell tinkling.

From the outside, the General Store looked like it would be all polished wood shelves and people in striped pinnies; instead, the place was a long, open space, divided up with metal shelving – piled high with tins and bottles and containers and boxes. An array of confectionery sat by the till, along with a collection of charity collection boxes and a heated display case with pies in it.

Edward followed Bigtoria in, past about half a dozen racks and carousels of what could only be described as 'craft-stall tat'.

A man and a woman busied themselves behind the counter – laughing and gossiping as they labelled up a crate of beans with a price gun. He was rangy, thin, with long black hair that couldn't be natural at his age, dangling in a limp ponytail. Minimum of four piercings in each ear, stud through his squint nose. But the *most* distinctive thing about him were the tattoos. Heaps of them. Most of which were straight out of the *So You Want To Disfigure Yourself In Prison?* handbook. They stained the back of his hands, reaching up his neck where it poked out of a tartan shirt, covering both cheeks and most of his forehead.

His companion was late forties, tall, her grey hair falling in curls around a heart-shaped face. The kind of person who wouldn't have been out of place in the boardroom, on the golf course, or chucking her car keys in a bowl at a swingers' party.

The man looked over as the bell's tinkling chime faded. 'Goodness, are these new residents I see before me? Welcome to Glenfarach, my lovelies! Come in, come in. Don't worry, we won't bite, will we, Wendy?'

She raised her eyebrows, and produced an accent posh enough to feature in yet another BBC Jane Austen adaptation. 'Well, I might if you ask nicely.'

They both laughed.

Edward and Bigtoria didn't.

A flash of warrant card. 'Detective Inspector Montgomery-Porter. You Kevin Clarke? I need to ask you some questions about Geoff Newman.'

'Oooh.' The tattooed man leaned his elbows on the counter. '*Fascinating.* I do declare the gossip has been quite delicious this morning. Is it true he was burned alive in his cottage?'

Ms Hamilton clasped imaginary pearls to her chest, eyes wide. 'I heard he was *dis-mem-bered.*'

'Newman was here, in your shop, the day before yesterday.'

'He was indeed.' Kevin made a spiralling gesture with one web-covered hand. 'As I recall it was baked beans, a packet of sausages, and a loaf of sliced white.' A sigh. 'Why I bother stocking prosciutto crudo, panettone, and truffle oil is beyond me.'

His companion shook her head. 'Some people just don't appreci-ate the good things in life.'

'How often did he—'

'Beans and sausages on toast. I mean, *honestly*.'

The DI's back stiffened. 'How often did Geoff Newman—'

'God knows we try to educate their palates, but what can we do if they refuse to *better* themselves?'

Bigtoria turned to Edward. 'DC Reekie, I need you to take Ms . . . ?'

She stepped out from behind the counter. 'Hamilton.' Then offered her hand to kiss. 'Charmed, I'm sure.'

Bigtoria ignored it. 'Take Ms Hamilton somewhere *else* and ask her some questions about Mr Newman.'

Great, now he was the distraction.

Still, might as well do a good job of it: have another bash at that honey-and-shite thing. Even if it hadn't worked on Dr Singh. 'Guv.' He hooked his arm into Ms Hamilton's. Putting a camp bounce into his voice to echo Kevin Clarke's. 'Shall we? I love your hair, by the way, very chic.'

She giggled, and allowed herself to be led away.

Bigtoria's standard, less-than-friendly tone growled out behind them. *'Right, Mr Clarke, let's try this again: Geoff Newman . . .'*

The epitome of charm.

Wendy Hamilton leaned against the worktop. 'I'd offer you a cup of tea, but . . . ?'

The galley kitchen was tucked away through a door at the back of the shop, off a wee corridor that smelled of cumin and lentils.

Edward kept up the friendly camp act. 'I'll make it, if you like?'

She waved him in the general direction of the kettle.

He filled it from the little sink. 'Kevin's a bit of a character, isn't he? Big guy, all those tattoos, you'd expect him to be a proper scary hardman.'

'Milk, no sugar for me: I'm sweet enough.'

'Especially with his rap sheet.' The kettle went on to boil.

Her voice hardened. 'We don't talk about things like that. It's bad manners.'

'Right. Understood. My apologies.' Edward picked two mugs off the draining board and threw her a disarming smile. 'I'm a bit new to all this. Still finding my feet.'

She stared at him, head on one side, watching as he plonked a teabag into each mug. Then, 'You're forgiven.'

He turned the camp up a notch. 'Bet you see *all* sorts, working here. What was Geoff Newman like?'

'It's my cross to bear, that I'm reduced to rubbing shoulders with the likes of Geoff Newman.' Ms Hamilton flared her nostrils. 'A *child* molester – I mean, *really*.'

Oh, so it wasn't 'bad manners' when *she* did it.

'Must be quite a thing.' The kettle sputtered to a halt, and he filled the mugs. 'People like that.'

'Of course, he was *forever* trying to get us to sell him drink. I told him, I said, "You can't have alcohol, Geoff, it's here on your file."' She dropped her voice and leaned in. 'We have to keep files on all our customers, in case they try to buy things they're not allowed. And it's nearly *always* booze.'

'Wow.' Not really, but it was a non-committal word that sounded like agreement.

Seemed to go down well too.

'And just between you and me, Monday wasn't the first time he came in here reeking of cheap spirits and paint-stripper wine.'

'Oh God, yes, I heard he'd been sneaking drink from some-where.' Squishing the teabags against the mugs with a spoon. 'How *terrible*.'

'I *know*, and he's not getting it from us, so who *is* he getting it from? We're the only place licensed to sell beers, wines, and spirits. I mean, you *can* have some at the hotel, but only with a meal, and only if it's allowed on your file.'

'Wow.' A splosh of milk in each mug.

'If you ask me, that young man was brewing his own. Well, a

certain class of person does that, don't they? Make "prison wine" in their radiators, when we sell a perfectly reasonable Merlot right here.'

'Very true.' He handed her a mug. 'Milk, no sugar, because you're sweet enough.'

'Aren't you a *charmer*.' She took a sip, eyeing him over the rim of her mug the same way a cat eyes a bird on the windowsill. 'He's not the only one, if you know what I mean. There's *several* people on the "no alcohol" list who come in here three sheets to the wind.'

'No!'

'They're probably in a syndicate, or a ring, or something. Running an illicit still, like hillbillies in the woods.'

Shaking his head. 'That really *is* terrible.'

Mind you, it kinda made sense. Geoff Newman leaves his house Monday morning, disappears into the forest, visits his private brewery, gets tanked up on moonshine, and heads off into town to do a bit of shopping. That would explain the missing two hours, anyway.

Edward had a sip of tea. *Much* nicer than the cheap-and-nasty teabags back at the station. 'Would it be OK to see the footage from the security cameras? If it's no trouble, I mean.'

Ms Hamilton pursed her lips, then nodded. 'Why not, as you asked nicely.' She led the way out of the kitchen, into the cumin-and-lentil corridor, and through a door marked 'STOCKROOM'.

Inside lurked a warren of floor-to-ceiling wooden shelves covered in massive catering packs of tins and packets, boxes of bottles, and crates of all three. A stack of those bath-mat-sized rafts of fresh eggs. A chest-high mound of lumpy potato sacks. Rows of toilet cleaner and bleach and deodorant and socks. A big metal door leading off to a walk-in fridge and freezer.

Even more craft-stall tat was crammed in here – a whole bay given over to half-arsed ashtrays and paintings and things made from wood and feathers and shells. If someone with no artistic aptitude could make it out of bits of old crap, it was here.

Ms Hamilton must've noticed him grimacing at it, because she grimaced too. 'I know, *horrific*, right?' She dipped into a cardboard box, producing a ceramic vase that didn't *entirely* look like a drunk primary-school kid had made it. Then a knitted dragon that was actually not bad. 'I mean, some of it's OK, just, but dear Lord, do we *have* to stock so much of it?' She popped both back in the box and wiped her hands on her trousers. 'But that's our Kevin for you. Such a softie. "There's only so many jobs to go round, Wendy", "The people need something to fill their days, Wendy", "We're supporting local artists, Wendy."' She took Edward's arm again. 'Don't get me wrong, I absolutely *love* the man to bits, but "artists"? Half this lot wouldn't know Monet from Mondrian.'

'That's so *true*. It must be . . .' Edward froze, looking up at the lights as they buzzed and flickered. Dimmed. Then slowly brightened to full strength again. 'OK.'

Ms Hamilton gave his arm a squeeze. 'Don't worry, it does that sometimes when the weather's foul. Last winter, the entire village didn't have any power for a *week*. Did a roaring trade in candles and thermal socks.'

They buzzed and flickered again.

'Riiiiiight.'

She led the way to a wooden door with 'KEVIN'S OFFICE' printed on a smart brass sign, and motioned Edward into a cramped room, with shelving on three walls and a desk on the fourth. Topless pictures of Jude Law and Russell Crowe were pinned up everywhere, either cut from magazines or taken from calendars. They were joined by other male movie stars, all in various stages of undress, showing off unrealistic six-packs and arms like hams.

Sinking into the room's only chair, she poked at the keyboard of a creaky old computer until an image of the shop floor appeared on the screen. The camera was mounted above and behind the till, looking down the rows of shelves towards the front door. A grey lump in the bottom left-hand corner looked like the back of Ms Hamilton's head.

The real Ms Hamilton smiled. 'Now then: day before yesterday, Monday afternoon . . .'

Onscreen, the footage jumped forty-eight hours into the past – going by the timestamp – then whizzed fast-forward through various comings and goings until it was just before four and Geoff Newman entered the store.

She slowed the recording to normal speed.

Newman was all bundled up in his padded jacket and woolly hat, hands deep in his pockets. He grabbed a basket and shambled around the shop for a couple of minutes, before approaching the till. Not making eye contact with Ms Hamilton as she rang up the three items he placed on the counter.

Her polished fingernail tapped the screen. 'He was in here once or twice a week, buying *exactly* the same thing: sausages, beans, and a loaf of sliced white. Occasionally a pint of milk, or a box of cornflakes, and *once* a tub of Quality Street, but that was as adventurous as he got.'

'Wow.'

'I mean, what was he saving his social credits for? I told him: "Splurge once in a while, for goodness' sake," I said. "Live a little!"'

'And what did he say?'

She rolled her eyes. 'You'd think I'd suggested a foursome with him, Kevin, and a cocker spaniel.'

Onscreen, Newman packed his shopping into a tote bag.

She curled her lip. '*He* should be so lucky. As if I'd have *anything* to do with someone who owned a hideous bag like that. Honestly: look at it.' Tapping the screen again. 'Is that supposed to be a horse? Because it looks absolutely *nothing* like a horse. More like a constipated badger. Gustav Spiers makes them, and we can only hope he was a better necrophiliac than he is an "artist".'

Urgh . . . There was an unwelcome image.

Edward squashed it down. 'Isn't that the *worst*?'

'Not that Geoff Newman would know the difference.' She dropped her voice to a whisper. 'Don't tell anyone, but I think he was on *drugs* too. His pupils were big as bowling balls, and he was all twitchy.'

'*Never.*' Well, it made a change from 'Wow'.

'Kept looking over his shoulder, as if someone was following him.' A nod. 'But then, cocaine does that to you, doesn't it? *Pa-ra-noia.*'

'Gosh.' Edward shook his head. 'I bet he was a complete junkie, right?'

She blinked, like Edward had just said something completely weird and off-script. 'Oh no, it was the first time I'd ever seen him like *that*. God, they'd throw you out of Glenfarach in a heartbeat if they thought you were taking—'

'Constable!' Bigtoria poked her head in from the stockroom. 'We're leaving.' And she was gone again.

Edward sagged against the desk. 'Sorry. She can be a bit . . .' – he made a vague hand gesture – 'sometimes? But it's been lovely meeting you, Ms Hamilton.' Which wasn't even vaguely true. Not after what she'd done to those poor starving kids. But: honey and vinegar.

'Aw . . .' She smiled, then leaned in and gave him two '*mwa, mwa*' air kisses. Like they were old friends on the ladies-who-lunch-and-embezzle circuit. 'You can call me Wendy.'

Nope.

Back in the Big Car, Edward started the engine and pulled away from the kerb. The tyres made that worrying crumping noise as they fought their way through the thickening snow. Wouldn't be too long before the roads here were undrivable.

Bigtoria was a lump in the passenger seat, going over yet more paperwork.

'Guv?'

She grunted and kept on reading.

'How did you get on with Kevin Clarke: any joy?'

She turned the page. 'Not really. You?'

'Ms Hamilton thinks Geoff Newman was drunk and/or stoned when he came in.'

The DI's eyes narrowed. 'Does she now? And here's us just discovered four lots of drugs in a missing social worker's bedside cabinet . . .'

'And he's not allowed to buy alcohol, so he had to be getting it from somewhere.' A frown as they took the corner onto Thistle Lane, going at a walking pace. No point taking stupid risks, after all.

'Maybe that's why Caroline Manson killed him? Drug deal gone wrong.' Bigtoria lowered her paperwork and stared out through the window. 'Maybe Manson smuggles it in and Newman was dealing for her? She finds out he's getting high on her supply and things get ugly.' More frowning. Then a huffed-out breath. 'No, I don't buy it. Not unless she was in a Mexican drug cartel. There's got to be more to this than just drugs. Something bigger.' Bigtoria looked off to the left, like she could see through the rows of little granite houses to Sanctuary House. 'Wonder what we'd find if we searched *all* the Social Work Team's rooms.'

'Or maybe he was making his own moonshine? Ms Hamilton thinks a bunch of them are running a hillbilly distillery in the woods. Think we should take a look, Guv?' He let the Big Car roll to a halt and took out the map Sergeant Farrow had given him – the one with the wandering red line. Held it out, pointing to Newman's first stop on the printout. 'He walks out of his house, turns left, and disappears into the woods for two hours. Might be the still? Or where they stash the drugs? Could be why he was killed – to keep whatever-it-is secret.'

'Or perhaps Sergeant Farrow was right and he just went for a walk and a wank in the woods.' Bigtoria took the map off Edward and gave it a good frowning at. 'If that idiot Samson hadn't got himself battered over the head last night, we'd know what was out there by now.' The creases between her brows deepened. 'How many more stops do we have?' Tracing the red line around the village with a finger. 'Library, some sort of workshop, and the baker's. Then we check the woods.'

Edward's stomach grumbled. 'Can't we visit the baker's *first*, Guv? Been ages since breakfast and we've not even had tenses.'

'No: library.' She thrust the map back across the car at him. 'And if you didn't drive like someone's granny this wouldn't be taking all day.'

Better than wrapping the thing around a lamppost.

But Edward took a deep breath and put his foot down anyway.

Might as well live a little . . .

12

No way Glenfarach was big enough to have a library this size. The three-storey building looked like it'd been built around the same time as the police station's extension – a vast Borg cube of glass and steel, packed with shelves and books and reading nooks.

OK, on the inside, those shelves were a bit rundown; and the carpet tiles faded to a tatty shade of brown, worn at the edges and curling free of the floor in places; but at least it had lots and lots and *lots* of books. They stood, shoulder to shoulder, in slouching categorized rows, dog-eared and scuffed, the paperbacks' spines lined with creases. They weren't here for decoration: they'd been *read*.

The whole place sat on a small rise, its floor-to-ceiling windows looking out over Glenfarach's twee houses and shops on one side, and down a hill to a burn on the other – the land sloping upwards beyond the stream and into the woods, fading away in the falling snow.

Security cameras stared down from every corner, and from those decapitated, upside down, shiny-Dalek-head things mounted to the ceilings.

About a dozen people had taken refuge from the weather, populating the ground floor in monastic silence: some perusing the shelves, others cloistered alone, or in pairs, in the reading nooks. Sitting in sagging armchairs, their heads buried in Trollope or King or Dostoevsky.

Soon as Edward and Bigtoria set foot through the library doors and into that hallowed space, the hush changed from sacred to hostile. Everyone turned to look. And this time, none of them were smiling.

Well, none of them except for Sergeant Farrow.

She stood in the middle of the floor, hands tucked into the pockets of her black Police Scotland fleece. A nod. 'Inspector. Constable.'

Bigtoria's jaw tightened. 'Sergeant. Shouldn't you be organizing a search party?'

'Why I'm here, Guv. I've got two *small* teams going door to door already, but the library's always a good bet if you want to find people.' She pointed at the readers. 'Need a hand, before I start rounding them up?'

'Might as well.'

She led the way across the scuffed carpet tiles to a curved reception desk with an old beige computer on top and an elderly man plonked behind it like a becardiganed toad. His combover was truly Trumpian in its folly, and little round glasses perched on the end of his nose. Wet lips pursed as he perused a volume of poetry.

Sergeant Farrow knocked on the desk. 'Theodore.'

He didn't look up. 'Sergeant.'

'You been on duty all week?'

'Where else am I going to go?' Theodore dabbed the tip of one finger against his pale pink tongue and turned the page. 'Now, do you want something, or can I get back to Louise Bogan?'

'Geoff Newman was here Monday.'

Nothing. No response whatsoever.

She leaned her fists against the desk. 'Theodore, do I need to remind you that you're already on your second strike? One more, and not only will we be looking for a new Chief Librarian, *you'll* be packing your bags and finding somewhere else to live.'

His head snapped up at that, the colour fading from his saggy cheeks.

'Now, do you want to put your book down and cooperate, or shall I get the paperwork started?'

He dropped Louise Bogan like she was radioactive, and pulled on a beaming smile. Threw his arms wide. 'Sergeant Farrow! What a delight to have you with us. How can I help? Perhaps the latest

E. L. James would be of interest? I understand it's appallingly written, but quite filthy.'

Bigtoria produced her warrant card. 'Did you serve Newman or didn't you?'

His mouth pursed. 'I *believe* so.'

The pause grew as they stared at each other.

Over in the corner someone sneezed.

The snow fell.

Edward shifted his feet.

Bigtoria blinked first. '*And?*'

Theodore turned to Sergeant Farrow. 'There's no need for your "friend" to be so rude, Sergeant. I'm *trying* to be helpful.'

'Try harder.' Bigtoria loomed. 'What – did – Newman – do – here – on – Monday?'

'I see.' Theodore closed his eyes, slouched, sighed at the ceiling, then sat upright and harrumphed out a breath. 'Mr *Newman* came in to return a number of books, two of which were overdue, so I had to fine him. He was not happy about this and I had to threaten to revoke his library privileges before he calmed down.'

Wow. That sounded like a high-stakes stand-off to rival *Reservoir Dogs*. Revoked library privileges? Heady stuff.

Edward leaned against a display of Western paperbacks. 'Seems pretty tame.'

A sniff. 'No one wants to be cut off from the library, Unknown Constable Person. Death itself would be preferable.'

Bigtoria gave up on the looming. 'That it?'

'You must understand, Inspector Whoever You Are: there's no Sky TV or Netflix here, nothing that could be deemed salacious or invigorating in a sexual way. Not even CBeebies. In Glenfarach, books are *life*.'

'So he didn't do anything else? Didn't talk to anyone? Didn't fight or fall out with anyone?'

Theodore drew himself up to his full toad height, glaring at her over the top of his glasses. 'Certainly not! We don't put up with that kind of nonsense in the library. You follow the rules, or you're barred.'

'All right.' An icy smile. 'Thank you *so much* for your time.' She turned and stomped off towards the main doors again.

Edward stayed where he was. 'Can I just ask, what books was Mr Newman returning?'

Theodore checked the computer. 'Two volumes of *Harry Potter and the Unedited Adverbs of Exposition*, for the umpteenth time. Honestly, you wouldn't believe how many copies we get through of those terrible novels. Coming back with the pages all stuck together . . .' A shudder. 'His copy of *The Scientific American Boy* was overdue, and so was the N-Five Physics textbook.' Theodore donned a patronizing smile. 'Like most of our patrons, he believes . . . *believed* he could better himself through further education.'

Bigtoria was out through the door now, but Sergeant Farrow hung back, lugging in on the conversation.

'Hold on' – Edward pulled his chin in – '*The Scientific American Boy*?'

'Oh, it's not as bad as it sounds, Unnamed Constable Person – it's a how-to manual for building ridiculous things like bridges and canoes and theodolites out of old sticks and bits of canvas, all dressed up as a fictional boys' camping expedition. It isn't even vaguely pornographic.'

That was a relief.

'He take anything new out?'

'In order to emphasize the importance of returning one's library books on time, I restricted him to a single tome. Which is just as well, given he managed to burn his house down with *that* book in it.'

Wow. Talk about *cold*.

'And what was it?'

'Vladimir Nabokov: *Lolita*.'

Edward's eyes widened. '*Lolita*?' How the *hell* did . . . 'If you're not allowed "salacious things" on TV, how come you're allowed to lend smutty books?'

'*Literature* isn't "smutty", young man!' The chins came up and Theodore glared down his nose. 'What a terribly *vulgar* way to view the world of books! Next thing you know you'll be burning them in the street, like a Nazi.'

'No, but *Lolita*? For someone with Mr Newman's record?'

'Literature *isn't* smutty.' Theodore made a big show of picking up his poetry book. Back straight, elbows out. 'Good day to you, sir.'

'Right.'

Unbelievable.

Edward marched for the door.

Sergeant Farrow fell in beside him. 'Don't let Theodore get to you, Edward, he's been like that since Belmarsh.'

They pushed out through the library doors, into the shelter of a concrete veranda overlooking the road. The Big Car was the only vehicle out there, its lone occupant sitting in the passenger seat, head stuck in yet more bits of paper.

The snow was still falling, slow and relentless, turning the world into a ghost. Silent as an owl's wing. Cold as a shallow grave.

'What did he do? Theodore?'

'He used to review books for the *Guardian*.' There was a pause. Then Sergeant Farrow's eyebrows jumped up her head. 'Oh, you mean what did he *do*.' She bared her teeth and cringed. 'You're probably better off not knowing, unless you really don't want to sleep tonight. It's—'

The Big Car's horn slashed through the feathery air as Bigtoria glared at them through the windscreen.

All the social skills of a rabid weasel.

'Yeah . . . she does that.'

Sergeant Farrow patted him on the shoulder. 'Good luck.' Then turned and headed back inside, leaving Edward standing outside on his own.

The Big Car's horn blared again.

Edward waved, throwing in a cheerful smile – just like one of the residents. 'COMING!' Lowering his voice as he descended the stairs, even though there was no way she could hear him with the windows rolled up. 'You rotten, scum-flavoured, angry, turd-faced tosspot.'

Because it was important to enjoy the little victories.

Wilkins' Joinery Workshop was about the size of a double garage, lined in chipboard, with deep racks along one wall – loaded down with different sized bits of wood. Workbenches hugged the other three walls, with more sitting out on the concrete floor, stuck in a frozen waltz with chunks of free-standing machinery that probably did interesting/important woodworking stuff, if you knew about that sort of thing. Could've been anything, to be honest.

Loads of hand tools were mounted above the workbenches, each one framed in its own Sharpie-drawn outline.

A wood-burning stove popped and crackled in the corner, filling the room with heat and a light, toasty scent of smoke.

Slightly less pleasant was the screeching howl of whatever bit of machinery the big woman in the dungarees had going full pelt – shrieking parallel grooves in a pale pine plank. Difficult to tell, with her all hunched over like that, but from here she looked about the same height as Bigtoria, but even more muscly, her curly flame-red hair tied back under a blue kerchief. Heavy brow, and a slight underbite. Broad, calloused hands. Wearing safety boots, safety goggles, a face mask, and ear defenders.

Edward shuffled closer, fingers in his ears. 'MS WILKINS? MS SIOBHAN WILKINS! HELLO?'

No response.

He tried standing on the opposite side of the woodworking machine, waving his arms.

Finally, she looked up, squinting at him through the safety goggles, before flipping a switch – making the screeching din whine down through the scales and octaves till there was blessed silence She removed her ear defenders, but kept her distance. Chest out, head lowered, hands clenching into fists. 'Who are you?'

'Detective Constable Reekie This is DI Montgomery-Porter. We need to ask you some questions about Geoff Newman?'

'Oh aye?' She took the plank of wood off the machine and carried it over to a large workbench, marooned between a bandsaw and what might've been a lathe.

Bigtoria gave her warrant card another outing. 'Newman was here: day before yesterday.'

'If you say so.'

'What did he want?'

She glowered at Edward. 'What does any *man* want?'

Bigtoria did a bit of glowering of her own. 'Would you like me to have a word with Sergeant Farrow about you not cooperating? Three strikes and you're out, isn't it? How many are you on, Ms Wilkins?'

She sighed. Then unfurled a tape measure and marked off half a dozen ticks on her plank with a flat red pencil. 'He wanted advice on a stupid book he was reading. Said he was thinking of building a bridge or some nonsense.'

'A *bridge*?' Checking to make sure that Edward was writing all this down, like he was an amateur.

'You're here a long time: you need things to do. Hobbies. A sense of purpose. Something to fill your days.' She busied herself with a metal square, drawing out a rectangle between the grooves. 'He was going to build a bridge; he was going to get a degree in physics; he was going to write a crime novel; he was going to blah, blah, blah.'

Edward took his notebook for a wee wander around the workshop. Lots of different wooden things, in various stages of construction, littered the space. Chairs. An ottoman. A sideboard. 'Did you make these? They're really good.'

Ms Wilkins ignored him. 'I *work* for a living. Always have. Always will.'

'And did he say where he was going to build this bridge?'

She plucked a chisel from its allotted slot on the wall. 'Out in the woods somewhere.'

Edward looked over at Bigtoria and she was looking straight back at him. A nod of her head. So she'd picked that one up too.

The chisel carved a perfect curl of pine from the plank. 'Wanted to know if I'd sell him an axe.'

'And did you?'

'Course I didn't. What if he used it on someone?'

Edward went wandering again, heading for a wee poke about the workbench that ran along the far wall. 'I've always fancied making a rocking horse, myself. I had a book when I was a kid about a little boy with a magic rocking horse and they went on all these adventures.' He liberated a saw from its outline. 'Think that would be hard to do?'

Ms Wilkins thunked her chisel down and marched straight over there. Took the saw from his hands and returned it to its proper place. 'Don't touch that!' She moved down the bench, five or six feet, and rested her bum against it – arms stretched out to either side, fists resting on the working surface – and forced a smile. 'It's sharp. You might hurt yourself.'

Edward retreated a couple of paces, hands up.

Bigtoria threw him a less than happy look, then went back to glowering at Ms Wilkins. 'So? What did you tell Newman about the bridge?'

'Told him it was *possible*. But on his own? No chance. You've got the sections to build and carry and arrange and hold in place while you lash it all together . . . But you know what men are like.'

Another glance at Edward. 'Don't I just.' Pause. 'Did Newman ever talk about Caroline Manson?'

'You think she killed him and buggered off?' The silence stretched. Then Ms Wilkins shrugged. 'Sergeant Farrow came past looking for search volunteers. It's my job to put things together.' Her smile was as cold and sharp as her chisels. 'Social worker murders a piece-of-shite ex-cop turned paedo? Isn't a single person here who wouldn't throw her a parade.'

Now there was something interesting – all this time, and Ms Wilkins hadn't moved one inch. Abandoning the whatever-it-is she was working on.

Interesting and suspicious.

Edward tipped his head to one side, watching her not moving.

Ms Wilkins nodded to herself. 'There'll be a line a mile long to piss on his grave when they finally bury what's left of him.'

Edward wandered over to the bench she'd been using. Picked up the pine plank with the weird grooves in it. Then helped himself to the chisel, turning the long, thin blade from side to side. 'I've never been any good with these things.'

And still Ms Wilkins stayed where she was. 'Don't touch that!'

'Always end up gouging great chunks out the wood. It's like—'

'*Constable!*' Bigtoria thumped the bench. 'Will you *please* shut up!'

He pulled on his innocent face. 'Sorry, Guv.' Then placed the plank back where he'd found it and lined the chisel up with one of the pencil marks. Tongue poking out the corner of his mouth as he shaved a sliver of wood off. 'Wow, that's *sharp*.'

'Don't!' Ms Wilkins stayed put, one arm stretching towards him, fingers splayed. 'It's delicate, you'll ruin it!'

'Constable, I won't tell you again.'

'Sorry, Guv.' Another sliver curled away from the wood.

And *still* Ms Wilkins didn't move.

Bigtoria jabbed a finger in his direction. 'What on earth are you doing?'

'Being really annoying, Guv.' He turned the chisel and had another go.

Ms Wilkins' eyes bugged – the sight of him fannying about with her work clearly causing a lot of pain, but even that wasn't enough to shift her.

Edward nodded. 'You see, all this time, Ms Wilkins has been working on . . . whatever this is. When I touched the saw, she rushed over, stopped me, then shoogled along a bit and stood *right* there.' Pointing at her. 'And she hasn't moved since. Not so much as an inch.'

His cunning revelation was met with silence.

No?

'Isn't it pretty obvious?'

Still nothing.

Ah well, better spell it out then. 'What is it you don't want us to see, Ms Wilkins? What are you hiding?'

Bigtoria turned to stare at Siobhan Wilkins.

He tilted over to the side, peering between Ms Wilkins' legs. 'What's in the box?'

It was cardboard, about the size of a microwave oven, with 'USED OIL RAGS' written on it in black marker pen. It'd been pushed to the back of a shelf beneath the workbench. Nice and out of sight.

Ms Wilkins licked her lips. 'Nothing?'

Bigtoria raised an eyebrow in Edward's direction. 'Maybe you're not so useless after all.'

'Step aside, please, Ms Wilkins.'

She buried her face in her hands, then sagged forward, shoulders curling in. Hollowing out her body like a spoon. Voice barely audible. 'I'm sorry.'

That's right, folks: Detective Constable Edward Reekie strikes again.

He stepped towards her, ready to take the box and—

Ms Wilkins went from nought to a full-on sprint in just a couple of paces. Shoulder-charging Edward on the way past, bulldozing him off his feet and sending him crashing down on his arse. Fireworks going off in both cheeks as they slammed into the concrete.

Bigtoria bent her knees, hunching forwards, arms out, like she was a rugby player, but Ms Wilkins jinked left, grabbed a stack of long, wooden battens and heaved it sideways.

It collapsed onto Bigtoria – she covered her head with her arms as the rods bounced off her, spinning and clattering against the concrete floor. And Ms Wilkins was past, sprinting full speed ahead.

She barged out through the workshop's back door, leaving it swinging.

Bigtoria shoved the last battens of wood away and hurried after her. Hurling the door open to *boom* off the wall. Disappearing into the snow.

God's sake.

Edward struggled to his feet, one hand clutching his aching bum. Looked left, looked right.

No point just following Bigtoria, she was faster than him anyway, with those long muscly legs. But *surely* there had to be a better way of catching up with the pair of . . .

Aha.

He turned and legged it in the opposite direction, making for the front door instead.

13

Edward burst through the workshop's front door and into the flurrying snow. Breath catching in his throat as it turned to steam.

He spun around on the spot, searching the . . .

There – off to the right, Bigtoria's back flashed in the gap between a blacksmith's and a dilapidated building. Sod. The Big Car was pointing in the opposite direction.

OK.

He ran for the driver's door and scrambled into the driver's seat. Cranked the engine. Hauled the steering wheel around. And jammed his foot to the floor, making that huge diesel motor roar.

The rear-end slithered as the tyres fought with the snow, nearly performing a full three-sixty, before he wrenched the wheel into opposite lock and gave it even more oomph.

Eyes wide, knuckles white. A strangled, gargling scream trapped in the back of his throat.

He peeled one hand off the wheel and wrestled his seatbelt on as the car surged forwards.

A glance to the side and there was Ms Wilkins, still running through the snow, behind the buildings, parallel to the street. Widening the gap between her and Bigtoria.

At the end of the road, Edward hit the brakes and turned right.

The back of the car kicked out in a wide skid, leaving him scrabbling at the wheel, trying to stop the thing from spinning. Jaw clenched as a lamppost made straight for the Big Car's bonnet.

Please, please, please, please, please . . .

Six inches to spare and the Big Car righted itself, shooting forward, closing the gap on Ms Wilkins and Bigtoria as Edward raced down a row of quaint little cottages, past a hairdresser's and a bakery.

The engine howled like a bandsaw cutting through tin.

Only trouble was: they'd run out of village. The street ended at a line of bollards, with nothing but the forest beyond. Ms Wilkins wasn't heading for the woods, though: instead she took a sharp left, careering down a long snowy hill with a burn at the bottom. The land rose on the other side, disappearing into the trees. Think that would've slowed her down a bit – the drifts must've easily been twice as deep as anything in town – but she just kept on running.

Bigtoria put on a spurt of speed, elbows and knees pumping as she dived off the road and hammered downhill. Didn't hurt that Ms Wilkins was clearing a path to follow.

Edward hauled in a deep breath.

'You can do this . . .'

He turned left and the Big Car parted company with the street, bumping over what was probably the kerb, buried under the snow, then over the brow of the hill.

'Bad idea! Bad Idea! BAD IDEA!'

The Land Rover's nose rose for a moment as all four wheels abandoned the ground, then dipped as it barrelled down the hill, sending up great gouts of white on either side. It curled in over the bonnet too, covering the windscreen, obliterating all sight of Bigtoria and Ms Wilkins. And everything else too, because the wipers were making sod all difference.

He was driving blind.

'AAAAAAAAAAAAAAAAAAAAAARGH!'

A juddering thump. The Big Car's nose rose again – like a small dog bounding through tall grass – and the spray cleared for just long enough to see he'd overtaken both Bigtoria *and* Ms Wilkins.

Edward pulled the Land Rover into a sweeping curve to cut her off, then—

BANG.

An almighty jolt shook the car and bits of what looked like picket fence sprayed into the air – bouncing off the bonnet with murderous clangs, smashing into the windscreen, leaving spider's web cracks behind.

'AAAAAAAAAAAAAAAAAAAAAAAAAAAAAAAAAARGH!'

He slammed on the brakes and the Big Car slithered to a halt, buried wing-mirror-deep in the snow.

Holy mother of *shite*.

Edward sat there, rigid, breathing like a ruptured accordion. Hands trembling as he unclenched them from the steering wheel.

Come on.

Move.

He unclipped his seatbelt and shoved the driver's door. It opened about an inch, then *thunked*. Wouldn't go any further. Pinned in place by the volume of snow outside.

Could *nothing* go right?

'Sodding, bloody, dirty, snowing . . .' He wound his window down and clambered out through the opening, and – *whump* – disappeared face first into the stinging, crunchy drifts of white.

Frozen wasps attacked both cheeks, sinking icy barbs into his forehead, setting his nose and ears buzzing with venomous cold.

He struggled back to the surface, flailing about like a drowning man, coughing and sputtering out great plumes of breath. Bloody stuff was chest deep. And most of it was stuck to him.

Ms Wilkins kept going, forging her way through the snow far quicker than any real person should've been able to. She'd clearly clocked the Big Car, because A: the thing was pretty sodding hard to miss, and B: she'd changed direction. Her path curved leftwards now, meaning she'd blast past the back of the Land Rover, off to the burn, up the slope and away into the woods beyond.

Oh no you don't . . .

Arms up at shoulder height, Edward waded towards the point where their paths would cross. 'Bloody hell . . .' It was like fighting through bleached treacle. 'STOP, POLICE!'

The Big Car had ploughed a square-edged canyon through the snow, littered now with shattered bits of picket fence. Ms Wilkins burst into it. Staggering as the resistance suddenly eased, making for the far wall, when *bam* – Bigtoria exploded into view behind her. The DI threw herself forward, arms reaching out in a classic rugby tackle.

She slammed into Ms Wilkins' waist and the pair of them walloped into the other side of the canyon. Vanishing into the snow. Reappearing in a knot of thrashing limbs as their struggles carved a hole out of the wall. Grunting and swearing.

Edward lumbered across the littered floor to the increasingly large hollow Bigtoria and Ms Wilkins were making. 'ALL RIGHT, THAT'S ENOUGH! Siobhan Wilkins, I am arresting you under Section One of the Criminal Justice, Scotland, Act 2016 for . . .'

What was the point? Nobody was listening to him.

They just kept on fighting and grunting and swearing.

'I've got pepper spray, Ms Wilkins; do you want pepper-sprayed? Cos I *will* pepper-spray you!'

More struggling.

For goodness' sake.

He put on his cajoling voice. 'Don't make me spray you, Ms Wilkins. You won't like it, and I'll have to fill out heaps of paperwork.' He sighed. 'It's over.'

Well, that seemed to work; the fighting came to a halt.

Blood dribbled down Bigtoria's face, oozing out of her squint nose – dripping off her chin to patter down on the back of Ms Wilkins' head. Who couldn't get out of the way, because Bigtoria had her in an armlock. Shoving Ms Wilkins' facedown into the snow.

Ms Wilkins was saying something, probably very rude, but thankfully it was muffled into nothing more than angry mumbling.

All three of them were clarted head-to-toe in white.

Bigtoria's voice growled out, all bunged up and nasal. 'Ond your feedt!' She hauled her prisoner upright, then snapped on the cuffs. And turned her attention to Edward instead. 'Loog whadt you've dund to dhe Big Car!'

He backed away. 'It wasn't my fault! I was in hot pursuit . . .'

'Surrounded by *idiots*.' She shoved Ms Wilkins into Edward's arms, then waded over to the Big Car and fought with the driver's door, hauling it back and forth until it crumped open far enough to let her squeeze inside.

The engine spluttered and coughed, then finally caught.

Edward pulled Ms Wilkins out of the way as the reversing lights snapped on. He needn't have bothered, though, because when Bigtoria put her foot down the wheels just spun and *vwipp*ed on the compacted snow. The Big Car wasn't going anywhere.

The driver's door bashed open again and out squeezed a glowering Bigtoria.

He tried a smile. 'Sorry, Guv.'

She stood there, glaring at him for a moment. Then stomped over, grabbed Ms Wilkins's arm and marched her back along the gouged trench – the pair of them limping. 'Afder all thiz, whadtever you were hidig bedder be wort it!'

Bigtoria hobbled into the joinery workshop, dragging Ms Wilkins with her. Edward brought up the rear, shutting the door behind them as the warmth of that wooden stove greeted him like a lonely Labrador.

All three of them were still covered in snow, but it was finally starting to melt.

He bustled across to stand in front of the crackling blaze, warming his purple fingers. If there was any justice he'd never leave this spot, he'd just—

'*Consdtable!*'

Of course.

Edward abandoned the stove and slouched over to where Bigtoria held Ms Wilkins, right next to the cardboard box with 'USED OIL RAGS' on it.

The DI gave their prisoner a wee shoogle. 'You wandt to say somethig before we open idt?'

Ms Wilkins' shoulders went back, chin jutting. 'I want a lawyer. I've done nothing wrong.'

'Consdtable Reekie?'

He pulled the box from its shelf, and placed it on the worktop.

A sneer. 'Never seen that box in my life. Someone else must've put it there.'

Edward huffed a breath into his aching hands, then fumbled a couple of nitrile gloves from his jacket, struggling them on over his sausage fingers. Opened the box. Wrinkled his nose at the jumble of greasy rags inside – which seemed to be a mix of old T-shirts and pants, that kind of thing – all marinating in the fatty, bitter scent of linseed oil. He dug the rags from the box and dumped them on the floor. 'You shouldn't store these in cardboard, they can spontaneously combust. You know that, don't you?' More rags joined the growing pile. 'You need a metal tin. And keep it away from anything flammable, otherwise you're just asking for . . .'

OK. Wasn't expecting that.

Bigtoria peered. 'What?'

There, nestling in the bottom of the box, was a collection of children's things. A stuffed toy penguin, a sippy cup, a faded-pink Babygro, an Action Man, a plastic digger, a plastic tractor, a plastic doll, and two moulded-plastic blister packs.

He took those out first.

Each one imprisoned a pair of walkie-talkies – one set shaped like a cartoon tiger and a lion, the other shaped like a teddy bear and a clown, held fast in their clear-plastic cell. New and unused. He popped them on the workbench, then, one by one, lined up everything else.

Ms Wilkins stiffened. 'I've never seen *any* of that stuff before.'

'Don't know about you, Guv, but I was expecting drugs, or a gun, you know? This is all a bit . . . Oh.' Something else lurked in there, a large brown-paper envelope, the same colour as the box, almost invisible against the cardboard. He held it up. 'Guv?'

'Open it.'

It wasn't sealed – the flap just folded over. He peered inside.

Cleared his throat.

Closed the flap again.

Then slid it across the workbench towards Bigtoria as something cold slithered about in the pit of his stomach. 'Might want to see this.'

She snapped on a pair of gloves of her own and took a look. Standing there, silent and still. Then her face hardened and she shut the envelope.

Ms Wilkins shuffled her feet. 'Whatever you've found, it's *nothing* to do with me.'

'Is that so.' Bigtoria's voice was calm, flat, expressionless. 'Thank you, Constable.' She handed the envelope back to him. 'Do it.'

'Yes, Guv.' He slid the horrible thing into the box again. 'Siobhan Wilkins, I am arresting you under Section One of the Criminal Justice, Scotland, Act 2016 for possessing indecent images of children.'

'This is bullshit. I want a lawyer!'

'The reason for your arrest is that I suspect that you have committed an offence and I believe that—'

She was struggling now. 'I'm not a paedo! Everyone knows that!'

'—keeping you in custody is necessary and proportionate for the purposes of bringing you before—'

Ms Wilkins tried to jerk away from Bigtoria, but the DI held her firm. 'I WANT A BLOODY LAWYER! THIS IS A FIT-UP!'

'—a court or otherwise dealing with you in accordance with the law. Do you understand?'

'GET OFF ME!'

Bigtoria tightened her grip. 'Hold still!'

'Do – you – under – stand?'

Ms Wilkins let loose a bellow of rage, hauling her shoulders forward, then back again, head whipping around – trying to catch Bigtoria with a skull-ringing headbutt. It didn't connect. Instead, the DI hauled her over backwards, sending her thumping onto the concrete floor with a *whumph*. Then pinning her down. Grunting with the effort of holding her there as she thrashed and swore and yelled and bit and roared.

You know what?

Sod this.

Edward pulled out his pepper spray. And that's when the screaming *really* started.

Ms Wilkins limped past the custody desk, wobbling slightly – cheeks and eyes puffy and red, tears rolling down her face, breath all laboured and rasping – as Sergeant Farrow led her to a nice cosy cell.

Edward shrugged, pulling the damp fabric of his trousers away from his partially numb legs. 'Said you wouldn't like it.'

'Hmmph.' Bigtoria hunched over one of the stainless-steel sinks, dabbing at her eyes with a wet paper towel. A wee twist of it was wodged up each nostril, stained dark with blood. But at least she'd lost the comedy accent. 'I wasn't too sodding keen, either.'

'I shouted "clear!", Guv. You heard me shout "clear".'

More dabbing. 'And then you didn't let me *get* clear.'

True.

'Sorry, Guv.' Doing his best to sound like he meant it.

Sergeant Farrow frowned her way out of the cell, fiddling with the handcuffs, and *slammed* the door shut behind her. Then checked to make sure it was locked. 'I can't believe Siobhan would do something like that.'

Edward tapped the cardboard box with 'USED OIL RAGS' written on it.

She waved that away. 'I know, but . . . you think you know someone.' Looking back towards the shuttered cell. 'Siobhan Wilkins isn't a sex offender. She's here because she ran drugs for Malk the Knife's crew in Edinburgh. Punishment beatings a speciality. Examples made for cash.' A grunt, a shake of the head, a disgusted face. 'And now *this*?'

Bigtoria straightened up from the sink, blotting her cheeks dry. 'Did I see that idiot, PC Harlaw, when we parked out front?'

'Hmmm . . . ? What? Oh, right: yes. He did the lunch run.'

That rumbling, *ominous* tone was back in the DI's voice. 'Did he now?' She marched across the custody suite and barged through the internal door.

Edward tore his gaze from the door to Sergeant Farrow. She grimaced at him. Then they both grimaced at the door for a breath or two, before hurrying after Bigtoria into a narrow breeze-block corridor – painted in two shades of sharny grey.

At the end of the corridor, Bigtoria clanged up the stairs. Open metal treads ringing beneath her boots.

Sergeant Farrow bustled after her. 'Don't suppose there's any chance Siobhan's telling the truth about that stuff being planted?'

'Nah.' Edward brought up the rear. 'Ms Wilkins was trying to hide the box. She knew fine well it was there.'

'Urgh . . .'

The DI's voice echoed off the breeze-block walls. 'She told us Geoff Newman stopped there, Monday, to pick her brains about building some half-arsed bridge in the woods. When in reality they were trading obscene bloody images!' Glancing over her shoulder. 'You've got an active paedophile ring in Glenfarach.'

Sergeant Farrow slowed to a halt, face sagging as that sank in. 'Oh God . . . They're going to shut us down, aren't they?'

'Need to round up everyone on the register: grill them, search their homes and places of work. Someone will crack eventually.'

'Erm . . .' Edward stood on his tiptoes, peering over the sergeant's drooping head. 'That's, like, a hundred and eighteen people, Guv. And there's only four of us. And we've got Caroline Manson to find and Geoff Newman's—'

'I know what the situation is, *Constable.*'

Sergeant Farrow scuffed her way up the stairs again. 'Mind you, maybe it's not a bad thing? Escape from this fudge-hole and get back to proper police work for a change.'

The DI swung around the landing and onto the next flight of metal steps. 'The Duty Inspector can pick it up when he gets here. *We* have a killer to find.'

OK, being stuck behind Sergeant Farrow was getting him nowhere fast. 'Scuse me, Sarge.' He squeezed his way past, half jogging to catch up with Bigtoria. 'What if being in the ring is what got Mr Newman tortured in the first place?'

Behind them, Sergeant Farrow's voice slumped out like a defeated slug. *'Glenfarach's like being trapped in amber. Nothing happens for years and years . . .'*

Bigtoria paused, wrinkles deepening on her forehead. 'Could be. And if Dr Singh's right about Caroline Manson's past . . . ?'

'That would do it.'

She turned and bellowed down the stairs. 'HAVE YOUR SEARCH TEAMS FOUND ANY SIGN OF OUR MISSING SOCIAL WORKER YET?'

'What?' Pause. 'No, they're still looking. They've got a lot of out-buildings to go through . . .'

'Typical.' Bigtoria marched on.

'And the career progression is rubbish. Six years I've been here, and there's no chance I'll ever make inspector, is there?'

Edward followed the DI out onto the ground floor, then round and onto the next flight of stairs. 'So Ms Manson's definitely our number-one suspect?'

'Just in case, we need to search the records: see if anyone else was a victim of historical abuse.'

'Guv.'

'Have to admit, it'll be nice to deal with a better class of criminal for a change.'

Edward was struggling to keep up, thighs burning after wading through all that snow, then walking halfway across town. 'Maybe we should try . . .' He slowed to a halt.

Hang on.

He turned and looked down through the open treads at Sergeant Farrow with her rounded shoulders and hanging head.

Bigtoria kept going. 'Then check up on Harlaw. See if the useless idiot's actually managed to find out which of Caroline Manson's clients saw her last.'

But Edward stayed where he was, watching as Sergeant Farrow slouched into view from below. No, not watching: staring, his eyes narrowing as she climbed.

She scuffed her way up the steps. 'And it's not like the top brass can blame me, is it? I mean, I'm not in charge here, Inspector Draper is. He should be the one carrying the can, not me.'

'And I want regular updates on the search teams' progress.' Bigtoria's boots clanged away up the steps, leaving them behind. 'Caroline Manson's out there somewhere.'

Sergeant Farrow lumbered towards Edward, focusing on her own feet, voice a miserable monotone. Wallowing in it, a bit. 'He'll probably try to pin the blame on us, though. You know what senior officers are like.'

'CONSTABLE!'

Edward jerked back to life. 'Holdall!'

Of sodding course.

The *holdall*.

Edward scrambled up the remaining stairs and out onto the first-floor landing, past the usual array of Police Scotland notices, crappy motivational posters, memos, and the rest.

Behind him, the sound of heavy feet clumped down the metal steps again, followed by Bigtoria's favourite word. '*What?*'

What indeed . . .

Edward grinned at the big composite screen. 'Ha! I was right.'

They'd gathered around the central console in the CCTV room, watching as Geoff Newman walked up the street, crossed the road, and disappeared into the Glenfarach General Store. Just before four in the afternoon, going by the timestamp in the corner.

Sergeant Farrow turned to Bigtoria. 'You got any idea what he's on about?'

Edward waved a hand. 'No, look. Rewind a couple of seconds.'

She pressed some keys, twiddled the dial thing, and Newman reversed out of the shop and froze, just outside, reaching for the handle.

Hard not to sound smug when you were so *comprehensively* right. 'Notice anything?'

Bigtoria glowered, voice a low, dark warning. 'Constable . . . ?'

'Split the screen, Sarge, and bring up when he left his house.'

Fingers clacked across the keyboard and the image divided in two, one half sticking with the General Store, the other showing Newman Cottage on Gallows Row as the man himself wandered down the garden path and out onto the pavement.

'Freeze it there.' Edward smiled. 'See?'

Stony silence.

Bigtoria rubbed at her bloodshot eyes.

'Nope.' Sergeant Farrow puffed out a breath. 'I don't get it.'

OK, time to lay it out for the slower members of the team.

'It was you talking about a "better class of criminal", then that thing about someone carrying the can, and you, Guv, saying Geoff

Newman was in a ring.' Edward gave them a 'ta-daaa' hand gesture, but they *still* hadn't twigged. 'See, *Ms Hamilton* was complaining about the class of criminals she has to associate with, and then she showed me the security camera from the store and there's Geoff Newman buying bread, and sausages, and a *tin* of beans. Which means he's *literally* carrying the can: in – his – ugly – tote bag. So, *I* was wondering . . . ?'

Surely they had to get it *now*?

It was sodding obvious.

'Ah.' Took a while, but the scowl evaporated from Bigtoria's face. 'He's got a red holdall when he leaves his house in the morning and disappears into the woods, but at the General Store . . . ?'

And Sergeant Farrow finally caught up. 'Yes: no holdall!'

Sometimes you just had to sit back and let them work it out for themselves.

'And the store was his last stop for the day. Which means he left it somewhere.'

Edward nodded. 'Which isn't suspicious *at all*.'

Bigtoria raised an eyebrow, looking him up and down. 'Well, aren't you full of surprises today.' She turned to Sergeant Farrow. 'I need you to bring up the CCTV footage of everywhere Newman went on Monday. Start at the General Store and work backward.'

A grimace. 'Fingers crossed that wasn't erased too . . .' She fiddled with the keyboard and the screens merged into one enormous image again: outside the General Store.

The timestamp flickered backwards, and Newman reversed out the shop door, carrying his hideous tote bag as he backed across the road, took a left and retreated out of shot.

Sergeant Farrow prodded the controls and the picture cut to Newman moonwalking past a bunch of other Glenfarach businesses. It looked almost normal: second-hand clothes shop, charity shop, craft shop, café, butcher's, hairdresser . . . He vanished off-screen, then everything jumped to a different camera.

The joinery workshop appeared. No holdall going in, backwards, and no holdall when he reversed out of there either.

Half a dozen more CCTV sequences and he was unvisiting the library.

No holdall.

Another chunk of shots and there was still no sign of it.

In and out of the baker's: no holdall.

Sergeant Farrow winced. 'You know what this means?'

Newman backed through screen after screen; reversed across a road, past a row of overwintering allotments; and retreated into the trees beyond.

Bigtoria folded her arms. 'Told you: *someone* has to search the woods.'

The pair of them turned to look at Edward.

Oh, for . . .

How was that fair?

A groan slipped free and he sagged.

He'd spotted the missing holdall! Should be getting *rewarded*, not given the crappy jobs.

Bigtoria headed for the exit. 'But before you go: we need to see an idiot about a lawyer.' Thumping out into the corridor.

The door swung shut again, leaving them wreathed in the glow of the TV screens.

So much for his Hercule Poirot moment.

Honestly, made you wonder why you bothered.

Sergeant Farrow patted him on the shoulder. 'Well done, Edward. That was some smart policework.'

Nice to know someone cared.

She hooked a thumb at the door. 'So, what's that all about?'

'No idea, Sarge.'

But it probably wasn't going to be anything good.

14

Bigtoria was on the top floor, grumbling her way past the control room like an angry bear, by the time Edward caught up with her.

'Guv? Why are we—'

She stopped dead, right in front of him, *very* nearly causing him to rear-end her. Then she stood there, head on one side, listening.

The sound of someone whistling 'Scotland the Brave' echoed out of the open door.

'That does it.' Bigtoria turned, pushed past Edward, and stomped into the control room.

He followed her.

The place looked empty, but an overlarge toolbox sat on a desk near the windows, which could only mean—

'CONSTABLE HARLAW!' Bigtoria flexed her shoulders. 'When I give you a job, I sodding well expect you to *do it*!'

But it wasn't Harlaw who popped up from behind one of the desks – holding an RJ45 Crimping Tool and a length of Cat6 cabling – it was Jenna Kirkdale, all four feet six of her. She'd stripped off her outer layers, leaving jeans and a low-cut vest top that was big on cleavage and short on subtlety. 'Dave's not here. It's . . .' Then her eyes latched onto Edward and a slow smile put dimples in her cheeks. 'Hi, handsome.' A saucy wave. 'You here to give a girl a *hand*?'

'Errr . . .'

'Hmmph.' Bigtoria plucked a handset from its cradle. 'You fixed these phones yet?'

'God, I *wish*. Been running diagnostics, but there's nothing wrong this end.' She held up the crimper. 'Trying to knock up a line tester, but everything points to a fault somewhere out in the wintery world. All it takes is some rotten branch, weighed down by too much snow, and snap, bang, wallop, the line's borked.'

She put down her crimper and sashayed over to Edward, standing *far* too close, looking up at him with big doe eyes. Wrapping him in the musky scent of soldering and peaches and warm cinnamon. Jenna bit her bottom lip. 'Did you miss me?'

'Errr . . .' Why did it suddenly feel uncomfortably hot in here?

Bigtoria dropped the handset back into place. 'The CCTV system needs—'

'Do me a favour, Eddie, and have a *rummage* in my toolbox.'

That was a euphemism, wasn't it. One that made sweat prickle across the back of his neck.

'Errrrr . . .'

She winked. 'You're cute.' Then reached over, opened her toolbox, and pulled out a rectangle of circuit board. Most of it was that artificial grass green, spidered through with little wires, speckled with transistors and chips and thick with dust. But nearly a quarter had gone dark as burnt toast. 'This is what happens when you're too cheap to install surge protectors, Inspector. Looks as if there's been a fluctuation in the power supply – sensitive electronics don't like that very much.' Her eyes locked on Edward's again as she ran a finger around the neck of her low-cut top. 'Do you know what *I* like very much, Eddie?'

He backed away, but the doorframe brought him up with a thump. 'Eek.'

A growl from Bigtoria. 'Just . . . fix the phones.' Then she grabbed Edward by the collar. 'Constable, with me.' Pulling him after her as she marched from the room.

Oh, thank God for that.

The station's records department sat at the end of the top-floor corridor. The lights were off, but thin bands of grey filtered in through gaps in the venetian blinds, doing little to alleviate the gloom.

Ranks of dusty filing cabinets marched down the middle of the long low room, in back-to-back formation. More standing sentry against the side walls. Three cubicles skulked at the far end, bordered with fraying blue felt – just visible through a pox of curling notices and scraps of paper. Each cubicle had its own bulky desktop computer and an old-fashioned CRT monitor that wouldn't have looked out of place in a museum, their plastic casings faded to a mushroomy magnolia colour.

PC Harlaw sat in front of the middle one, headphones on, nodding his head to whatever beat he was listening to, nibbling on a prawn-mayonnaise sandwich as he poked at the keyboard. Hunched forward to squint at the screen.

Bigtoria slapped a hand on his shoulder. 'Constable Harlaw!'

A high-pitched squeal burst free in a spray of breadcrumbs. Then Harlaw scrambled around in his seat, eyes wide, breathing hard. 'Guv. Bleeding *heck*. Frightened the willy off me.' He slumped in place. Took another bite from his lunch. Gathered up a stack of printouts and held them out. Chewing through the words: 'Here's that list of residents and the map you wanted.' Creases formed between his eyebrows. 'What happened to your nose?'

She stepped closer, causing him to shrink back against the desk. 'You're *supposed* to be visiting Caroline Manson's clients.'

'I was. I did!' He stuck the sandwich in his gob, freeing up both hands to rummage through another stack of paperwork. Emerging with a single sheet. Holding it up like a crucifix to ward off Count Dracula. Mumbling the word around his mouthful. 'See?'

It was a list of names and addresses. About a third of them were scored through in wobbly blue biro, but not in any sort of apparent order – plenty of gaps between the lines. Harlaw removed the sandwich. 'I went through her calendar and worked backwards from her last appointment, until—'

'All right, we don't need to know the mechanics. Who'd she see last?'

'Ah. OK . . .' He turned the sheet to face him again, then pointed. 'Adrian Bedwin: ran a single-sex faith school in Lanarkshire, so you can guess why *he's* here. Says Caroline visited him round about two-ish.'

'And she didn't seem agitated, or angry, or anything?'

Harlaw shrugged. 'Same as usual. Said she'd see him tomorrow, which would be today, and off she went.' The constable pointed at another name. 'Laura Dundry was . . .'

The room's lights flickered on, even though no one had flipped the switches. Buzzed. Then flickered off again, returning the records department to its Stygian gloom.

Everyone stared.

'Oh dear . . .' Harlaw cleared his throat. 'That's new.' He nibbled a bite from his sandwich. 'Anyway, so: Laura Dundry. You remember that thing about thirteen Afghan refugees suffocating in the walk-in fridge at a chicken factory? This is her. Says Caroline Manson didn't show up for their appointment at quarter past.'

Edward peered at the list of names. 'What about Dr Singh?'

'She saw him at one fifteen.'

Which was a relief.

Bigtoria frowned. 'What?'

'Just checking.' Wouldn't be the first time some dodgy bastard inveigled their way into an investigation when *they* were the one who'd committed the crime.

She pocketed the list. 'Of course, we could've simply reviewed the CCTV footage and found out what happened to her, if you hadn't *broken* it.'

Harlaw cowered in his seat. 'It's not my fault, Guv! Jenna says the circuit-board control something-or-other's fried, and—'

'What about getting Geoff Newman's case files from the Met?'

He blinked at her. 'But—'

'You were supposed to request—'

'I *can't*!' Bottom lip wobbling a bit. 'The phone lines are down.' He waved his half-eaten sandwich at the monitor. 'So I'm going through the database trying to see if anyone here was in London when Geoff was still a cop.' His eyes moistened as his mouth puckered. 'I'm doing my best, Guv . . .'

Edward shot her a look.

She sighed. Then her face softened. 'OK.' Patting Harlaw on the back. Awkward and stiff, like she didn't really know how the gesture

worked. 'Good lad. You've done well. Meanwhile: your two hundred residents—'

'Hundred and ninety-nine, now.'

Bigtoria removed her hand, that soft expression replaced by
something much colder. 'Your *hundred and ninety-nine* residents:
how many of them were lawyers in a past life?'

'Let's see . . .' He returned to his keyboard. 'Sure we've got a
couple somewhere.'

Edward leaned against the cubicle wall. 'Lawyer, Guv?'

'Here we go: Lewis Nichols, former advocate.' Harlaw tapped the
screen. 'Taking bribes, perverting the course of justice, and causing
death by reckless driving.'

Bigtoria nodded. 'He disbarred?'

'Probably? Doesn't say. Suppose they all will be.'

'He'll have to do. Get him in here.'

'Erm, Guv?' Harlaw gazed up at her. 'If he asks why . . . ?'

'Because Siobhan Wilkins wants a solicitor, and I can't interview
her without one. Disbarred or not: get him in here.'

'Yes, Guv.' He stuffed the last of his sandwich in his mouth and
scrambled out of his seat. Scurrying off through the ranks of filing
cabinets.

Edward checked his watch. 'Lunch wouldn't be a bad idea. It's
gone two o'clock already.'

'Put your stomach away, Constable.'

'But we could check out the *bakery*. You know, Geoff Newman's
first stop on Monday? Last place on our list before the sodding
woods?' Well, worth a shot, wasn't it? And it'd been a long, *long*
time since breakfast. 'If we're going there anyway, we could kill two
birds with one scone.'

She stood there, staring at him. Then, 'Unbelievable.' Before
turning and marching off.

Edward grinned. 'Oh, come on, I thought that was kinda good.
Guv? Guv!'

Snow swirled down in sharp little flakes, caught up in gusts of arctic
air that whipped them into icy tornadoes.

Edward lumbered along the pavement, hands jammed deep into the pockets of his borrowed high-vis, shoulders up around his ears. Nose – a frozen lump of raw mince and black pepper. Breath streaming out, tugged this way and that by the relentless wind. 'Buggering hell, it's *freezing*.'

Bigtoria marched beside him, like the cold didn't matter at all. Because God forbid she show any *human* weakness. 'And whose fault is that?'

Off in the middle distance, a line of residents shuffled across the street, slow and steady, peering up ginnels and into doorways. That would be one of Sergeant Farrow's search teams.

Edward shivered. 'I didn't make the weather, Guv.'

'No, but you broke the Big Car.'

'It's not "broke" broke, it's just . . . a bit stuck. Anyway, nothing wrong with a brisk walk, eh?' Sod brisk walks, *especially* in the sodding freezing sodding cold sodding snow.

Still, at least they were nearly there: Lisa's Country Bakery glowed up ahead.

It didn't have the olde-worlde charm that many of Glenfarach's business premises enjoyed. Instead of picturesque mullioned windows, it played host to a big single lump of glazing with vertical blinds pulled open, showing off a display of baked goods that actually looked pretty impressive. A handful of jagged-edged circles, cut from bits of cardboard, advertised today's specials, screaming things like 'BAPS – 4SC A DOZ!!!', 'NEW: FONDANT FANCIES!!!', and 'SOURDOUGH ROWIES!!!'

The baker's was sandwiched between two houses and opposite a funeral home, complete with black-draped coffins and a mannequin dressed in the full mourning get-up with matching top hat.

Suppose they'd be getting a bit more business than usual right now . . .

One of the search team stood clear of the others, watching Edward and Bigtoria crunching their way along the pavement. Then marched over.

Mid-fifties, with a no-nonsense haircut and matching face.

Shrewd eyes and a thin-lipped mouth. Holding herself like someone used to wielding power. The soft, lilting Highlands accent
didn't really go with her hard-as-nails look. 'You Montgomery-
Porter?' Not waiting for a reply. 'DCI Miller, Lothian and Borders.
What's the state of play?'

Edward marched on the spot, trying to get some circulation
back into his aching feet. 'We're going to inter—'

'Lunch.' Bigtoria straightened up to her full height. 'We're getting lunch, Ms Miller.'

The newcomer's eyes narrowed. 'That's *Detective Chief Inspector*
Miller.'

'No, it *was*, but you're a resident here now, aren't you?' She
pointed across the road at the line of people. 'I take it Sergeant
Farrow put you in charge of this little search team?'

Miller's face hardened.

The snow swirled around them like frozen sandpaper.

Edward shivered.

Then Bigtoria took some stapled-together sheets of paper from
her jacket pocket and skimmed through them till she found what
she was looking for. 'I see you beat a man to death, Ms Miller, then
hung his body from the railings in Princes Street Gardens.'

Muscles bunched along Miller's jaw, like they were holding
something very nasty inside.

Bigtoria's smile went with the weather. 'So you'll forgive me if I
don't tug the forelock.'

Because she couldn't meet someone and just talk to them, could
she? It always had to be a competition in how quickly she could
alienate *everyone*.

Miller's chin came up. 'Five women killed in three years, all on
Calton Hill. Sandy Ettrick's DNA was all over them. A taxi driver *saw*
him at the scene of the third murder. He confessed before he died.'

'And yet . . . here – you – are.'

'He *confessed*.'

Bigtoria tilted her head on one side. 'How's the search progressing, Ms Miller?'

The answer was forced out through gritted teeth. 'Nothing so far.'

'In that case, we won't keep you from your important work any longer.'

Colour flushed Miller's cheeks, her gloved hands clenching into fists. This was it – she was going to kick off. And they'd be returning to the station all bruised, cold, and stinking of pepper spray. *Again.*

Edward nodded.

Time to shine.

Defuse the situation, or wave goodbye to lunch.

He went to open his mouth, but it seemed the moment had passed.

Miller's fists unclenched; she straightened her shoulders, turned, and marched off towards her search-line. Not so much as a backwards glance.

He huffed out a long misty breath. 'Did you *have* to, Guv?'

'Nothing worse than a dirty copper, Constable.' Bigtoria pushed her way into the bakery.

Edward slumped, grimaced at the iron-grey sky, then followed her.

Inside, Lisa's Country Bakery was every bit as old-fashioned and basic as its façade. A tiled floor, glass cabinets showing off pastries, pies, and fancy pieces, with angled racks on the walls displaying various breads. Nothing swish. No gimmicks. And the whole place *seriously* needed a fresh coat of paint.

A mountain gorilla of a man stood behind the counter: head buried in a copy of Proust's *À la recherche du temps perdu* in the original French, wearing a striped pinny and a badge with 'HELLO, MY NAME IS ADAM!' on it.

He looked more like a Kurt, or a Clint.

Other than him, the place was empty.

He glanced up as Edward and Bigtoria bustled in from the snow, stomping their feet on the mat as the door's *bwip-bwop* chime faded.

Adam put his book down, his voice a flat, nasal, Central Belt drawl. 'What can I get you?'

Edward blew warm breath into cupped hands. 'Got anything hot?'

Bigtoria flashed her warrant card. 'Did you know Geoff Newman?'

'Can do tea, coffee, lentil soup, or microwave you a pie.'

She nodded. 'Hot steak pie, lentil soup, raisin whirl. And did you know Geoff Newman?'

A snort. 'Aye, Geoff used to come in here sometimes. Dirty kiddy-fiddling shite that he was.' Writing down her order.

Edward cleared his throat. 'I'll have a macaroni pie, soup, and one of those maple plait things. Oh, and a tea, please.'

'Hmmph.' He wrote that down too.

Bigtoria rapped her knuckles on the display case. 'You didn't like Newman?'

'*Nobody* liked him. Bad enough he was into kids, but an ex-cop too?' The smile went from suave to shark's tooth. 'Hope he was still alive when they torched his house. Hope he *burned*.' He tore the top sheet off his notebook and thumped it down beside the till. 'That's six credits for the macaroni, and seven for the steak.'

Edward dug out his wallet. 'Cash?'

'What use have *I* got for cash?' Adam ripped up their orders. 'Lisa's rules: no social credits, no pies.'

Edward shuffled closer to the counter. 'But we're *police* officers; you can trust us, can't you?'

Adam frowned, making a big show of mulling that over. Then a shrug, like he'd reached some sort of conclusion. 'No.'

Bigtoria knocked on the display cabinet again. 'People are saying Newman was drunk on Monday. Was he?'

'Wouldn't know. I only work Tuesday, Thursday, Saturdays. Shouldn't even be in today, but Pauline didn't turn up this morning. Useless cow.'

'They're saying there's a paedophile ring operating in Glenfarach.'

Adam's shoulders went back, flexing that gorilla-barrel chest. 'Dirty bastards. Living here with decent, *normal* folks? Ought to be locked up for the rest of their nasty, manky little lives.'

The baker's door *bwip-bwop*ed again and someone backed into the shop, bringing with them a howl of cold air and the squeak of an unoiled wheelchair.

Edward hurried over. 'Here, let me help.'

'Aye, thanks, Wee Man.' Mr Richards grinned at him.

Mr Bishop blinked up from the wheelchair – wrapped up in multiple layers, a thick padded coat, and a tartan blanket dusted with snow. So was his Russian-style fur hat. His oxygen mask was fixed in place by its elastic strap. Hissing and *whoooch*ing with each laboured breath.

Together, they hauled Mr Bishop in over the step and onto the tiled floor.

Adam was still at it: 'Better yet: bring back hanging. I had my way, we'd string the bastards up' – pointing through the big advert-studded window – 'one dangling from every sodding lamppost.'

'Hi.' Edward hunched over, giving Mr Bishop a quick check. 'How you doing?'

Not well, going by the look of him.

It was like he'd aged twenty years since yesterday. The confident tosspot who'd been smoking in the HMP Grampian car park replaced by a shrivelled-up auld mannie who probably wouldn't be around for long.

Mr Bishop's trembling hand emerged from beneath the tartan blanket and removed the mask. His wheezing voice was barely there at all. 'Cold as a witch's fanny out there . . .' Then a barrage of rattling coughs set him rocking in his wheelchair.

'And whose fault is that?' Mr Richards helped Mr Bishop put the oxygen mask on again, fussing over him like an indulgent mother. '*Telt* you this was a daft idea. But you're a stubborn old bugger, aren't you?' Pulling a face at Edward. 'Wanted to see a bit of Glenfarach before the snow closes everything down. Get a feel for it.' A sad shake of the head. 'I telt him, "Whole place is *Doctor* sodding *Zhivago*, the day," but will he listen?' Mr Richards waved at Adam. 'Hey, Big Man. Gie's two granary torpedoes, a pack of them sourdough rowies, and half a dozen pies. Three mince, three mealie.'

'Yes, Mr Richards. Got those eclairs you like, fresh made this morning?'

'Aye.' He plonked a tote bag on the counter. 'See's two of them an' all.'

Bigtoria did her best to reclaim control. 'Who's dealing illegal booze in Glenfarach?'

'Wouldn't know.' Adam got to work: wielding his tongs to gather Mr Richards' order into a series of paper bags.

'Don't know much, do you?'

He moved onto the pie cabinet. No expression in his voice at all, like he'd rehearsed the life out of it: 'I am cooperating with the appropriate authorities, to the best of my abilities, as per the terms of my residency.'

A snort from Bigtoria. 'I'll bet you are.'

Mr Richards tucked Mr Bishop in again. Nodded at Edward. 'You out catching the sights, son?'

Before he could answer, Bigtoria leapt in. 'We're investigating a *murder*, Mr Richards. That just coincidentally, as if by magic, occurred on the very day Mr Bishop arrived in Glenfarach.' Looming. 'I don't suppose either of you would know anything about that?'

A grin. 'Not a scoobie, hen.'

She glowered down at Mr Bishop. 'What about you?'

That shivery hand came up to remove the mask again. 'I was . . . was with you . . . you neep.' He pulled in a rattling breath. 'Been through this . . . already . . . with the wee lad . . . Besides, have you seen . . . my hands?' He held up a trembling, arthritic claw. 'Can barely . . . wipe my own arse   never mind . . . kill someone.'

Bigtoria turned her baleful glare in Edward's direction.

He shrank back. 'We were chatting, and it sort of came up.'

'I'll deal with you *later*.'

Great. That was something to look forward to.

Mr Bishop reached out and patted Edward on the sleeve. 'If I think of anything . . . son, I'll . . . let you know.' His head wobbled up to take in Mr Richards and Adam, his eyes pinched and his mouth hard. 'I'm not . . . clyping on anyone . . . but I'll not have some . . . *bastard* screwing up . . . my last bloody days . . . running around killing folk!'

Adam nodded and looked away. 'Yes, Mr Bishop.'

Mr Richards squeezed his bony shoulder. 'Aye, don't you worry, Marky. We'll no' let that happen.'

Bigtoria went in for another loom. 'If you have *any* evidence or information, you'll come to me first. Understand?'

The only things that broke the ensuing silence were Adam, busying himself behind the counter, and Mr Bishop's tortured breathing.

She gripped both arms of the wheelchair and leaned in, till her face was inches from Mr Bishop's. 'I said: do you understand?'

'That's *enough*: the man's no' well.' Mr Richards pulled the wheelchair back a bit, forcing her to let go, his scarred sneer twisting as he stared at her bloodshot eyes and the bits of towel poking out of her nostrils. 'No' surprised someone belted you one.' He got Mr Bishop into his mask again. 'It's OK, Marky, nice deep breaths.' Scowling at Bigtoria, teeth bared. 'Should be ashamed of yourself.' Before making sure Mr Bishop was all wrapped up. 'Let's get you home.'

Edward grimaced. 'I'd offer to give you a lift back to Jenkins House, but we don't have the car. Sorry.'

'*Bishop* House, now Mrs Jenkins is six feet closer to Satan.'

Mr Bishop's muffled voice Darth-Vadered out from the oxygen mask. 'Least she'll be bloody warm.'

'All right, Constable, that's enough community policing. We've got work to do.' Bigtoria dug out her list of residents and flicked through it. Glancing up at Adam: 'This Pauline who didn't come to work today, she have a surname?'

He placed a collection of paper bags on the countertop. 'Thomson, with a "TH" and no "P". And if you see her, tell her I said she was—'

'A "useless cow". I heard.'

He bustled the order into Mr Richards' tote bag. 'There you go; on the house. Hang on and I'll do you a couple of teas, too.'

Edward's stomach let loose a cry of hollow, piteous envy. 'But we only wanted two little pies . . .'

Bigtoria marched for the shop door. 'Soon as you like, Constable.' *Bwip-bwop*, and she was gone.

Some days it just didn't pay to get out of your cell.

15

Filigree woodwork dripped from the eaves of Ms Thomson's house; a black-cat weathervane poked up from the chimney; and small mullioned windows peered out at the wintery world. That, the brown harling, and a liberal coating of snow gave it the uncomfortable whiff of gingerbread cottage, only it wasn't buried away in the middle of the woods: it occupied an overgrown garden on the edge of Glenfarach, the end of a row of four equally twee gingerbread cottages. The forest loomed in front and to the side, adding to the whole here-comes-a-wolf vibe.

This was the last house before you disappeared into the wilderness, never to return.

Bigtoria and Edward waded along the pavement. Whoever was in charge of the snowblower, they hadn't been arsed to come past this bit of the village today, letting it build up shin-deep. Meaning they both had to high-step their way through the snow.

'I'm sorry, OK?' Cold and wet seeping through Edward's trouser legs; meltwater trickling down to soak into his socks. At this rate they'd be going home with frostbite *and* trench foot.

Bigtoria turned and poked him with a rock-hard finger. 'You do *not* talk to suspects without my say-so!'

'I didn't! OK, maybe *kind* of, but I was asking him how he was doing, because he wasn't looking well, and it sort of came up. He doesn't think it's got anything to do with him, but if it does, it might be a message or a present. No idea which, though.' Edward shrugged. 'He's never met Geoff Newman. Never even heard of him. So . . . ?'

She closed the gap till she towered over Edward. 'I'm the one running this investigation. Are we clear, Constable?'

'At least he's going to keep a lookout for us, right? We've got someone onside.'

'Are – we – clear?'

What was the point?

'Yes, Guv.'

She grunted, then shoved open the gate to Thomson Cottage. The garden path was even worse than the pavement. Bloody thing had to be hidden under a good two feet of snow.

Bigtoria waded her way to the front door.

Edward slouched after her, sticking to her footprints – which at least made the going a little easier. And the fairy-tale cottage's fili-greed porch offered a bit of cover from the relentless, tumbling flakes.

Which was nice.

She leaned on the doorbell, then stood back, one finger exploring the paper towel bungs in each nostril. Probing. Wiggling them from side to side before easing them out and pinging them away into the Witch's Winter Wonderland masquerading as a garden. Wincing as she dabbed her pinkie across the bottom of her nose and examined its tip – presumably for signs of fresh blood.

Then she froze, and looked up to find Edward had been staring at her. 'What!'

How best to put it . . , ?

He licked his lips, turned his gaze towards the forest's hungry darkness, lurking beyond the garden wall. Not sure if it was a good idea to broach this now, but she was already pissed off at him, so might as well. 'It's just, and I say this with the *utmost* of respect, Guv, but your interview technique seems a bit . . . adversarial?'

She abandoned her nostrils and loomed instead. 'What?'

He held up his hands. 'Don't get me wrong. I mean, there's a time and a place for the old Good Cop, Bad Cop routine, but people *might* be more inclined to cooperate *if* we didn't go out of our way to put those people's backs up.' Shuffling his feet. 'Hypothetically speaking.'

Her eyes narrowed as she stepped closer, bringing with her the smell of stale house fires and more than a hint of impending violence. 'Are you questioning my professionalism?'

'Me? No, not me, nope, not a bit of it.' Looking away. 'Sorry I brought it up.'

Still no response from Thomson Cottage, so he had a bash at being helpful and rang the bell again.

Bigtoria loomed some more. 'I do *not* get people's backs up.'

'Course you don't, Guv. Silly me.' Come on, answer the bloody door. He mashed his finger on the button. 'Only, you know, like Mr Bishop says, you catch more flies with honey and shite than vinegar. I speak to him: he wants to help. You growl at him: he tells us to bugger off. And you growl at *everyone*!'

She stepped forward, glowering down at him. 'You're sailing very close to the wind, Constable.'

Well, can't say he hadn't tried.

'You win: I give up.' Edward banged on the door with the flat of his hand. 'MS THOMSON, POLICE! OPEN UP!' *Bang, bang, bang.* 'MS THOMSON? MS THOMSON!' A pained smile. 'She's not answering.'

'I can bloody *see* that. Check the windows.'

Of course, Bigtoria stayed where she was, on the path, while he had to wade out into yet more sodding snow, trouser legs sticking to his pins-and-needles skin.

Standing on his tiptoes, he peered in at a dusty lounge. Then a dusty box room. 'Don't think anyone's lived here for a while.'

'Then try round the back.'

Urgh . . .

Edward waded his way to the front of the house again, snow caked up to his waist. 'Sod all. Kitchen, bathroom, and two bedrooms;

everything's dusty and abandoned.' Kicking the sides of his shoes against the top step sent a small avalanche of second-hand flakes tumbling down to pile up around his frozen feet. 'And before you ask, yes, I *did* try the back door: locked.'

She stared out into the slow-motion swirl of cold white slivers, adding their weight to the smothered world. Then stuck out her hand. 'Give me your Airwave.'

He did what he was told, and she pressed the buttons.

'Sergeant Farrow from DI Montgomery-Porter. Safe to talk.'

Sergeant Farrow's voice crackled from the handset's speaker, sounding a lot more distorted than last time. *'Golf Foxtrot Four to Alpha Charlie One, go ahead.'*

'We're outside Pauline Thomson's place. She's not answering her door.'

'Have you tried Millbrae Cottage? She's probably there.'

Bigtoria dug out two bits of paper, then slapped them against Edward's chest. 'Find it.' Back to the Airwave. 'What's the status on those search teams?'

'Don't know yet.'

Her face darkened. 'You're *supposed* to give me regular updates!'

Edward skimmed a finger around the map before giving up and looking for a 'Millbrae' in the list of residents. After all, that seemed to be the way Glenfarach's naming scheme worked.

'I'd love to, Guv, but I'm stuck here, at the station. We can't leave a prisoner in the cellblock without supervision. What if something hap-pened? The hell to pay.'

Millbrae, Millbrae, Millbrae . . . Ah, there you go: Kerry Millbrae, Millbrae Cottage, Soldier's Row. Piece of cake.

The Airwave handset creaked in Bigtoria's paw – her knuckles turning white as her voice got louder. 'Then get that *idiot* Harlaw to do it. Out!' She ended the call and stood there, seething at the snowy woods. 'I swear to God . . .'

Edward gave her a couple of minutes to fume before clearing his throat and pointing down the road. 'If it helps: Millbrae Cottage is this-a-way.'

She grunted, thrust the Airwave into his hands, then turned and trudged back down the garden path and off into the snow.

Honestly, it was like wrangling an angry toddler . . .

Soldier's Row was a quiet little street with houses on one side and a view of the hills and forest on the other. Both slowly disappearing beneath a thickening white blanket.

Another search team was just visible in the middle distance, moving in a line, heads bent, poking at the drifts with sticks. All noise muffled by the winter's hush.

Edward checked the map and pointed. 'That's us.'

This row of cottages wasn't anywhere near as twee as the last lot. Bigger, but more utilitarian, with double glazing, loft extensions, and grey walls. And it looked like someone had shovelled all the paths too, which was a bonus.

Didn't even have to wade their way to the front door of Millbrae Cottage.

Bigtoria rang the bell. 'Homeowner?'

'Right: Kerry Millbrae . . .' Edward checked the list. 'Says here, she ran a chain of Edinburgh brothels for the Russian mafia. Set fire to one of them when the police raided the place. She was inside it at the time; nobody else got out alive.' He grimaced. 'Sounds lovely.'

The searchers kept searching.

The snow kept falling.

Bigtoria tried the bell again. Gave it a count of three, then whacked the side of her fist against the wood. 'KERRY MILLBRAE, OPEN UP RIGHT NOW! POLICE!'

Edward shuffled along the path and peered in through the nearest window. A living room: cosy-looking, with a big fat ginger cat washing itself on a neat-freak coffee table. 'Lights are on.'

She gave the door another couple of whacks. 'OPEN THIS DOOR, MS MILLBRAE! WE'RE NOT KIDDING AROUND!' And again. 'POLICE!'

Edward sniffed. 'What do you think the regulations are for entering a resident's home without their permission?'

'Let's find out.' She twisted the handle and pushed. It wasn't locked, leaving them looking at a pastel-pink hallway lined with framed prints of intensely coloured flowers. Polished floorboards. Nice geometric rug.

'Sergeant Farrow said they had to cooperate with being searched, Guv. So, maybe we're just searching?'

A grunt, and Bigtoria stepped inside. 'KERRY MILLBRAE: POLICE!'

He followed her in, clunking the door shut in the ensuing silence. Stood there, one hand resting against the painted wood. 'You starting to get an itchy feeling about this?'

Edward tried the first room off the hallway.

It opened on the lounge with its yoga-position cat, now working away at the back of a ginger knee. Guess you could call it a 'feminine' space, with an overabundance of couch pillows heaped up on a violet sofa. An armchair draped with Indian-print throws. Flowers on the mantelpiece. Standard lamps in pastel shades, with dangly tassels. Nice framed prints.

The cat stopped licking its kneepits to stare at Edward, then returned to the task in . . . tongue.

Edward peered behind the sofa. 'Hello? Ms Millbrae?' Checking under the coffee table, *just in case*. 'Ms Thomson?' No one.

Back out to the hall.

Bigtoria stood in the doorway of what had probably started life as a dining room, now transformed into a craft-space-come-artist's-studio. 'Where the bloody hell are they?' Deep breath. 'PAULINE THOMSON, POLICE!'

Wait, was that . . . ?

He raised a hand, head tilted. 'Shhh . . .' Straining his ears.

'Don't you "Shush" me!'

'No, Guv, *listen*. Can you hear that?' A sort of creaky, faint, jagged noise. Someone crying? If it was, they were either far away, or doing their best to not make any sound.

Bigtoria held her breath, ear cocked, then her eyes narrowed and she burst through the door at the end of the corridor.

Soon as it banged open, the sobbing stopped and the unmistakable stench of raw meat collapsed out into the hallway. Ripe as a butcher's shop.

She froze on the threshold. 'Hello? Is someone in there?' Then stepped inside.

Edward joined her.

The kitchen was every bit as well furnished and cosy as the lounge. Homely. Comfortable. Traditional, but not in a fusty way. The kind of kitchen where you could rustle up a delicious quiche, or have your palm read by a middle-aged lady in a gaily patterned headscarf. Which only made what was in the centre of the room even more horrible.

A woman lay on her back on the kitchen's central island; wrists and ankles tied to the cupboard-doors' hinges; head hanging over the edge to stare, eyeless, at the burgundy-coloured Aga.

She'd been stripped to her underwear, leaving a bony corpse with protruding hip bones and ribs. Ancient scars of self-harm writhed around her forearms and thighs, but they were nothing compared to what'd been done to her here. Cuts and bruises covered nearly every inch of pale, blood-streaked skin. More blood had flowed and dripped down the island's cupboard doors. A puddle of dark, sticky red reaching out across the kitchen tiles.

She was still wearing her ankle tag.

Just like Geoff Newman.

Edward took a breath. Hissed it out again. 'Jesus . . .'

Bigtoria froze. Blinking. Face hardening.

He pulled out his Airwave. 'Alpha Charlie Two to Golf Foxtrot Four. Doesn't matter if it's safe to talk or not: urgent, over!'

A shuddering grunt, and the DI dug a pair of blue nitriles out of her pocket. 'Glove up.' She stepped further into the kitchen, picking her way around the obvious spatters of blood.

Edward lowered the handset. 'Are you sure you should be doing that, Guv? What about the policies and—'

'We sodding lost everything last time.' She produced her phone, holding it up in landscape mode, filming the scene. 'I'm not making that mistake again.'

Fair enough.

He pinned the Airwave between his cheek and his shoulder, freeing his hands to snap on a pair of nitrile gloves.

Sergeant Farrow's voice squawked into his ear, even more distorted than before. *'Safe to talk, Alpha Charlie Two. What's up?'*

'We've got another body, Sarge.' He swallowed, trying not to gag at the warm-copper taint of raw meat that laced the air. 'Same MO as Geoff Newman.'

'Fudging hell . . .'

Bigtoria's tour of the kitchen came to a stumbling halt and she stood there, staring at something hidden behind that block of free-standing units. Her voice was eerily calm, like a monster was lurking just out of sight. 'Constable Reekie, can you come here for a minute?' She kept her gaze fixed on whatever she'd found, only now she was making rapid, sweeping gestures with her left hand, trying to waft him around the other side of the central island.

'Guv? Shouldn't we minimize contaminating the scene, and—'

'Now, Constable.'

OK . . .

He edged his way past the blood puddle, skirting the island and its gruesome trophy, then came to a stumbling halt of his own.

A woman sat on the floor, with her back wedged into the corner between two sets of kitchen units, knees drawn up to her chest. She wore a pair of bloodstained socks, bloodstained jeans, and a bloodstained pink sweatshirt. Her face tight and shiny with webs of scar tissue as tears streamed into the creases from her lopsided eyes – one of which was a solid ball of milky grey. Nose little more than a stub with elongated nostrils. That long, black hair was definitely a wig: no eyebrows, no eyelashes.

Exactly what you'd expect if someone set fire to a brothel, and barely made it out alive. Framed photos freckled the kitchen wall, featuring her and a woman who *might* have been the victim. It was difficult to tell, what with all the blood . . .

'Kerry Millbrae?' Keeping his hands where she could see them, making no sudden moves. 'Ms Millbrae, we're here to help. Is that OK? Will you let us help you?'

She rocked quietly in place. Her right hand was little more than a club – its fingers and thumb reduced to stumps, pressed against her trembling mouth – while the other formed a curled claw, missing a couple of digits, clutching an eight-inch chef's knife. Staring straight ahead, like she could see straight through the central island and off to another country, where nothing nasty, violent, and blood-drenched ever happened . . .

Bigtoria crept closer. 'I need you to drop the knife.'

No response.

'DROP THE KNIFE!'

It was like Ms Millbrae didn't know they were there.

Edward shuffled towards her from the other side, keeping his voice soft and warm as he squatted beside her. 'We're not going to hurt you, OK?' Inching closer. 'Shhh . . . Shhh . . . It'll be OK.'

He reached out, moving as slow as possible, and slipped the knife from her ruined fingers. Oh, thank the buggering hell for that. She hadn't even *tried* to stab him. His breath wobbled out. 'There we go.'

Then Edward backed away, taking the knife with him, making sure it stayed out of reach.

Bigtoria stepped up, voice hard as a rottweiler and twice as dark. 'Kerry Millbrae, I am arresting you under Section One of the Criminal Justice, Scotland, Act 2016 for the murders of Geoff Newman and Pauline Thomson.'

As soon as Pauline's name left Bigtoria's lips, Ms Millbrae threw back her head, howling out her pain and tears. Sobbing and screaming as the DI hauled her to her feet and snapped on the cuffs.

—don't move—

(don't even *breathe*)

16

A dull grey glow oozed down from the darkening sky as PC Harlaw bundled himself in through the front door. Stamping the snow from his boots. Shaking it off his padded high-vis jacket. Staring as Bigtoria escorted Ms Millbrae out of the kitchen. 'Sodding hell. Kerry?'

Not sure the handcuffs were *strictly* necessary, given she was nearly catatonic.

Edward brought up the rear. 'You got that knife tube?'

Harlaw produced a clear plastic cylinder with a black stopper at one end, and held it out. 'Had to ransack the entire evidence cupboard for that. Don't think we've ever used them before.'

'Ta.' He took it back through into the abattoir kitchen, doing his best not to look at what was left of Pauline Thomson. Assuming it *was* Pauline Thomson; still hadn't had an official ID yet.

Difficult to know whether to breathe through his nose or his mouth in here. One way, you got the meat-and bowels stench of butchered human being. The other you got the taste – iron and iodine, salt and bitter eggs.

He pulled on his last pair of nitrile gloves and slid the eight-inch chef's knife into the tube. Wedged the stopper into place. And eased out of the room again, closing the door behind him. Hiding the horror within.

They'd draped a duvet-style jacket on over Ms Millbrae's top half, zipping it up with her handcuffed arms trapped inside. Slipped a woolly hat on over her wig, leaving it slightly squint.

Bigtoria poked Harlaw in his uniformed chest. 'Constable: you will guard this crime scene. You will not leave it. You will not let anyone in. You will not let anyone *set fire* to it. And most important of all: you will *not* trample all over the bloody thing!'

'Yes, Guv!'

She pointed at Edward. 'You: with me.' Then hauled her prisoner out through the front door.

Edward followed, taking deep cleansing breaths of sharp night air as the streetlights flickered into life, casting their stark, icy glow into the swirling flakes of grey and white.

'Take her. Give me your Airwave.'

He did what he was told.

The cold singed the tips of Edward's ears, burning its way across his cheeks, making those cleansing breaths thick as woodsmoke in the LED light, but Ms Millbrae wasn't even shivering. Or looking where she was going. Not really – staring blankly into the middle distance didn't count.

Bigtoria pressed the button. 'DI Montgomery-Porter to Sergeant Farrow. Safe to talk.'

They scrunched their way along the pavement, passing from one glaring white orb of streetlight to the next. Leaving footprints that probably wouldn't last more than thirty minutes as the snow spiralled down.

A small row of shops lined the other side of the road, windows warm and inviting with their displays of craft-fair tat, second-hand furniture, and mediocre watercolours.

Finally, Sergeant Farrow's voice hissed and sputtered from the speaker. *'Guv? How's Kerry, is she OK? I can't believe she'd—'*

'Has that bloody solicitor turned up?'

'Lewis? He's in with Siobhan Wilkins now. Are you sure Kerry's—'

'And I want an update on the search teams.' Wiping the snow from her face.

'Well, they haven't all reported in yet, and I'm stuck here, so—'

'Then you'd better do something about it, hadn't you?'

Even distorted and crackling, there was no mistaking the pained sigh. *'Yes, Guv.'*

Bigtoria killed the call and thrust the Airwave handset back to Edward. 'Place is a complete disaster . . .'

'Sorry, Guv.'

And on they trudged.

At least the cellblock was warm. Edward guided Ms Millbrae to the custody desk and Sergeant Farrow booked her in. Which wasn't easy, given the only noise she could make was a high-pitched keening moan, followed by sobbing. Her one good eye not focusing on anything, shoulders hunched, mouth going from a tourniquet grimace to slack-jawed misery. They helped her out of her woolly hat and puffy jacket; her shoes and belt went in a tray on the desk.

Bigtoria unzipped her own high-vis, shaking the snow from it. 'Siobhan Wilkins?'

Sergeant Farrow pointed at a blue door with a little round porthole in it. 'Consultation Room One.'

She stomped over there and peered through the window. Grunted. Turned. 'You done yet?'

'Almost, Guv.' Sergeant Farrow completed the last form. 'And there we are.' She looked at Edward. 'Watch the desk for me?'

'Sarge.'

Then she gathered up a bundle of evidence bags and an SOC suit in its plastic wrapper. Put a gloved hand on Kerry's shoulder, and guided her over to Cell Six. 'Come on, Kerry, let's get you out of those dirty things.' Soon as they were inside, she shut the door behind her.

Had to wonder, didn't you? What made someone *do* something like that? What went through their mind to make it OK to butcher another human being? Not surprised she'd slipped off the rails afterwards. How would you even *live* with yourself?

Pfff . . .

Might as well get a brew on.

By the time he returned from the back office, bearing three mugs of builders' finest, and a plastic cup of the same, the DI was nowhere to be seen. Which, let's be honest, was a sodding relief.

Cell Six's door swung open and out came Sergeant Farrow, still carrying those evidence bags – only now they were filled with Ms Millbrae's bloodstained clothes. She dumped everything on the custody desk, her face creased, mouth a downturned line that didn't speak of joy.

Edward handed her a mug. 'Did you a tea.'

A sigh. 'Thanks.' She had a sip, then looked around the cellblock, dropping her voice to a whisper. 'Where's the Huge Harridan Horror of Old Aberdeen?'

Hard not to smile at that. 'Sarge, I'm shocked you should say such a thing!' He picked up the plastic cup. 'Shall I . . . ?' Nodding towards Cell Six.

'Please.'

He took the tea over there, opened the door and stepped inside, leaving it open so Sergeant Farrow could keep an eye on things. Just in case.

Ms Millbrae sat on the cell's mattress, knees drawn up to her chest – like she'd never left the kitchen – dressed in a crisp new SOC suit, with the hood thrown back. Exposing the scarred swathe of skin covering her head and the nubs of twisted gristle where her ears used to be.

Sergeant Farrow had confiscated the wig.

Well, of course she had. Why wouldn't she? But that didn't make the sight any less raw. Any less sad.

Edward squatted down. 'Hey, Kerry. Is it OK if I call you Kerry?'

No reply.

'Got you a nice cup of tea.' He placed the plastic cup on the floor, beside her. 'There we go.'

She didn't move. Didn't even blink.

'I know this all seems scary, but we'll sort it out, OK?'

Nothing.

'Do you remember what happened, Kerry?'

Her reconstructed lips twitched, then she rocked forward a teeny bit and back again. Forward and back. Forward and back. Weeping quietly. Looking like her whole world had died.

'Kerry? Hello? Can you hear me?'

Forward and back. Forward and back.

'OK . . .'

He eased the door shut behind him as he left, so it barely made a sound.

Sergeant Farrow was signing the evidence bags into the productions log when he scuffed his way across the grubby terrazzo floor. 'You do any better than me?'

Edward shook his head. 'Might want to get your Duty Doctor to take a look. Pretty sure she's in shock.'

'Probably right.' Sergeant Farrow picked up the phone. 'Never would've thought Kerry could *do* something like that. To Geoff Newman, *maybe*, but not Pauline.' Poking at the keypad, handset to her ear. 'Come on, Doc.'

Edward sidled up, helping himself to a fistful of nitrile gloves from the box on the counter. 'Sarge?' Stuffing them into his pocket. 'Any chance you can give us some social credits? The baker's wouldn't take cash and I'm *starving*.'

'Hello, Doc? It's Louise. We need you down the station; Kerry Millbrae's taken a bit of a funny turn . . . Definitely . . . No, she's pretty unresponsive . . . What happened? Might've murdered Pauline Thomson and Geoff Newman . . .' A sigh. 'Yup, that's what I said . . . OK, thanks . . . Bye. Bye.'

Bigtoria thumped back through the door, into the custody suite. Face flushed and clenched. 'Bloody outside lines *still* aren't working.'

He held up a mug. 'Made you a tea, Guv.'

She took it without so much as a thank you. Turning to Sergeant Farrow instead. 'Hit the CCTV, see if it caught anyone going in or out of Millbrae Cottage. Not that I'm holding my sodding breath.'

'Ah . . .' Sergeant Farrow sucked air in through her teeth. 'I can try, Guv, but Jenna says until we get the bits in to fix it, it's not actually recording anything.'

Bigtoria stared at her. 'Oh, for *God's* sake.'

'Yup.' She plonked a ration book on the counter in front of Edward. 'One week's social credits. Just don't blow them all on beer and sweeties.' A glance at the clock. 'Now grab your coat, we need to see an ex-DCI about a search team.' Raising her eyebrows at Bigtoria. 'If you're OK looking after the cellblock, that is, Guv?'

All she got was a grunt in return.

Because, you know: people skills.

The howling snow softened the streetlights' glare, blurring it around the edges as wind strafed its way across the square – whipping the flakes into dervishes and billowing sheets that obscured everything more than a dozen feet away.

Edward and Sergeant Farrow huddled in the lee of the clock tower/monument thing, hands deep in pockets, shoulders up, Police Scotland woolly hats jammed on tight, headtorches shining bright but not achieving much.

He stamped his soggy, half-frozen shoes, and leaned in closer to the granite monument. Face screwed up where he could still actually *move* it. Nose and ears stinging from a million tiny needles.

Whose stupid idea was it to join the police force? Whose stupid, half-arsed, idiot idea was it to do this for a living? Whose—

'Are you OK?'

A shiver rippled its way across his shoulders. 'Ever wonder about your choice of career, Sarge?'

'I'm sure Jane won't be long.'

'I wanted to be an astronaut, or a football player, or a rock star. Now look at me.'

'Yup.'

A gust of wind sent thick white flakes whipping around the monument to crackle against their high-vis jackets, sparkling in the headtorch glow.

'Sarge? That thing you gave Mr Bishop: the welcome present?'

'Same gift every resident gets – their name on a nice custom-made wrought-iron sign, with "house" or "cottage" or whatever. Our way of making them feel wanted. Giving them a bit of ownership.'

Suppose that made sense. If they felt part of the community, maybe they'd be less likely to screw it up for everyone else? Mind you, it wasn't exactly working right now. Not with tortured—

Sergeant Farrow's elbow jabbed into Edward's side. 'Here we go.'

A lone figure lurched out of the blizzard. Getting closer.

'Cutting it a bit fine, aren't we, Jane?'

Ex-DCI Jane Miller was even more wrapped up than they were, her nose and ears an angry pink where they stuck out of the heavy-weather gear. 'That's what happens when you do a thorough job.' Bracing herself against the wind as she glanced up at the red line marking curfew time on the clockface. 'Let's make this quick. We covered everything from Flesher's Brae to Gallows Row: no sign of Caroline Manson in any outbuilding, garden, or shed. And we've spoken to every resident we could: no one's seen her. Or at least no one that'll admit to it.'

Sergeant Farrow nodded. 'Fudge. Kind of expected that, though.'

Edward stuck up his hand. 'What about the derelict houses and cottages and things?'

'Do you think I became a detective chief inspector by not knowing how to organize a search, *Constable*?' Ex-DCI Miller turned to squint into the driving snow. 'Assuming she's out there somewhere, she's survived one night in the open. She won't survive another. If she's still in Glenfarach? My advice: tomorrow morning you give me a team of deputized individuals with official powers to search residents' homes.' Pointing east, west, and south. 'Establish roadblocks on all major routes. Then go house to house. Tear the place apart, if we have to.'

'I'll pass that on to DI Montgomery-Porter.' Sergeant Farrow stepped forward, then staggered a couple of paces as the wind snatched and shoved at her high-vis. 'Thanks, Jane, I appreciate your help.'

The Ex-DCI took one last look at the curfew line, and loped off into the storm. Fading like a ghost into the swirling snow.

Edward waited till she was *definitely* out of earshot. 'How come, soon as anyone gets promoted above sergeant, they become an utter dick?'

Sergeant Farrow staggered into the teeth of the wind, face turned away from the battering icy flakes, heading back to the station. Voice raised above the storm: 'ONE OF THOSE UNFATHOMABLE LAWS OF NATURE, I SUPPOSE . . .'

*

Steam rose from the legs of Edward's trousers, bringing with it the sharp-sour-vinegar stink of fabric that had gone from wet to dry to wet to dry to wet again far too often. The gritty, smoky remnants of last night's house fire added to the general pong. Making him smell a *little bit* like a burning urinal.

He was leaving a puddle on the cellblock floor: snow melting from his shoes, soaking *out* through the lace holes. Socks squelching every time he moved.

Bigtoria had her back to him, standing there with her arms folded as a florid-faced man in his mid-sixties talked down to *her* for a change.

His bouffant grey hair curled around the collar of a tailored three-piece suit in deep inky purple, with a crisp white shirt and old-school tie. The kind of deep, rumbling lawyery voice that was pitched loud and arrogant enough to batter a jury into submission a dozen buildings away. 'I'd like to point out that my client isn't permitted to be outwith her domicile after curfew, and as it's currently' – he made a big show of consulting an oversized, flash Rolex watch – 'four thirty-six – sixteen minutes *late* – I suggest you release her on her own recognizance.'

The DI shook her head. 'No chance.'

'And what about *me*, Detective Inspector? I'm not allowed to be out after curfew either.'

'You've been granted a special dispensation, Mr Nichols. In lieu of a fee.'

One eyebrow scurried its way up his forehead, leaving a sneer behind. 'My client has prepared a statement.' Then his eyes drifted to Ms Millbrae's cell. 'And I see you have arrested another poor, unfortunate soul. Do they also require representation? Because if they do, I'm expecting *reasonable* compensation for my efforts.'

'Of course you are.' She paused. Then turned and frowned at Edward. Maybe his smoky-vinegar scent had reached her? 'What are *you* still doing here?'

He backed off a step. 'I was just—'

'You have a Big Car to dig out.'

Now hold on a minute.

'But, Guv, it's pitch dark, blowing a gale, and *snowing* out there! We—'

'You got it stuck – you can get it *un*stuck. And as you clearly can't be trusted to do anything unsupervised, Sergeant Farrow's going with you.'

Sergeant Farrow stared at her. 'With all due respect, Guv, Constable Reekie's right: there's a blizzard out—'

'Oh, and while we're at it: someone still needs to search the woods. I want to know what Geoff Newman was up to for two hours the day before he died.' She pointed at Kerry Millbrae's cell. 'Just because we got distracted by another murder, doesn't mean it's slipped off the priority list. You can do that while you're out.'

Edward opened his mouth. Closed it. Tried again, 'But—'

'Did that sound like a *request*, Constable?' Squaring her shoulders.

Urgh . . .

'No, Guv.'

Edward crunched along the pavement, following Sergeant Farrow, leaning back against the gusting wind that clawed at his back. Snow whipping past, making a swirling tunnel of vertigo in the harsh white LED lights of Gallows Row.

The wellies he'd commandeered from the stores were a bit on the big side, but that just meant more space to pad them out with extra socks – filched from the locker room. Nice, warm, thick, woolly, *dry* socks.

And better yet: gloves! OK, so they were ancient and falling apart – liberated from the station's dusty old Method of Entry kit – and every time Edward flexed his hands, little crusts of perished leather tumbled from the wrinkled black surface. But it was a massive improvement on having painful, curled, purple sausages for fingers.

He gripped the snow shovel across his middle, the blade turned scoop-side away from the howling gusts. Once smacked in the chest with a snow shovel, twice shy.

Sergeant Farrow had hers tucked under her arm, freeing her other hand up so she could stick the fingertips of her glove between her teeth and pull the thing off. Then fiddled with her phone for a bit.

The fire engine had gone from outside Newman Cottage, leaving nothing but the house's charred remains behind. The granite walls were intact, as were both gable ends, but everything in between was a blackened ruin. Still steaming gently as the snow fell and fell and fell . . .

Lights glowed in the three other houses' windows. Ex-DCI Miller was in her living room, staring out at them.

Edward gave her a smile and a small wave. Then lowered his hand. Only been here a day and a half, and he was already acting like a creepy resident.

But ex-DCI Miller didn't move, or even acknowledge his presence. Just kept on staring.

So sod her.

When they reached the last intact house on the street, Leonard Walker watched them go by from the safety of his own personal library, a book in one hand. Then pulled the curtains shut, hiding himself and his children away.

Sod him too.

Sergeant Farrow stopped on the pavement outside Newman Cottage, bracing herself as she stared at the ruins. Raising her voice over the wind. 'SIX YEARS I'VE BEEN HERE AND WE'VE NEVER HAD ANYTHING LIKE THIS.'

'STILL THINKING ABOUT LEAVING?'

She scrunched up her mouth, nostrils flaring like she was taking in the scorched smell of defeat. 'LOOK AT IT.' Waving her phone at the wreckage. 'BET THEY'LL TWIST EVERYTHING, SO IT'S ALL *MY* FAULT. MIGHT AS WELL JUMP BEFORE I'M PUSHED.'

Edward leaned over the garden wall and drove the blade of his shovel down into the snow, so the handle stuck up like a grave marker.

She blinked at him.

A shrug. 'NO POINT LUGGING THEM ALL THE WAY INTO THE WOODS AND BACK AGAIN, IS THERE?'

'SUPPOSE.' She stabbed her shovel in beside his.

They stood there for a moment longer, then turned – wind shoving at their shoulders, as they tromped through the knee-deep snow towards the forest.

'BETTER GET ON WITH IT.' She put her phone away and grimaced.

He poked away at his headtorch – not easy with the thick armoured gloves – until the thing clicked on, casting his own private spotlight through the screeching whirl of flakes.

Sergeant Farrow did the same, then pulled her glove back on. 'MAYBE I'LL GET A TRANSFER SOMEWHERE WARMER, LIKE GLASGOW?' They stepped off the end of the road into deeper snow. Wading through it towards the waiting darkness. 'OR THE OUTER HEBRIDES ARE PROBABLY NICE.'

Edward shoved his way past a smothered whin bush, causing a mini-blizzard of his own and setting the seedheads rattling. 'I HEAR THEY'VE GOT PALM TREES AND WHITE SANDY BEACHES. VERY SWANKY . . .'

He stopped at the edge of the forest.

From here on in, the only light came from their headtorches, leaping from frosted trunk to frosted trunk. Tracing the outlines of long-dead bracken, twisted bramble, and jagged gorse. Their shadows writhing and dancing like pagan beasts.

Yeah . . .

This was the kind of place mankind had been telling cautionary tales about for centuries. Go not into the deep, dark woods, for there are monsters waiting to devour you

Edward huffed out a cloudy breath. Pulled his shoulders back. 'THIS IS A REALLY BAD IDEA, ISN'T IT?'

'COMPLETELY.'

Right.

They waded into the forest.

17

Trees crowded around them as they worked their way deeper into the woods. On the upside: the further they went, the thicker the leaf canopy above them, which meant a *lot* less snow. It never disappeared completely – well, maybe under the biggest pines – but at least it wasn't knee-deep any more.

Sadly, the low-hanging branches and crunchy loam of the forest floor made walking just as difficult as it had been out in the blizzard. Much quieter, though. Well, if you ignored the creak and groan of shifting branches, and the distant haunted susurrus of wind through the needles.

This wasn't your usual Forestry Commission plantation, where everything was laid out in ordered rows, waiting for harvest: this was *properly* old. Vast, twisted trees, their branches drooping under the weight of snow, their trunks scabbed with frosty lichen that glittered in the headtorches' beams.

A screech rang out in the darkness, somewhere off to the right, echoing through the woods before being snatched away by the darkness.

. . . all the streams ran red . . . Legend has it, on a quiet night . . . you can still hear their ghosts screaming . . .

Edward froze, then turned a full, slow three-sixty, headtorch scanning the trunks and branches, breath misting around his head. No sign of whatever it was. Somehow that wasn't as reassuring as it could have been.

He licked his lips. Moved a couple of steps closer to Sergeant

Farrow. 'Is it just me, or does this feel like the start of a horror film?'

She launched into a whistled rendition of 'Teddy Bears' Picnic', but not the normal jaunty, child-friendly version – she'd dropped it a couple of octaves and slowed it *way* down, drawing each note out to its full ominous potential. Then grinned. 'Bags you get eaten first.'

She had her glove off again, holding her phone, the map app glowing – underlighting her features. Which did nothing to detract from the horror-film feel. The printout of Geoff Newman's last movements was in her other, MOE-gloved hand as she turned left, then right, eyes fixed on the screen. A nod and she moved off, following what might or might not have been a track through the trees.

Difficult to tell with all the snow.

Edward hurried after her. 'I can't get eaten first: I've got a note from my mum.'

'Well, don't look at me. I'm the attractive, virtuous female character – that makes me the Final Girl. I survive and live happily ever after, while you're monster-meat.'

Had to admit, that was worth a smile.

She frowned. 'What?'

'Nothing. Just nice to work with someone who has a sense of humour for a change.'

'Really? And DI Montgomery-Porter always comes across as so *warm* and *approachable*.'

They crunched on, deeper into the woods.

Good job they still had a GPS signal, because this was the kind of place people got lost in, never to be seen again. Not even their picked-clean bones . . .

Edward did another three-sixty, but his torchlight barely made it ten feet before the forest devoured it. 'What do you think we'll find when we get there? Be pretty disappointing if it's just a half-arsed bridge.'

She didn't stop. 'There won't be a bridge. Why would he build a bridge? Where's he going to build it *to*? Fiver says the whole thing's a cover story for buying and/or trading child pornography. Plus the . . .' She cleared her throat. '. . . you know: pleasuring himself.'

'Lovely.' Edward picked his way around the paddling-pool-sized root ball of a fallen pine tree. 'But what if he really *was* building something? He borrowed that book about it, right: *The Scientific American Boy*?'

'So?'

The ground dropped away in front of them: a wide bowl scooped from the forest floor, trees thinning out to form a round clearing. Which, of course, meant there hadn't been enough leaf cover to stop the snow accumulating until deep drifts smothered everything.

'Well, I mean . . .' – Edward waded down the slope – 'does that not *worry* you? Maybe it's, you know, a project he's doing with his fellow ring members? Maybe they're building something together? And if it's not a bridge . . . ?'

She stopped. 'What, a sort of clubhouse for perverts?'

'Could be.' Edward's headtorch scanned the snowy depression surrounded by that dark forbidding woodland. Tiny flecks of ice sparkling in the torchlight as yet more of the stuff tumbled from the sky. 'Mind you, you'd have to be off your nut.'

He struggled across the clearing, Sergeant Farrow crumping through the drifts beside him.

Wading downhill was hard enough, but *uphill*?

Dear God . . .

Every step a fight.

Breath whoomping his lungs, burning in his throat.

Pulse battering in his ears like a malfunctioning drum machine.

He staggered to a halt at the top of the hill, peching and heeching out great billowing clouds of white in his headtorch's glow.

Sergeant Farrow bent double, back heaving. 'Urgh . . .' Wheezing, coughing, then straightening up, all shiny-faced and flushed. 'You . . . you OK?'

'No.' Edward raised his face to the snow, sweat trickling down his spine and into his underwear. Shirt clammy against his skin. 'God, I hate . . . I hate Detective Inspector . . . Montgomery-Porter . . .'

'Yup.' Sergeant Farrow checked her map and phone. 'Not . . . not long . . . now.'

He slumped forwards again, catching his breath. 'This building project: what if it's not a clubhouse? What if Ms Hamilton's right and they're making moonshine?'

'I'd buy that.' Sergeant Farrow battled her way along the lip of the bowl, stopping every six or seven steps to peer at her screen.

Edward lumbered after her. 'Or maybe it's somewhere to . . .' – waving his hand in a vague, circular gesture – 'drugs?'

'Could be.' She lurched to a halt. 'This is us.' Unzipping her high-vis and flapping out steam.

'*Here?*' He performed a slow, staggering circle, his headtorch's beam leaping from tree to tree, sweeping back along the ridge and down the twin grooves they'd gouged through the snow, up the bowl again, across yet more trees, until the light fell on Sergeant Farrow's sweaty face once more. 'You sure?'

'See?' She held out her phone and the map. 'These are the *exact* GPS coordinates.'

'But there's sod all here!'

No half-arsed bridge, no clubhouse for perverts, no illicit still. Nothing but miles of darkness, forest, and snow.

He sagged back against the nearest tree – a big Scots pine, with its warty bark and drooping branches heavy with white – puffing and panting till his breath and pulse returned to something less heart-attacky.

Sergeant Farrow kicked a drift, sending clumps of white up to fluoresce in her headtorch's glow. 'It's a wild fudging goose chase.'

Bloody Bigtoria *knew* this would be a waste of time. A horrible, cold, nasty, exhausting, awful waste of time.

His head rolled back against the tree trunk.

And she did it just to punish him for *accidentally* getting the Big Car stuck. During an active pursuit. Which was definitely not his fault, by the way, but did she care?

What an absolute . . .

He frowned up at a weird-looking branch not far above. It poked out of the bark like normal, then angled almost straight up. Which wouldn't have been anything remarkable if it hadn't been whittled away, leaving a six-inch stump that bore more than a passing resemblance to an erect willy.

Ew . . .

Edward curled his lip and retreated from the Cock Tree. 'OK: let's be logical about this. You tromp all the way out here: what do you do for two hours?'

Bitterness dripped into the snowy night. 'You know this is your DI getting revenge on me because the CCTV isn't working, and the search teams didn't find Caroline, don't you? Like *I* control the fudging budget, or the snow, or *anything*. I'm a sergeant, not the Chief Constable!'

Wow. Way to make it all about yourself.

He held his hand out. 'See's the printout, Sarge.'

She passed it over and he squinted at the map. Each stop on Newman's last outing was marked with a time and duration. Edward's thick-gloved finger followed the line from Newman Cottage – '11:50, 19H 26M' – into the woods to where they were now: '12:05, 2H 17M'.

Sergeant Farrow held her arms out, like she'd been crucified. 'How many times have I put requests in to get the system upgraded? Hundreds, *that's* how many.'

'According to this, he was here for two hours seventeen minutes. What's the resolution on this?' Peering at the map in the head-torch's glow. 'Should've got you to print off a close-up, Sarge. No idea if he's just standing in the one place or moving about doing stuff.'

She kicked the drift again, sending up a flurry of sparkling white. 'Beginning to think he only came out here to make us look like fudging idiots.'

Nah, Newman *had* to be up to something, didn't he?

Edward scuffed about in the snow around the Cock Tree, clearing it away. No sign of that red holdall, or anything else suspicious, come to that. Just stones, twigs, dirt, and urine-yellow grass.

You'd think there'd be a pile of wanky used tissues at the very least.

Unless they'd all dissolved?

He frowned up at the whittled penis. 'Or *maybe* Newman was waiting for someone? Maybe Caroline Manson met him, right here, and he gave *her* the holdall?' And given what he'd found in her sock drawer? 'Bet it's something to do with drugs.'

Sergeant Farrow puffed out her cheeks. 'Might be worth looking into. Go through Caroline's clients again: see if she's unaccounted for while Geoff was out here.' A grunt. 'Doesn't help *us*, though.'

Abandoning the tree, Sergeant Farrow stomped back along the track they'd made in the snow, following it downhill.

Ah well, Bigtoria couldn't say they hadn't tried.

Not that it would stop her, mind.

She'd still find some way to make this all his fault . . .

They staggered out of the woods, breathing hard.

Sergeant Farrow bent double, grabbing her knees and panting, while Edward stood, tilted backwards, hands on his ribs, huffing great clouds of white up into the unrelenting snow.

God almighty . . .

Her voice came out muffled and ragged. 'Let's . . . let's never . . . do that . . . again . . .'

Took a while, but they finally got themselves together and trudged over to the remains of Newman Cottage.

Edward reached over the garden wall and grabbed the handle of his snow shovel, drawing the blade free and holding it high. Putting a bit of theatrical flourish into it: 'Excalibur!' Grinning. 'Now I'm King of the Britons, I officially outrank you and you have to make the tea.'

She shook her head, extracted her own shovel, and crumped away down the pavement.

'Sarge? I thought we were having a bonding moment. Sarge? Sarge!'

Pfff . . .

Only trying to lighten the mood a bit.

So much for finally working with someone who had a sense of humour.

Turned out sergeants were just as bad as detective inspectors.

Every *single* step was a sodding struggle as they waded their way off South Street and onto Meadowburn Lane, snow up to their knees, and still it kept on falling.

Edward had his high-vis open, letting the steam swirl out in the streetlight's LED glare. Breathing like a rusty crack pipe. Toes icy and stinging in his borrowed wellies. Trousers soaked through, sticking to aching-numb-tingling-hot-and-frozen-all-at-the-same-time legs.

Knee-high. And that was on the pavement – it was even worse when they had to fight their way across the road.

'We should've commandeered that sodding snowplough.'

She trudged on. 'This bit's your fault, remember?'

They slogged past Wilkins' Joinery Workshop. All shuttered up now that they'd got Siobhan Wilkins in custody.

'Seriously: the snowplough would make things much easier.'

'How? You'd still have to fight through all this to reach it.' She pointed at a big shed-like wooden structure down the end of the street, with 'GRAMPIAN ROADS DEPARTMENT' stencilled along the side. 'And before you ask: Shammy's the only one who can drive the thing.'

On they crunched.

'Could give it a go?'

They'd reached the final streetlight – everything beyond here was pitch grey, devoid of features and details. The wind had picked up too; without the screen of houses and buildings to get in the way, it howled in from the wilderness, bringing fistfuls of stinging flakes with it. Battering them. Whipping the surface into a ghostly fog and sending it drifting across the road to pile up against anything it could find. Edward hauled up his zip and curled his left ear down to his shoulder, leaning into the storm.

'ARE YOU INSANE?' Sergeant Farrow waded on into the gloom,

her shadow fading before her. 'YOU'RE NOT ALLOWED TO RIDE A FUDGING BICYCLE WITHOUT DOING AN OFFICIAL POLICE SCOTLAND TRAINING COURSE. THINK THEY'LL LET YOU LOOSE WITH A *SNOWPLOUGH*?'

'AT THIS POINT THEY CAN FIRE ME, SARGE. DON'T CARE.'

They stopped at a dip in the snow – marking the point where the Big Car went off-roading. Drifting had softened the edges, as had the unremitting build-up of fresh flakes. From here the ground fell towards the burn at the bottom of the hill, not that the visibility was good enough to see more than eight or nine feet.

They paused at the top, leaning on their shovels as they clicked on their headtorches.

Edward turned sideways-on to the raging wind, making himself a smaller target. 'THIS IS GOING TO BE A NIGHTMARE, ISN'T IT?'

She patted him on the arm. 'THAT'S MY BRAVE, OPTIMISTIC LITTLE SOLDIER.' Then she stepped off the path and into the wild beyond.

Ah well, he'd come this far.

More snow had settled into the channel he'd gouged out with the Big Car, chasing Siobhan Wilkins, but it only came up to mid-shin. And it was fluffy, rather than crispy, and it didn't clutch at his wellington boots anywhere near as much. Which was a bonus. Drifting flakes curled in over the lip of the chest-level trench, though – a semi-solid mist that hit his sweaty skin like frozen sandpaper. 'I CAN'T FEEL MY FEET. CAN YOU FEEL YOUR FEET?'

'THIS BIT IS *STILL* YOUR FAULT.'

'IF I PROMISE NEVER TO DO IT AGAIN, CAN EVERYONE STOP BANGING ON?' He slipped and stumbled, thumping his shovel into the side wall, nearly going flat on his face. 'AAAAARGH! SODDING SNOW!'

'WILL YOU HURRY UP?'

Easy for her to say.

He stomped on through the snow, following the curved canyon. Swearing under his foggy breath.

A flash of light glimmered up ahead – yellow and red. The chevrons on the Big Car's boot. Thank God for that.

And best of all, as they shambled closer, the wind just . . . stopped. Not everywhere – look back the way they'd come, and it was still howling – but by some weird, lucky contrivance of trees and topography, there was little more than an enthusiastic breeze here. The snow didn't hammer down, it spiralled in fat lazy flakes.

He staggered to a halt and leaned on his shovel, head resting on his arms. 'Oh, thank . . . thank Christ.'

Sergeant Farrow nudged him with an elbow. 'Nearly there.'

'No offence, Sarge, but I *hate* Glenfarach.'

'Come on.' She scooped an arm around his back, propelling him forward. 'If it helps, Glenfarach seems to like you. Jenna was very keen.'

'Ms Kirkdale? Your IT fixer?' He faked a shrug. 'Didn't notice.' Which wasn't just untrue, it was unbelievable. You could've seen her putting the moves on him from the *moon*.

'Aye, right.'

'Do I want to know what she did?'

'Oh, she's not so bad, really. Fell in with a dodgy crowd, ended up money laundering for a bunch of drug dealers, Kremlin stooges, and Conservative MPs.'

Not sure if that made things better or worse.

They'd finally reached the Big Car. A six-inch-blanket of crispy white covered the roof and bonnet, pyramiding on top of the spare wheel, crusting the wing mirrors and spotlights. The drifts on either side had gone from waist-deep to the middle of his chest. And it was *everywhere*.

Sergeant Farrow thumped her shovel into the snow at her feet and slumped against the handle. 'Looks like you were right: it *is* going to be a nightmare.' Hanging her head and puffing out a glowing fogbank of pale grey. 'Get our breath back first. Then we dig out the doors, and after that, we do a turning circle. OK?'

A *turning* circle?

He pointed. 'Can we not just reverse out of here?'

She didn't move. 'Yes, Edward. That's a much better idea. We'll simply reverse, through deep snow, seven, eight hundred feet, uphill, in a blizzard, in the dark.' Sergeant Farrow gave him a sarcastic thumbs up. 'Piece of cake.'

Urgh . . .

Anyone who liked snow was an idiot.

Edward's shovel scrunched into the wall of white, and he hauled it upwards, lifting a lump the size of a tea chest that towered above the blade, before hefting it over the lip of the canyon and out of the way. Face slick with sweat. More dribbling between his shoulder blades. Black leather gloves sodden and sticky. Steam rising from his open high-vis, because you couldn't zip the sodding thing up or you'd bloody melt . . .

Then he went in for yet another shovelful.

Sergeant Farrow was at it too – every bit as sweaty as he was – digging, throwing, digging, throwing, digging, throwing.

Been at it for ages, and only managed half a turning circle. This was going to take *hours*.

What they needed was a flamethrower. That'd shift the freezing, horrible, Christ-forsaken—

Sergeant Farrow's Airwave gave three bleeps, then a posh Dundee accent burst out into the snowy air.

'Louise? It's Dr Singh. Are you free for a chat?'

She dropped her shovel and snapped upright. Scrabbled the handset from her jacket. 'Kuwarjeet? . . . Is that . . .' Slumping back against the Big Car, breath wh-whooping out in worried clouds that whistled slightly at the edges. 'How did you get . . . get an Airwave? You're not . . . supposed to have phones . . . or radios!'

'I know, but I had a visit from two police officers today, a DI Montgomery-Porter and some DC or other.'

Edward rammed his shovel into the snow and sagged over the handle. 'Nice to be appreciated.'

'They wanted my help with the murder of Geoff Newman, but there wasn't much I could do because they didn't have crime-scene reports, or photographs, or post-mortem results.'

She used the armoured pad on the back of her MOE glove to

wipe the sweat from her flushed pink face. 'Still not hearing why you've got an Airwave handset, Kuwarjeet.'

'I'm getting to that. So, I had a think, and then a brainwave. The young DC: he said they didn't take photos of Newman's body on their mobile phones because it isn't allowed any more. But what if there were someone else *at the crime scene who was perhaps a little less . . . professional?'*

That pink, shiny face tightened. 'You're talking about PCs Harlaw and Samson, aren't you?'

'Aha! Yes indeed!' Sounding like that was the most *delightful* thing he'd heard for years. *'I see great minds think alike. And I know I'm not supposed to violate curfew, but I thought, given the circumstances – in order to help you and your colleagues with your inquiries – it was my duty to risk it.'*

'Where are you?'

'Enjoying a nice cup of tea with Dr Griffiths at his medical establishment. PC Samson is a little groggy, but he was *able to let me into his phone to see the photographs and videos he took of Mr Newman's somewhat . . . grisly end.'*

Sergeant Farrow pressed the Airwave against her chest while she scowled up at the hostile sky. 'I'm going to kill the pair of them.'

'So, if you'd like to tell DI Montgomery-Porter: PC Samson's footage is *available, should she need it? And in the meantime, I shall head back to my humble abode and begin work on some behavioural evidence analysis.'* An indulgent chuckle. *'That is, assuming you're happy for me to breach curfew once more by heading home from the good doctor's?'*

Her jaw tightened. Like she was trying *very* hard not to say something. Then pulled on a fake smile and forced it into her voice. 'Yes. Of course. Thank you, Kuwarjeet.' She ended the call, stuck the Airwave in her pocket. Let her head thunk back against the Big Car. And groaned.

Edward straightened up. 'Well, at least that's progress, right?'

'Ever get the feeling you work with a bunch of *fudging* idiots?'

'All the time.' He wiggled his shovel free of the snow. 'Sarge, don't take this the wrong way, but if people can just wander about after curfew, what's the point of—'

'Oh, there'll be a little red light winking away in the control room right now, maybe a wee alarm in the CCTV suite, and no one there to see it.' Baring her teeth. 'Because we only need *three* officers to look after a town with two hundred dangerous ex-cons in it! What could *possibly* go wrong?'

He kept his mouth shut, letting her seethe in silence for a bit. Not making a target of himself. Because, once again: not an idiot.

Eventually she hunched over, both gloved hands covering her eyes. Then sighed. Voice flat and heavy as breeze block. 'Come on, this thing's not going to dig itself out.'

They collapsed back against the Big Car's bonnet, breathing hard as the snow fell and fell and fell . . .

Edward wiped his sweaty face, huffing out great cumulonimbus clouds that glowed in the light of his headtorch. Soggy and hot and uncomfortable and why the *hell* did he ever agree to join the police force?

Sergeant Farrow flapped the front of her unzipped high-vis again, wafting the steam away. 'Fudging heck . . .' She ditched her gloves, then dipped into a pocket and came out with a tin of Irn-Bru, *tsssskd* the ring pull and took a good long swig. Sighed, like that was the most satisfying fizzy beverage she'd ever tasted. Held out the can. 'Want a scoof?'

Oh Christ, yes.

'Thanks, Sarge.' He drank deep, gulping down that sweet, carbonated, weirdly-unidentifiable-fruity-flavoured nectar. Half a second later, an enormous, diaphragm-rattling belch exploded out a billow of tangy fog.

Oops. Maybe not the best of ideas, given the po-faced reaction to his Excalibur act.

He clapped a hand over his mouth. 'Sorry, Sarge!'

Sergeant Farrow nodded, chin wrinkling in appreciation. 'Bit of an echo on that one.' She took the can back and drank again. This time, instead of a refined sigh, she opened her jaw wide and let a massive burp clatter free – about twice the volume of his.

Edward gave her a round of applause. 'Ooooh, great technique.'

Then accepted the proffered tin, but there was only enough Irn-Bru left for an apologetic, foamy *urp*.

She shook her head. 'So close. The plucky youngster from NE Division, falling there at the last hurdle.' Throwing her hands into the air. 'THE WINNER!'

'And the crowd goes wild!'

'I'd like to thank my mum and my agent and the good people at Barr's . . .' Crumpling the empty tin in her clenched fist of victory. 'Come on then: let's do this.'

Edward swept the thick layer of snow from the car's bonnet and windscreen while Sergeant Farrow chucked their shovels in the back.

Then they both clambered inside.

She stuck the keys in the ignition and – miracle of miracles – the Big Car started first time. 'Now, if we've done this right . . .' She put it in four-wheel drive, low, and hauled the steering wheel around, full-lock. Gave the throttle a tickle.

The car juddered and complained, crumping forward about three feet, following the line of their hard-won turning circle, then came the ominous *vwwwwwwwwwwwwwwipp*ing noise of tyres slipping on packed snow and ice.

Sergeant Farrow killed the engine and sagged over the wheel. '*Fudge.*' Deep breath. 'Right.' Sitting up again. 'There's a set of snow chains in the boot.' She climbed out into the night. Then stuck her head back into the car. 'Well? Come on then.'

Groan.

'Yes, Sarge.'

18

They climbed into the car again, and Sergeant Farrow started her up. 'Let's give that another go.'

The windscreen wipers clunked and moaned, clearing twin arcs through the spiralling snow.

Edward crossed his fingers, and this time the Big Car *didn't* conk out after three feet: it scrunched and lurched around their turning circle, till they were facing back the way they'd come. Crawling forwards, but moving. 'We are the champions!'

She kept it at a walking pace, but even with the chains on, the rear end slithered, making horrible grinding noises where it bounced and scraped against the canyon walls. 'Don't even *think* about stopping, you fudging fudger . . .'

The further along the gouged-out path they went, the bigger the bow wave of fresh snow that built up in front – until it spilled over the bonnet, juddering with the engine's vibrations.

Then they were past the flat bit and heading uphill again.

Sergeant Farrow bared her teeth as the sound of slithering tyres grew, swinging the steering wheel from side to side, trying to keep the car straight. 'Don't do this to me!'

Come on, lovely Big Car. Don't stop. Good little Land Rover. You can do it. You can—

They weren't moving any more. Not forward anyway. Just stayed where they were while the rear end walked from one side of the canyon to the other then back again.

'Sod.'

They were stuck.

'OK.' Sergeant Farrow undid her seatbelt. 'Shovel time.'

'Have I mentioned how much I hate Glenfarach, Sarge?'

'Yes.'

'I know, but *recently*?' He opened his door . . . only it wouldn't shift more than a couple of inches before the compacted snow stopped it going any further. 'Arse.'

He wriggled out through the window and plummeted, face first, into the crunchy drifts of white once more. 'I HATE GLENFARACH!'

Digging and shovelling.

Swearing and sweating.

Sticking anti-slip mats in under the wheels.

Getting another ten/fifteen feet forward.

More skidding.

More digging.

More swearing.

Repeat and repeat and repeat and repeat . . .

Edward keeled over backwards into the snow and lay there, wheezing like a dying buffalo, blinking up at the scudding flakes that whipped overhead.

Dear God . . .

Everything ached.

Everything was wet.

Everything was horrible.

The Big Car's engine growled and roared, straining, singing an angry counterpoint to the winch's electrical whine. Slowly climbing the hill.

He let his head flop over to the right.

The winch cable was taut as a guitar string, one end hooked around the last lamppost on the street, the other end disappearing down the slope. Thrumming with the strain as searchlights speared up into the howling blizzard. Until *finally* the Big Car's nose inched into view, followed by the rest of it, headlights glaring full-beam, wheels *vwipp*ing up flurries of compressed snow. The back end slithering about like a snake in a sack of milk.

And then the whole thing was on the road. The engine's out-raged growl dropped into a knackered, rattly idling, and the garrotte-tight winch cable became a flaccid droop.

Hurrah.

Just a shame he was about to die any minute.

Which, to be honest, right now would be a blessed relief.

Maybe they could—

The Big Car's horn blared out into the blizzard, and when he raised his head, there was Sergeant Farrow, pointing at him, then at the lamppost, mouth moving like he could actually hear her from all the way over here.

Urgh . . .

Come on: count of three.

Two.

One.

He rolled over onto his side, then struggled upright, using the snow shovel as a lever. Creaked out the stiffness in his back and shoulders. Groaned. Then limped across to the lamppost.

Edward unhooked the cable and gave Sergeant Farrow a thumbs up.

The winch whined, spooling in the wire, then the Big Car purred forward until it was right alongside.

He stayed where he was, still breathing like a malfunctioning balloon.

She honked the horn again.

Great.

Edward clambered into the passenger seat and pulled off his woolly hat – flicking soggy lumps of snow into the footwell.

Sergeant Farrow frowned across the car at him. 'Look at you: all horrid, pink, and shiny. Like a microwaved pervert.' A smile. 'That'll teach you to crash the Big Car.'

Didn't have the energy to come up with a witty retort, so he flipped her the Vs instead.

'Let's get you back to the station.'

The Land Rover scrunched along the crisp, smothered street. Those snow chains might not have made a heap of difference when they were off-roading through massive great-big drifts, but at least they worked on the road.

Bloody roasting in here too. Well, that or someone had set fire to Edward's face and ears and neck and everything else without him noticing. Sweat trickling down all the places sweat had no business trickling. He hauled off his gloves and used them as a makeshift fan, wafting the steamy air about.

Sergeant Farrow sat forwards, peering through the windscreen as the wipers cleared it again. 'Getting deep out there.'

That thick blanket of snow glittered and shone in the headlights' glow – not quite knee-high yet, but working on it.

It was meant to be a sweeping gesture, but it ended up as a knackered flop of the hand on the end of a sagging arm. 'Snnn . . . Snowplough . . .' Struggling to haul enough air into his barbed-wire lungs. 'Won't be . . . be able . . . to drive . . . in this . . . much . . . much longer.' Letting the hand fall back into his lap. 'Urgh . . .'

'You know: you might actually be right about that.' She leaned across the car and nudged him. 'Had to happen eventually.'

'With all . . . all due . . . respect, Sarge . . .' He flipped her the Vs again. Then fumbled off his clip-on tie, undid the top three shirt buttons, copying her flapping-the-sides motion to get some air in there as Glenfarach drifted past the slowly steaming windows. 'Bloody drenched . . . My underwear's . . . floating . . .'

'Yes, thank you for that lovely image. We can break into the second-hand shop: I've got a master key.' She wrinkled her nose. 'Plus, and please take this in the spirit it's intended, you *stink*.'

'Thanks . . . Sarge . . . very nice.'

'Honestly, it's like someone's set fire to a teenager's sweaty pants.'

She pressed the button on the steering wheel, setting her Airwave bleeping. 'Golf Foxtrot Six from Golf Foxtrot Four, safe to talk?'

PC Harlaw's voice cracked and popped, fizzing and distorted. *'Hey, Sarge. Can you hear me? Everything's quiet here. Starting to smell a bit . . . ripe, though. You know, what with . . . ?'*

Edward shoogled a hand in the air. 'Tell . . . tell him to . . . central heating.' Miming turning it down. 'Body.'

She went back to the handset. 'Turn down the heating, Dave, that'll help.'

'Ah, cool. Thanks, Sarge. Great idea.'

And yet did Edward get any credit for it? Of course he didn't.

Sergeant Farrow took them up a little road and onto Market Square. 'Keep your eyes peeled, OK, Dave? Don't want that cottage burning down with you in it.'

'Roger that.' Not sounding the least bit concerned. *'Any chance someone can drop round some food? Starving. Pretty sure the DI would wring my neck if I went into the crime scene and raided the fridge.'*

Soon as the word 'food' floated through the ether, Edward's stomach growled loud enough to be heard over the Big Car's diesel engine.

'OK. Stay safe, Dave. Out.'

'At least he had sodding lunch. I've had nothing since *breakfast.'*

She chewed on her lip for a bit. Then, 'Can't leave Dave there on his own all night. What if something happens?'

'True.' Edward wiped a fresh slick of sweat from his face. 'What if Caroline Manson comes back.'

'Exactly.' She parked in front of the police station and killed the engine. Looked up at the concrete-and-steel monstrosity. 'Then there's this place. We've got two prisoners in the cells, so we need at least one person on-site to make sure nothing happens to them.'

'PC Samson?'

'Shammy?' Her brow furrowed. 'Depends what Doc Griffiths says, I'm not having him back on duty if he's going to drop down dead.' Pulling the keys from the ignition. 'A: it'd be a total waste of a good bloke, and B: my bum would be for the fudging chop.'

She climbed out and Edward followed her. Then froze.

Soon as the cold air got hold of his soggy shirt it sank its claws deep into his chest. Nipples like tiny stinging unicorns. Goosebumps rampaging up his arms and neck. He zipped his high-vis back up, trapping at least *some* of the heat inside. Pulled on his damp woolly hat. And hurried after Sergeant Farrow. 'Worth a try, though. Can't see Bigtoria being happy about babysitting your cellblock.' There had to be someone else who could . . . Ah. Perfect: 'What about the Social Work Team?'

She unlocked the doors. ' "Bigtoria"?'

Oh crap.

Oh no, oh no, oh crap, oh no . . .

He hauled in a breath. 'No! *Definitely* don't call her that. And if you do: *don't* tell her I told you! Say it was Mr Bishop: she hates him already.' Edward bustled inside. 'Actually, forget you heard anything, OK? We'll never speak of this again.'

'Bigtoria.' Sergeant Farrow locked the doors behind them. 'Big-*toria.*'

Why could he never learn to keep his stupid mouth shut?

'Seriously, Sarge, she'll go *ballistic*. Intercontinental.'

A grin. 'And now I have power over you: Bwahahahahaaaaa!' Unzipping her coat and giving it a shake. 'But we can't get the social workers to man our cellblock: they're stretched tight enough as it is. Ten minutes a visit, remember?' The grin faded. 'Only, with Caroline missing, they won't even have that.'

Two hundred offenders, divided by *four* social workers, fifty offenders each, which made it . . . 'Less than eight minutes a visit.' He followed Sergeant Farrow down the stairs. 'If this snow doesn't let up, they're going to be stuck at home anyway. No one's driving round town in that. He said. Hint, hint.'

She paused halfway down, head back to groan at the open treads above them. 'All right, all right. First thing tomorrow morning: snowplough.' Then she sniffed, pulled her chin in, and hurried away from him. 'But even more importantly, we need to get you destinkified.' Marching down the breeze-block corridor and into the cellblock.

Edward pushed through after her.

All but two of the cell doors hung open, and Bigtoria was sitting behind the custody desk, scowling at some paperwork. Other than that, it was lovely and warm.

He peeled off his high-vis and scuffed over there, steaming

slightly. 'Car out of ditch.' Slumping against the chipped Formica. 'Can we *please* go get something to eat now?'

Sergeant Farrow popped behind the desk and dug about underneath it. 'Here.' She tossed a small bundle of keys to Edward. 'Duncan's Second-Hand Delights: Farmer's Lane. Alarm's by the door: seven, three, three, five, one. Make sure you arm it on the way out.'

He jingled the keys for Bigtoria. 'Going to get a change of clothes.'

'And you think that's an appropriate use of police . . . ?' A pause. Then the DI had a good sniff of herself. Curled her top lip. 'You're probably right.' She folded up the paperwork and stuck it in her pocket. 'What time's the hotel stop doing food?'

'*Technically*: curfew.' Sergeant Farrow wriggled her way out of her fluorescent-yellow jacket and hung it up to drip. 'There's no point cooking meals when no one's allowed out to eat them. But Andy and Charlie live there, so maybe if you ask them nicely? If not, it's back here for whatever you can scavenge from the vending machine. And that's not been restocked since pre-Covid times, so you're taking your life in your hands.'

Sod that.

Edward grabbed his coat again.

He waded his way down Farmer's Lane.

The snow was up to his knees, well over the top of his wellies, every step dragging at his sodden trousers, the chill seeping right down to the bone. Legs aching from all the buggering about today.

Bigtoria lumbered along beside him, because apparently he was a 'complete lazy bastard' if he let her go first so he could follow the path she'd cleared.

Farmer's Lane was proper Dickens territory – a narrow street with cast-iron lampposts and mullioned windows. Some of which had embraced the cliché and gone for bullseye glass. A couple of craft shops faced off across the lane, their displays full of wool and crepe paper and pre-formed things for decoupage and painting. Some houses at either end. And right in the middle: Duncan's Second-Hand Delights.

It had a purple-and-gold frontage, with the shop's name in a ye olde English font. The lights were off, but those cast-iron lampposts produced enough LED glare to make everything in the window clearly visible: mannequins, dressed up in jumpers and chinos and cardigans and floral blouses; piles of yellowing magazines; displays of general household items – frying pans, kettles, one of those ancient carpet sweeper things . . .

Didn't exactly look promising, to be honest.

He struggled his way to the front door. 'Could we not've taken the Big Car?'

'Operational necessity takes priority, you know that, Constable.'

Doubt the thing would've made it down the street anyway. Wouldn't take much more snow before the entire village was impassable.

Didn't stop him having a moan and a mutter, though. 'Freezing, wet trousers. Catch my bloody death, here.' Especially now he'd had to ditch the MOE gloves, because they were too soggy to wear. He worked his way through the small bundle of keys until one of them turned in the lock. Opened the door. And half collapsed into the shop, bringing a wee avalanche of snow with him.

Inside, it didn't look quite as welcoming.

The only light spilled in through the window between the mannequins, silhouetting them, casting vampiric shadows across the linoleum floor. Leaving the kind of darkness that *things* lurked in.

It wasn't a huge space. Lined with clothes on one side, shelves on the other three. A handful of display racks formed a cluttered nest in the middle of the room – all of them weighed down with yet more arts-and-crafts tat. Only a few books, but loads of plates and glasses and casserole dishes and slow cookers and a collection of dusty fondue sets and—

A harsh *bleep-bleep-bleep* cut through the gloom – the alarm.

Sod.

He hurried over to the glowing control panel and punched in the five-digit code he'd copied down on the back of his hand.

Silence.

Bigtoria stepped inside and clicked on the lights, stomping her newly requisitioned Police Scotland wellington boots, shaking the snow off her high-vis as the fluorescent tubes pinged and flickered into life.

Urgh . . . strip lights: guaranteed to make *everything* three hundred percent more depressing.

Edward let out a long, low whistle. 'God, would you *look* at this stuff?' Pointing at a shelf laden down with awful filigree gold blobs. 'My granny had that very clock.'

Bigtoria turned on the spot, taking it all in, something like appreciation on her face. 'Our Prop Department would love it here. Save a fortune on hiring period kit.'

Maybe she could see the beauty and potential in a velvet painting of a weeping Elvis, but Edward couldn't. He hung his high-vis on a free-standing coat stand – making it rock to one side – and had a rummage through a rack of clothing marked 'GENTS!' Rattling the hangers along the metal rail. 'So, it's a period piece then? Your play?' Pulling out a cheerful black-red-blue-and-yellow shirt. 'What do you think?'

'Too Hawaiian.'

Yeah, she was probably right.

It went back on the rail.

Bigtoria delved into a different rack. 'It's a serial-killer thriller: someone abducts teenaged girls just before their thirteenth birthdays, then sends their parents a homemade card every year, showing them being slowly tortured to death.'

'Sounds horrible.' He plucked a suit from the row of clothes and held it against his chest, like he was wearing it 'How about this?'

'Pinstripe? No.'

Fair enough.

The only sound was the clitter-clack of hangers.

Bigtoria took out, then rejected a couple of shirts. 'I'm playing this really vicious gangster woman.' She adopted an Irish brogue – hard and aggressive. '"Yez'll do what yer told, or I'll have yer langer in flitters!"'

He raised his eyebrows, face all open and innocent. 'Didn't know you could do a Welsh accent, Guv.'

That got him a scowl.

'It's a joke! I was joking.'

She harrumphed, then picked a petrol-blue shirt and another in cream from the rack and dumped them on the counter by the till.

Edward worked his way past a trio of ugly sports coats to a swanky black suit. 'Ooh.' Now *that* was more like it. 'Armani!' He held the jacket up and gave her a twirl.

A nod. 'Much better.' She selected a pair of dark-grey trousers. 'I find the whole process fascinating. The stage design, lighting, sound, practical FX, costumes, props . . .'

He helped himself to four OK-ish shirts that were probably a reasonable fit. 'Last thing *I* was in was the school nativity play.'

'Eventually I'd like to direct.' She grabbed a no-nonsense black jacket. 'But I think, to do it properly, you've got to really understand what every department does. Get a bit of experience.'

'Hmmm . . .' He slipped out of his dirty suit jacket and tried on a brown leather one instead, posing in front of a gilt-edged mirror. It gave him an air of a young James Dean. If James Dean had been pasty. And Scottish. With a Vandyke. And no motorbike. 'Can you imagine being stuck here for the rest of your days? Well, not *stuck*, stuck, cos it's all voluntary, but still.' Not sure about the jacket. But what the hell. Wasn't like they were paying for any of this stuff. 'You're not allowed to go out after sundown, you're told who you can and can't be friends with, no phone or internet.'

'Tough.' She hummed and hawed over a dark jacket that screamed middle-management-at-a-garden-centre-near-Peebles. 'If they don't like it, they can take their chances in the real world.' The jacket went on the counter. 'There are consequences for rape, and murder, and child abuse.'

'Suppose.' He had a wee wander around, peering into shelves and boxes. 'What about underwear? Socks and pants and that?'

She stared at him. 'Second-hand underwear? In a village with one hundred and eighteen sex offenders? Think it through.'

Good point.

Just have to wash the current lot in the cellblock sink, before bed. Hang them up to dry in his 'room'.

'Now, *that's* more like it.' Bigtoria pulled a burgundy T-shirt free from a row of pastel-coloured ones. It had a cartoon black cat on the front, which, for some unfathomable reason, was wearing an eye patch and bow-tie, posing in a James Bond kinda way with a sucker-dart gun.

No accounting for taste.

She must've felt him staring, because she turned, eyes narrowed. 'What?'

'Nothing.' He retreated a couple of paces. 'Well, maybe it's a bit—'

'I *like* cats.' Shoulders back, chest out, chin up. 'That OK with you?'

'Yup, absolutely. A-OK with me. I think it looks great. Really stylish. Wish I had one too.'

'Hmmph.' She folded it neatly and placed it with her other finds.

Edward pulled out the black plastic binbag Sergeant Farrow had given him back at the station, and bundled all his 'purchases' into it.

Bigtoria unfurled a binbag of her own, carefully folding her new clothes before placing them inside.

They both tied the tops.

He hefted his bag over his shoulder: a cut-price Santa Claus in a soot-stained stinky suit. 'Food?'

She had a last look around. Probably fantasizing about her Prop Department again. Then nodded. 'Food.'

Oh, thank God.

19

They sat at a corner table in the empty dining room, bathed in the not-so-romantic glow of a flickering candle and glaring overhead lights. Both nursing a pint of beer, with their binbag on the seat next to them.

Turned out the Glenfarach House Hotel was a tartan-carpet-and-curtains kind of place. Highland scenes punctuated the orange walls – stags and waterfalls, capercaillies and heather, men in kilts rounding up sheep, the usual roaming-in-the-gloaming nonsense – but they were all really . . . amateurish.

The only professional-looking thing up there was the laminated A4 sign: 'THE POOL TABLE IS FOR *EVERYONE*. STOP STEALING THE BALLS!!!'

Edward fiddled with his pint. 'Guv? I've been thinking . . .'

'Have you now.' Not in the least bit interested.

A man's voice boomed across the tartan landscape. *'Hello, hello, hello, hello.'* And their host appeared, striding out from the door marked 'KITCHEN', bringing with him a couple of plates and a beaming smile. He'd strapped a Black-Watch pinny on over his billowy scarlet shirt, and the wispy ends of his shoulder-length grey hair wafted about as he passed beneath the blow heater. Didn't do a thing to the big bald bit on top of his head, though. 'Ta-daaaaaaaaaa!' Placing their plates on the table like they were a magic trick to be applauded. 'One spicy chorizoburger – extra bacon, no mayo – and sweet-potato fries for our new friend, DI Montgomery-Porter; one macaroni cheese and chips for her delightful sidekick,

DC Reekie. Your onion rings'll be out shortly.' Rocking on his sensible brogues and grinning. 'Can I get you folks anything else?'

Bigtoria grunted, then hunched over her burger and set to work.

No people skills at all.

'Wow.' Edward smiled. 'Thanks, Mr Haig, this looks delicious.'

Their host slapped a hand over his heart. 'Andy's a *miracle worker* in the kitchen, isn't he?' Hovering. 'Would you like some tomato sauce or mustard?'

The DI didn't look up. 'Ketchup. Lots of it.'

Edward dipped a fork into the macaroni. Cheesy and rich and stringy. 'Mmmm . . . Very tasty.'

'Oh, I *am* glad.'

'Compliments to the chef.' He pulled on an open, friendly face. 'So, Mr Haig, have you been here a while?' Making a vague gesture with another forkful of macaroni. 'I mean, Glenfarach?'

'Since eighty-four.' A sigh, and a smile. 'Ah, the folly of youth.'

'Wow. Nineteen eighty-four? So you must know everyone, then.'

'I suppose I do. Well, you have to when you're running a bar-slash-restaurant, don't you? Playing' – he wobbled his head – '"mine host".'

'Did you know Pauline Thomson?'

Mr Haig's eyes widened. 'Oh my God, yes, I heard all about it from Adam! Adam Kirkwood? He's part-time at the baker's, on account of his back.' Mr Haig dropped his voice to a conspiratorial whisper, leaning in, like this was *the* most exciting thing ever. 'They say she was chopped up into little bits. How terrible is *that*?'

OK, two could play at that game.

Edward mirrored their host's tone and body language. 'Oh, I *know*. What about anyone else? Any fights, any grudges?'

'Ooh, now you're asking.' Chewing on his bottom lip, frowning up at the corniced ceiling for a moment or three. Then, 'Not really. Kept herself to herself. Well, people do here, don't they. You should ask Kerry Millbrae, though, she and Pauline were like that.' Crossing his fingers. 'Anyway, listen to me, gossiping away and you still waiting for your onion rings! Let me go chase those up.'

He swept off, leaving them alone at the table.

It'd been worth a try.

And at least he *had* tried.

Edward had another chip, frowning as he ate. 'What was I . . . ? Ah, right: Guv, I've been thinking—'

'No, you can't have the rest of the evening off.' She ripped a bite out of her burger. 'We've got an investigation to run, remember?' Mouthful of beer. 'After this we talk to Dr Singh again, see if he's come up with anything, then back to the station to work out a plan of attack for tomorrow. Expand the murder board. We need to widen our search grid, maybe try going door to door? Caroline Manson has to be *somewhere*.'

'Ex-DCI Miller said the same thing.' He gave her an icicle stare. 'And I wasn't *asking* for the evening off; what I've been *thinking* is: we know Pauline Thomson's been staying at Kerry Millbrae's place, right?'

Bigtoria looked at him like he was daft.

'No, listen, Guv. Thomson Cottage is just sitting there, all empty and unloved . . . ?' He held up the master keys.

She blinked. Frowned. Then something sly crept its way across her face. 'An empty house, just sitting there.' An actual, genuine smile followed. 'I don't have to sleep in that *bloody* cell tonight.'

'And maybe Pauline Thomson's got a spare room?' Scooping up another forkful of macaroni. 'You know, as it was my idea?'

She shrugged one shoulder, then went back to her burger.

'Guv? Come on, Guv, it's not like I snore or anything!'

'God, you're such a whinge. All right, all right. If there's a spare room, you can have it. But *only* if there's a spare room.'

'Cool.' More chips. 'Thanks, Guv.'

'And you'd *better* not snore.'

Mr Haig reappeared with his customary flourish. 'Onion rings and tomato sauce for my favourite guests.' Placing both on the table. 'Now, can I get you anything else? More drinks? No? OK, super. Enjoy your meal.' And he was gone again.

Bigtoria grabbed the squeezy bottle of off-brand ketchup, curled her lip as she contemplated the label, then squirted a vast glollop of bright red onto what was left of her burger, almost drowning it. Smiled. Then took a bite.

Urgh . . .

It was like something off Shark Week.

She looked up. 'What?'

'Nothing, Guv.'

Edward didn't bother covering his mouth, just let the yawn creak and groan free as he stepped out of the hotel's front door into their own private winter hellhole again.

Snow, snow, and more snow.

At least the stuff wasn't hurtling sideways any more; instead, it drifted down in slow heavy flakes – the world tinted blue and grey around the puddles of harsh white streetlight.

Bigtoria clomped out behind him, zipping up her high-vis. 'Which way?'

He checked the map, pointed off in the vague direction of Old-mill Road, then tucked his hands back in his pockets before frostbite set in. The snow was up over the top of his wellies as he lumbered off. 'How do penguins do this every day? Seriously, it's sodding—'

Three Airwave bleeps sounded in his pocket.

Edward pulled out the handset just in time for Sergeant Farrow's voice to growl and *squonk* from the speaker – almost buried under the weight of furry static. Bloody things were getting worse.

'*Golf Foxtrot Four to Alpha Charlie Two, safe to talk?*'

'Full of macaroni cheese, thanks, Sarge.'

'*You got the DI with you?*'

Bigtoria plucked the Airwave from his hand. 'What?'

'*Guv, Doc Griffiths says you can speak to Kerry Millbrae if you keep it brief. She's in Interview Two with Lewis now, if that helps.*'

Bigtoria sucked on her teeth for a while, gazing off up the street towards Oldmill Road and Dr Singh's house, then back across Market Square to where the police station glowed like a neon bunion. 'Stick the kettle on; we'll be there in a minute.' She held the Airwave out towards Edward. Not so much as a 'thank you'.

He put it away. 'Change of plan?'

'Change of plan.'

*

The interview room was a lot less scruffy than ninety percent of the station, probably because it'd never been used. Or not very often, anyway. A claustrophobic box with a table in the middle – bolted to the floor – a bank of recording equipment that wouldn't have looked out of place in a period drama, four chairs, and four cameras. They stared down from the corners of the room, their all-seeing eyes cataracted by dust.

Kerry Millbrae sat, hunched on the other side of the table, her white Tyvek suit rustling as she picked at one sleeve with her remaining fingers. Then the shoulder seam. Then the zip. Then the front of the suit. Then the legs. Like the very feeling of it against her scarred skin was unbearable. She had the hood thrown back, and while, obviously, Sergeant Farrow couldn't return her wig because it'd been signed into evidence, Ms Millbrae now wore a Police Scotland black-fleece beanie hat.

Beside her, Lewis Nichols had a leather-bound pad and a fountain pen at the ready; immaculate in his ink-dark three-piece pinstripe, one eyebrow raised as he watched Edward and Bigtoria like they were sticky children. 'You don't have to answer that, Kerry.'

The DI had changed into her new black jacket, dark-grey trousers, and cream shirt, but Edward still rocked his soot-dirt-and-sweat-stained fighting suit. A bit on the funky side, but tough. It would have to do for now.

Ms Millbrae nodded, dabbing at her eyes with a clean hanky. Her voice rough and breathy, tight, and slightly mushy. 'No, I want to.' Trembling. 'I . . . I was asleep. I get these headaches and Doc Griffiths gives me pills. I was asleep.'

Stony silence radiated out of Bigtoria.

OK, if she was going to play Bad Cop, yet again, then there was only one thing for it.

Edward kept his voice soft. 'And what happened when you woke up?'

'I went . . . I went through to the studio. Pauline likes to paint in the afternoon, but she wasn't . . .' Ms Millbrae's face barely moved because of the scar tissue, but there was definitely a change, maybe a frown? 'I don't smell too well, since the fire, but the house had this strange . . . iron and copper? And Pauline wasn't in the living room, but Captain Fluffingham wanted fed, so I took his dish and opened the kitchen door and . . .'

Silence.

Mr Nichols nodded. 'It's all right, Kerry, we can stop here and take a break, you don't have to—'

'And . . .' Her good eye narrowed, like she was looking through Edward and off into the middle distance. 'I couldn't . . . I . . .' Struggling with the words. 'Everything's grey and fuzzy and then I'm sitting on the floor, trying to escape from the thing on the unit, but the cupboard doors won't let me and there's a handle sticking in my spine and . . .' Ms Millbrae shook herself, tears welling up over the lip of her taut eyelids. 'And there was a noise at the front door and what if it was them? What if they came back to do . . . *that* to me too? And I . . . I grabbed a knife off the worktop and . . .' She blinked. Licked her rebuilt lips. 'Then I was here.'

Bigtoria yawned. 'So, you *claim* you didn't kill Pauline Thomson. You expect us to believe that?'

Mr Nichols tapped his fountain pen against the pad. 'My client told you what happened, Inspector. Move on.'

'If you didn't kill her, who did?'

'My client's not here to do your job for you, Inspector. That's what we pay our taxes for.'

Bigtoria reached below the table and produced a blue folder. Opened it. Pulled out a handful of printouts. 'Pauline Thomson: eighteen stretch in Cornton Vale for abducting and murdering Eloise Linton.'

God's sake

Edward gave her a pained glance. '*Thank you*, Guv.' Back to Kerry. 'If you know who killed Pauline, you have to tell us, Ms Millbrae. You owe her that, don't you?'

The DI stretched out in her seat. 'I remember the headlines: "Sadist Sicko Tortured Straight-A Student". Nineteen years old. She was studying to be a nurse.'

'Inspector!' Mr Nichols poked the table. 'I fail to see how this is helping. My client isn't—'

'Your partner broke every bone in that wee girl's hands and feet, didn't she, Kerry? Caved her ribs in. Shattered her knees and elbows.'

'It . . . It wasn't *like* that.' Dabbing at her eyes again.

Edward had another go. 'Ms Millbrae, I know it's hard, but—'

'How could anyone *do* that?' Bigtoria curled her lip. 'I saw the post-mortem photos at a forensics conference in Glasgow. She looked as if she'd been run over by a combine harvester.'

Mr Nichols stood. 'All right, that's quite enough. My client has just lost her life partner and we don't have to sit here and listen to you maligning Pauline's memory.'

'Poor Eloise must've been glad when death came.'

Tears glistened in the webs of scar tissue. 'Pauline was . . . oh, God . . . and now she's gone.'

'I want this interview suspended immediately!'

Why did Edward have to be the only grown-up?

He pulled on his reassuring voice. 'Ms Millbrae, we're going to do everything we can to catch whoever did this. I promise.'

A bitter, gargling laugh scraped its way out of Kerry Millbrae's throat. '"Whoever did this"? You haven't got a bloody clue, do you? The only person I've ever loved is *dead* . . . and I'm still here: ON MY OWN!' She shook her head. 'Forever . . .'

Mr Nichols closed his leather-bound pad. 'Come on, Kerry, we're getting out of here.'

'I *told* her to stay away from those people, but she wouldn't listen. Pauline always had to know best. Stupid, and stubborn' – wailing it out in the soulless little room – 'and now she's gone!' Sobbing. Curling forward. Her fingerless hand pressed against her forehead.

He tried to help her to her feet, but she shoved him.

'DON'T TOUCH ME!'

Mr Nichols recoiled like he'd been stung.

Bigtoria raised an eyebrow. 'Stay away from who, Kerry?'

'All those years . . .' Choking down the sobs. 'Who'd think you'd have to come somewhere as awful as *this* to find the other half of your soul?'

'Who should she have stayed away from?'

Ms Millbrae sat forward, watery eyes fixed on Bigtoria. 'None of you understand: Pauline didn't do it! She didn't torture Eloise Linton, it was that bastard Rupert Fraser. Pauline just abducted the girl – that was her job.'

Disgust slithered across Bigtoria's face. 'So, this Rupert Fraser paid her to find a victim he could abuse and kill?'

'Have you not been *listening*?' Kerry Millbrae's stump of a hand banged down on the tabletop. 'Eloise Linton's mother was a bigwig at Newtonmore Asset Capital Finance. Pauline was part of a four-man team; Fraser was the muscle. He was just supposed to rough Linton up for the ransom video. Make it look convincing. And you know how *that* turned out.' She stared at the tabletop. 'But they found Pauline's DNA on the body, so she's the one who went down.'

Edward puffed out his cheeks. 'Bloody hell.'

'Are you saying she was *innocent*?' Lewis Nichols thumped back down into his seat. 'So, Pauline was demonized in the papers; everyone thinking she's a monster; eighteen years in Cornton Vale; and she was innocent? Good grief . . .' He blinked, mouth hanging open. Then shook himself. 'People always *say* they didn't commit the crimes they were convicted for, but I've never encountered anyone who was telling the *truth* before.'

Ms Millbrae kept her head down. ' "You don't clype on your team, Kerry. You keep your gob shut and you do your time." ' A small, sad smile. 'And if she hadn't done that, I never would've met her. Pauline couldn't understand how she'd screwed up so badly – leaving DNA on the *victim*? She was far from careful for that.'

Nobody liked to think ill of the dead.

Edward put as much kindness into his voice as possible: 'Everyone makes mistakes.'

'Not Pauline. She was the best in the business: you needed someone snatched? She was the person you called.' Ms Millbrae pulled at the scratchy SOC suit again. 'One of the team must've set her up. Insurance in case your lot found Linton's body.' It clearly took a lot of work, but Kerry bared her teeth. '*Bastards*.'

Edward turned the page on his notebook. Pen poised. 'Are there any members of Pauline's gang living here in Glenfarach?'

No response.

It was like she'd been frozen.

'Ms Millbrae? Did Pauline ever speak to you about Geoff Newman?'

Her head snapped up. 'That prick?' A sharp, cruel smile twisted her scarred cheeks. 'I hope he *suffered*. Serve him right, homophobic piece of shit.' Then she turned to her temporary solicitor. 'I'm tired now. I don't want to talk any more.'

'Of course.' He helped her to her feet. 'This interview is over, Detective Inspector.' A nod. 'Constable Reekie.'

The DI didn't move. Just sat there, letting the silence grow. And grow. And grow ... Then stood. 'Fine. Interview suspended at twenty-one sixteen.' Bigtoria marched from the room, only pausing to point a finger at Edward. 'Take her back to her cell.'

20

Edward slouched into the control room, mug of coffee pressed against his chest for the warmth, a jaw-shuddering yawn fading on his lips.

The internal lights were off, but enough of Glenfarach's ever-present LED glare shone through the grubby windows to see Bigtoria, standing there with her back to the room, looking out through a portal she'd wiped in the dust.

He scuffed his way over, not bothering to hide an aftershock yawn that was nearly as powerful as the first. 'That's Mr Nichols away.' Slumping his bum against a desk. 'Ms Millbrae's not doing so well. Maybe we should . . .' What? 'I don't know.' A sip of bitter, black coffee. 'You think she did it?'

Bigtoria's voice was flat as a concrete car park. 'Doesn't matter what I think. We can't let her go home – not with Pauline Thomson's tortured corpse strapped to her kitchen unit. She's safer here.'

'Fair enough.' Especially after what happened to Geoff Newman's cottage. 'Still want to see Dr Singh for an update? Or shall we call it a night?' Checking his watch. 'Nearly half nine.'

Her shoulders dipped and a long breath slid out, misting the glass. 'Been here a day and a half and we're on our second murder already.' Groaning as her head sank forward to rest against the frosted window.

Edward picked himself off the desk and wiped a porthole of his own. Outside, the relentless fall of white smothered the world, sparkling as it tumbled through the streetlights' glare, covering everything. It was almost pretty. In an ominous, something-horrible-is-about-to-happen kind of way. 'You know what I—'

'Right: arses in gear.' She stood up straight and turned. Top lip curling as she looked him up and down. 'What was the point of getting clean clothes if you won't wear them? Get changed.'

'You don't put clean clothes on a dirty body, Guv: not hygienic. When we *finally* finish tonight, I'm having a long hot shower and *then* I'll get changed.'

For a moment it seemed like she was going to make it an order, then she grunted and shrugged. 'As if I care.' Marching for the door. 'Grab your filthy coat, Constable, we've got a forensic psychologist to visit.'

Dr Singh added a hefty slug of booze to his mug. 'Sure I can't tempt you?' Waggling the bottle of cheap brandy.

The study was lovely and warm, with a coal fire crackling in the grate. The doctor was in a pair of smart paisley pyjamas, suede slippers, and a silk dressing gown. Edward and Bigtoria had slipped out of their high-vis jackets and wellies, which wasn't *really* the same kind of vibe. But he'd turned up the heating and made them both a mug of Bovril, which was an improvement on most welcomes they'd had since arriving in this godforsaken village.

Edward covered his drink with a hand. 'Can't: on duty.'

'Very dedicated of you.' He took a sip of boozy Bovril. 'The footage on PC Samson's phone was quite revealing. Now, if I can visit the *scene* of Pauline Thomson's death, that would really put things into—'

'Here.' Bigtoria produced her phone and poked at it for a bit, before holding the screen out. It was the video she'd shot at Millbrae Cottage – Pauline Thomson's tortured body, tied to the central island.

Dr Singh smiled. 'I see you overcame your "professional squeamishness" about breaking the rules. Good. Good.' Swapping his seeing glasses for his reading ones, then peering at the recording. 'Interesting . . . May I?' Hand out.

She passed it over and he watched the footage through three

times, then hit pause. Opened a drawer and produced a scratched old iPhone. Unlocked it. Then fiddled with the screen before placing both mobiles side by side on the desk.

The iPhone showed Geoff Newman, tied to the kitchen table in his own house. Bloody. Bruised. Blinded. And very, very dead. The picture Dr Singh had chosen was from almost the exact same angle as the image of Pauline Thomson on Bigtoria's phone.

'You'll agree that the pattern of bruising and cuts is virtually identical? I had speculated that the torture was deliberate, but freeform: without a set plan of attack. Now that we can compare *both* bodies, however, it's clear that every single curve of the blade, or blow with a hammer, has been deliberately placed in the same location to cause maximum pain. Twice. Then there's the bruising around the throat – reminiscent of a garrotte being tightened and released several times, don't you think?' Dr Singh chewed his lip for a moment. 'Professional guess? Loosen it off to ask questions, tighten it again to muffle the screams.'

Lovely.

Edward grimaced. 'Could Kerry Millbrae do something like that?'

'*Conceptually?* Definitely. Practically? No.' Another sip of Bovril. 'You've seen her hands, I assume? Or what's left of them. I doubt she'd be physically capable of even tying the knots around our victims' wrists and ankles. This' – pointing at the phones as one screen went black – 'is the work of an expert.'

Bigtoria unlocked her phone again. 'Hammer.'

'Sorry?'

'You said they used a knife and a *hammer.*'

'The contusions all have a circular centre point, approximately twenty millimetres wide.' A smile. 'I have a *lot* of experience with this kind of thing.'

Edward screwed up his face. 'Sod . . .' When he opened his eyes, they were both looking at him. 'Not the "hammer": Caroline Manson. Anyone believe she's an expert in torturing people?'

Dr Singh looked impressed for a moment. But it passed. 'I fear we may have to embrace the possibility that poor Caroline has either come to some sort of harm, or suffered what you laypeople might refer to as a "breakdown".' Making quote marks with his fingers. 'If the stress has proven too much for her normal coping mechanisms . . . Who knows?' He shook his head. 'The fact that she went missing so close to both murders makes me very concerned about her safety.'

Bigtoria grimaced into her Bovril. 'Wonderful.'

'OK' – Edward had a bash at making some *actual* progress here – 'so we're looking for someone who knew Geoff Newman, Pauline Thomson, and *maybe* Caroline Manson? And also knows how to torture people.'

The doctor flicked through the remaining photos on PC Samson's iPhone. 'Did you find any sign of self-stimulation at either scene? It's difficult to tell from the videos. Perhaps a small bundle of used tissues, for example?'

Used . . . ?

Ew. OK, so *that* kind of 'self-stimulation'.

'You see, it's important to know if this was *sexually* motivated – in which case we're looking at Yellow, *maybe* Orange Flag residents – or if the purpose was to extract information from our victims. Which means we look at Green and Blue Flag ones.'

'No.' Bigtoria abandoned examining the contents of her mug to frown off into the middle distance instead, like it was a lot more interesting than what was happening here. 'There's still the problem of the ankle tags. It *has* to be one of the Social Work Team. Or the Duty Doctor. Or the police officers.'

The fire glowed.

The meaty scent of Bovril mixed with Edward's funky smell.

Bigtoria moved away a couple of paces.

Weird, but OK: if she wasn't going to take charge . . .

Edward opened his notebook. 'It's safe to say that Ms Thomson and Mr Newman were connected in some way, right? Otherwise, why torture them? What we need to know is who else might be linked . . .' He held out his hand. 'Can I borrow that list again, Guv?'

But Bigtoria just stared off into space.

Dr Singh peered at him over the top of his reading glasses. 'List?'

'Of every Glenfarach resident.'

'All up here, my dear Detective Constable.' Tapping his forehead. 'For whom do you seek?'

'When we interviewed Kerry Millbrae, she said Ms Thomson didn't kill that student nurse, it was a man called *Rupert Fraser*. And I was wondering—'

'Rupert Fraser?' Dr Singh scooted his chair over to the filing cabinets and had a rummage. 'Now then, Fraser, Fraser . . . Ah, here we are.' Scooting back to plonk a file on the desk. 'Rupert Daniel Fraser. Beat two young women so badly they never regained consciousness. Put another three in traction.' He opened the folder and flicked through it. 'There's been a number of incidents – violent ones – involving Mr Fraser over the last year or so. Nothing ever happens, of course, because those on the receiving end of Mr Fraser's temper are reluctant to involve the authorities.'

See? Not just a pretty face.

Edward allowed himself a little preen. 'So, Rupert Fraser's here, he's got a history of violence, and he knew Pauline Thomson had something over him.'

Bigtoria snapped back into the room. 'What – maybe she was blackmailing him, and he killed her for it?'

'Don't suppose he was one of Caroline Manson's clients, was he, Doc?'

'That would make things nice and neat, wouldn't it? But no.'

Ah well.

'You know what *I* find interesting?' Dr Singh abandoned his chair and walked over to the map of Glenfarach. 'Just because Mr Fraser was involved in all those kidnappings and Post Office jobs, everyone thinks he's nothing but a violent thug, but you mark my words: the man's a sex offender.' He took hold of the sides of his silk dressing gown, pacing in front of the map like an Oxford don. 'His violence against women is a clear psychosexual expression of his *hunger* to dominate. Presumably because his mother belittled his father and dominated *him*. I'd be surprised if Rupert Fraser's sexual identity isn't entirely buried in the murky intersection of female as "nurturer", "whore", "gatekeeper", and "punisher". It's no surprise he—'

'No one needs his psychobabble backstory. Where is he?'

A pained expression. 'Please, Inspector, don't take this little pleasure away from me. It's always been my *favourite* part of a case: briefing the team, painting contextual portraits of people and events, holding the assembled officers' rapt attention.'

She pulled out the list. 'Fine: I'll find him myself.' She marched from the room, not bothering to shut the door behind her.

Standing in front of his hand-coloured map, Dr Singh sagged like a three-day-old party balloon.

'Yeah . . .' Edward scrunched up his nose and shrugged. 'Sorry about that. She can be a bit . . . brusque? . . . at times.' He wandered over and patted Dr Singh on the shoulder. 'You did good.' Hooking a thumb at the door. 'I'd better get after her.' But he only got half-way across the floor before turning back. 'Just out of interest, who else here is connected to Rupert Fraser?'

'Erm . . .' It took a breath or two for Dr Singh to focus. 'Well, Mr Fraser spends a lot of time with Anna Radcliffe and Catherine Johansson. I'm sure he's simply venting his sexual spleen with Radcliffe, but I know Johansson was part of his gang at some point. And Joseph Ivanson, of course, you'll often see them huddled together in the library.' That party balloon deflated again. 'Back in the day, I'd have a room of officers hanging on my every word, and *now* look at me.'

'Don't let the DI get to you. She means well, but sometimes . . .' Wait a minute: '*Who* did you say he hangs out with? In the library?'

'Joseph Ivanson?'

'Not "*Black Joe*" Ivanson?' Because, let's face it, 'Ivanson' wasn't exactly a common name.

'They meet up three or four times a week.' Dr Singh bustled back to his files again. 'Here we go: Joseph Ivanson, AKA: Black Joe. Eighteen years in HMP Kilmarnock. Sent down for a tiger kidnap that went *very* badly wrong: MSP's daughter and grandson. A lot of it didn't make the papers, but they came to a particularly unpleasant end. And I'm led to believe he, Geoff Newman, and Rupert Fraser were part of a syndicate that took down the Clydesdale Bank in Fraserburgh. Of course *they* don't know that, but' – tapping his forehead – 'you'd be surprised what the observant, trained professional can deduce.'

'How could they not know they were on the same job?'

'Apparently Newman was focusing his criminal activities north of the border, because his friends in the Met were getting suspicious.'

'Doc: how – could – they – not – know?'

'Hmm? Oh. The gentleman who arranged it, "Big Craig" McPherson, was a very cautious soul. He gave each member of the syndicate a codename, forbidding them from using their real ones. And everyone had to wear a mask at *all* times. That way, if one of them was picked up by the police, they couldn't identify anyone else.' A shrug. 'Of course, if the residents here weren't so reticent about discussing their criminal pasts with each other, it would have come out years ago. But they are, so it didn't. Does that help?'

It kinda did. It kinda did a *lot*.

Not about what happened to Pauline Thomson and Geoff Newman, or even Caroline Manson, but it still helped. And asked a whole heap of new questions.

Dr Singh tilted his head to one side. 'Is everything all right?'

'Got to go.' Edward patted him on the shoulder again. 'Thanks for the Bovril.' Hurrying from the room, down the hall – grabbing his high-vis and stuffing his feet into his wellies – then out into the chilly night air.

Bigloria was already halfway down the street, leaving twin lines gouged into the snow behind her.

He waded after her as yet more of the bloody stuff plummeted from the unseen sky. 'Guv? Guv! Guv!'

She didn't even slow down. 'If there's one thing I hate more than a bent copper, it's an up-himself forensic psychologist.'

'Check the list, check the list!'

'I *know* where Rupert Fraser lives.'

'No, check it for Joseph Ivanson.' Already getting out of breath, because running through deep snow in wellington boots was harder than it looked.

She scuffed to a halt, turned, stared. 'And *why* would I do that?'

'Joseph Ivanson? AKA: *Black Joe* Ivanson.'

Nope, no reaction.

He lumbered to a halt, right in front of her. 'On the way to Glenfarach, when we stopped for a pee? Mr Bishop told me *Ivanson* killed Emily Lawrie, only he *also* told me Mr Ivanson was in a nursing home with dementia. Till he caught Covid and *died*.' Edward raised an eyebrow. 'Only if Mr Ivanson died of Covid—'

'What's he doing living here.' Her mouth pursed. 'Interesting . . .'

'Why would Mr Bishop lie about Mr Ivanson being dead? Unless he doesn't know, of course. I mean, he only told me about the murder because he thought Ivanson was dead.' Ooh, now *there* was an idea: 'What if Ivanson's here on some sort of witness-protection thing? I know, they all are, kind of, but what if the powers that be faked Ivanson's death so he could live out his days in Glenfarach without anyone knowing?' Mind you . . . 'Bit daft to use his real name, though. But if you weren't a resident, or someone who works here, how would you find out?'

Bigtoria stared off into the distance, silent as a standing stone.

'And from what Dr Singh says, Mr Ivanson and Mr Newman were both part of that Clydesdale Bank job in Fraserburgh. So we can clear Emily Lawrie's murder *and* that off the books.' Edward smiled. 'The Boss'll be pleased.'

Nothing.

Snow settled on her hair and shoulders. Whirled gently through the streetlights' glow. Killed all sound but Edward's breathing.

'Guv?'

Her voice, when it came, was calm and quiet. 'Yes, I imagine he will . . .'

You'd think she'd be a bit more excited about it. A twofer – murder and a big bank heist. But it was like he'd told her about a nice sandwich he'd had three weeks ago.

'Guv? Is everything OK?'

She marched on through the snow again, leaving him behind.

'Guv!' He dropped his voice to a whisper. 'You're A: very welcome, and B: an absolute sodding nightmare.'

But he hurried after her anyway.

Byre Road wasn't *quite* as swanky as the street Dr Singh lived on. Two derelict cottages sagging in crumbling isolation, their gutters drooping, windows boarded up, saplings growing out of the drains. They faced a short row of four houses that looked like they were heading the same way. To be fair, one of them did have an upper floor, but the harling had partially crumbled, exposing the granite beneath.

Edward slogged through the crisp grey wall of snow, breath streaming out in thick, pale, *laboured* whumps. Sweat trickling down his spine – again. 'Should've . . . should've gone back . . . to the . . . station . . . for the keys . . . the keys to that . . . sodding snowplough!'

Even Bigtoria's face glowed a ruddy shade of beetroot in the streetlights' LED blaze. 'Stop whinging.'

'I'm not "whinging", I'm *complaining*. It's different.' He staggered to a halt in front of the two-storey building. A solitary light shone in a downstairs window, and a hand-carved sign was mounted on the garden wall: 'FRASER HOUSE'. 'This is us.'

The other three cottages had their curtains drawn, but one by one those twitched, then opened, and silhouettes peered out. Watching them. Motionless.

No one waved.

OK, because somehow that was even creepier.

Edward huffed out another tortured breath. 'When we get home, I'm never walking anywhere again.'

'See? Whinging.' She fought with the gate: hauling it back and forth, back and forth, carving a small semicircle through the knee-deep snow. Before giving up and just stepping over the thing. 'You should try being a bit fitter.' She forged a path to the front door and leaned on the bell.

'Pffff . . .' He scrambled over the gate – not being freakishly tall had its drawbacks – and stumbled after her. 'Cold. Wet. Knackered. And I *smell*.'

Bigtoria tried the bell again. 'We need those reinforcements. How am I supposed to catch a killer with just you, Sergeant Farrow, and that idiot Harlaw?'

Edward bent over, clutching his knees, hauling in lungfuls of frigid, peppery air. 'I suggested drafting in the Social Work Team, but Sergeant Farrow says they're stretched too tight as it is.'

'I don't care *what* Sergeant Farrow says, unless it's "Yes, Guv." Besides, it's . . .' – she checked her phone – 'gone ten o'clock. They'll have finished their rounds hours ago.' Teeth bared, she took it out on the bell – mashing the thing with her thumb like she was trying to kill it. 'What on earth's taking so long?'

He levered himself upright again. 'Maybe he's lying flat on his back in there, tied to a kitchen table, with his eyes gouged out.'

'Don't even start.' She hammered on the woodwork. 'OPEN UP! WE KNOW YOU'RE IN THERE!'

The epitome of tact and community engagement as ever.

Edward waded his way off the path and through the snow to that glowing downstairs window. Stood on his tiptoes to peer over the sill. Which didn't help much. The only thing visible from down here was a corniced ceiling, a handmade lampshade dangling from the middle of it, and a trio of grubby magnolia walls – wallpaper peeling in the corners.

'Not seeing anyone moving about in there, Guv.'

'RUPERT FRASER! POLICE! OPEN THIS DOOR!'

He lumbered back to the trampled path. 'Place looks a bit of a tip, though.'

'IF YOU DON'T OPEN UP, RIGHT NOW, YOU'RE IN BREACH OF YOUR CONDITIONS!'

'What if he's on the bog? Or in the shower?'

Bigtoria pounded her fist against the woodwork. 'I'LL HAVE YOU THROWN OUT OF TOWN! THAT WHAT YOU WANT?'

Edward hooked a thumb towards the gap between here and the nearest cottage. 'Maybe we should check round back?'

He shoved through the drifts and had a squint down the side of the building, but instead of a path, or gate, through to a garden behind the house, an eight-foot-high stone wall blocked the way. It was topped with another foot of snow. And, knowing old Scottish towns like this, probably a good three-to-four inches of broken glass.

OK, try the other side.

As he scuffed past, Bigtoria gave up on the banging. 'Beginning to think you might've been right. He's lying dead in there.'

An identical snow-capped eight-foot stone wall.

Sod it. Time for plan B.

He trudged back to the front door, dug the master keys from his pocket and held them up. 'Just a thought.'

Bigtoria snatched them out of his hand and fiddled with the lock till it swung open, revealing a grubby hallway wreathed in gloom. She stepped inside and clicked on the lights.

It'd probably been pretty swanky in its heyday, with a high ceiling and elaborate tilework on the floor, big mahogany panelled doors leading off to other once-grand rooms. The wallpaper was peeling in here as well, dirt building up along the side of the skirting boards, dust everywhere that didn't get touched or used on a regular basis.

She sniffed. 'Can you smell that?'

Edward squeezed in behind her, nose twitching. 'Smell what?'

'Me neither.' Marching straight for the door at the end of the hall, clumps of snow falling off her wellies to melt on the grubby tiles. 'The other two bodies – their houses stank of raw meat.'

'Ah, I get you.'

She shoved the door open, revealing nothing but darkness. Bigtoria stayed on the threshold, bracing herself against the architrave to reach an arm in, fumbling along the wall

Click

Light buzzed and flickered across a large, old-fashioned kitchen with more dust than furniture. A handful of worktops and units barely made a dent in the space. An ancient refrigerator; a battered kettle; an antique range cooker; pots and plates piled up in the cracked Belfast sink.

The most important thing, though, wasn't there.

No dead body, tied to the rickety wooden table.

Which was a relief, to be honest.

Edward followed her inside – checking the fridge while she nosied around. Its glass shelves boasted two packs of sausages, a bag of mince, about a dozen non-alcoholic beers, and a loaf of bread. Fishfingers in the freezer compartment. No fruit. No vegetables. Not even *oven chips*. The fridge door clunked shut like a coffin lid. 'Don't think Mr Fraser has the healthiest of diets.'

A set of switches sat next to the back door and Bigtoria flicked those on, too. Must've been exterior lights, because a soft amber glow oozed across the garden, getting slowly brighter as the bulbs warmed up.

He scuffed over to the window and peered out.

It was a good sized plot – bushes and sheds and things almost buried in white – and someone had clearly waded their way from the house to the fence at the bottom, disappearing off into the night.

Bigtoria's face tightened. 'Sod.' When she tried the back door, it swung open. Not locked. 'Search the rest of the house. Search it *now!*'

The living room was every bit as post-opulent-rundown-dirty as the hall and the kitchen, only with a stained carpet instead of filthy tiles. A sagging sofa lumped in front of the hollow fireplace, a standard lamp on either side. No TV. No stereo.

Edward did a quick circuit, then checked out the dining room. Looked like it hadn't been redecorated, or cleaned, for thirty years. Big table, eight chairs, sideboard.

No Rupert Fraser.

Every step creaked beneath Edward's feet, all the way upstairs to a landing where the carpet was worn down to the underlay in the middle. Four doors leading off.

Door One opened on what was probably the main bedroom. As the low-energy lightbulbs cast their miserable glow, Edward had a poke around, peering into the twin mahogany wardrobes and matching chest of drawers. Poking his head under the double bed – with its manky duvet cover that clearly hadn't been washed in ages – and avoiding the discarded tissues slumped by the headboard.

Urgh . . .

Dr Singh would've *loved* that.

Door Two: a smaller version of the big bedroom, struggling in the gloom of more cheap old-fashioned energy-saving bulbs. A queen-sized divan, buried beneath piles of smelly clothes and general bric-a-brac.

Door Three: the lighting here was a massive improvement: one flick of the switch and the place lit up like a football pitch. It had probably started life as another guest bedroom, but been transformed into an artist's studio. White-painted walls bounced back the LED glow, showing off loads of stretched canvases, jars of pens and paintbrushes, and a whole heap of oil paints in various boxes. An easel sat in the middle of the room, featuring a large canvas that was a mass of visceral reds and blacks and purples with a woman's torn body at its heart.

Dr Singh was right about Rupert Fraser: that man was *disturbed*.

Door Four opened on a family bathroom. Probably just as well the lights in here didn't do an awful lot to dispel the darkness. The smell was bad enough.

A claw-foot bath dominated one wall, topped by a mildewed shower curtain. Crusts of dark-orange and brown limescale around the drain. Lid *and* seat up on the toilet, showing off a whole Formula-One-season of skid marks . . .

Rupert Fraser was a catch, all right.

Edward creaked down the stairs.

Pushed through into the kitchen again.

Bigtoria was where he'd left her – still scowling out through the open back door, her breath misting the air. 'Anything?'

'He's not here.'

'Hmmph.' She slammed the door shut and turned. 'This ankle-tag-enforced curfew is a complete and utter . . .'

The lights buzzed and flickered. Then darkness swamped the room.

'Guv?' Now the only light was the night-time pale-grey luminescence of snow outside – just bright enough to turn the smothered garden into lurking animal shapes. Bears and wolves, stalking into town from the fairy-tale woods that surrounded Glenfarach. Searching for fresh meat.

'*Great.*' A narrow beam of white pierced the chilly air, bouncing off the kitchen window, casting a reflection in the glass that showed Bigtoria holding out her phone's torch. 'That's all we—'

The lights crackled back on, flickered again . . . but didn't go out this time.

Edward dug into his high-vis, feeling for the headtorch. 'Yeah, this is really giving me confidence.'

Bigtoria killed the app on her phone and held out a hand. 'Airwave.'

Edward passed it over and she poked at the buttons, getting a harsh squeal of feedback in return.

She had another go. 'DI Montgomery-Porter to Sergeant Farrow: safe to talk.'

A horrible electronic *squonk* shattered the air, followed by a loud fizzing crackle and a barely audible voice. '. . . *fff Foxtrot Fffff* . . . Hello? . . . hear me? . . .' Then a wall of hissing static. And then silence.

She pressed the button again.

Nothing. Not even malfunctioning noises.

A couple more tries produced the same result.

She tossed the handset to Edward. 'Get back to the station and tell Sergeant Farrow to fire up her GPS-tag tracker while the power's still on. I want to know where this bastard is.'

'What about you, Guv?'

A nasty, sharp-toothed smile lowered the temperature another five degrees. 'I'm going to wait here' – rolling her shoulders and flexing her fists – 'and make sure Mr Fraser gets a warm welcome home.'

Oh dear . . .

21

What sort of stupid town didn't have phones? How were you supposed to get *anything* done if you couldn't call anyone? What if
there was an emergency? Which, let's be one hundred percent
clear, there sodding was.

Edward trudged through the thigh-deep drifts on West Main
Street, every *single* step a struggle. Snow scrabbling its way in between
his trousers and his wellies to melt and soak into his socks. Again!
What was the point of wellington boots if they were no better
than his soggy shoes? Squelching, cold, frozen, uncomfortable, *bastarding* Glenfarach.

'I hate this bloody place . . .'

The only bonus was that the storm had given up on the massive
dinner-plate-sized flakes for teeny drifting ones instead.

So: on he fought, all alone in a blue-grey world, lit by the eye-
stinging glare of LED streetlights. Cameras watching as he passed.

'"Oh, you *have* to join the police, Teddy", "It's a family tradition, Teddy", "Don't you think your brother would love to be in
your shoes? He's *so* disappointed, and he's in a *wheelchair*, Teddy",
"You're so *ungrateful*, Teddy."' Edward hauled in a deep breath – it
tasted of ice and woodsmoke and frustration and winter.
'AAAAAAAAAAAAAAAAAAAAAAARRRRGH!'

Edward shivered his way along the breeze-block corridor, through
the door and into the glorious warmth of the custody suite. Limped

straight over to the portable radiator sitting in the middle of the room and more or less tried to climb inside it.

Teeth chattering as the heat leaked in through his deep-chilled, soggy trousers and into his purple, clawed hands. Cheeks, nose, and ears aching. Which was more than he could say for his numb toes.

Be lucky if he didn't lose half of them to frostbite.

He unzipped his high-vis, bending forwards so the edges dangled either side of the radiator, letting the heat flood into his torso.

OK, so it was undignified, but sod it: he was the only one here.

Well, maybe not the *only* one. Two of the cell doors were closed, so Kerry Millbrae and Siobhan Wilkins were still in residence. But other than that, he had the place to himself.

'Whole sssssodding t-t-t-town is a g-g-g-ghost sssssship. Should never have v-v-v-volunteered for thissss stupid bloody—'

'Having a moan, are we?' Sergeant Farrow emerged from the little room hidden away behind the custody desk, carrying two plastic cups of something hot. She frowned, then turned, gaze following the trail of meltwater he'd left from the door through to the rest of the station. 'You're dripping all over my nice clean cellblock!'

'It's-s-s-s a f-f-f-flipping f-f-f-f-f-freezer out there. And the pow-w-w-wer's all wonky. D-d-d-d-did you get the f-f-f-f-flickering lights here? Wh-wh-wh-what if there's a p-p-p-power cut? Place is like *D-d-d-d-deliverance* meets *The Th-th-th-thing* at the best of sssssodding times. *And* the Airwaves are knackered again!'

'Only so much Jenna can do with string and bogies. I'll get her to have another go tomorrow.' Sergeant Farrow marched past, pausing to thump him on the arm. 'Now, shift off that heater, you twit: you'll give yourself chilblains.'

No chance.

He was staying here till they prised him off with a crowbar.

She knocked on one of the closed cell doors, then flipped up the sneak-peek window. 'Siobhan? Tea for you.'

Edward shuffled his knees against the warm metal. 'Rupert F-f-f-fraser's missing.'

Sergeant Farrow stood there, still as a snowman, for a moment.

Then opened the cell door and placed the cup on the floor, inside. 'Watch: it's hot.' Shut the door again. Turned. Licked her lips. 'When you say "missing", you—'

'We went to his housssse and he wasn't there.'

Her eyes bugged. 'What do you mean, "he wasn't there"? Of *course* he's there – it's after curfew!'

'Had-d-d-d to let ourselves in with the m-m-m-master key. No sign of him anywhere.' Edward gave the radiator a wee shoogle. 'C-c-c-can we turn this th-th-th-thing up?'

'Oh, for *fudge's* sake!' She clenched her jaw, turning her head away for a moment. Took a couple of deep breaths. Then knocked on the other cell, her voice all calm again. 'Kerry? Would you like some tea, Kerry?'

He hugged the radiator harder. 'How's she feeling?' At least his teeth had stopped chattering.

Sergeant Farrow winced. Pulled her shoulders up. Shook her head. Then opened the cell door. 'Come on, Kerry, maybe a nice cuppa will help?'

Ms Millbrae was just visible in the gap between the sergeant and the doorframe. She was still in her white SOC suit, lying on the cell's plastic mattress with her back to the room. She didn't move. Didn't say anything. Didn't even cry.

'OK. Well, in case you change your mind.' Sergeant Farrow placed the tea by the mattress, then backed out and closed the cell door. Huffed out a breath. 'Poor wee soul . . .'

'Dr Singh doesn't think she killed Pauline Thomson. Thinks it was a professional job.'

Sergeant Farrow stayed where she was, her shoulders drooping, voice flat. 'It's all fudged up, Edward. Used to be so *easy* working here – everyone so well behaved, never any aggro or burglaries or drunken brawls.' She blew out a long, sad breath. 'Now look at us.'

Yup.

Edward straightened up, pulling his knees away from the radiator. Getting a bit burny there. 'I have a message for you from DI Montgomery-Porter—'

'Bigtoria.'

'No. *Definitely* not that. She wants you to track Rupert Fraser's ankle tag so we can wade through yet more sodding snow, find him, and arrest him. And she says you have to call in some of the Social Work Team to cover the cellblock and guard Millbrae Cottage. Free up you and PC Harlaw for other stuff.'

'Ah . . .' Sergeant Farrow wandered back to the custody desk. 'Not loving the sound of that, to be honest, Edward.'

'Just the messenger here, Sarge. And speaking of which: where's your productions store?'

She pointed at the ceiling. 'First floor. Why?'

'Any chance of the key? I need to get something.'

Sergeant Farrow was on the phone when Edward squelched his way back into the custody suite, carrying his prize – a large brown-paper evidence bag.

'I know, but what can we do?'

He dumped it on the desk and placed the productions-store key beside it. Waiting while she wound up the call.

'True . . . Thanks, Ian, I owe you one . . . OK. Bye. Bye.' She hung up. 'That's Ian on his way to relieve Dave at Kerry's house. Clive will take over here, even though he's not done *any* of the training courses.' Raising a finger. 'Which once more, for the record, I said was a *fudgingly* bad idea, OK?'

'Again: just the messenger, Sarge.' He patted the brown-paper bag. 'I need you to sign this out of evidence and into my custody.'

'Do you now?' She took the key and returned it to a drawer beneath the desk, then pulled the bag over and frowned at the handwritten label. Looked at him. Then back at the bag again. 'Why?'

'Call it a result of unforeseen operational complications, requiring these items for the support of ongoing investigations and to facilitate the security of residents.'

'And the *real* reason?'

He opened the thing and tipped out its contents – two blister packs, each containing a pair of brand-new children's walkie-talkies. The ones recovered from Siobhan Wilkins's joinery workshop.

She blinked at him. 'Are you suffering from hypothermia? Is that what this is?'

'No, think about it' – struggling his way into one of the clear-plastic casings – 'our Airwaves are buggered, there's no mobile signal, and we can't use landlines, because the residents don't have any. Hence: walkie-talkies.' He winkled the clown's head and teddy bear free of their see-through prison, then broke out the lion and tiger too.

Sergeant Farrow picked up that last one, turning it over in her hands. 'Don't think these'll have *much* of a range.'

Edward helped himself to the teddy bear. 'Better than nothing, though.' He popped the shiny brown back off his brand-new walkie-talkie, revealing a cavity.

Sod.

'Got any batteries, Sarge?'

'Bloody snow. Bloody sodding cold snow that's bloody cold and snowy and sodding bloody—'

A harsh, electronic, monophonic rendition of 'Teddy Bears' Picnic' burst out of his high-vis pocket as Edward fought his way back along West Main Street in the swirling eddies of yet more *bastarding* snow. You'd think, having just waded down the road half an hour ago, that the going would be easier, sticking to the tracks he'd made, but *no*. Because everything always had to be *more* difficult in this horrible place.

He dragged the teddy bear walkie-talkie out and stabbed a thumb into its tummy, making it bleep. Holding it up in front of his face. 'Doctor Zhivago's I-Hate-Bloody-Snow Emporium, polar bears our sodding speciality!' He released the bear's tummy, freeing up the transmission.

Sergeant Farrow's voice was a bit buzzy and distorted, but still a lot better than the Airwave system, before it stopped working. '*Golf Foxtrot Four to Alpha Charlie Two, safe to talk?*'

Edward struggled on, pressing the button again. 'There's only the two of us got walkie-talkies, Sarge.'

'*We have procedures for a reason, Edward.*'

Like that mattered in this situation. Still, no point arguing with someone who outranked you, was there. They never listened.

'Yes, Sarge.' He took a right, retracing his path onto Byre Road.

'I've run Rupert Fraser's ankle tag. According to this, he's at home. Hasn't been out since yesterday morning.'

'Ha. Ha. Ha.' Putting zero energy into it.

'Did you check the whole house? Maybe Rupert's hiding in the basement or the attic? Cupboard under the stairs? Somewhere like that?'

Sod.

'Well . . . we were . . . kinda in a hurry.'

A groan rumbled out of the teddy bear. *'Then tell Bigtoria to have another look!'*

He closed his eyes, curling into himself as the snow clattered against his back and shoulders. 'Sarge, I'm *begging* you. If she hears you saying "Bigtoria", she'll pop a rivet.'

'And that, my dear Constable Reekie, is why we say "safe to talk?" at the start of every radio call. Golf Foxtrot Four, out.'

Everyone was a bloody comedian.

He returned the teddy bear to his inside pocket and struggled on. Past the dilapidated cottages – with their boarded-up windows and sagging roofs – and over to Fraser House. Resplendent in all its manky glory.

Imagine being stuck out in *this* – had to be below freezing, and it'd only get colder as the night wore on . . .

No wonder everyone thought Caroline Manson was dead already. Even if Rupert Fraser *hadn't* killed her, she'd be well on her way to hypothermia by now. Unless she'd found a place to hole up.

Or someone had stashed her somewhere.

Edward stopped at the gate, one hand hovering over the metal latch. Then turned to peer through the veil of tumbling snow at the two knackered buildings opposite.

If you were Rupert Fraser, renowned violent, misogynistic toss-pot, and you'd abducted a social worker, would you keep them where they were easy to access, or far away so no one would suspect you?

Worth a try, wasn't it?

And it's not like he could get any colder. Or wetter.

Edward followed his own footsteps back out into the road, then clambered over the knee-high wall separating the nearest cottage's garden from the pavement, wading his way to the front door.

It was impossible to see anything, what with the windows being covered in a thick skin of bloated plywood. Still, you had to wonder, didn't you?

He tried the handle, but the door was pinned in place with about a dozen massive rusty nails – driven right through the wood and into the frame, holding it solid. Which meant Rupert Fraser couldn't have got in this way.

The neighbouring cottage was sealed up too, but battling a path around the back revealed a window where the plywood sagged from a single nail, meaning you could hinge it open.

Who was the idiot now?

Edward heaved the thing, setting the swollen wood squealing against its rusty fixing, until it exposed the dark uninviting hole where the glass used to be.

His headtorch's beam slipped through the gap and onto the cottage floor. Only the floor wasn't there: just an eight-foot drop to a square of rough earth, littered with chunks of rotten timber. Nearly every joist had gone, leaving a solitary beam reaching out into the gloom.

A pair of glittering eyes peered back at Edward from about a third of the way along it. They were attached to a large brown rat that stared at him, like it was daring him to enter its domain.

Nope.

He pulled his head out into the snow and let the chunk of plywood squeal shut again.

Of course there were rats. Because the only thing this sodding place needed to round off the cheery, welcoming, romantic atmosphere was a pack of disease-spreading, slithery-tailed, big, fat rodenty bastards. Whole bloody village was probably crawling with them.

The back doors of both cottages were boarded up too, and the other windows impenetrable. So if Rupert Fraser had stashed Caroline Manson somewhere, it wasn't here.

Besides, the only footprints in the snow were Edward's.

So much for saving the day . . .

He let himself into Fraser House, and banged the door closed behind him. Leaned back against it and expelled a shuddery breath. Then knocked a flurry of white from his wellies. 'GUV?'

Her voice echoed down the hall: '*In here.*'

He scuffed his way to the kitchen, wellington boots squeaking on the filthy tiles.

Bigtoria was filling the dented kettle – having to tilt it nearly sideways to get it in under the tap, because of all the dirty dishes in the sink.

'You sure that's a good idea, Guv? Not exactly hygienic.' Unzipping his high-vis. 'I got Sergeant Farrow to run Mr Fraser's tag and—'

'He hasn't left the house.' Each word chipped out of granite.

Oh no, not again.

'You didn't find a body, did . . . ?'

She held up a grey ankle tag. It looked pretty much identical to the one Sergeant Farrow had fitted to Mr Bishop, only instead of being fastened tight, a little rainbow of wires crocodile-clipped the band and the unit together. Making it more than big enough to slip free of. 'It was in the master bedroom.' Her lip curled. 'And if *one* resident's doing it, you can pretty much guarantee they all are.' The ankle tag clattered down on the grubby worktop. 'This whole place is a *joke.*'

And not a funny one.

He wandered over and peered through the window. 'Where do you think Mr Fraser's gone?'

'Given his criminal record? Freezing to death in a ditch would be an excellent result.' Slamming the kettle down and plugging it in.

'So, we've got a misogynistic, violent tosspot – who really, *really* loves to hurt women – running about out there, with no way to track him, and Caroline Manson is still missing.' Edward sagged against the nearest kitchen unit. No prizes for guessing what that meant: 'We're looking for her dead body tomorrow, aren't we.'

The kettle pinged and clunked.

'That's about the size of it.'

'Cock.'

The angry song of boiling water was the only thing to break the silence as Bigtoria stood there, jaw flexing, face creasing, teeth bared. Then something went *snap* and she snatched the kettle off the worktop – the cable jerking tight, then ripping the plug from the wall – snarling as she hurled it across the kitchen to smash into the tiles above the range cooker. Metal buckling, water spewing everywhere, before it clanged against the hob, bounced, and its battered carcass tumbled to the floor.

Yeah . . .

That was a good sign.

Maybe a little present would cut through the homicidal mood?

He dipped into his pocket. 'Here.' Holding out the clown-head walkie-talkie, with its big cheery smile, red nose, curly hair, and wee pointy hat.

She looked at it, then at him, like he'd lost what few marbles he had left.

'No, it's good, see?' He produced the teddy bear and pressed its tummy. 'Alpha Charlie Two to Golf Foxtrot Four, safe to talk?' Then let go.

His voice echoed out of the clown, about three words behind. *'Alpha Charlie Two to Golf Foxtrot Four, safe to talk?'*

Sergeant Farrow sounded like she was sitting in the bath, but other than that the sound quality was pretty good. *'What can we do you for, Edward?'*

'We've—'

Bigtoria stuck her hand in his face and pressed the clown's nose. Clipped and angry 'Rupert Fraser's slipped his ankle tag and sodded off into the snow.'

A pause.

Then silence.

He pointed. 'You have to let go of the button, Guv, or the person on the other end can't talk.'

A shrug. 'They're a bit basic: if more than one handset's in transmit mode none of them work. Better than nothing, though. Right?'

She released the clown's nose, and a low groan crackled out into the kitchen.

Followed by, *'For . . . In the name of . . . fudge.'*

'Your whole town's compromised, Sergeant.'

'How the heck's he done that? Rupert Fraser's not exactly MENSA material.' Then the implication must've sunk in, because a slash of horror cut into her voice. *'Oh, God. If he can do it . . .'*

'As of now he's our number-one suspect. And don't be surprised if you're down another resident by daybreak.'

Edward waved at the DI. 'We could go door to door: warn everyone? See if anyone else is AWOL?'

Her scowl darkened. 'As if we didn't have *enough* to do.' She pressed the clown's nose again. 'Sergeant, I want you and Harlaw out there checking residents' homes. You do everything west of the square, Constable Reekie and I will do everything east.'

'Soon as Clive Fox-Johnson gets here to mind the cells, I'll go fetch Dave and we'll crack on.'

'You do that. Out.' She released the button and frowned down at the clown's head. 'Was this meant to be some sort of coded message, Constable?'

Really?

She was going to take his *completely* brilliant bit of initiative and make out like it was an insult?

'Sergeant Farrow bagsed the lion and tiger, and she outranks me, so . . . ?' He shrugged. 'You can be the teddy bear, if you want? Only I thought, as that's what my mum used to call me when I was little . . . "Teddy", I mean. Not "Teddy Bear".' Heat surged up his neck and cheeks. 'Though she did do that sometimes' – the words tripping out faster and faster – 'but I probably *shouldn't* have mentioned it cos it's really embarrassing, so if we all forget I said anything we can go see if everyone else is home.' He cleared his throat. 'Sorry, Guv.'

'Hmmph.' She slid the clown's head into her jacket pocket. Then marched for the door. 'We've got a stop to make first.'

22

Brindle Lane was one over from Byre Road – little more than a narrow alleyway wedged between two buildings. Which meant, holy day, dance round the sodding mistletoe, the snow wasn't anywhere near as deep in here. Or at least not to start with. Soon as they passed the gable ends and moved onto the bit bordered by back gardens, the drifts were up to Edward's knees again.

A small terrace of three narrow houses was squeezed in, halfway down the lane, opposite the crumbling remains of a stable block – roof gone, glass cracked, wooden partitions rotting. The houses looked cheery enough, though, light oozing around the edges of their closed curtains. Dormer windows poking from their snow-covered roofs: happy, shining eyes with fluffy white eyebrows.

The front doors opened straight onto the street, so for once Edward didn't have to wade up an uncleared garden path.

Ivanson House sat in the middle – boasting a plain white PVC door with a row of three Yale locks lined up like the pips on a chief inspector's epaulettes. In a normal village that would be considered overkill, but given the kind of people who lived in Glenfarach? Surprised everyone wasn't doing it.

Bigtoria mashed the bell. Then slammed her palm against the wood. 'JOSEPH IVANSON, OPEN UP! POLICE!'

Nothing like exercising a little patience and restraint.

Boom, boom, boom.

'IVANSON! OPEN THIS DOOR, NOW!'

Boom, boom, boom.

A muffled voice growled from inside, getting louder. *'All right, all right. Christ's sake. I'm coming, OK?'* A rattle, a series of clunks, and the door yanked open. 'What the bloody hell do you want?'

Joseph 'Black Joe' Ivanson was a lairy wee nyaff of a man in a prison-style blue sweatshirt and jogging bottoms. Flip-flops on his feet. Grey moustache and homemade haircut – complete with tight-trimmed dundrearies. His back had the traditional auld-mannie stoop to it, hands thin and bony.

Even Edward could've picked him up and chucked him across the road . . . but there was something about Mr Ivanson that whispered of broken bones and savage beatings. Something that radiated menace.

He regarded Edward and Bigtoria with an expression that implied he was bored with them already. 'Well?'

Bigtoria clearly wasn't worried about the undercurrent of violence. 'Geoff Newman.'

'Wrong house.' Pointing a gnarled finger at the wrought-iron sign mounted on the wall.

He went to close the door, but Bigtoria slapped her hand against it, holding it open.

'You were part of his crew. You were his friend.'

A sniff. 'Never heard of him.'

'You've *never* heard of Geoff Newman. Despite living in the same village as him for the last five years.' She turned to Edward. 'Well, that sounds perfectly plausible to me. What about you, Constable?'

Edward scrunched his nose. 'Bit sceptical, to be honest, Guv.'

Back to Mr Ivanson. 'And I suppose you've never heard of Rupert Fraser either?'

The bored look slipped towards a glower.

'Caroline Manson?'

The glower deepened.

'How about *Emily Lawrie*? Surely you remember her?'

His left eye twitched, jaw tightening, and then the jaded-hardman veneer slid into place again. 'There a point to this?'

Edward stuck his hand up. 'Everyone on the outside seems to think you're dead, Mr Ivanson. Any reason for that?'

Silence.

He pulled his lips in.

Bony fingers curled into fists.

Nostrils flared.

Then his hands disappeared into his pockets, and Mr Ivanson gave them a shrug. 'You got any idea what time it is? I need my beauty sleep. Not as young as I was.'

Bigtoria leaned in for a loom. 'You *are* aware of what happens if you don't cooperate with the police, Mr Ivanson?'

'I am cooperating with the appropriate authorities, to the best of my abilities, as per the terms of my residency.' The exact same words Adam at the bakery had used, delivered with the same flat, practised intonation as well.

A smile broke across Bigtoria's stony face. 'Then you won't mind if we search the place. Constable?'

'Yes, Guv.'

It didn't take long to search Ivanson House, because it was tiny and there was nearly sod all in it.

Every wall had been stripped down to the plasterwork – the various dings and holes filled in with Polyfilla, ready for redecorating.

He'd ripped all the carpets up, leaving the gripper rods with their jagged little teeth behind, exposing a patchwork of floorboards. Making each step echo back and forth between the bare walls.

The only furniture in the house was a mattress on the floor in the bedroom and a camping chair in the living room. Even the kitchen cabinets were gone.

Bigtoria nudged the chair with her wellington boot. 'What a *lovely* place you have here. Fallen on hard times?'

He stuck his chin out, dundrearies bristling. 'Traded all my furniture back to the exchange, *actually*. Getting a whole new set when the carpet and wallpaper's done.' One shoulder rose, then fell again. 'Well, new to *me*, anyway.'

'Touchy.' She snapped her fingers. 'Constable. I think it's about time you rummaged through Mr Ivanson's attic and crawl spaces, don't you? And don't forget the cupboard under the stairs.'

Thanks a sodding heap . . .

And they were back out on the street again, Bigtoria and Mr Ivanson squaring off across the threshold while Edward wiped dust and cobwebs and what looked suspiciously like mouse droppings off his high-vis jacket and low-vis trousers.

She tilted her head in a sarcastic nod. '*Thank you* for your cooperation.'

He glared, bared his teeth, then slammed the door shut.

But before he could lock it, Bigtoria twisted the handle and pushed it open a crack. 'A word to the wise, Mr Ivanson: Rupert Fraser's friends and accomplices have a habit of turning up dead this week.'

One eye glowered out at them through the opening. 'I'm nobody's "friend".'

A cold smile. 'Be sure to lock your doors and windows.'

She let go, and he slammed the door shut again. Followed by a brief performance of Ivanson's Symphony for Yale Locks and Deadbolts.

'Wasn't he lovely?' Edward dug a double handful of snow from the nearest window ledge, using it to wash the yuck off his fingers – the cold stinging all the way down to the bone. 'And thanks for making me rummage through all the dirty bits.' Shaking off the slush and stuffing his hands deep into his pockets. 'Very kind of you.'

But Bigtoria didn't rise to it. Just stared at the closed door, like she could see through it to the bare hallway and the vicious old man beyond. Then nodded. Sniffed. And marched off into the snow.

Some DCs got *nice* detective inspectors to sidekick for. Some DCs got sent to *nice* towns and villages. Some DCs got to deal with *nice* members of the public. While some poor sods got stuck with DI Montgomery-Porter, in a winter-bound hellhole full of sex offenders and thugs, going door to door, *in the middle of the night*, to make sure none of them were out and about wandering the streets killing people . . .

Edward sighed, slumped, groaned, sighed again, then lumbered after her.

White Cottage, 23:28

Edward waded up the path to a front door besieged with slithery, black-leafed ivy and rang the bell. Then risked a glower in Bigtoria's direction.

She just stood there, on the pavement, staring off into space. Couldn't even be bothered watching to see how this went.

And how come *they* weren't doing the west side of Glenfarach? They were already *on* the west side of Glenfarach – Rupert Fraser and Mr Ivanson *both lived* on the west side of Glenfarach. But no: they had to tromp all the way over here, and leave Sergeant Farrow and PC Harlaw with the easy bit. This half was bigger too. It was like she *wanted* them both to freeze to—

A short man in a shiny, expensive-looking silk robe answered the door. Mean narrow eyes and a squint nose. He took one look at Edward and tied his robe tight. 'I don't care what they told you: I didn't do it. They're all lying.'

Edward forced a bit of jollity into his voice, pretending he wasn't freezing his nuts off out here. 'Just checking that you're OK, Mr White, and you've not seen anything suspicious?'

Mr White pulled his chin in. 'What kind of suspicious?'

'Well, maybe—'

Bigtoria's dulcet tones thundered out through the snow. 'HAVE YOU SEEN RUPERT FRASER, OR HAVEN'T YOU?'

'What, tonight?' Eyebrows pinched, mouth a scrunched line, like that was the most baffling question he'd ever faced. '*No*. It's after curfew.'

Greeb Cottage, 23:50

A fat man with a tattooed face leaned on the doorframe, wafts of cardamom and cloves and bitter-onion BO coiling around him. SpongeBob SquarePants T-shirt, boxer shorts, hairy legs. 'Rupert Fraser? Nah, not for ages. The man's a prick.'

Silverman House, 00:00

'Suspicious?' Ms Silverman peered at Edward through a thick-framed pair of milk-bottle-bottom glasses that made her eyes huge. Big, beige hearing aids in her big, beige ears. A set of false teeth that seemed two sizes too large for her head. Brown cardigan on over threadbare buttoned-up jammies.

Which, for some weird reason, brought wolves and forests and Little Red Riding Hoods to mind.

Edward shuffled his wellies, trying to get some feeling into his toes. 'No, Ms Silverman, let's go back to the—'

'Why would I have done anything suspicious? I'm a model citizen!'

Oh, for God's sake . . .

'No, not you. Have you *seen* anything suspicious tonight?'

'I've been here twenty-nine years and not a single complaint against me.'

'OK. Look, maybe we should start again . . .'

Barrow Cottage, 00:10

Mrs Barrow leaned forward and fixed Edward with a wide-eyed gaze. 'Have we seen Rupert Fraser?' She pulled the knot on her dressing gown tighter. Red checks, which didn't go with the blue-and-white striped pyjamas, or the leather slippers.

Her husband stood at her elbow, in an identical bedtime outfit. His hair slicked into an immaculate side parting. He had the same intense stare too. 'We haven't seen Rupert Fraser, have we, Marion?'

Oh, this pair weren't straight out of a horror film *at all*.

Edward licked his lips. 'Maybe you—'

'No, we haven't, Peter. We haven't seen Rupert Fraser or Caroline Manson.'

He backed away a couple of paces. 'OK . . .'

Mrs Barrow stepped forward, slippers crunching into the fresh snow. 'But do you know who we *have* seen?'

Mr Barrow was right behind her. 'Tell him who we've seen, Marion.'

'We've seen Our Lord and Saviour, Jesus Christ.'

'Have *you* seen Our Lord and Saviour, Jesus Christ, Constable Reekie?'

'Actually, I'd probably better . . .' Edward pointed over his shoulder. 'Think I can hear the DI calling me. We've got a *lot* of houses to check.'

Mr Barrow's slippers shuffled closer. 'Maybe you'd like to come in out of this terrible weather and learn how to let Our Lord and Saviour, Jesus Christ, into your heart?'

Mrs Barrow reached for him, her bitten fingernails searching, searching. 'I've made a cake!'

No way in *utter* hell he was eating anything this pair had touched.

'OK, thanks. Bye.' Edward marched down the path to join Bigtoria again.

Mrs Barrow's voice slithered through the air behind him. '*Come back any time, Constable Reekie, we'd love to have you.*'

And when he turned, they were both smiling and waving at him.

A shudder skittered down his spine. He hurried away, keeping his voice low so the weirdos wouldn't hear. 'I don't know what they did, and I don't *want* to know.'

Bigtoria nodded. 'Probably just as well.'

Stourbridge House, 00:25

Edward fought his way along yet another snowy garden path as a little old lady with a history of child abduction smiled and waved at him.

'Come back soon. I don't get many visitors!'

No wonder, you creepy old bag.

Bigtoria was waiting for him on the pavement. Or at least, on the knee-deep strip of white where the pavement should've been. Scowling as Mrs Stourbridge shuffled inside again and closed the door. 'Well?'

'Hasn't seen anyone for weeks. Apparently the residents "aren't as friendly" as they used to be.' He sagged. 'Knackered.'

The only plus side was that the sodding snow had finally stopped. There was even a wee break in the clouds – wide enough to let a handful of stars flicker away in their coal-dark shroud. It should've been reassuring, but something was . . . unnerving about it, like they were being watched.

Getting colder too – his breath was nearly opaque as it hit the unforgiving gaze of the streetlights. Ice crystals glittering across the drifts, spidering the window glass, dusting the back of Bigtoria's high-vis jacket, sparkling on Edward's fluorescent-yellow sleeves.

Bigtoria crunched her way down Flesher's Brae, forging a path through the snow, shoulders rolling like an angry bear. Edward slouched along behind her, stifling a yawn.

Actually, you know what?

Sod stifling.

He stopped and let it rip, head back, jaw wide, shuddering and slumping when it passed.

Pfff . . .

His breath billowed out, glowing, then flickering, then disappearing altogether as the streetlights died, plunging everything into blue-tinged darkness.

OK, that wasn't good.

Bigtoria stared up at the nearest lamppost and its crown of CCTV thorns.

'Guv? Maybe we should . . .'

The lights fizzed and buzzed, and though they *did* come back on again it was at barely half strength. That bright-white glare reduced to a soft grey glow.

No idea why that would make it even colder, but somehow it did.

Edward hunched his shoulders up around his ears, hands buried deep, body clenched. This whole exercise was a waste of time. Tromping round house after house, talking to child molesters and murderers and rapists and arsonists and thugs and bent coppers and every horrible combination along the way.

What did they have to show for it?

Probably frostbite.

And sod all else.

A shiver clattered his teeth for a moment, then passed. Taking with it the last ounce of heat he had.

Come on, there *had* to be a better way to do this . . .

'OK, so maybe Rupert Fraser *isn't* off torturing someone to death, maybe he's . . . I don't know. Dr Singh said Fraser was having sex-and-violence with Anna Radcliffe, so maybe he's at her house, banging away? Or, or maybe he's plotting something with his old gang mates? We know he's not at Mr Ivanson's, but . . .' Edward pulled out the map, skimming it for Radcliffe Cottage. Pointing in the vague direction. 'Ms Radcliffe's that way.' He swung his finger around. 'Catherine Johansson's this. We could cut the crap and just go *see* them.'

No reply from Bigtoria. She hadn't even stopped.

'OK, if you're not keen on *that* idea, maybe we could . . .'

She was still going – wading away through the snow like nothing he said mattered.

Oh, for Christ's sake.

He ran a hand across his face, somehow cold and sweaty all at the same time.

'Guv?'

Still nothing.

'GUV!'

She finally lumbered to a halt, but didn't turn around. 'What?'

Seriously?

'It's well past *midnight* and we've been at it since seven this morning!' Clenching his fists and glowering at the frigid expanse of snow, piled so deep it was over the top of his wellies. Who cared if he sounded whiny? He had every reason to whine. 'I'm cold, I'm knackered, I'm hungry, I can't feel my feet, and I just want a nice cup of tea and a sit-down for five *bloody* minutes!'

Bigtoria gazed off into the distance, back expanding and contracting, long slow curls of breath haunting the air around her head, their faded spectres replaced by the next apparition.

Then she nodded. And crumped away through the snow in *none* of the directions Edward had pointed.

Because *God forbid* his opinion was worth listening to.

Only now there was a droop to her shoulders that hadn't been there before. A heaviness to her gait as she forged a path through the thick blanket of white.

'Guv?'

Like something had gone seriously wrong.

'Guv, you OK?'

Because she didn't look OK.

He lurched after her, struggling even though he stuck to the trail she'd left. 'Where are we going?'

Her voice was cold and flat as the snow. 'It's time.'

Why did that sound horribly ominous?

23

The two-storey building, opposite the graveyard, hadn't changed much since they'd dropped Mr Bishop off yesterday afternoon. The only real difference was the brand-new wrought-iron sign mounted in place of the old one: 'BISHOP HOUSE'.

All the lights were off.

Because, presumably, like sensible bloody people, they were all in sodding bed. Not tramping about through the arctic cold of a Scottish winter in the middle of the *bastarding* night.

Bigtoria lumbered her way up to the front door and pointed. 'Bell.'

God almighty: detective inspectors.

'Can't feel my fingers now.' He shoved the heel of his hand against the button, setting chimes ringing inside. 'Honestly, Guv, it's not too late for a nice hot tea and—'

'What are you, seventy?'

'No, I'm *human*, OK? Just cos you're immune to the cold doesn't mean I am!'

She turned, looming over him. 'You got something to say, *Constable*?'

'Damn right I do!' Chin up, finger out – poking it into the middle of her chest. 'I'm not your bloody slave, *Detective Inspector*. I'm a police officer. And soon as we're back in Aberdeen, I'm going straight to my Federation Rep and . . .'

Light glowed through the glazed panels flanking the door, fading on one side as someone came closer, casting their shadow across the glass. Then a harsh, bunged-up Glaswegian accent growled out, *'Bugger off! You got any idea what time it is? He's in his bed!'*

'DAMN RIGHT I KNOW!' She banged her fist against the wood, setting it booming. 'WAKEY, WAKEY! RISE AND SHINE! IT'S TIME FOR A RECKONING!'

OK, this was sounding worse and worse.

'Reckoning?' Edward checked over his shoulder – no one there, but he lowered his voice anyway. 'Guv? What reckoning? Any chance you can clue me in? Do we need to call for Sergeant Farrow and PC Harlaw?' Fingering the teddy-bear walkie-talkie in his pocket. 'Is this some sort of—'

The door yanked open and Mr Richards glared out at them, with a wee drip hanging off the end of his nose. It was hard to look intimidating when dressed in flannel jammies and a terry-towelling dressing gown. Bare hairy feet splayed like an extra set of hands on the hall carpet. He curled his lip. 'You're keen buggers, I'll give you that.'

Bigtoria shoved past into the house. 'Get him up, Razors, I've got the final piece of the puzzle and I *wouldn't* want Marky to miss the big reveal.'

He scowled at her, eyes moving up and down, taking in the grubby high-vis, the snow-clarted wellingtons, the clenched fists. Then Mr Richards snorted, turned, and limped away down the hall.

Edward stopped at the doorway. 'Guv? Seriously, I haven't—'

'*Inside*, Constable.' Both words cold and hard, straight from the freezer.

OK . . .

He followed her into the living room.

The wall sconces boasted naked energy-saving bulbs – stripped of their shades – which was just as well, given they were suffering from the same problem as the streetlights. Doing their best on half power. Making the shadows darker. But it was still bright enough to see that someone had been busy with a load of reddish-pink emulsion; a stepladder, brushes, rollers, and some tins of paint sat in the corner, ready for the next coat. Masking tape skirted every bit of woodwork and all the sockets and switches; a swathe of plastic sheeting protecting a sizeable chunk of the old carpet.

They'd got rid of all the furniture and decorations, leaving nothing behind but that squeaky wheelchair. OK, so maybe not as stripped to the bone as Mr Ivanson's house, but it still had that fusty, cigarettes-and-mildew scent – not quite bludgeoned to death by the paint's chemical tang.

'Come on!' Mr Richards jabbed a finger at their wellies. 'Dee's a man a favour, yer dripping all over the place! I have tae clean this!' Swinging the finger around to point at the sheeting. 'Go on, shift. Over there.' Then he blew his nose and scurried out again, like an angry rat, grumbling away to himself as he thumped up the stairs. *'Bloody messy police buggers, crashing about, making everything harder than it needs to be . . .'*

They shuffled onto the plastic, water pooling around their boots as the snow melted.

Edward sniffed. Turned in place, taking in the new colour scheme. 'Not keen on the decor. Like living inside a wart. Or someone's colon.'

Nothing from Bigtoria.

'For God's sake, Guv, can you . . .'

The lights flickered, bulbs dimming until they were barely more than a firefly's glow.

'Uh-oh . . .'

But they didn't go out this time. It took seven or eight seconds, but eventually they worked their way up to half strength again. Maybe slightly less.

'Ms Hamilton – you know: at the General Store? says last winter the power was out for a whole week.' Edward shuddered. 'God, can you imagine this place in total darkness?'

But Bigtoria didn't answer. Instead, she made a brief circuit of the plastic sheeting, hands in her pockets, head tilting from side to side as she passed light fittings and architraves and anything else that jutted out of the wall.

At the end of her tour, she came to a halt right back where she'd started, just behind Edward. Looming.

'Are you going to tell me what's going on here, Guv?'

'And spoil the big surprise?'

Ooh, that didn't sound good.

Got the feeling Mr Bishop was in for a shock when he finally arrived.

Still, rather him than Edward.

The whine of the stairlift gurgled through the silent house; then Mr Richards helped Marky shuffle into the living room. Holding his arms and lowering him into the wheelchair like he was made of eggshell. Which was probably just as well, because Mr Bishop looked two shambling steps away from tumbling through Death's final door.

The oxygen mask *hissssssss*ed and *whoooooomph*ed with every echoing breath, that red tank from earlier swapped for a natty new green number.

Edward waved. 'Evening, Mr Bishop. Getting the place redecorated?'

Mr Richards snarled, one hand on his dying friend's shoulder. 'What's it to you?' Chin jutting. 'Man's got a *right* to live somewhere nice.'

Mr Bishop fumbled the mask off with trembling fingers. 'Spent all those . . . years looking at prison walls, son . . . If I'm going to die here . . . want it to look . . . look . . .'

'It's OK, Marky' – Mr Richards gave that shoulder a squeeze – 'the boy's an arse.'

That's what you got for trying to be kind to people.

'Leave the . . . wee lad alone . . . Razors . . . He means well.' He smiled at Edward. 'We've . . . been asking about . . . your Geoff Newman . . . son.'

Because: more flies with honey.

'Thanks, Mr Bishop. Did anyone say anything?'

'Think we're close . . . to discovering . . . who's behind . . . the whole thing.' He sucked on the oxygen for two laboured, rattling breaths. 'Won't be long . . . now . . . Promise.'

'If you've *quite* finished?' Bigtoria folded her arms. 'Let's get back to the topic in hand. I've been out and about, doing my job, *Mr* Bishop. And guess what I found.'

A dismissive wave. 'Tired.'

'Oh, you'll wake up for this.' She pointed. 'We have Constable Reekie to thank; asked the right question at the right time. Connected the disparate dots.' Nodding at Edward. 'Have to say, I'm *actually* impressed.'

Wonders would never cease.

Mr Richards stuck his chest out. 'You've got two minutes, then I'm taking him back upstairs. And I'm already putting in a formal complaint, hen, so make it good.'

'Black Joe Ivanson isn't dead after all. He's right here.'

'Oh, for . . .' Mr Richards rolled his eyes. 'You buggerin' *numptie*. I kent that the whole time! He's over on Brindle Lane; works in Duncan's Second-Hand Delights, Mondays and Thursdays.' Peering down at Mr Bishop. 'Told you she was a waste of skin.'

Here it came . . .

Whatever it was.

'What you maybe didn't "ken" is that Rupert Fraser's slipped his ankle tag and done a runner. Probably heard you were after him for the Fraserburgh Clydesdale Bank job. But guess who *else* was part of the team: the – very – last – member?'

'Black Joe?' Mr Bishop struggled upright in his seat. 'You've got him?'

'No, but he's home right now. Ripe for the picking.'

Ripe for the picking? What was that supposed to mean?

Edward turned. 'Guv?'

'Ha!' Mr Bishop sounded more alive than he had since they'd picked him up from the prison car park. 'After all this time.' Rubbing his arthritic claws together. 'Black Joe Ivanson . . . you sneaky wee bastard . . . Should've *known* you'd be in on it.'

Edward stared at Bigtoria, then at Mr Bishop. 'OK, what *exactly* is going on here?'

Mr Richards shook his head. 'Christ, you're slow on the uptake, son.'

And that's when Bigtoria lunged – her front pressing into Edward's back, her right hand formed into a blade that slipped around his neck, pulling her arm with it, leaving his throat caught in the crook of her elbow, chin forced up by her high-vis sleeve. The right hand grabbed her left biceps, her other hand pressed against the back of his head, forcing it forward. Trapping him in a choke hold.

All done in less than three seconds.

Her muscles flexed, and little dark specks popped in from the edges of the world.

Edward's hands snatched at her arms, slapping, fingernails getting no purchase on the slippery fluorescent-yellow jacket. 'GUV!'

She squeezed and the pressure behind his eyes built and built till they were ready to pop.

'Guv! Gggggg . . .' Feet kicking out. Stamping. Trying to land a blow on her shin or foot, but his welly boots just skiffed off hers like they were Teflon.

Bigtoria's lips brushed his ear. 'Don't move, don't even *breathe*.'

Mr Bishop held up a finger. 'Let's not rush things, Bigtoria . . . The wee boy did find our man . . . after all.'

She relaxed her grip, but only enough to let blood pulse back into his brain like a malfunctioning jackhammer. Breath wheezing in his squashed throat.

'You sound worse than me, son.' Mr Bishop grated out a whispering laugh. 'Thanks for everything . . . I appreciate your help, I genuinely do . . . Only, we're already splitting this thing . . . four ways . . . and one more really doesn't . . . work for me.' A wink. 'You understand . . . right?'

Edward tried for 'Don't! Don't do this!' but Bigtoria shoved his head forward again, clamping his jaw shut, so only a guttural 'GNNNN! DNNNGNNNNNDDDDGGGGGNNNN!' escaped.

Mr Bishop took a hit of oxygen. 'See, son? . . . I promised you'd find out . . . who was behind all this . . . didn't I?' He raised a palsied hand. 'Oh, the two and a half million's . . . not bad, but it's what's *in* those safety-deposit boxes . . . that's the real payday.' He shuffled forward in his wheelchair's seat. 'And it's not just money, it's *power* . . . You've no idea how long it's taken me . . . to get here . . . working my way through every bugger . . . connected to that bank job . . . All those little feelers and tentacles . . . slithering out into the wicked world . . . Paying folk to hunt them down . . . and ask them "nicely" for me . . . Each one pointing . . . the finger at the next poor sod in line . . . Each one with their own piece of the secret.'

Mr Richards' liver-spotted hand dipped into the pocket of his dressing gown and came out with a delicate curve of engraved ebony – two fingers thick and six inches long. 'Been a regular treasure hunt, but.' He held the thing in front of his face, like a religious object, then pressed a tongue of metal sticking out one end, unfolding the blade of an old-fashioned cut-throat razor.

The polished steel caught the sconces' half-strength glow, sending a chip of cold light sweeping across the wall, along the arm of Bigtoria's high-vis coat, flaring as it hit Edward's eyes, then off into the darkness again. His own private mirrorball, for this last horrible dance.

No.

No, no, no, no, no . . .

Edward wriggled and writhed and kicked out and struggled, but Bigtoria held him firm.

Mr Bishop nodded. 'A treasure hunt . . . that's led us all the way here . . . to Glenfarach . . . Fitting the pieces together like a . . . blood-soaked jigsaw puzzle . . . And now, thanks to *you* . . . we know who's got the last bit!' He smiled at Mr Richards. 'Razors, you went to all . . . the trouble of putting this . . . plastic sheeting down . . . Be a shame to waste it.'

'DNNNNNN! DDNNNNNNTDOOOOTHGHHHHH!'

'Oh aye . . .' Mr Richards stretched his neck from side to side, all his dentures on show like a grinning death's head, eyes wide. 'You ready to *scream*, Wee Man?'

'NNNNNNNNNNNNNNNNNNNNN!' Hands battering at Bigtoria's massive arms, feet flailing, thrashing against the strangling grip on his throat. 'NNNNNNNN! DNNNGGG DDNNNNNNNTTTT!'

'Stop wriggling!' Bigtoria retreated a step, taking Edward with her. 'And you can put that stupid razor down, sunshine. This annoying little shite's been a pain in my arse since yesterday morning. He's *mine*.'

The pressure vanished from the back of Edward's head as she removed her left hand. When it reappeared, it was wrapped around the thick handle of a four-inch hunting knife.

Her lips brushed his ear again. 'Goodbye, Constable.'

'NNNNNNNNNNNNNNNNNNNNNNNNNN!'

Something hard slammed into the small of his back, splinters of ice exploding inside. Another blow, and fire tore through him, curling his feet up from the plastic sheeting. One more and his whole body jerked.

She held up the knife, its blade dripping with dark-red blood. Scarlet smeared across the fluorescent-yellow sleeve of her high-vis.

She'd stabbed him.

SHE'D FUCKING STABBED HIM!

Mr Bishop shrugged. 'I'm sorry it couldn't work out . . . son. I liked you . . . I really did.'

GET OUT OF HERE.

MEDICAL . . .

DOCTOR . . .

THERE HAD TO BE SOMETHING—

Bigtoria's left hand slapped onto the back of his head again, the warm blood soaking into his hair. Then she must've straightened up to her full height, lifting him off his feet, the pressure on his throat growing and growing and those dark spots swarmed out of the corners and filled his eyes as a high-pitched squeal rang in his ears and his pulse thumped and battered . . . and faded . . . and his legs didn't work any more . . . and his arms dangled at his sides . . . and the dark spots . . . and then it was all gone.

. . .

She'd killed him.

—detective inspector—

(Victoria Elizabeth Montgomery-Porter)

Twenty-Four

Victoria let DC Reekie's body slide to the plastic sheeting. Lying there, still as a shallow grave, covered in blood.

Razors *stared*, mouth moving around his dentures, clearly working his way up to a petulant sulk. 'Hmph . . .' He put his cut-throat away. 'Was looking forward to that.'

She released a long, happy sigh. 'So was I.' She arched her back, stretching out the kinks and knots that had clustered about her spine for the last two days. Then spread her arms wide, revelling in it. 'Ahhhh.' What a lovely relief.

Marky Bishop's grin bordered on the obscene as he winked at his henchman. 'And to think, you said we couldn't trust her.'

'Still don't.'

As if she hadn't just *proven* she was one of the team.

There was no pleasing some people.

Victoria pulled the edges of the plastic sheeting in from the wall, using them to make a loose parcel around DC Reekie's body. Taking care to ensure that none of the blood leaked out onto the carpet. It wouldn't do to leave any evidence, after all. This was one crime scene Forensics wouldn't be going over with DNA swabs and fingerprint powder.

Marky rubbed his gnarled old-man hands together. 'She found the last piece of our puzzle, Razors.' He pointed a finger that bent outwards at the second joint. 'She killed the wee loon for us.'

She plucked a roll of masking tape from the stepladder and its collection of decorating materials. 'Last piece? What about Rupert Fraser?'

Razors sniffed. 'Don't you worry your pretty little head about him, hen. Threw the old bastard a farewell party this afternoon. He was *very* moved. Went all to pieces, like.' The leer that followed made clear exactly what that meant.

'What about Caroline Manson? You throw her a party as well?'

'Eh?' Pulling his chin in, setting the scar tissue wrinkling up the side of his face. 'Never touched the soppy cow.' Razors waved a hand at her efforts. 'And what the hell are you doing? That's no' how you wrap a body! Are you retarded?'

You know what? There was only so much misogynistic, patronizing, ignorant nonsense one person could take.

She tossed the masking tape over to the body and squared her shoulders. 'You looking for a stiff kicking, "Paul"?' Putting a bit of menace in her voice. 'Because I'd be happy to help.'

He flicked out his cut-throat's blade. 'I've coughed up scarier things than you.'

Perhaps it was time to put that to the test?

Victoria stuck her chin out, clenched both fists and stepped forwards. 'Soon as you like, old man.'

'Oh aye?' He licked his leathery lips. 'How 'bout now? How 'bout I—'

'THE PAIR OF YOU: *BEHAVE*!' Marky trembled in his wheelchair, dark pink flushing his cheeks, eyes bulging as he rocked back and forward, gasping and rattling. He grabbed his oxygen mask with a shaky hand and clasped it to his mouth. Shuddering as he hauled in tortured breath after tortured breath.

Razors kept glaring, as if that was impressing anyone.

Eventually Marky surfaced with a wheeze. 'Razors, stop being . . . a sexist prick. Bigtoria . . . stop being such a touchy cow. Don't care if . . . if it *is* your time of the month; we're a team.'

Who on earth did this wizened old . . . fart of a man think he was calling 'Bigtoria'?

And what bloody right did he have to speak to her that way?

Her '*time of the month*'?

Oh, Razors wasn't the only one in need of a stiff kicking . . .

But if she did that, she'd never get hold of the loot. Not even a quarter-share.

The silence built.

She didn't move.

Then Razors lowered his eyes and shuffled his horrible naked feet on the ugly carpet. More *importantly*, he folded the blade back into its handle.

Fair enough, then.

She'd bide her time.

Victoria stepped back and let her fists relax into hands again.

Marky glared at them. 'You can kill each other . . . when I say you can . . . Not before.' He took another deep draught of air from the oxygen mask. 'Black Joe Ivanson: I want him.'

Razors put his cut-throat away. 'You want him *here*, or you want him seen to?'

Marky looked at Victoria. 'You got a vehicle?'

'No.' She returned to DC Reekie's body, using the masking tape to secure the joins – laying it on thick to keep anything inside from dribbling out.

Razors pointed. 'This pair of tits were on foot.'

Another layer of tape secured the sagging bag of plastic that enshrouded DC Reekie's head. 'Sergeant Farrow's got the Big Car. But doubt it's going anywhere in this weather.'

Not given how deep the snow was already.

'Bastard . . .' Marky's eyebrows dipped and he chewed on his top lip for a beat or two. 'Can't bring him here: too much   forensic risk as it is.' Taking a pointed look at the body. 'We'll have to go to him.'

'Come on, Marky! Big Man, *no*. You're no' going anywhere. You're staying here in the warm and—'

'Don't be an arse.' He levered himself upright, hissing and grunting all the way, as if it were a complicated thing to get out of a wheelchair, until he was standing hunched over beside it. 'Fit as a sodding fiddle, me.'

He didn't look it.

He looked like a wizened old man, slowly making his inevitable journey towards the grave.

'This is daft, Marky, you're no'—'

'Aye, I *am*.' He waved a hand at Victoria. 'Get rid of that.'

Oh no.

She drew herself up to full height, glaring down at both of them. 'If you think I'm letting the pair of you go carve your secrets out of Black Joe Ivanson without me, you're dafter than you look.'

'We've got an *agreement*, remember?'

Victoria laughed, rich and loud, a proper thigh-slapper. 'I don't *trust* you.'

He stood there, in silence, watching until she'd finished. 'Don't care if you do or not . . . Bigtoria; long as I'm . . . in charge, you'll do as you're told.' That bent finger of his came up again to jab at the plastic-wrapped remains. 'Now, get rid of that.'

She gritted her teeth.

Bit back the reply.

Because sooner or later, Marky Bishop would find out just how unwise it was to be on her shit list.

Razors helped him into the wheelchair, and pushed him from the room, followed by the slow-motion electric moan of the stairlift, returning Marky to the first floor. Where, no doubt, Razors would dress him in suitable outdoor attire for their trip to Black Joe Ivanson's.

Which meant she probably *just* had time to ditch DC Reekie and hurry over to Ivanson House before they arrived.

Right . . .

Victoria scooped up the body in its plastic cocoon, hefted it over her shoulder like a sack of tatties, and marched into the hall, barging through the front door and out into the endless snow.

She slipped the master key into the back-door lock, turned it, and shoved her way into the gloom-smothered kitchen.

It could stay gloom-smothered too, because she wasn't turning the lights on.

A pale-blue haze bounced off the snow outside, filtering in through the open door and the window, robbing all colour from the small room. Old-fashioned but serviceable. A mammalian pelt of furry dust covered every horizontal surface, spiders' webs bulking out the corners and hanging from the light fittings.

The smell wasn't particularly pleasant, either. A sharp malt-vinegar-and-raw-sewage stench that tainted the air with its dark-brown tang.

Palm-sized chunks of snow tumbled from her wellington boots, slapping onto the cheap tiles, making mini-icebergs.

It wouldn't have been so deep if she'd come in around the front, but then someone might have seen her lumbering up the street with a plastic-wrapped body thrown over one shoulder. There'd been no witnesses so far, and that was how it was staying.

She strode across the kitchen and out into a narrow hallway with four doors leading off it. The first opened on a living room; the next: a small bedroom, just big enough for a double divan, a wardrobe, and more dust; but the third one she tried led into an even smaller bedroom, with a single bed against the wall beneath the window.

Pauline Thomson hadn't bothered to strip the beds when she moved in with Kerry Millbrae. Maybe she'd thought it wouldn't last, and wanted somewhere to escape to, just in case? A bolthole against disappointment and heartache.

It *hadn't* lasted, of course. Marky Bishop and Razors Richards had seen to that.

Still, this was as good a place as any.

Victoria dumped her burden on the bed, the springs groaning and complaining as DC Reekie's weight crashed down – sending up a *whoomph* of dust that filled the air with its gritty scent.

At least no one would find him here. Not that anyone would be looking.

She checked her watch. Then scowled at the body. 'If I'm late because of *you*, and they've killed Black Joe Ivanson before I get there . . .'

Well, that didn't bear thinking about.

She charged through the falling snow, knees pumping, elbows too, not slowing down for the drifts – sending up gouts of sparkling grey to glimmer in the dimmed streetlights. The cold air roared in her throat, burning in her lungs, legs aching as she ran up Brindle Lane.

Victoria skidded to a halt outside Ivanson House, breath hammering out in great chest-racking clouds. The houses on either side were in darkness, but a faint glow seeped out through an upstairs window.

Difficult to tell if anyone else had been here, given the gouged trails she and DC Reekie had left on their last visit, but there was no sign of any wheelchair tracks.

Which meant she'd got here first.

Oh, thank goodness for that . . .

She sagged forwards, grabbing her knees and breathing hard. Coughing as if her lungs were trying to escape. Then spitting out a gobbet of yuck into the snow.

'Fusty . . . old bastard . . . must've slowed . . . slowed them up.'

All those years playing rugby hadn't been for nothing.

She released one knee, curled her fist, and held it aloft. 'Go Team . . . Go Team Victoria.' Another bout of coughing. 'Argh . . .'

Finally, her lungs agreed to stay where they were and she straightened up. Then scuffed her way through the fresh snow to the front door and tried the handle.

It wasn't locked.

Three Yales, and none of them were locked. And Black Joe Ivanson had made a big show of locking every single one when he'd slammed the door in her face.

This was *not* a good sign . . .

She pushed the door open and stepped into the stripped-bare hallway.

Then froze as two voices sounded on the other side of the bedroom door: a nasal Glaswegian and a wheezy old man.

Razors Richards and Marky Bishop.

She hadn't got here first.

But *maybe* she wasn't too late.

She grabbed the handle and barged through the door.

Then froze again.

Christ . . .

Twenty-Five

The only furniture in here was the mattress on the warped floor-boards. Duvet and pillows thrown into the corner. Bare walls, their orange-pink plasterwork patched with white Polyfilla; the single light fitting dangling from its wire, its naked bulb only just bright enough to reveal the tableau. No curtains to shut out the funereal glow of the snow-covered garden, but a small CD player sat on the windowsill, burbling out cheerful ceilidh music.

Marky was sitting on the camping chair – last seen in the living room – suckling away on his oxygen mask as though it were the teat of a huge hissing beast. Skin pale and loose on his skeletal head. Looking closer to death than ever.

But not as close as Black Joe Ivanson.

He lay on his back, stripped down to a pair of faded-blue Y-fronts, the white hairs on his chest stained a darker shade of red. Somehow, they'd tied his wrists and ankles to the corners of the mattress, holding him spreadeagled as Razors had gone to work. Leaving a mess of blood and cuts and bruises and agony behind.

A thick length of rope was wrapped around his throat, pulled tight enough to make all the tendons stick out on the flushed skin. Teeth bared, scarlet spittle bubbling up between them; head jerking up and down; one eye socket nothing more than a leaking ragged hole.

The butcher's-shop stench of raw meat enveloped her, every breath tasting of cold iron and warm copper.

Razors whistled along to a jaunty Eightsome Reel as he placed a gloved hand on Ivanson's forehead and forced it down against the mattress. Then dug his cut-throat's blade deep into the poor bastard's one remaining eye. Twisting it left and right, scraping around the socket's edges as Ivanson's body bucked and writhed.

The only sound that made it out past the garrotte was a muffled, strangled gurgle.

Victoria hauled in her first breath since opening the door, then whispered it out again. 'For *fuck's* sake . . .'

Marky reached up with a shaky hand and pulled the mask away from his mouth, exposing a thin smile. 'You're late. Missed all the fun.'

'How did . . . ?' Unable to rip her gaze from Ivanson's blood-smeared, tortured face. 'Was . . . ? How . . . ?'

Razors slid his blade free with a wet *schloppp* that made the chorizoburger curdle in Victoria's stomach.

He wiped it clean on the duvet. 'What you doing here? You were *told* to ditch that dead cop.'

On the mattress, Ivanson's chest heaved once, twice, three times – his arms and legs trembling as every muscle in his body contracted . . . then he sagged back and his final breath hissed out in a froth of deep dark red.

It was as if the lights in the room had dimmed even further, stealing the last of the warmth with it.

Victoria swallowed. And finally managed to look away. 'Did he . . . ?'

'Course he did, hen. The buggers always do' – he held up the cut-throat, making the now-clean blade glint – 'when *Mortimer* comes out to play.' He patted the body's shoulder. 'Aye, Black Joe was a tough old bastard, but we got there in the end.'

This wasn't . . .

How was she supposed to . . .

She blinked.

Swallowed the bitter metal taste.

Gave herself a shake as Marky looked up at her.

'What did you do with the wee boy?'

Force it down. You can do this.

She put a bit of steel back in her voice. 'Don't worry: his body's in a safe place.'

Marky took a hit of oxygen. 'No, no, no, no, no. You didn't like it when *Razors* said that, so why should I?' His tone darkened. 'Now: where – is – the – boy?'

Victoria pulled her chin up. Time to take charge again. 'Stashed him.'

'No. You *bury* a body. You *burn* a body. You wrap it up with chicken wire and stones and dump it in the *North Sea*. You *don't* leave it lying about for people to find. Especially when it's a police officer!'

Razors creaked his way to his feet. 'See, that's the trouble getting into bed with amateurs, man.' Pointing at her with his blade. 'It's morons like her that get you caught.'

Come on: losing this.

She stuck her chest out and put on a proper growl. 'That kicking's still on offer, "Paul".'

'Think you scare me, hen?' Gesturing at Black Joe Ivanson's tormented remains. 'Think *you* scare *me*?'

He was a little old man; that cut-throat would be easy enough to take off him. Block with her left, open-palm strike to the nose, grab the wrist, break the arm.

She bent her knees, lowering the centre of gravity. Ready. 'Get fucked.'

'Spoken like a true dyke.'

Her jaw clenched. '*What* did you call me?'

He crept closer, 'Mortimer' weaving from side to side in a shining figure eight. 'You heard me, *dyke*.' Clearing the edge of the mattress. 'You're a stupid amateur dyke. You wouldnae know how to hide a body if your life depended on it.' The cut-throat slashed through the air – nowhere near close enough to catch anything – then returned to its glittering dance. 'And believe me, hen, your life *does*.'

Sod open-palm strikes, this Neanderthal bastard could have the full fist. 'I don't need lessons from some *baldy*-headed, *limp*-dicked old fud!'

Spittle arced in the gloom as his eyes bugged. 'NOBODY SPEAKS TO ME LIKE THAT!'

Marky's voice barked out through the metallic air. 'Oh, for Christ's sake, will the pair of you GROW UP!' The effort left him slumped over and wheezing into his oxygen mask. Shoulders trembling like Ivanson on his deathbed.

Pink flushed Razors' cheeks and he lowered Mortimer.

Victoria unclenched her fists.

They both took a step back as Marky fought for every breath he could gasp from the oxygen tank. Finally, his breathing settled and he surfaced. A drowning man, returned to dry land. 'Pair of *children*. We're done, understand? . . . We've got . . .' – pointing at the bloodied body – 'we've got everything we need. Now all we have to do is . . . sit out the snow . . . Soon as the road's passable, we're gone.' His lips twitched up in a tired smile. 'Sand, sea, surf, and more money than you'll see in a lifetime.'

The adrenaline still buzzed through Victoria's veins, making the blood *whoosh-whump* in her ears. Making her stand just that bit taller. Making everything sharp and hard. 'I need more than vague promises from a dying man.'

'Fine.' He took another swig of oxygen. 'HMP Grampian, three years ago, and there's this warty old grandad comes onto the wing. Transferred up from Glenochil, on account of him chibbing an ex-copper in the exercise yard. Only it turns out this warty old grandad is Big Craig McPherson.'

Marky paused, eyebrows raised, as if he expected that to be met with a gasp of surprise and recognition.

Well, he'd come to the wrong place.

Never heard of the man.

A disappointed sigh rattled from Marky's mouth. 'God's sake. Big Craig *McPherson*? He was the brains behind a dozen bank jobs! Man's a legend.'

She shrugged. 'New to me.'

'That's cos he was clever. Careful. Very fond of his wee tricks and games: like not letting anyone use their real names. Masks and gloves to be worn at all times – aye, even when they weren't robbing. Everything hidden behind codewords . . . He was the only one knew who the whole team was.' Marky shook his head. 'If it hadn't been for a schemie tosser from Birmingham turning Queen's evidence . . . you bastards would never've laid a hand on him . . . Anyway: Big Craig was the man who organized . . . that Fraserburgh Clydesdale Bank job . . . Now I'd heard *tales* of what they made off with – never believed them, though . . . not till Big Craig McPherson told me the truth.'

Marky took his time, sipping on his oxygen as if it were a fine wine. 'Of course, the good stuff was too hot to shift for at least a decade, so he and his seven-man team sign . . . the pledge: each gets a piece of the puzzle, you know, like a treasure map, and they don't touch the loot till it's cooled down.'

A snort burst free. 'What a load of old *bollocks*.'

'Hoy!' Razors squared his shoulders again. 'You take care.'

'Oh, come on!' She threw her arms wide. 'It wasn't a decade ago, it was *twenty-six* years. And they haven't touched their magnificent haul in all that time?' Victoria turned back to Marky. '*How?* How'd they keep it a secret this long? Why not just spend it all?'

'Cos they were scared, my dear Detective Inspector. Scared of what they'd got their sticky little fingers on. They lacked vision. They lacked *balls*.' Another languid oxygen breath. 'Course, Big Craig McPherson had a *terrible* accident, moments after I "encouraged" him to share his bit of the secret.' A bony shrug raised Marky's skeletal shoulders. 'Just a shame his poor heart was weaker than I'd thought. If I'd known it'd conk out, I would've . . . gone easier on the old fart, and maybe he'd've lived long enough to name his whole team. Still, it gave me a hobby, didn't it? . . . Something to fill my days – working . . . on my wee treasure hunt.' That monologue must've taken it out of Marky, because he sounded increasingly breathless as he waved a wobbly hand at the bedroom-come-abattoir. 'And here we are . . . all done. The last piece . . . slotted into place.'

'And we're just supposed to believe you, are we?'

The hand flopped back down into Marky's lap and he drooped slightly. 'Don't worry, Bigtoria . . . I keep my promises. I said you'd be in for a quarter . . . you're in for a quarter. Soon as . . . soon as we're on that . . . fishing boat for Norway . . . you're golden.' This time the oxygen wasn't sipped, it was gulped. His voice echoed inside the mask as he gestured to Razors. 'It's . . . it's late, and . . . I'm tired . . . Take me . . . home.'

Razors put Mortimer away, then helped Marky to his shaky feet. 'Come on, Big Man.'

'Three of us here . . . Forensics . . . DNA. Soon as . . . police arrive. Going . . . to ask questions.'

And he'd only just realized that?

Not quite the master criminal he liked to believe. Or perhaps all that palliative-care medicine had blunted the old sod's killer instinct?

Razors zipped up Marky's coat, fussing to make sure he was tucked in, cosy and warm. 'Aye, very true. But don't you worry, Big Man, I can sort that, no problem.' Then he helped Marky shuffle from the room.

Victoria stayed where she was, eyes drawn back to what they'd left of Joseph 'Black Joe' Ivanson. Breath catching in her throat, as if it were made of greasepaint and sealing wax.

It was one thing, seeing bodies like this, after the fact. When they were on the cutting table in a stainless-steel mortuary. Or at a crime scene, with the yellow-and-black 'DO NOT CROSS' tape rippling behind her and someone on hand to take photos and DNA. When everything was sanitized by procedure and protocol. But to stand there and *watch* it happen . . .

Watch someone's life torn from their body by unimaginable pain.

See their whole frame twist and writhe and convulse as the blood—

Razors' voice echoed in from the hallway. 'Better shift it, hen. Going to get *very* hot in there in a mintie.'

She pulled out her phone.

Took three quick photographs.

Then got out of there fast.

Twenty-Six

A warm orange glow flickered through the gaps in the curtains as the fire in Ivanson House spread. Smoke swirled out of a dormer window – opened for that very reason – disappearing up into the ink-dark sky.

Soon the sticky-sweet scent of rendering fat would join it.

Victoria kept her eyes on the building, watching as the flames took hold. 'Why didn't you burn Pauline Thomson's body?'

A sniff, then a sneeze burst out of Razors, followed by a honk in a handkerchief and more sniffing. 'Cos I'm no' a monster, you blood-thirsty bitch.' He stuck out both hands, warming them on the blaze. 'Kerry Millbrae's suffered enough without me setting fire to her house. Poor cow's ninety-five percent scars as it is.'

The smoke became darker, thick and greasy against the heavy, snow-swirling sky.

She cleared her throat. 'What about the other houses?'

'Nah.' He pointed left. 'You got a murdering rapist on *that* side.' Pointed right. 'And an ex-MP sex offender over here. No bugger's gonnae miss either of them.'

Marky's face didn't look healthy at the best of times, but the light emanating from Ivanson House gave his features an oily, jaundiced glow. He was only just upright, leaning heavily on his horrible companion's shoulder. 'I want . . . the boy's body . . . buried tomorrow morning.' A tote of oxygen hissed through the mask, and he stood there, wheezing it in, eyes closed. 'One fire . . . one fire a night's . . . probably enough . . . to be getting on with.'

You wouldn't think an empty house would go up so quickly. Maybe the wooden floorboards were a lot more flammable than they looked? Or the thin slats of birch woven through the lath-and-plaster walls. Or maybe Razors was just a really good arsonist?

Whatever the reason, the flames were spreading fast.

Ivanson House was like Ivanson's corpse – mesmerizing. She could barely tear her eyes from the growing blaze. 'It doesn't matter what they did, we should still tell the neighbours. Chap on their doors: give them a chance to—'

'Razors will keep an eye on you tomorrow, Bigtoria. Make sure there's no . . . complications. Won't you, Razors?'

'Oh aye. A *real* close eye.'

She blinked, breaking the fire's spell. 'I don't need a babysitter.'

'You'll get one, hen, and like it.'

This again.

Victoria turned, squaring up to the vicious little git. 'Pucker up and kiss my—'

A jaunty rendition of that circus tune jingled deep in the pocket of her high-vis. She pulled out the child's walkie-talkie as Farrow's voice crackled free from the clown's open mouth.

'*Golf Foxtrot Four to Alpha Charlie One, safe to talk?*'

She let Razors marinate in the full force of her glare for a beat, or three, then pressed the clown's nose. 'Go ahead.'

'*I'm on Farrier's Lane, Guv. Are you outside? Are you seeing this? Looks like another fire!*'

'Hold on.' She eyed Marky – standing there, *hissssssss*ing and *whooommmmmph*ing breaths in and out of his oxygen mask. 'I can see it now.'

'*Sodding heck. We're going to need the Fire Engine Team out again . . .*' A pause. '*Fudge! I forgot: Ian's watching Kerry Millbrae's place – we can't pull him from that. What if our arsonist hits there next?*'

The light was flickering in the dormer windows, which meant the flames had either travelled up the stairs or through the ceiling from the floor below.

'*Guv, you're closer to Sanctuary House than we are – can you get there*' *and raise the alarm? There's a secondary team: Helen and Aggie. Tell them we've got a code black!'*

Only she wasn't closer, was she: she was all the way over here, on the west side of Glenfarach, when she should've been on the east. If it hadn't been for Joseph Ivanson . . .

Marky lowered his oxygen mask and nodded at Victoria, mouthing the words 'Yes. I will!' in exaggerated silence.

Which was probably just his way of getting rid of her, but what choice did she have?

She pressed the clown's nose again. 'Roger that.'

'Thanks, Guv. Be there soon as we can. Out.'

Marky patted her on the arm, as if she were a well-behaved poodle. 'Good girl. And make sure you take your time. Don't want them putting anything out . . . till every last bit of forensics is gone.' He gripped Razors. 'Come on, the rozzers are coming. We need to go.'

'Aye, let's get you home.' He turned and helped the old git shamble away through the snow – following the path Victoria had forged when she'd dashed over here.

Speed they were going, it would be next Thursday by the time they got back there.

Razors glanced over his shoulder. 'Don't forget, hen: first thing tomorrow, you and me get rid of the wee dead boy.' A smile. 'Don't make me come get you, but.'

As if that scared her.

Black Joe Ivanson, shuddering and thrashing, screams strangled by the rope tourniquet around his throat, as Razors drove Mortimer's blade into his one remaining eye.

He was just a little old man.

The blood welling up in that tortured socket, streaming down the side of his face, soaking into those ridiculous dundreary whiskers, dribbling into the mattress and spreading like poppies.

She could take him with one hand tied behind her back and the other in a plastic bag.

Trembling arms and legs, convulsing as the last agonized gasp tore free from his bloodied mouth . . .

Didn't scare her in the least.

She huffed out a wobbly breath, watching as they lumbered away down Brindle Lane.

Show a little backbone, for God's sake.

Victoria made a loudhailer from her cupped hands. 'And you better not do a runner in the night. I want my twenty-five percent!'

Marky's gravelly voice came wafting back through the tumbling snow. 'Good things come to those who wait.'

And they disappeared around the corner, onto West Main Street.

Jesus . . .

She sagged.

Scrubbed a hand across her face.

Gave herself a shake.

Better go rouse the fire team.

But she had something to take care of first.

Victoria hammered on the pervert MP's door. 'YOU IN THERE! GET OUT YOUR BLOODY BED, DON'T YOU KNOW THE HOUSE IS ON FIRE?' Then did the same with the murdering rapist. 'FIRE! GET UP! COME ON, OUT OF THERE!'

The lights flickered on in both houses.

Good enough.

She waded through the unbroken snow, making for North Street. With any luck she'd be long gone before Farrow or the idiot Harlaw arrived.

Because there was no way in hell they could *ever* find out what had happened here tonight.

Twenty-Seven

Ow. Ow. Ow.

Stitch . . .

Victoria staggered her way onto Brindle Lane again, face hot and damp, breath grating out of her throat in huge grey gusts. Sweaty. Tired. Aching. One hand clutching the ribs on her left side, trying to squeeze the pain away through her high-vis.

Ivanson House was ablaze, flames raging in all the broken windows, black smoke belching out – coiling upwards like a vast, venomous snake, impervious to the blizzard. The inferno hadn't restricted itself to the one property either – it had spread to its two terraced neighbours. Creeping along the rafters, probably, sneaking into the adjoining loft conversions. Spreading the misery.

Had to hand it to Razors: when he set fire to somewhere it *burned*.

The half-light lampposts cast their wretched glow across the narrow street, no longer able to compete with the burning spotlight of Ivanson House, but providing a pseudo-safe haven for the residents of Brindle Lane to gather beneath and watch their lives be devoured.

PC Harlaw was stopping them from going back into their homes, presumably to rescue whatever tat they'd collected over the years – standing there with his arms outstretched. 'Come on, guys, you *know* it's not safe.'

And right on cue something collapsed in Ivanson House, a crackling boom reverberating out as the last remaining windows shattered and a thick gout of flame scoured the front of the building.

Farrow flinched back from the surge of heat, one arm up, shielding her face.

There was no point arousing suspicion, so Victoria slipped off her high-vis, slinging it over her shoulder with care – making sure that the bloodstained sleeve was hidden in the folds of reflective yellow. Then limped over. Every breath whooping out and rattling in. Sweat soaking through the underband of her bra to trickle down her sides. 'Everyone get out OK?'

The sergeant nodded. 'Where's the . . .' She frowned. 'Are you not cold?'

Victoria undid another button on her shirt, giving the material a shoogle. 'After running all the way to Sanctuary House and back? Plus this?' Pointing at the blaze. 'Sodding boiling.'

That seemed to do the trick.

'Fire engine's on its way, though, right?'

'They have to dig it out. Don't know when it'll get here.' Which would please Marky Bishop.

'Fudging heck!' Farrow glared at the blaze, flickering light chasing shadows around her features.

Another crashing bang and a chunk of Ivanson House's roof caved in. It was spreading through the other two houses much faster now, but then they had more to burn. Doubt anything was going to survive beyond the outer walls at this rate.

Farrow pointed at the residents – pervert MP, and murdering rapist. 'What am I supposed to do with this pair?'

'Urgh . . .' Victoria bent over, holding herself up by grabbing both knees and locking her arms. Back heaving as she wheezed. 'Stick them in the hotel's dining room, stick them in the library, or stick them in the cells: don't care which.'

'You OK?'

A bitter laugh barked out. 'Been a bloody long day. It's . . .'

The streetlights' half-hearted glow dipped even further, accompanied by a wasp-edged buzzing noise that faded away, as the LEDs dimmed, and dimmed, and dimmed.

Then died.

Now the only light came from the burning houses.

Everyone stared at the lampposts, but *this time* they didn't sputter on again.

The fire roared and crackled.

Smoke belched into the dark sky, underlit by the flames.

The snow fell, circling that column of hot rising air.

And still the lights stayed off.

Victoria took a deep breath and shoved herself upright. 'Well, that's just great.' She pointed at the blaze. 'Can you deal with this?'

Farrow bared her teeth. 'Guv?'

'Because I'm going to go lie down – before I fall down.' Her hand dug into her high-vis, coming out with the clown's-head walkie-talkie. 'Only if it's an emergency.'

'Sorry?' Farrow blinked at her, then at the burning houses for a moment or three. 'This *isn't* an emergency?'

'From what I can tell, it's an average bloody weekday.'

Victoria slumped her way into Thomson Cottage, one hand over her mouth to cover the yawn as she kicked the door shut with the heel of her wellington boot.

Then locked it.

Because Glenfarach wasn't exactly what you would call a 'safe environment'. And who knew what the neighbours had been up to.

Well, there was a simple way to *tell* what they'd been up to – she had a list in her jacket pocket, after all – but sleep would probably come more easily if she didn't look.

It took three steps down the hall before the niggling voice in the back of her head made her return to the front door and stick the key in the lock again. Twisting it a half-turn to ensure no one else could unlock it, or pick the damn thing.

Another yawn juddered its way through her, and she reached for the light switch, flicking it up and down three times before the fact it wasn't going to work filtered through the hot cotton wool currently masquerading as her brain.

The – power – was – out.

'God's sake . . . I *hate* Glenfarach.' She levered off her borrowed wellingtons, then padded her way to Pauline Thomson's bedroom on sweaty-stockinged feet, leaving damp footprints behind.

It wasn't really big enough for the queen-sized divan; two bedside cabinets; and heavy, dark-wood wardrobe that had been squeezed in here, but at least the bed was still made. Even if the duvet cover had far too many horses on it to belong to anyone over the age of twelve.

It would probably be a good idea to find some clean sheets, pillowcases, and a duvet cover for adults, but . . . nah.

Victoria timbered down onto the bed, creating a small cloud of gritty grey particles that hung in the air like her own personal fogbank. Another yawn tasted of burnt plastic and faded white pepper. Could sleep for a year.

She plucked a framed photograph from the bedside cabinet: Pauline Thomson and Kerry Millbrae, enjoying a picnic somewhere, surrounded by sunshine, daisies, and buttercups. The town library just out of focus in the background.

Kerry was wearing a vest top, exposing the scar tissue that twisted its way up her arms and across her shoulders, then up her neck and face, disappearing under a wavy auburn wig. Pauline had a T-shirt on, featuring four portraits of Sandi Toksvig in the style of Warhol's Monroe screen-prints.

They looked happy, Kerry and Pauline, as if life had finally smiled on them. As if their Happily Ever After was guaranteed.

Victoria turned the photo face down.

In Glenfarach *no one* got a Happily Ever After.

She groaned her way over onto her back and sagged into the duvet. 'What a day . . .'

Hold on.

Another groan rattled free and she covered her eyes with both palms, fingers squeezing her forehead as if it were about to explode. First thing tomorrow morning, before the curfew was even lifted, she had to carry DC Edward Bloody Reekie's body out into the middle of nowhere and bury it under the watchful beady eye of Paul 'Razors' Richards.

Why did crap like this *always* have to happen to her?

Twenty-Eight

Victoria hefted the last shovel of dirt onto the filled-in grave, then topped it off with a layer of snow. Just enough to hide it should anyone happen by.

Not that anyone would.

It had taken half an hour of slogging through the sodding forest, with DC Reekie's body thrown over her shoulder, to get here. A secluded glade in the woods, with a burn gurgling its way between the snow-covered grass and bushes. Knife-blade icicles hanging from rocks bordering the water. Crystals of ice furring the twisted skein of dying brambles and slumping mounds of long-dead bracken.

Would be quite peaceful, if it weren't for all the digging.

She chucked the spade to one side and stood, hands on her hips, head thrown back, breath making delicate plumes of white in the thin morning light.

No sign of the sun, but there was a glow to the heavy grey clouds that probably counted.

Fat icy flakes of snow settled on her skin, melting away as steam rose from her bare arms and new secret-agent-cat T-shirt.

Still, couldn't hang about here all day: there were things to be getting on with.

She crumped through the drifts to the branch and got back into her petrol-blue shirt and jacket. Which didn't seem *quite* as nice as they had last night in the second-hand store. Should've carried on looking till she found something a bit classier, better quality. Shoplifter's remorse.

Ah well. Too late to worry about that now.

She grabbed the pick and the shovel, throwing one over each shoulder as she forged her way up the slope again. Shame she couldn't have kept the high-vis. Probably get colder on the long trudge back to town, but at least the aftermath of all that digging would keep her warm for a bit.

A glint of light sparkled from the brow of the hill.

Victoria narrowed her eyes.

There he was: Razors. Standing watch over her. Making sure she didn't mess this up.

As if.

His figure became clearer the further she climbed: the crooked shape of a skeletal old man, wearing a dark-green parka jacket with a rabbit-fur collar. Tweed bunnet. Navy waterproof trousers. Thick padded ski gloves: one clutching that teddy-bear walkie-talkie, the other holding a pair of binoculars to his eyes as he followed her progress.

He was still gazing through the bloody things as she drew level, even though he was less than a dozen feet away. Idiot.

She waded past him and kept going.

He fell in beside her. 'Your gravedigging is shite, by the way.'

Nope. Not rising to it.

He let the binoculars dangle around his neck. 'You have to *cut the buggers up* before you bury them. And you don't do it all in the same place either . . .'

Some people were just in love with the sound of their own voice. And it was always the ones with the least to say.

Victoria upped the pace, leaving him behind.

'Hoy, I'm talking to you!'

Good for you.

Still, it would be rude not to *acknowledge* his presence. She didn't stop, but she *did* lower the pickaxe, swinging the shovel sideways so it rested across both shoulders, meaning he had a good view of her right hand as she raised the middle finger in his direction.

That circus theme tune jingled out from her pocket.

She ignored it and kept on wading through the snow. Heading back towards town.

Razors' Weegie accent blared out from the depths of Victoria's second-hand jacket. *'You think I left Rupert Fraser in a shallow grave, but? Naw, hen: he's in pieces.'*

OK. She dug out the walkie-talkie after all.

'Cos I know what I'm doing. Cos I'm no' a—'

She pressed the clown's nose, silencing him, and raised her voice loud enough that it didn't *need* a walkie-talkie to carry, clear as a bell, to the old bastard's oversized ears. 'FEEL FREE TO GO FUCK YOURSELF!'

Then she switched the radio off, stuffed it back in her pocket, and continued on her way. 'Should never, *ever* have agreed to this, complete and utter load of bloody' – hauling in a deep breath for the grand finale – 'AAAAAAAAAAAAAAAAAAAARGH!'

—take a deep breath—

(it may be your last)

29

The snowplough's engine growls like a broken Wurlitzer, blowers bellowing, windscreen wipers fighting a losing battle with the snow – howling sideways in near impenetrable sheets, flickering orange and white as the warning beacon and headlights fight for supremacy.

A curling bow wave of gritty white erupts before the plough's blade, flung aside as it powers on. Shame visibility's less than a dozen feet, especially given the speed the thing's going.

It isn't one of the modern, neon-yellow snowploughs with a fancy gritting hopper built in, it's some sort of converted truck. At least thirty years old, if the layer of dust clarting the dashboard is anything to go by. The interior's tatty too, the black vinyl peeling off the steering wheel, both seats Frankensteined together with silver duct tape. Sweet wrappers rolling about in the footwell.

To be honest, the only non-ancient bit about it is the tiger's-head walkie-talkie attached to the driver's-side sun visor. A cheery, smiling face amidst the dust and grime.

Though, given everything that's been going on, it's not the strangest thing about the snowplough.

No, the *strangest* thing is who's driving it.

I never really wanted to be a police officer, but it's kinda too late to worry about that now. Things have moved on a bit . . .

*

Edward looks like crap – covered in dirt and scrapes – and his high-vis is torn around the shoulders, letting the white kapok stuffing poke out in a fuzzy pale-grey prolapse.

Dark-red smears stain the jacket's chest, muting the fluorescent-yellow fabric, making it smell of hot batteries. Which doesn't really go with the roasting dust belching out of the blowers at full force.

Blood stains his top lip too, but at least it's stopped dripping off his chin. His nose is maybe a bit less straight than it used to be. Scrapes and bruises run rampant across his cheeks and forehead. And his nice new Armani suit is all torn around the collar.

Now you're probably wondering why I'm still here and not a lot more on the dead side. You know: what with the shallow grave and everything.

Edward hauls the wheel right and the snowplough swings, wallowing like a boat, jolting as it bumps over something hidden beneath the snow. Hopefully not a person. But given the way things have been going in Glenfarach for the last three days, it's anyone's guess.

And the stabbing, of course – mustn't forget about that. Oh, and the strangling. But mostly the shallow grave, right?

A vague shape materializes up ahead, swimming in and out of view as the blizzard hurls sheets of flickering orange and white flakes to snarl against the windscreen and the wipers struggle to catch up.

The shape resolves into a thick grey line with a bulky square behind it, topped with a spire that disappears into the low birling cloud. Growing ever larger as the snowplough speeds towards it.

Well, it's a long story . . .

Thirty

Thomson Cottage, 01:30 (last night)

Victoria dumped her burden on the bed, the springs groaning and complaining as DC Reekie's weight crashed down – sending up a *whoomph* of dust that filled the air with its gritty scent.

At least no one would find him here. Not that anyone would be looking.

She checked her watch. Then scowled at the body. 'If I'm late because of *you*, and they've killed Black Joe Ivanson before I get there . . .'

Well, that didn't bear thinking about.

She dug her fingernails into the plastic covering DC Reekie's face – fogged up after the death march through the snow all the way over here from Bishop House – and tore it open with one sharp tug.

His skin was pale and smeared with deep-dark red. No motion. No sign of life.

Please, not this. Not after everything she'd been through . . .

And she'd been *careful*. She'd left plenty of gaps and air holes when she'd wrapped him up, even though Razors was standing there moaning on about what a crap job she was doing.

But . . .

What if she hadn't been *quite* as careful as she'd hoped? What if

DC Reekie had suffocated on the way over here? What if he really *was* dead?

'Don't you bloody dare.'

Hauling back a hand, she took aim, then lashed out – catching him full on the cheek, snapping his head to the side as the slap reverberated around the horrible little room. Well, what was the point of pussying about?

DC Reekie's eyes sprang open, then his face whipped around till he was staring straight at her, jaws gaping, as breath roared in his throat, the sharp, leading edge of a scream just making it past his lips before she clamped her hand over his mouth, trapping the rest of it inside.

'Will you shut up, you idiot? Do you want everyone to know you're not dead?'

30

What the actual, bloody, sodding, *fuck*-buggering hell?

Edward glared up at Bigtoria, looming overhead, with one of her big, calloused paws covering his mouth – forcing his head down into the plastic sheeting as fire and broken bottles scorched their way across his left cheek.

He hissed a deep breath in through his nose and howled it out again: 'YOU KILLED ME! YOU STABBED ME AND YOU KILLED ME!' But all that came out was an angry, incoherent mumble.

Something else was holding him down, not just the murderous scumbag masquerading as a detective inspector, something that held his arms tight to his chest and stopped his legs from moving.

'AAAAAAAAAAAAAARGH!'

Thrashing about, struggling to get free, but whatever the bloody stuff was it gripped him like . . .

God's sake – it was that bloody plastic sheeting from Mr Bishop's house.

'YOU STABBED ME!'

That must've got through, because she frowned. 'Of course I didn't stab you, you idiot.' Bigtoria's right hand dipped into a pocket and came out with the scary-looking hunting knife she'd rammed into his back. She held the point of the blade against her forearm, just above where her left hand was clamped over his mouth, and stabbed herself.

Only the blade didn't sink through the high-vis jacket and into the skin beneath: it retracted into the handle, sending a teeny squirt of scarlet out to splash against the fluorescent yellow sleeve.

She held the knife up again, twisting it in the gloom. 'It's not even metal.' Pushing it *sideways* against her arm this time, causing the whole blade to bend like a banana. 'Chromed rubber. Professional theatrical productions, remember?' Bigtoria released her makeshift gag and sat back. 'See?'

He stared.

Stared at her.

Stared at the knife that wasn't a knife.

Stared at the droplets of dark red dripping down her sleeve.

Stared at her again.

'But . . . It . . . You . . .'

'Fake blood. My own recipe. It's—'

'You stole that tomato sauce from the hotel, didn't you? I knew it!'

Of course – *now* it all made sense.

She must've pocketed it before the dessert arrived, slipped it into her high-vis when he wasn't looking.

'What?' She pulled her chin in, eyebrows pinched. 'No! Don't be ridiculous, ketchup's *nothing like* blood. How thick would you have to be if you saw a pool of ketchup and thought it was blood?' She curled her top lip. 'It doesn't even *smell* like blood. How could anyone possibly mistake it for blood?'

'All right, all right. That's not the—'

'Corn syrup; cornstarch; red, green, and blue food colouring; splash of water. Mix them in the proper quantities and you've got perfect stage blood.'

She huffed out a breath, shoulders rounding as she scrubbed a hand across her face. 'And yes, I've had to improvise a bit, but I wouldn't be doing that if DC Sodding Guthrie hadn't fallen down the stairs, pissed as a skunk.' Sagging back to grimace at the ceiling. 'This was all meant to be *so* straightforward: I "kill" Guthrie, Marky Bishop thinks I'm a bona fide bent cop, and I stick with him till we find out where those bloody safety-deposit boxes are.'

'Right.' Edward nodded – well, as best he could in the circumstances. 'That makes perfect sense.' Relaxing a little. 'Especially now you've *explained* everything.' Then thrashing about like a dying herring in his plastic cocoon. 'YOU COULD'VE SODDING TOLD ME YOU WERE GOING TO—'

She slapped her hand over his mouth again. 'I didn't know if you could be trusted. I didn't know if we were being watched. I didn't know if they had hidden microphones . . . or some other James Bond shite.'

It was a shame Bigtoria couldn't hear anything other than indignant muffled noises, because he had a lot of extremely rude words, phrases, and choice bits of anatomically challenging advice to share.

Eventually, he ran out of steam and sagged back into the bed.

She raised an eyebrow. 'Are we finished?'

He glared. Then closed his eyes and nodded.

She removed the five-fingered gag. 'Good.'

'How could . . .' Forced out through gritted teeth. 'I thought I was *dying*!'

Bigtoria waved that away. 'Simple Naked Reverse Choke Hold. Knocks you out for ten, maybe fifteen minutes tops. Very few people ever die from one.'

Very few?

'Is that supposed to be reassuring?'

'*And* I saved you from Razors, didn't I? He would've slit your throat. *If* you were lucky.'

That wasn't the point.

Well, maybe it was.

But only partially.

And she still could've bloody well told him what was going to happen.

How would *she* feel if he killed *her*, then brought her back to life in some crappy little bedroom that stank of mildew and . . . farts?

Bigtoria tore off a layer of the thick, clear plastic sheeting. 'You're welcome.'

'You should've *told* me.' And who cared if he sounded sulky: he had good sodding reason. Edward sat up, looking around at the dusty wardrobe, the dusty bedside cabinet, the dusty windowsill, the dusty duvet, and that horrible sewagey smell . . . 'Where are we?'

'Pauline Thomson's house. Your idea, remember?'

Somehow he hadn't imagined it being this manky.

'I know this is all messed up.' Bigtoria flexed her fists, frowning down at them. 'But whatever's in those safety-deposit boxes – the powers that be are bricking themselves. Securing access to them is our number-one priority; everything else is secondary.' A smile dimpled her cheeks. 'If it's any consolation: your performance was perfect. Oscar-winning stuff.'

'Oh, thanks. Thanks a bloody heap.'

She ripped through the last layer of plastic, setting his limbs free. 'Marky and Razors think you're dead, and they think I'm on their side. Let's keep it that way.' She stood. 'Now, I've got to hot-foot it over to Black Joe Ivanson's house before they get there and kill him, too.'

He sat up. 'What am I supposed to—'

'You stay here, you keep the lights off, and you play *dead*. Understand?'

He shoved himself backwards till he bumped against the headboard. 'I nearly sodding was!'

Bigtoria didn't move. 'Do you have any idea how long this operation took to put together? What I've had to do to get here? To earn these bastards' trust?' A thick finger came up and pointed straight at Edward's forehead. 'You are *not* screwing this up for me.'

She turned on her heel and marched out into the hall.

He kicked the plastic sheeting onto the floor. 'Those safety-deposit boxes better be worth it!'

'Just lie low and let me do my bloody job.'

Her wellington bootsteps thunked across the hall; then came the sound of a door opening. Then another one, much fainter this time. Then the same door clunking shut.

And that was it.

He was alive again, but all alone. In the darkness of a dead woman's house.

Great.

Edward sagged back against the headboard.

This week really wasn't going all that well . . .

Kinda weird.

Knackered, but too tired to sleep.

Shouldn't be surprised, really – given everything that had happened over the last couple of days. What with the dying and the murders. And the cold.

God knew when Pauline Thomson abandoned house to shack up with Kerry Millbrae, but the heating probably hadn't been on in months. Place was like a sodding fridge. Even with that dusty single duvet wrapped around his high-vis jacket.

Not to mention the whole threat of Mr Richards and Mr Bishop finding out Bigtoria didn't *actually* kill him, and them turning up to finish the job. Carving bits off him with that bloody cut-throat razor . . .

No wonder he couldn't sleep.

Edward rubbed the grit out of his eyes and turned the volume down on his phone till the song playing was barely audible – saving what little battery he had left. Which wasn't much. And there was no way to charge it, of course, because all the sodding power was out.

It was a bit eerie, creeping into the living room to peer out over the windowsill, like a pervert, at Glenfarach's unlit streets. No LED glare, no lights in the windows. Just the ghostly blue-grey glimmer of snow, seeping its way through the gaps in the curtains, dimming as his breath misted the cold glass.

Mind you, there *was* a glow in the sky, somewhere over on the other side of town. Yellow and orange and red, catching the underside of a pall of oily black smoke.

That would be another house fire, which *probably* meant a crime scene being erased. The tally had been: two murdered residents, a missing-presumed-dead social worker, and a police officer with a fractured skull. What were they covering up this time: one more tortured sex offender? Or maybe it was Caroline Manson's remains going up in smoke? Making sure nothing remained for the forensics team to examine.

Assuming they ever got here.

At this rate, everyone would be dead long before that happened, and there'd be sod all left of Glenfarach but a pile of smouldering rubble.

And good riddance to it.

He let the teeny gap he'd opened in the curtains fall shut again. Turned. Huffed out a breath as the Foo Fighters whispered in his ear.

God, it stank in here: a sour, brown, uncleaned-toilet stench that coiled its way out of the kitchen and bathroom. Not exactly inviting.

But he didn't have any choice. When nature called, you either heeded the summons or you wet yourself. He took a deep breath and tiptoed into the bathroom, closing the door before clicking on his headtorch.

Flipping the toilet lid and seat up revealed a clean empty bowl. Well, except for that ring around the porcelain where it dipped into the dry U-bend. But nothing to explain the horrible smell.

Edward was mid-flow when a thump sounded from somewhere behind, throwing him off his game, and the pitter-patter of shame spattered up from the tiled floor.

Then a clunk.

Front door closing, maybe?

OK.

Don't panic.

Well, maybe a little.

He clicked off the headtorch, finished quick as possible *in the dark*, tucked Little Ted away, and pulled out the paring knife he'd liberated from the kitchen. Dumped the single duvet in the bath – stealth and mobility being more important than warmth right now.

The creaky squeal of hinges meant whoever-it-was must've gone through to one of the other rooms.

He felt his way along the wall to the bathroom door, easing it open just enough to peer out into the hallway.

No one there.

It was Mr Richards, wasn't it. With his bloody cut-throat. Come to finish the job.

Well, he was in for a nasty shock, because no way Edward Theodore Reekie was giving up without a bloody fight.

He tightened his grip on the knife.

You can do this.

A floorboard creaked, somewhere off to the side. Then another one.

Edward snuck over to the kitchen, eased his head around the corner . . . Nope. Then tried the living room . . . Nope again. Spare room . . . Third time nope. Which only left the main bedroom.

Gritting his teeth, he yanked the door open and barged inside, knife in one hand, the other clicking his headtorch on – its beam slashing through the gloom. 'POLICE! STAY WHERE YOU ARE!'

'Jesus!' Bigtoria was spreadeagled on the bed as the light caught her. She thrashed over onto her side – high-vis jacket flashing like a radioactive lemon – then slipped off the edge and crashed to the floor.

Oh.

She leapt to her feet, eyes wide, fists up. Face smeared with soot and dirt. Hair a bit frizzy and crispy at the edges, where it wasn't wet with melting snow. The stench of smoke rolling off her was enough to drown out even that weird kitchen-toilet smell.

'Guv?'

'Don't *do* that!' Holding a hand up, blocking the torch beam. 'And turn that bloody light out!'

'Sorry, Guv.' He did what he was told, plunging them into darkness – almost impenetrable now his night vision was shot.

'Are you *trying* to get us both killed?'

'Well, I didn't know if it was you or some other thug, did I?' His knife-free hand dug into his high-vis pocket. 'You should've called me on the . . .' Ah. No teddy bear.

She shook her head. 'Razors has your walkie-talkie.'

Bugger.

He pointed at the rounded silhouette where her hair would be. 'There's been another fire, hasn't there?'

'Do you *think*?'

Little bits of detail appeared out of the gloom as his eyes started to adjust. Enough to see Bigtoria peel off her high-vis jacket and dump it on the floor, where it landed with a suspiciously heavy and metallic *clunk*. She sank down on the end of the mattress, sounding like she'd just run three marathons and would never be happy again. 'I was too late. Joe Ivanson was already dead. Almost.' Rubbing at her face with both hands. 'Marky Bishop wants your body disposed of tomorrow morning. Razors is going to "keep an eye" on me to make sure I do it right.'

'Now wait a minute: get rid of my *body*?'

'Yup.' Bigtoria removed her jacket and socks. 'I'm thinking shallow grave.'

Edward retreated a couple of paces and nearly fell over something lurking in the murk. A metal rectangular something, covered in stickers. That stupid toolbox of hers. 'With all due respect, Detective Inspector Montgomery-Porter, get sodding bent.'

'You're such a drama queen.' A small laugh. 'And I should know – worked with enough of them.' She fished about over the side of the bed, coming up with her high-vis again. 'Here.'

Bigtoria must've had deeper inside pockets in her jacket than he had, because she pulled out a brown oxygen cylinder as long as her forearm. Looked like the tank Mr Bishop had with him on Tuesday, when they'd picked him up from HMP Grampian. It even had a mask and tube attached. 'Doc Griffiths does a refill service for residents with breathing problems. Luckily, he's got spares.'

What the hell did *that* have to do with anything?

Didn't matter, because he was having sod all to do with this . . . utter bollocking nonsense.

Edward pulled his chin in. 'No. Nope. Not doing it.'

'Shut up.' Her voice hardened. 'It's just you and me here; there's no backup. We're snowed in; there's no escape. We do this, or they come for us and we die for real.' Bigtoria's shoulders drooped. She ground the palms of her hands into her eye sockets, like she was trying to squeeze a bit of life into them. Then hissed out a long, knackered sigh. 'So, here's the plan . . .'

—snow, blood, death, pain—

(here comes the storm)

31

Edward checked his phone in the darkness.

Wasn't easy in the cramped space, lying on his side, curled up like a foetus, with all that weight heaped on top of him, but he managed.

The screen glowed '09:50' for about a second, then went black and wouldn't come on again.

Out – of – sodding – battery.

Of course it was.

Ha. Ha. Ha . . .

God, life was hilarious.

He hissed in a deep breath and bellowed it out, the scream muffled and echoing in the oxygen mask. Then lay there with his forehead pressed into the folds of Bigtoria's high-vis – more of it wrapped around his curled body, like he'd crawled the wrong way into a sleeping bag.

Claustrophobic, uncomfortable, but at least he was still alive.

Mind you . . .

This was a stupid plan.

Should never have agreed to it. To hell with the 'mission', to hell with the top brass, to hell with the mysterious safety-deposit boxes, to hell with Glenfarach, and to hell with Detective Inspector Victoria Elizabeth Montgomery-Porter.

Urgh . . .

The extra high-vis kept *some* of the cold out, but it still seeped in through his bum and feet, turning his wellies into foot-freezers that had shuffled well past the point of numb and into nipping-throbbing-aching territory.

Bet frostbite was helping itself to his toes, right now.

Pfff . . .

And there was nothing to do. Which probably seemed like a tiny problem compared to being buried alive, but he'd been down here for ages, lying still and *bored out of his mind*.

Didn't help that his face was all tight and slimy from the grease-paint Bigtoria had slathered on, back at Pauline Thomson's place. Oh, you have to look the part, Constable. They'll expect you to look like a corpse, Constable. I know what I'm doing, Constable.

Yes, OK, maybe she *had* done a good job of transforming him into a waxy-pale lump of cadaverous stab-victim, but that wasn't the point. It stank too – the reek of rancid candles filling his oxygen mask, because God forbid there should be any fresh air down here in this dark, cold, *miserable* hole.

Sod it: nine fifty, plus a bit, meant it'd been nearly an hour now. Anyone watching would've buggered off long ago.

He shuffled over onto his front, slip-sliding in the high-vis sheath, forced his arms and knees underneath his chest, and did the mother of all push-ups. Gritting his teeth, closing his eyes. Shoving and straining . . . all that soil and rocks and crap had probably frozen solid in the never-ending snow. He'd be stuck down here forever, and the oxygen in the tank would run out and he'd suffocate and die and no one would ever find his body and it would all be *bloody* Bigtoria's fault!

Then the ground above shifted.

Not much to start with, just a couple of inches. Then more and faster, the additional high-vis slipping off his back as he got his wellies beneath him, forcing his numb feet to cooperate as he heaved and struggled and gave it another full-throated bellow.

His head broke free, followed by his right arm, clawing its way out of the fusty grey-brown earth like something out of a zombie film. Then his left arm.

Ha!

Punching the sky and letting loose an oxygen-mask-muffled 'FREEDOM!'

Oh, thank God . . .

He ripped the mask off and hauled in a lungful of pepper-tinted snowy air. Coughing and spluttering, hacking away, because, apparently, he'd never tried breathing before. Or couldn't remember how it worked.

Jesus . . .

Buried in a shallow grave.

Now there was an experience *never* to try again.

He shoved at the soil around his chest with fingers that were already going the same colour as frozen beef sausages. Stinging like he'd wrapped the bloody things in nettles, then set fire to them. But it only took a minute to make a hole big enough to wriggle out of.

He lay there, on his back in the snow, blinking up at the falling flakes of soft white, steaming the air above him.

Didn't take long before the cold sank in through his exposed skin and trousers, though, as the heat of exertion evaporated away in the frigid Thursday morning. Leaving him shivering.

Or maybe that was the shock?

Or maybe it had something to do with not having more than a couple of hours' uninterrupted sleep since arriving at Glenfarach?

Either way, it was bloody horrible.

It took three goes to lever himself upright, stomping his feet in the thickening snow to get some life back into the damn things. Then he turned on the spot, frowning out at the ice-smothered landscape . . .

OK, that wasn't good.

Where was the track?

It hadn't been easy, watching what route Bigtoria had taken deep into the woods while A: thrown over her shoulder, and B: wrapped in a fusty-smelling sheet from Pauline Thomson's linen closet, but he'd done the best he could. And even if he couldn't remember every twist and turn, Bigtoria had left a nice wide trail when she waded her way through the snow. All he had to do was follow that back to town.

Edward did another three-sixty.

More thick white flakes drifted down from the faded-charcoal sky. Just like they'd probably done for the last hour. Erasing any sign that she'd carried him out here.

He folded forwards and clutched his frozen hands over his burning face. 'AAAAAAAAAAAAAAAAARGH!'

Then straightened.

Wait, it was OK: didn't matter if he couldn't find her tracks, because even without a mobile signal the *GPS* still worked. Sergeant Farrow proved that when they were out looking for Geoff Newman's 'bridge' yesterday. All he had to do was fire up the map on his phone and follow the digital road all the way to Glenfarach.

Only when he pulled out his mobile . . .

'Buggering hell!'

The battery was flat, remember? You sodding moron? Lying in your shallow grave, checking the time every five bloody minutes like an *idiot* instead of saving power for something far more important. How are you supposed to find your way home now?

Edward bit his bottom lip and let his head fall back. Blinking up at the falling bastarding snow.

He was going to die of exposure out here, in this stupid winter wonderland of shite.

'I HATE THIS BLOODY VILLAGE!'

The woods echoed the words from trunk to trunk, mocking him with his own voice: '*Village. Village. Village. Village. Village.*'

God's sake.

Come on, Edward.

You're not going to die here.

You're a big, brave, resourceful boy, right?

Course you are.

Glenfarach's built in a valley. That means all you've got to do is head downhill till you get to either the village or the road.

No problem.

Assuming you don't die of hypothermia on the way.

Yeah . . .

Well, there was one thing that would help – he dug his Police

Scotland beanie from his pocket and jammed it onto his head, pulling it down as far as it would go, so it covered most of his ears.

Actually, there were *two* things:

Edward shivered over to the edge of the grave and rammed a hand back into the hole he'd made climbing out of the damned thing. Aching fingers scraping through the dirt and stones until they latched onto a chunk of slippery fabric.

He hauled Bigtoria's high-vis out of the earth and gave it a shake. Part of the inside was smeared with grey-green greasepaint from his forehead and cheeks. He buried his face in the jacket's lining and scrubbed and scrubbed and scrubbed till that fusty candle scent faded. At least he'd be a bit less *Dawn of the Dead* now.

That done, he pulled her fake-blood-and-corpse-make-up-stained high-vis on over the top of his own. Because, luckily, she was freakishly large.

Zipping it up probably made him look like a fluorescent Michelin Man, but it was better than freezing to death.

OK.

Eeny, meeny, miney, mo.

He picked a direction and crumped off into the snow.

How were you supposed to find your way through this crap?

Edward waded through yet another knee-deep clearing, following the line of trees around the edge. Trailing breath behind him like an old-fashioned steam engine. Puffing and huffing. Hands stuffed into the outer high-vis's pockets. Shoulders up, head down.

Past dirty-big boulders and half-buried whin bushes as even more of the horrible stuff drifted from the granite-coloured sky. Burying the world. Deeper and deeper. Till the only thing left was a solid plain of featureless white and mankind was wiped from the face of the earth.

This was all bloody DI Montgomery-Porter's fault.

He laboured up the hill, breathing hard, using the trunks of partially buried beech trees to haul himself through the hip-deep snow. Every step a struggle. Sweat dribbling down his face, chest, and spine. Socks squelching in his wellington boots. Soggy trousers clinging to his shins and thighs.

Tired.

Knackered.

Thirsty . . .

Should've thought of that back at Pauline Thomson's stinky house. Got himself a bottle of water. Or wine. Or gin.

A great-big, *massive* gin would go down very nicely right now.

But there wasn't any, so he scooped a handful of snow from the drifts around his legs and stuffed it in his mouth. Which was about as unsatisfying as it sounded.

So much for *Here's the plan* . . . Bigtoria wouldn't know a decent plan if it got up, stabbed her in the back, then buried her in the sodding woods.

It all looked the same. How could it *all* look the same? Surely there had to be *some* bit of this bastarding forest that didn't look identical to every other bloody bit. But no: it was all trees, snow, humps, and lumps, hidden in a vast, unremitting blanket of white . . .

Edward limped to a halt, turning slowly around. Trees. Snow. Humps. Lumps. That's all it ever was. Over and over and over again.

And never mind finding his way downhill, everything was downhill till it wasn't and then he was lumbering up another slope and why did he let sodding DI Sodding Montgomery-*Sodding*-Porter talk him into this?

'AAAAAAAAAAAAAAAAAAAAAARGH!' The howl drifted away in a ghost-grey cloud, to be swallowed up by the falling snow.

It had got to the point where every single step was like he had a breeze block tied to both legs.

Edward lurched out into a fresh clearing, getting slower and slower. Winding down to a dead stop. Which it probably *would* be in this weather.

You keep moving, or you die.

Oh, hurrah . . .

The ground dipped away before him, making a dent in the ranks and ranks of pine trees that stretched off into the white mist. Their tops scratching the clouds.

His breeze-blocked legs came to an unexpected halt and Edward pitched forward. And with both hands in his pockets there was no chance to break his fall or stop himself before—

Whoooooomph – face first, right into the snow.

Dragging his hands free, thrashing his way up to his knees, spitting out cold globbets of white, scrubbing more of the bloody stuff from his cheeks and eyes. Standing and staggering back a couple of paces. Trembling. Blood fizzing in his ears. Teeth clamped together like a table vice.

Hauling in a deep, shuddery breath and howling it out into the shitting, never-ending flurries of bastarding snow. 'WAS THAT *REALLY* NECESSARY? WERE THINGS NOT BAD ENOUGH?'

There – poking out of the ground where his feet had been when he'd pitched over – a bush. He'd fallen over a sodding *bush*. Some sort of stupid clump of stupid bloody heather, just lurking in the buried wilderness, waiting for someone to trip over it.

'AAAAAAAAAAAAAAAARGH!'

Kicking it, stomping on it, kicking it again. Slamming his wellies into the damn thing until little branches fell off. Then he stood there, ribs heaving, face hot as a burning coal, breath raw and fiery in his throat.

Just a bush.

He folded forward and grabbed his cold, damp knees. Tears of frustration hissing on his fiery cheeks.

See if he lived through this? And he got his hands on Detective Inspector Montgomery-Porter? No jury in the land would convict him. They'd give him a medal and throw him a sodding parade.

Edward straightened up. Wiped the sweat from his face.

Slumped.

Because this was the kind of place people got lost in, never to be seen again. Not even their picked-clean bones . . .

He gave himself a little shake.

Come on, you can do this, remember?

He turned.

There was probably some clever backwoods thing you could do with which side of the trees moss grew on, or where the sun was, to help you navigate. But he didn't have a single clue.

Should've borrowed that book from the library: *The Scientific American Boy*, same as Geoff Newman. Bet it had that kind of crap in it.

He was just about to embark on another three-sixty when a loud crack sounded and a branch plummeted to the ground, overloaded with snow, unable to bear the weight any longer.

Knew how it felt.

Now, back to . . .

Hold on.

Edward inched forwards. Eyes narrowed. Head on one side. Something weird lurked on the edge of the clearing, fifteen or twenty feet from where that broken branch had hit the deck. The closer he got, the more not-natural it looked – too regular for one thing: rectangular at the top, sloping on the sides.

Another three lumbering steps and it was clearly some sort of makeshift wooden structure: tree trunks and branches lashed together with hairy brown string. About the size of a small caravan, partially buried into the side of a hill, and camouflaged with clumps of broom and bracken. Their ragged green spines scratched the air, branches tied to the walls; a thick layer piled up on the snowy roof.

It even had a rough wooden door, complete with a toggle handle – like it'd been salvaged from a duffel coat.

Halle-flipping-lujah.

OK, so it might not be all that warm inside, but it would be *dry*, and the chance to sit on his backside for five minutes out of the horrible bloody weather would be the greatest luxury known to man.

He hurried over . . .

Then stopped.

A semi-circular groove was carved out of the snow in front of the door. Nice and sharp, barely softened by the permanent blizzard. It'd been opened recently.

That wasn't suspicious *at all*.

Edward crept over to the homemade door, and pressed his ear against it.

Voices. Well, one male voice, and one person crying.

'*Come on,* do *something. Fight a bit, for Christ's sake!*'

Right.

He pulled his shoulders back, grabbed the toggle handle with his purple-tinged fingers, and threw the door open. 'POLICE! NOBODY MOVE!'

A battery-powered camping light hung from a beam in the middle of the roof, casting a greasy yellow glow over a space about the size of a large shed. Shelves ran around all four sides, stocked with bottles of vodka and whisky; tinned food; packets of biscuits; a row of crepe bandages, plasters, painkillers, and liniment. A series of hooks were screwed to one wall, playing host to what looked like an extensive collection of DIY bondage gear: ball gags; handcuffs; leather paddles, straps, and restraints.

An assortment of grubby rugs covered what was probably a dirt floor, and right in the middle of them sat a mattress, complete with fitted sheet, a Postman Pat duvet cover, and Peppa Pig pillowcases.

And that was where the noises were coming from.

A woman shrank back against the rear wall, wearing nothing but a dirty old dressing gown and a pair of woolly socks. Her skin was flushed and bruised; fresh scabs on her cheeks, forehead, hands, and knees. Mouth swollen on one side. Her long straight nose wasn't straight any more, and a crust of dried blood surrounded both nostrils and caked her top lip.

With all the damage it took a moment to recognize her, but it was the dark-brown wavy hair that cinched it: Caroline Manson, their missing social worker.

Bloody hell . . .

A length of blue nylon rope tied her wrists together, while a thick chain – padlocked around her left ankle – hobbled her to one of the shack's thicker uprights.

What was it Sergeant Farrow had called it? *A clubhouse for perverts.*

Ms Manson's eyes drifted up towards Edward, pupils huge and black.

The man was a chunky, late-forties, ghost-pale wedge of lard, with a close-cropped haircut that was probably meant to disguise the sheer volume of baldness rampaging across his ugly head. He was wearing a thick blue jumper that looked like his nan had knitted it, but his trousers and underpants were down around his ankles. Showing off a hairy slab of flabby arse. His eyes widened behind steamed-up glasses as he fumbled to drag his breeks and pants up – trying to cover his rapidly deflating nub of a cock – scrabbling back from the flung-open door. Voice a high-pitched nasal whine. 'This . . . this isn't what you think!'

Edward stared. 'Christ . . .' He wiped a frozen hand across his mouth, then bared his teeth. Pointed at the half-naked bastard. 'YOU: FACE DOWN, HANDS BEHIND YOUR HEAD!'

'I was just walking in the forest, and I heard her crying for help, and . . . I must've *tripped* and my trousers fell down and—'

'I'M NOT TELLING YOU AGAIN! FACE DOWN, NOW!'

'I'm sorry, I'm sorry.' Face contorted into an obsequious, gurning slab of pink. Hands up like he was being held at gunpoint. 'I didn't do anything, I swear!' Trembling, on the point of tears. 'This is all a big misunder—'

'NAME?'

He flinched, covering his head, mumbling into the crooks of his arms. 'Adrian. Adrian Bedwin. But this is all—'

'YOU SIT THERE, *MISTER* BEDWIN, AND YOU SHUT THE HELL UP!' Not that the bastard *deserved* to be called 'mister' anything. He hadn't earned the title.

A little squeal and Bedwin curled up even further.

Pretty sure he was about to wet himself in terror.

Good.

At least, with his trousers around his ankles, he wasn't going anywhere. Still, better safe than sorry.

Edward grabbed Bedwin's left wrist, pulled out the cuffs and snapped one side into place. Looked up and gave Ms Manson a reassuring smile while he fumbled for Bedwin's other hand. 'It's OK, I'm a police officer. Are you all—'

Which was when the bald rapist bastard stopped cooperating. Violently.

32

Bedwin reared up, arms thrashing, and Edward went over backwards, the momentum sending the pair of them tumbling across the manky floor to crash into the open doorway.

Something hard slammed into his ribs. Then again. *Whump*ing the air from his lungs. Good job he had a double-thickness layer of high-vis padding on, because Bedwin wasn't messing about.

Then a sharp pain, barking through Edward's left hand – the bastard was *biting*.

No you sodding don't . . .

Edward jabbed an elbow into something soft and Bedwin whoomphed out a grunt. Then they were both shoving and kicking and sometimes landing a blow and most times not, but all the flailing arms and legs meant they were moving again, rolling out into the snow.

A fist battered off the side of Edward's head, setting his ears ringing as the loose bar of the handcuffs whiplashed in after it; the other fist crashed into his ribs for the third time in the last thirty seconds.

Bedwin was stronger than he looked – landing punch after punch. And the handcuffs, still fixed to his left wrist, weren't slowing him down any.

The ringing got louder, bringing with it searing bursts of black and yellow that swirled faster than the blizzard.

'Aaaargh!' Edward lashed out, but the swing went wide and that bloody fist cracked into his side again.

Even with his trousers round his ankles, Adrian Bedwin was kicking his arse. And Christ knew what would happen if he *won* this fight. But it wouldn't end well for Edward or Ms Manson.

Edward caught Bedwin a glancing blow on the shoulder, but another punch connected with Edward's cheek, complete with the stinging crack of the cuff's metallic bracelet as it clattered off his skull.

This really wasn't working . . .

Sod Marquess of Queensberry Rules: go for the balls!

Edward hunched his head into his shoulders, trying to make it a smaller target, and jammed his right hand into Bedwin's face, forcing it back, while the left hand forced its way between them, down to groin level.

Oh God . . . He was at full-mast again.

Deep breath. Edward reached past it, grabbed a handful of Bedwin's scrotum and *squeezed*. Digging his nails in. Yanking his fist from side to side, trying to rip the damn thing off.

A sharp nasal squeal tore through the air and Bedwin curled away. Breaking free of Edward's ball-killer grip. Face an agonized mask of puce and beetroot. Teeth bared, spittle rolling down his lips, tears sparkling in his bloodshot eyes.

Good.

Hope he'd ruptured *both* of them.

Edward flattened his palm and scrubbed it against the nearest drift, trying to wash off the greasy, sweaty, hairy sensation. Now all he needed to do was . . .

Wait a minute.

Bedwin was on his knees, forehead pressed against the trampled snow, left hand cupping his balls, a smile spreading across his features. What sounded like a cross between a growl and a giggle slithered from his mouth as he grinned at Edward. And his pupils were tiny pinpricks.

Oh great.

Ms Manson wasn't the only one on drugs.

Edward scrambled to his feet – almost getting there before Bedwin exploded towards him, battering into his stomach, sending him jack-knifing into the snow, his skull bouncing off the doorway on the way down. Leaving him flat on his back, half in, half out of the club-house while the world became a carousel – blurred and spinning, people screaming, nausea bubbling deep inside.

Then Bedwin was on top of him, giggling and hissing, fists flying left and right into Edward's head and chest and shoulders.

This was it.

He was going to die here.

Battered to death by a junkie pervert with their trousers around their ankles.

After all he'd been through?

Sod that.

Edward's hands shot up, grabbing Bedwin by the neck of his horrible jumper and hauling him forwards – off balance – bringing his face to the perfect point for Edward's headbutt to *clunk* right into the middle of it.

A muffled crack and Bedwin reared back, eyes half closed, nose a ruptured sausage, blood spattering out in all directions.

It barely even slowed him down.

Bedwin lunged again, dripping bright drops of scarlet in the wan glow of the clubhouse's camping light as he slammed Edward's head sideways into the doorpost. Then wrapped his hands around Edward's throat.

Squeezing.

The black and yellow dots were back.

Edward scrabbled at Bedwin's hands, hauling at the fingers, slap-ping at the wrists, making no difference whatsoever.

The handcuffs! Grab the thick, plastic bar and *twist*: break the bastard's wrist ... But even yanking at the bloody thing just made the giggling louder. Then the sound of whooshing blood – pounding through Edward's skull – drowned it out, building in force and volume, as dots crowded at the edges of his vision, pushing inward, narrowing everything until all he could see was Bedwin's coked-up, bleeding face grinning and dripping all over him and—

A pair of hands reached into view – tied together at the wrists with blue nylon rope – fingers curled into sharp-tipped claws, as

Ms Manson fell to her knees beside Edward and dug her fingernails into Bedwin's cheeks, just in front of his ears. She hauled, opening up deep scratches that sent even more scarlet blood dribbling off his flabby chin. Bringing with them a howl of pain.

'YOU BITCH!'

He let go of Edward's throat and backhanded Ms Manson, sending her crashing onto the mattress.

BREATHE.

Edward dragged in two burning, gritty lungfuls of blessed air, then threw a right – cracking his fist into Bedwin's cheek. 'Get off me!'

The bastard barely registered the punch. Instead, he thumped forwards, hands wrapping around Edward's throat again. Grinning as he bounced Edward's head off the manky-rugged floor. One, two, three times.

Edward went for his eyes, but Bedwin yanked his bleeding face back, just out of reach.

Could hardly force the words out as his throat compressed, but Edward managed: 'Help . . . me!'

Ms Manson appeared once more, rearing above them both. She had what looked like the ball-gag from the DIY bondage gear dangling from her bound hands – a leather strap with a metal buckle on the end, and a repurposed pool ball set in the middle. A white one, with a red stripe and the number eleven on it. Solid. Heavy.

She whipped it downwards, thwacking it off the crown of Bedwin's skull with a resounding *clunk*.

He grunted, rocking backwards under the blow, and she hit him again, snarling as she swung the gag so hard it split the skin on his temple.

Bedwin let go of Edward's throat, both hands coming up to defend his head, but not fast enough – the eleven ball smashed right into his face, caving in his left cheekbone.

He wobbled, gurgled, then tipped forwards – collapsing onto the clubhouse floor.

Oh – thank – God . . .

Edward sagged.

Still alive.

And lying underneath a half-naked rapist.

'GET OFF ME!'

He wriggled free, shoving the body off him, struggled to his knees, massaging the lumps and knots out of his tender throat. Coughing and wheezing. Getting used to breathing again.

Ms Manson dropped the ball gag – the sound it made hitting the floor disturbingly similar to the one it'd made slamming into Bedwin's skull – and staggered back a step. Her foot hit the edge of the mattress and she sat down hard. Face creasing as tears welled up and spilled over, bound hands covering her mouth as she stared at Bedwin's motionless body.

Edward gave her a thumbs up, then sagged against the clubhouse wall, gasping and puffing and coughing, the breath whistling and rasping in his throat.

Had to admit, it was nice not to be dead. Again.

No idea how long he slumped there, but eventually dragging air into his lungs didn't hurt *quite* as much and the world stopped its fairground impersonation. Only trouble was the dull thudding throb radiating across his scalp and cheeks where Bedwin's fists had smashed into them. Repeatedly.

Ms Manson's tears had turned into a dose of the shivers – probably a mixture of shock and cold, given what she must've been through. Her voice was heavy, fuzzy, like her tongue didn't work properly any more. 'Who . . . are . . .' – blinking at him through whatever it was they'd doped her up with – 'who are you?'

He shoved himself off the wall. 'Detective Constable Edward Reekie.' A barbed-wire cough scoured the lining off his throat again. 'Thanks for the help. You seriously *rock*.' He shuffled forwards on his knees, till he reached Bedwin's body.

Might as well get the formal stuff out of the way.

But when he pressed two fingers into Bedwin's neck, just below the jawline, what do you know: there was a pulse. A nice strong one too.

She stared. 'Is . . . is he . . . ?'

'Nope.' A smile. 'You didn't kill him after all.' Edward finally snapped the other side of the handcuffs over Bedwin's right wrist, then sat back on his haunches and frowned at the coked-up raping wee shite, then at Ms Manson, then up at the rough wooden ceiling. This was all *seriously* screwed up. So much for sneaking into Glenfarach and hiding out in Thomson Cottage until Bigtoria finished with Operation Whatever-This-Was-Called.

He couldn't just lie low after all this.

God knew what Ms Manson had been through, chained up here. By the look of those bruises and scrapes, this wasn't the first time Adrian Bedwin had paid her an unwelcome visit. She'd need medical attention, and heat, and help, and support, and everything else.

And speaking of Bedwin – assuming he survived his injuries, *he'd* need arresting and processing and locking up till the snow cleared enough to cart him off to jail again. Where, hopefully, they'd throw away the sodding key.

Nope, the plan was officially dead.

He had to get the pair of them back to Glenfarach, and Bigtoria would just have to lump it. Whatever was in those safety-deposit boxes wasn't more important than Caroline Manson. *Or* Adrian Bastarding Bedwin.

And yes, knowing Bigtoria, she'd find a way to make this all his fault, but tough. Sometimes a detective constable had to do what a detective constable had to do.

'How you feeling, Ms Manson? You hurt? Can you walk?'

'Of course . . . course I'm *hurt*. What do . . . do you think doing here!'

Fair enough. It *was* a stupid question.

'Sorry.'

He went through Bedwin's pockets, coming out with a pack of chewing gum; a snotty handkerchief; a wee box containing three condoms – past their sell-by date; a social-credits ration book; and a little silver key.

'Let's get you out of here.' He shuffled his knees over to Ms Manson and untied her wrists, leaving her rubbing at the dark-purple weals the rope had left behind as he slipped the key into the padlock and released the chain around her ankle. 'Right.' Sitting back and having a quick look about the place. 'What did this dick-head do with your clothes?'

'Don't . . . don't know.'

OK – time to go rummaging.

Edward struggled his cold hands into a pair of nitrile gloves and searched the clubhouse, working his way clockwise from the door. Other than the booze, tins, medical supplies, and bondage gear, the only thing he found was a stack of revolting self-published 'sex' fanzines, piled up in the far corner. Well, that and Adrian Bedwin's dark-blue parka jacket. Oh, and a very familiar red holdall.

He unzipped it.

After all the build-up, it was kinda disappointing that golden light didn't spill out, accompanied by a wee choir of angels going, 'Aaaa-AAAAA!' Instead, it contained what looked like a half-kilo block of cannabis resin; a large Ziploc pouch of weed that filled the clubhouse with its sweet-sweaty scent when he opened it to take a look; a heavy-duty freezer bag with a handful of white powder inside; several unmarked boxes of loose pills; another box full of empty, small, clear-plastic baggies, ready to divvy everything up into; and a brown A4 envelope.

Deep breath and he took a peek.

Then shut it again and dumped it back in the holdall.

Shuddered.

Good job he was wearing gloves, because . . . bloody hell.

Edward peeled his *contaminated* gloves off and stuffed them into a high-vis pocket. Gave himself a shake. 'OK: not solving the clothes problem.' How was he supposed to get Ms Manson all the way to Glenfarach when all she had were socks and a dressing gown?

Mind you . . .

He offered Bedwin a shrug. 'Well, you brought this on yourself.'

The handcuffs came off, then Edward struggled Bedwin's nasty blue jumper up over the unconscious man's head, before the cuffs went on again sharpish. No point taking any chances. Then he undid and hauled off Bedwin's boots and trousers. Leaving him in just his vest, pants, and socks.

There was probably something in the Geneva Conventions pro-
hibiting things like that, but tough. Better *Bedwin* had to scuff his
way through the snow in his stockinged feet than . . .

Hang on a minute.

Each pale hairy leg disappeared into the neck of a blue-and-grey
sock. Where was his sodding ankle tag?

'Hoy!' Edward nudged him with a foot. 'Where's your ankle tag?'

No reply.

Wonderful – so Bigtoria was right. Rupert Fraser wasn't the only
one who could wander around Glenfarach whenever he fancied.

'Here.' Edward popped the parka, jumper, trousers, and boots in
front of Ms Manson. 'You deserve these more than he does.'

She looked at the pile of clothes, then stared at Edward with
those big button eyes. Her face narrowed. She pulled the dressing
gown tighter.

Ah, right. Of course.

'Better idea.' Edward pointed over his shoulder, at the open door.
'How about I wait outside while you get changed? OK. Let's do
that.' He thumped the holdall onto Bedwin's back. 'Come on,
tosser, give the lady some privacy.'

He took hold of Bedwin's untagged ankles and dragged him –
face down – out into the snow, dumping him far enough from the
clubhouse to swing the door shut again.

Might have been the movement, or it might have been the sudden
plunge in temperature as Edward abandoned him in a snowbank,
but either way: Bedwin groaned. Moaned. Then rolled onto his side,
knees coming up to his chest as the holdall fell off.

His one good eye flickered open, not really focusing on anything, as a long, whispery, creaking noise grated out from his
throat. Bits of his head and face were already beginning to swell,
making purple-tinged eggs where the pool-ball-gag had whacked
into it. That broken cheekbone bulged out beneath an eye rapidly
darkening to Dracula-red. And blood from his ruined nose and
gouged cheeks soaked into the snow, turning it pink, then scarlet.

Served him right.

Could freeze to death for all Edward cared.

Little shite.

Edward kicked the nearest drift.

Rolled his eyes.

Sighed.

Fine.

He stripped off his outer layer – Bigtoria's high-vis – and man-handled Bedwin onto his arse, propping him up in a wobbly sitting position to get the jacket on over his torso like a bag. Zipping it up with Bedwin's hands still cuffed behind his back. A fluorescent straitjacket. Then helped him to his feet, where he swayed and staggered, but somehow managed to stay upright.

Just as well, because Edward had no intention of carrying the fat lump.

He was halfway through the official 'I am arresting you under Section One of the Criminal Justice, Scotland, Act' bit, when the clubhouse door swung open. Ms Manson stepped out onto the snow, moving slow and careful, like a drunk trying to pretend they were sober. Bedwin's clothes were baggy around the middle on her, and short at the ankles and wrists. Him being much shorter and fatter than she was. She was still wearing the dressing gown under his parka jacket.

Edward nodded. 'That looks better. We should get moving, though, cos . . .'

Ah.

She had a bottle of whisky from the clubhouse shelves in her hand. A *crick* sounded as she twisted the metal cap off, then took a big swig and poured the rest onto the snow at her feet. Soon as the bottle was empty, she grasped it by the neck and cracked the fat end against the doorframe. The glass shattered, spilling glistening green shards, leaving her holding a broken-bottle flower with razor-sharp edges.

'Whoa, whoa, whoa!' Edward held his hands up. 'I *know* he deserves it, but you can't cut his throat. Or his balls off. Or . . . anything else.'

Ms Manson marched straight past them both, pausing only to

spit a gobbet of blood-tinged phlegm into Bedwin's face as she headed uphill.

She stopped at the first tree she came to and used the broken bottle to carve an arrow into the bark – pointing back towards the clubhouse.

'Oh!' Edward nodded. 'Right. Cool. I get it: Hansel and Gretel.' He picked up the holdall and pulled it on like a backpack – using the handles as shoulder straps – then grabbed one of the empty sleeves dangling from Bedwin's high-vis. 'Come on, then: walkies.' Leading him away, up the hill, following Ms Manson, because she actually seemed to know where she was going.

Which made a lovely change.

33

They lumbered up another hill, fighting through yet more sodding snow. At least the forest was thick enough here that it was only ankle-deep, but that didn't stop each breath from sandpapering its way down Edward's throat to sink frozen claws into his lungs, before exploding from his lips in a ghostly pall of grey.

Ms Manson took the lead, crumping a path for Edward and Adrian Bedwin to follow. Every couple of minutes she'd carve another arrow into a tree trunk, then struggle onwards. Ducking under branches, skirting boulders, clambering over fallen trees . . .

Bedwin shuffled along on his sleeve-leash, making a strange slack-jawed whimpering sound, like he was trying to harmonize with the wind as it moaned through the treetops – teeth chattering a staccato beat. His naked legs had gone from pale and flabby to angry-red and flabby, to blotchy-purple and flabby, and had now settled on a sort of insipid blue. Which probably wasn't all that healthy, but what was Edward supposed to do, leave him at the clubhouse? Alone and unsupervised? With a possible fractured skull, given how hard Ms Manson had been swinging that pool-ball ball-gag?

Couldn't see *anyone* giving Edward a bollocking over that.

The slope levelled out, unremitting pines yielding to beech and oak, their bare branches and twigs offering sod-all shelter from the weather. So the ankle-deep snow soon became shin-deep, then knee-deep as they struggled on into the blizzard.

It howled down from the low ink-blot sky, whipped along by a ravenous wind that set the tail ends of Ms Manson's dressing gown flapping where they stuck out the bottom of her commandeered parka.

She seemed a bit better, like the drugs were wearing off. Steadier on her feet. More determined.

When she stopped to hack out another arrow with her broken-bottle knife, Edward pulled up alongside. Turned his back to the hungry wind.

'Are you *sure* you know where we are? I mean, you've had a big shock and everything.'

Her speech had lost that mushiness, too. 'WHAT?' Bracing herself against the gusts as she squinted at him.

Oh, right. He raised his voice over the wailing blizzard. 'ARE YOU SURE YOU KNOW WHERE WE ARE?'

'OF COURSE I DO.'

'COS I DON'T THINK YOU REALLY KNOW WHERE WE ARE.' Waving a hand at the snow and the half-buried brambles and the trees and the sodding wind. 'COULD BE ANYWHERE!'

'I *KNOW* WHERE WE ARE.' And she headed off again, zipping her parka's hood up till only her eyes peered out of the fur-trimmed periscope.

Fiver said they were walking around in circles.

Still, at least now he wouldn't freeze to death, all alone, in the woods of a remote Scottish glen. No, he'd have company when the Grim Sodding Reaper came for him.

He lurched after her, taking Bedwin for walkies again. Picking his words carefully 'MS MANSON, WHEN WE SEARCHED YOUR ROOMS WE FOUND SOMETHING IN YOUR BEDSIDE CABINET. THE BOTTOM DRAWER, TO BE PRECISE.'

Ms Manson paused for a moment, then the full meaning of that must've sunk in because her eyes narrowed in the depths of her hood. She pushed forwards again, skirting the root-ball of a toppled birch tree, mouth pinched.

'ANYTHING YOU WANT TO TELL ME, MS MANSON? ON ACCOUNT OF I SAVED YOUR LIFE?'

A snort. 'I SAVED *YOUR* LIFE.'

True.

'OK, SO WE BOTH SAVED EACH OTHER'S LIVES.' The snow was getting deeper, heading for mid-thigh as they battled their way up another slope. 'WHERE DID YOU GET THE DRUGS, MS MANSON?'

'THEY'RE GOING TO FIRE ME, AREN'T THEY?'

Probably.

Edward shrugged. 'DO YOU *REALLY* WANT TO KEEP WORKING HERE, AFTER THIS?'

They waded in silence for a couple of minutes, slowing as the drifts hit waist-deep, Bedwin's groans growing more juddery as his teeth clattered with the cold.

Then Ms Manson slashed another tree. 'GEOFF NEWMAN. HE WAS MY SUPPLIER.' Carving the arrow deep into the pale white bark of a silver birch, making it bleed. 'DON'T KNOW WHERE HE GOT THEM FROM – NEVER ASKED – BUT I GOT MINE FROM HIM.' She abandoned the scarred birch and struggled on through the snow. 'JUST A BIT OF COKE, THE OCCASIONAL UPPER, A DOWNER OR TWO IF I HAD TO DO A PRESENTATION OR SOME-THING. MAYBE SOME HASH.' She cleared her throat. 'MOSTLY HASH. LOTS OF HASH. WORKING HERE, IT TAKES THE EDGE OFF.'

Edward guided Bedwin past a jagged clump of prickly gorse. 'DID YOU KNOW HE'S DEAD? GEOFF NEWMAN?'

She stumbled to a halt. 'HE'S *DEAD*?'

'YOU DIDN'T KNOW?'

'HOW WOULD I . . .?' Ms Manson stared at Edward from the depths of her snood. 'YOU THOUGHT *I* DID IT?'

'SORRY. BUT YOU SEE: YOU DISAPPEARED AT PRETTY MUCH THE SAME TIME, AND WHOEVER KILLED HIM WASN'T WEAR-ING AN ANKLE TAG, AND BACK THEN WE WERE TOLD THE THINGS WERE IMPOSSIBLE TO REMOVE!' He hooked a thumb at Bedwin. 'BUT NOW IT TURNS OUT THEY'RE ALL AT IT.'

She seemed to think about that for a long, long moment. Before shaking her head and turning into the wind again. Marching away into the blizzard.

Well, it wasn't Edward's fault, was it? Dr Singh made the

connection between her horrible father and Geoff Newman's offences, not him. Mind you, to be fair on Dr Singh, no one knew Mr Newman was her dealer at that point.

Maybe it was easier for Ms Manson to overlook Geoff Newman's faults because he supplied her drugs? No matter how sodding horrendous those faults had been . . .

Edward headed after her, bringing the shambling remains of Adrian Bedwin with him.

Who wasn't looking all that good. His legs had taken on more of that blue tinge, and his face was heading that way too, even with the high-vis's hood unfurled from its collar and up over his head.

Starting to think that leaving him at the clubhouse might've been a better idea – all chained-up, so he couldn't go anywhere.

Yes, but what if he had some sort of internal bleeding and keeled over dead before Edward got back with help?

Well, what if he had some sort of internal bleeding and keeled over out here? Still end up just as dead.

Urgh . . .

Damned if you do.

And maybe being out here in the cold was *good* for him? You know, if you had internal bleeding, chilling things down would stop it progressing as quickly, wouldn't it? Slow the flow.

Yeah, you keep telling yourself that.

Edward lurched along the path Caroline Manson was forging through the deep, deep snow.

This was a complete disaster.

They *should* have stayed back at the clubhouse, all three of them. At least they'd be out of the storm. Someone would've come looking for them eventually, wouldn't they? A rescue party, armed with blankets and snowmobiles and hot soup?

Mind you, that could take days.

Weeks.

Stuck in that manky wee hovel, rationing out the booze and biscuits and tins of cold beans, just to survive . . .

Edward's stomach snarled like a hungry wolf.

Probably best not to think about food.

In the end, it didn't really matter how miserable it would've been back at the clubhouse – it'd still be better than *this*.

Because it was sodding obvious that they were now totally and utterly completely lost.

Up ahead, Ms Manson disappeared into a big hedge of whin that blocked the way, shoving at the branches, causing the snow to tumble from its spindly leaves, setting its seedpods hissing like rattlesnakes.

He pushed in after her, Bedwin groaning along behind him.

Maybe there'd be somewhere nearby to hole up and wait for the blizzard to pass? A cave or something. Or how about building a shelter with twigs and bits of whin? Find a fallen tree to creep beneath and fill in the gaps so the wind and snow couldn't get in.

Worth a go, wasn't it?

Edward shoved his way through the huge bush, emerging on the edge of a large clearing – the ground dropping away in front of him and up the other side, like a big scoop had been taken out of the earth.

Wait a minute.

Ms Manson kept on going, working her way along the lip of the bowl.

An ancient Scots pine towered overhead, barely a dozen feet from where he stood. Definitely seen it before, and the hollow, and . . . He did a slow three-sixty. Yup, definitely. This was where he'd ended up with Sergeant Farrow – when they'd been following Geoff Newman's final movements.

'I KNOW WHERE WE ARE!'

He dragged Bedwin over to the tree and stared up at the branches. There: just above head height, that weird branch with the upward hook – the one somebody had whittled to resemble an erect willy. This was the Cock Tree. Only now the cock had a ring: someone had hooked an ankle tag over it, the band fixed to the unit with a handful of crocodile-clipped wires. The same way Rupert Fraser's had been bypassed.

He slipped the ankle tag off its penis hook and stuffed it into the side pocket of Bedwin's high-vis straitjacket. Stuck two fingers in his mouth and let free a sharp ear-curling whistle.

Ms Manson stumbled to a halt, then turned the opening of her snood in his direction. 'WHAT NOW?'

He pointed, following the imaginary trail down the hill, across the clearing, and up the other side. 'TOWN'S THAT WAY.'

Sergeant Farrow was sitting behind the custody desk, head buried in a tatty paperback copy of *Outlander*, her brow crumpled as she slow-motioned salt-and-vinegar squares from the packet to her mouth, crunching as she read. Completely absorbed and apparently oblivious to the sound of gentle sobbing coming from one of the cells, the back-up generator's low diesel hum, and the door through to the rest of the station thunking shut again.

She didn't even look up as Edward scuffed across the floor, bringing Adrian Bedwin and Caroline Manson with him. Delivering them unto the promised land of heating, electric light, and hopefully a nice hot cup of tea – because all three of them were caked down the front with a thick layer of snow.

Bedwin hadn't improved on the way here from the woods. If anything, he looked worse. His socks left wet patches on the grey terrazzo; his bare legs – waxy, pale, and stiff as frozen butter; shivering so much he moved like cheap Soviet-era animation. A glob of slush slid down the front of his high-vis and plopped onto the floor, covering his feet.

Edward led him over to the custody desk. Then wriggled his own arms out of the red holdall's handles and dumped the thing beside the desk.

She *still* hadn't looked up.

He knocked on the chipped wooden top – *rat, tat-tat*.

Even then it took a couple of beats for Sergeant Farrow to tear herself away from tales of a time-travelling nurse and her frequently half-naked Highlander lover. The look of annoyance faded from her face as she frowned at Edward. 'I thought you were meant to be laid up with the squits. Bigtoria said . . .' She looked him up and down – taking in the bruises and the scuffs and the blood and the filthy high-vis. Like a manky Scott of the Antarctic. 'What the *fudge* happened to . . . ?' Her eyes drifted across to who he was with, and widened. 'Adrian? Caroline?' Dropping her book and standing. 'Is that . . . ? Is she . . . ? *What* . . . ?'

'I found what Geoff Newman was building in the woods.'

She hurried out from behind the desk, dithering as she stood there, clearly having difficulty deciding who needed her help more – Ms Manson or Bedwin.

Edward manoeuvred his shivering prisoner into position for processing. 'Adrian Bedwin, arrested for kidnap, illegal imprisonment, sexual assault, attempted murder, and anything else you can think of.'

Sergeant Farrow sidestepped Bedwin and helped Ms Manson into a plastic chair, kneeling in front of her and brushing the hair from her battered face. 'What did they *do* to you?'

Ms Manson's bottom lip trembled; then tears spilled down her cheeks as all that strength and bravery and bloody-minded tenacity evaporated. Finally safe.

Edward gave himself a shake, spattering the floor with more melting snow. 'They'll both need to see the Duty Doc. And Ms Manson should probably have . . .' – he lowered his voice and stared down at the puddle growing around his wellington boots – '. . . rape kit.'

Sergeant Farrow pulled Caroline Manson into a hug. 'I'm sorry. I'm so, so sorry.' Stroking her hair as she sobbed.

He cleared his throat. 'Mr Newman built himself a lair. There's a mattress in there with booze, drugs, the whole thing. He and his *little friends* have been sharing it.'

Sergeant Farrow raised her face to the ceiling tiles, mouth scrunched up, the lines deepening across her forehead. Like each word was a stabbing needle. '*Fudge!*' Then she was on her feet, bustling around to the other side of the desk and picking up the landline. Jabbing a finger at the buttons. 'Doc? . . . Doc, it's Louise . . . Doc, no: listen! I need you down here ASAP.'

Sergeant Farrow stopped on the threshold of Edward's cell, knocked on the open door, and held up a couple of mugs. 'You decent?'

Edward went back to drying his feet. 'How come we have to watch the cellblock, Sarge? What happened to the Social Work Team?'

'You smell a lot better, anyway.'

The joy of a quick shower in hot water. 'Another fifteen minutes wouldn't have hurt.'

'Don't be ungrateful. We've no power, and the boiler won't run off the generator.'

Fair enough.

He pulled on a pair of freshly pilfered socks – lifted out of someone's locker. Black, to go with the pilfered Armani suit. Which looked pretty damn sharp, thank you very much. Then followed them up with a pair of pilfered trainers, which didn't. But they were dry, so he wasn't complaining. 'Still don't see why we've got to watch the cellblock.'

'Social Work Team has rounds to do.' She handed him one of the mugs – tea, lots of milk, what tasted like a couple of sugars in there as well. 'Doc Griffiths says Adrian's got concussion, *possibly* a fractured skull, *definitely* a fractured cheekbone. Lucky he didn't lose the eye.'

'Poor baby.' Edward dumped his wet towel on the cell's blue plastic mattress. 'What?'

She was frowning at him. 'He's still a human being, Edward!'

'Yeah: a human being who tried to *kill* me.' Prodding, *gently*, at the bruises already darkening the skin across both cheeks. 'I'm kinda short on sympathy for the raping wee shite.'

The frown took on that 'not angry, just disappointed' edge.

Edward sighed. Sagged. 'OK, OK: pity poor Adrian Bedwin. I do so hope he gets well soon.' Sniff. More importantly: 'What about Ms Manson?'

Sergeant Farrow stared down into her mug. 'She's given me three names.'

Christ . . .

He shook his head. Kept his gob shut. Because what *could* you say?

Sergeant Farrow's eyes crept up again, narrowing as they came. 'What were you doing out there, on your own, in a blizzard?'

Good question.

And one that Bigtoria wouldn't want him answering.

But it was too late for that, wasn't it. The plan was buggered from the moment he discovered Caroline Manson in that horrible clubhouse, and now here he was, back in Glenfarach, alive and kicking for all to see. When he was supposed to be dead and buried in a shallow grave. And it wouldn't take long for word to reach Mr Richards and Mr Bishop. And as soon as *they* found out . . .

He took a sip of hot, sweet tea.

Sod it: he'd need help if this whole thing wasn't to go even more badly wrong.

Which meant he might as well tell Sergeant Farrow the truth.

'It's Mr Bishop. He and Mr Richards killed Geoff Newman, Pauline Thomson, and "Black Joe" Ivanson. Well, Mr Richards killed them, on account of Mr Bishop's dying of cancer, but he's the guy behind it all. They're after some safety-deposit boxes from a bank job – worth a massive fortune, apparently.'

She stepped up close and raised a hand in front of his face, sounding worried. 'How many fingers am I holding up?'

He pushed it aside. 'Don't be daft, Sarge: the DI's in danger. She had to pretend to kill me and bury me in a shallow grave, so they wouldn't guess she isn't *really* on the take. I was supposed to lie low at Pauline Thomson's place – which seriously stinks, by the way – because we've no idea who to trust, but then I found the clubhouse and that was all . . . you know.' He shrugged. 'And I had to come back here, didn't I? Couldn't leave Ms Manson and Mr Bedwin out there, they might've died.'

She blinked at him for a while. 'Wow.' Then gave herself a little shake. 'OK. Right.' Puffed out a breath. 'Fudging Nora.'

Edward followed her out of his cell, down the corridor and into the custody suite. 'Sarge?'

'Septic tank.'

OK, that wasn't what he'd expected. 'Eh?'

'That's why Pauline's house smells. The place hasn't been used for ages, so the water in the U-bends evaporates – toilets, sinks, baths, doesn't matter – and there's nothing to stop the sewage smell from seeping through the pipes into the house.' Sergeant Farrow wandered over to Newman's red holdall – still sitting on the floor where Edward had left it – and nudged it with her foot. 'What was Geoff hiding?'

Edward scooped the thing up and dumped it on the desk. Undid the zip, pulling back the edges so she could see the contents. 'Looks like cocaine, weed, resin, and a bunch of pills.' He curled his lip and pointed at the brown envelope. 'And a heap of revolting photographs. Kids. You know what Newman was into.'

'Fudge . . .' Sergeant Farrow buried her face in her hands. 'Kiddy porn, coke, and cannabis.' She deflated for a moment, then stood up straight – shoulders back – marched behind the custody desk and grabbed her tiger's-head-shaped walkie-talkie. Pressed its nose. 'Golf Foxtrot Four to—'

Edward lunged forward, flapping his arms and mouthing the word 'NO!'

She looked at him like he'd coiled one out on the floor.

He dropped his voice to a hissing whisper. 'Shhhhhhh! No! They've got my walkie-talkie, and they think I'm *dead*!'

Sergeant Farrow nodded. 'Golf Foxtrot Four to Golf Foxtrot Six, safe to talk?' Cool and calm, because there was *nothing* special going on and she hadn't just heard about a conspiracy to murder residents and kill a police officer.

PC Harlaw came through loud and proud. *'Safe to talk, Sarge.'*

'Nip back to the station, would you, Dave? Need someone to watch the custody suite for half an hour.'

'Roger Wilco.'

'And pick up a big thing of milk if you're passing the General Store. Maybe some biscuits too. This lot in the cellblock are eating me out of house and home.'

Oh, she was *good* at this.

Edward gave her a double thumbs up.

'Be about . . . fifteen minutes?'

'Don't forget the biscuits.' She released the button and put her tiger down. 'This whole thing is a fudging disaster, isn't it?'

Edward nodded. 'Pretty much, Sarge.'

'Then we'll just have to figure our way out of it.' Pointing. 'Drink your tea and we'll see what we can do.'

According to the dusty clock mounted on the control-room wall, it had just gone twenty past one, but the light was already fading. Blocked out by the thick layer of coal-scuttle clouds that blanketed the valley. Wind snarled and howled outside the windows, snapping its snowy teeth against the glass.

The only illumination came from a trio of headtorches as Edward, Sergeant Farrow, and PC Harlaw gathered around the map of Glenfarach that dominated one wall. The fact they were both in uniform only made Edward's new Armani suit look all the swankier.

Which was nice.

He stopped pointing at Bishop House and shrugged. 'That's as much as I know.'

Harlaw pulled his chin in. 'And DI Montgomery-Porter didn't tell you any of this until *after* she killed you?'

'Apparently my performance "wouldn't have been convincing" if I'd known.'

'Bloody hell.' The constable shook his head, causing a slow-motion strobe effect with his torch. 'Detective inspectors are a complete nightmare.' Then frowned. 'Wait, how come you didn't suffocate when she wrapped you in all that plastic?'

'Did a crap job of it on purpose – tight everywhere else, loose and full of air gaps from about here up.' Tapping himself on the shoulder. 'It's—'

'All right.' Sergeant Farrow scowled at the pair of them. 'Do you think we could get on with this, please?'

Harlaw's torchlight drooped. 'Yes, Sarge.'

So did Edward's. 'Sorry, Sarge.'

'Bad enough I've got three dead residents, another one missing, one in the infirmary with a cracked skull, not to mention Shammy with his battered bonce, and a traumatized social worker; now there's a secret perverts' clubhouse in the woods and a drug ring operating right under our fudging noses.' Her headtorch lit up a circle of grubby ceiling tiles as she dragged in a big breath and bellowed it out again, 'FUDGING HECK!'

Edward and Harlaw grimaced at each other as the echo was smothered by dust.

She covered her face with her hands, muffling out the words: 'Everything's ruined. Everything we've worked for all these years. *Ruined.*' Then she straightened up. 'Right, here's what we've got to do.' Counting the points off on her fingers. 'Number *one*: we arrest Razors and Marky. That'll put an end to their killing spree. Number *two*: we go to Geoff's lair and we secure the crime scene. Number *three*: we interview everybody and arrest anyone who's involved . . .' She stared at Edward's raised hand. 'What?'

'We should probably try and rescue DI Montgomery-Porter first, Sarge. I get the feeling Mr Bishop will find out she's not *really* on his side sooner rather than later.'

Harlaw hooked a thumb over his shoulder. 'And someone's got to stay and look after the cellblock.'

Edward shoved him. '*Sod* the cellblock! Doesn't matter how much of a pain in the arse she is; she's one of ours, and she's going to get herself killed if we don't *do* something!'

Sergeant Farrow groaned, then sagged. 'Fine.' She marched for the exit. 'Everyone grab your stabproof, high-vis, baton, pepper spray, wellies, and whatnot.' Thumping the door open with a dramatic flourish. 'We've got folk to bang up.'

Now that was more like it.

34

God's sake . . .

Edward pulled his chin in, tilting his head against the wind, letting the Police Scotland beanie take the brunt instead of his face. Each gust hurled icy shards against his skin, pelting his brand-new, straight-out-of-the-packet, so-fluorescent-yellow-it-almost-hurt-to-look-at high-vis with layers of fresh snow. Doing its best to batter him into submission as he waded his way along East Main Street.

OK, so it meant his headtorch could only illuminate the thigh-deep drifts a couple of feet in front of him, but visibility wasn't much further than you could spit anyway.

His breath didn't hang around long enough to fog – the gale ripped it away soon as it left his lips. On the plus side, at least his Method of Entry armoured gloves had dried out, even if the leather *was* seized nearly solid.

PC Harlaw led the way, fighting through the blizzard, one shoulder down and forward, an arm up to shield his face as he forged a path into the worst of it. Sergeant Farrow brought up the rear, sticking close, using Edward as a windbreak, her headtorch flicking from side to side, sweeping solid cones of swirling white all around them.

Harlaw lurched to a stop and turned his back on the wind, waving a hand off towards a narrow alley. 'SHORTCUT!' Then wallowed across the road.

Edward followed, into what was little more than a ginnel: two storeys high; rough granite walls; the roofs on both sides overhanging the space by a couple of feet, narrowing the gap above their heads even further. Which had the *massive* benefit of shutting out ninety-nine percent of the wind, and the same amount of snow. On East Main Street it was nearly up to his groin; in here it barely came halfway up his wellies.

Thank God for that.

Dark, though – almost pitch black in fact, those alley walls blocking the pale, blue-grey luminescence that pervaded the rest of the village.

He slumped back against the granite, breath pluming in his headtorch's beam, cold stinging his cheeks every bit as much as the screaming blizzard. 'What if Mr Bishop's not home?'

Sergeant Farrow wiped the snow off her chest with a gloved hand. 'Oh, he'll be home all right. Man his age, in his condition, in this weather? Be off his chump to risk it.'

'You guys ready?' Harlaw watched them both nod, then headed off again, trudging his way down the alley, leading them deeper into the silent darkness.

With any luck it'd spit them out on Church Row, not far from Bishop House. And they'd be in time to rescue Bigtoria from whatever horrible fate Mr Richards had in store for her.

Not that she'd be grateful. Probably blow her top and blame it all on Edward. *'How dare you come back from the dead and ruin everything by saving me and making sure I don't get carved up with a bloody cut-throat!'*

'Hang on.' Harlaw stopped in his tracks and stood there with his hand up. Head on one side. Lowering his voice to a whisper. 'Did you hear that.'

Nope.

Edward turned, ears straining against the relative silence, headtorch lighthousing across granite and brick as he rotated. They'd come about two-thirds, maybe three-quarters of the way down the lane, and other than a handful of blank doors there was nothing to see.

Sergeant Farrow was doing the same, keeping her voice down too. 'What am I listening for?'

'Shhhh . . .' Harlaw crept over to a red door – scuffed and

functional, with a sign screwed to the painted wood: 'Rosebark's Furniture Exchange ~ Employees Only'. He pressed his ear against the door. 'Thought I heard someone crying for help. Like, "Let me out!" Something like that. *Proper* crying, you know? *Small-child* crying.'

Sodding hell.

Edward raised his eyebrows at Sergeant Farrow. After what he'd found in the woods?

She nodded. 'Kick it in!'

Harlaw puffed out his chest, took a step back, and slammed the sole of his wellington boot into the wood, just beneath the round brass disk of a Yale lock. The whole thing *boom*ed and rattled, but didn't budge. So he had another try. And another. Putting his weight into it, arms at shoulder height every time his welly landed.

No success.

'Hold on.' Edward pulled off one glove and dug out the master keys. 'This'll do it.' It took a couple of goes, but key number three slid into the lock and turned. A *clunk*, and all he had to do was give the door a gentle push and it swung open.

'OK.' Harlaw went first, his wellies scuffing on what sounded like a concrete floor – the noise echoing softly in the darkness.

Edward was next, stepping into a low room with bare granite walls: long enough that his headtorch couldn't reach the end. The grimy scent of mildew polluted the cold air, clawing at the back of his throat.

Sofas and sideboards lurked in the gloom; chests of drawers, bookcases, and bedsteads materialized in the torchlight, then slipped away again. Some sat out on their own; others were draped in dust-furred sheets. Like old-fashioned ghosts, or a Klan meeting for racist, half-wit, out-of-fashion furniture.

He crept further in, torch pulling details from the darkened room. A vanity unit with a scarred top, an easel clarted in paint stains, a recliner chair with matching footstool. All of it slumping under layers of dust; all of it second-hand. This must've been where Black Joe Ivanson was going to furnish his house from, when the redecorating was done.

THE DEAD OF WINTER

Which it wouldn't be, now. Or at least, not by *him*.

Edward took a right at a three-seater leather sofa with cat scratches all up the sides. Edging his way along a row of TV units, ears cocked, trying to pick up the crying Harlaw had heard, but the whole place was silent. Maybe whoever was in here, had moved the child? Or maybe they'd slapped a hand over its mouth? Maybe they were only inches away, concealed under one of the dust sheets . . .

He pitched his voice not much above a murmur. 'What do you think, Sarge: somebody from Geoff Newman's ring?'

Silence.

Edward tried again. 'Does anyone live here – you know, in the building – or is it all just furniture?'

More silence.

'Sarge?'

He stopped beside a Welsh dresser and turned, looking back the way he'd come.

Darkness.

Not even a glow from their headtorches.

OK, that wasn't good.

He raised his voice a little: 'Sarge? Constable Harlaw?'

Maybe, whoever had the child, they'd crept up on Sergeant Farrow and PC Harlaw, taking them down one by one, till only Edward was left? Maybe they were sneaking up on him right now, and the only way he could save everyone was by not getting himself killed in the next couple of minutes. And after today, he'd had quite enough of shallow graves, thank you very much.

Question was: where was the bugger hiding?

And that's when Sergeant Farrow's voice slithered through the darkness. *'I'm sorry, Edward, I really am.'*

Oh no . . .

'Sarge?' Headtorch swinging in the direction the sound came from; finding nothing but haunted furniture.

'I'm afraid your journey ends here.'

Great – because things weren't screwed up enough already.

He turned left, then right, raking the dust sheets with torchlight. 'You saying what I think you're saying, Sarge? You're involved in a conspiracy with Mr Bishop and Mr Richards to murder multiple individuals? Because I'm *pretty sure* that's gross misconduct.'

'*Of course not! Had no idea the old scunner was on a rampage.*' A sigh echoed around the low room. '*I tried to keep you out of harm's way, I really did, but you had to go wandering about in the woods and find Geoff's stupid clubhouse.*'

Eh?

'Why does that—'

'*Who do you think he got the drugs from, Edward? Who do you think he was dealing for? I always ran such a tight ship, and then there goes Geoff, getting high on my supply.*'

'So you killed him.' Edward raised his voice a bit. 'Constable Harlaw, looks like it's up to you and me. Two against one!' He took a deep breath. 'Sergeant Louise Farrow, I am arresting you under Section One of the Criminal Justice, Scotland, Act 2016 for the murder of Geoff Newman—'

'*I didn't kill anyone, you muppet. But you know what, Edward? You're right about one thing: it* is *two against one.*'

Harlaw's voice came from somewhere nearby, much, much closer than Sergeant Farrow. Far *too* close. '*Only it's the other way around.*'

Oh . . . bugger.

Edward spun towards the sound, his headtorch making shadows dance among the shrouded furniture. Where the hell *was* he?

'*Geoff Newman was dead when we got there, swear to God. Only I didn't know what he had stashed about the place. Merchandise? Stuff with our fingerprints on it? Stuff he'd hidden away to blackmail the Sarge and me with? Stuff any competent forensic team would find when they searched his house . . . ?*'

A scraping noise, off to the left.

Edward whirled towards it, crouching down, arms out. Ready. But there was no one there. Just more shadows writhing in the torch's beam.

'*It's a shame about Shammy. I didn't want to hurt him, but I had to burn the place to the ground, and witnesses . . .*' Harlaw sucked air in through his teeth, making them *hissssssss*. '*But that's all taken care of now. Or will be in a minute.*'

Bugger, bugger, bugger, bugger.

'Think you scare me?' Edward rummaged through his pockets – or tried to with the stiff, thick MOE gloves. Pepper spray. Pepper spray. Where was his *sodding* pepper spray? 'Cos you don't!' Aha. Right. There we go.

Thank Christ for that.

'A lanky wee shite like you? I won't even break a sweat.'

Edward stuck his fingertips in his mouth and pulled the leather gloves off, letting them fall to the ground as he removed the safety catch from the little cylinder. 'You know you can't get away with this.' Holding the spray out like Dirty Harry's magnum. Unlocked and ready to rock. 'The Procurator Fiscal and your Duty Inspector and the whole circus is on its way!'

A laugh rang out from the darkness. And when the echo faded, Sergeant Farrow's voice took on a kids'-TV-presenter lilt: all singsong and amused and patronizing. *'Oh Eddie. Oh Edward. Oh Eddie McTedward . . . The cavalry isn't coming till the pass clears and that'll take* days. *By the time anyone turns up, you'll be long gone.'*

He edged back until there was nothing but granite wall behind him. Torch sweeping left and right, searching for Harlaw. Pepper spray at the ready. 'Come on, Sarge, you don't have to do this.'

'You see, you discovered that one of our greasier residents was up to no good – doesn't matter which, they're all disposable – and when you and I confronted them, they went . . . wild and attacked us.' Another sigh. *'Sadly, you both sustained fatal injuries in the fight, though you were terribly brave. Maybe I'll even say you saved me? That sounds inspiringly heroic, don't you think?'*

The woman was bloody deranged.

'You'll get a hero's funeral. I'll cut a deal with Marky Bishop and clype on your DI – earn myself a nice big share of that "massive fortune" you were on about. Then Dave and I will retire from Glenfarach very, very, very rich.' A rustling noise crinkled the darkness, a click, then a short monophonic rendition of 'The Lion Sleeps Tonight' jingled away on Edward's left.

He whipped around, pointing the pepper spray in that direction. Took a deep breath.

Sergeant Farrow grew an extra electronic echo as her words cut across the room from wherever she was, *and* crackled out of PC Harlaw's walkie-talkie. With enough delay to make the words mush into each other. *'Golf Foxtrot Four to Alpha Charlie One, safe to talk?'*

Bigtoria's voice replied in stereo – blaring simultaneously from Sergeant Farrow's tiger and Harlaw's lion. *'Safe to talk.'*

'I know what you did. And you are so *going to fudging pay for it.'*

Static buzzed from the walkie-talkies' speakers.

'Did you hear me, Bigtoria? *We know you didn't really kill the boy: you faked the whole thing. You're an undercover grass and Mr Bishop won't like that.'*

Still nothing.

'Hello? Are you there? Hello? Hmph . . .' Silence. *'Ah well. Dave, want to do the honours?'*

Harlaw's voice was much closer than it should've been, and instead of being in front of Edward, where the walkie-talkie was, it was right behind. *'Sorry, mate, I'll make it quick.'*

The bastard had set him up.

35

Edward whirled around, just in time for his torch to catch PC Harlaw leaping at him over a chaise longue.

They clattered to the concrete floor, rolling over and over, then slamming into a mahogany wardrobe. The impact was enough to separate them for a moment; it wasn't a lot of space, but it'd do.

He struggled to his knees and brought the pepper spray up, thumb on the trigger.

Harlaw slashed his hand sideways, knocking the cylinder from Edward's fingers – sending it bouncing across the concrete: *ping-clang-clonnng*. It rolled under a vanity unit with an oval mirror on top about a dozen feet away. Too far to reach, unless—

The hand slashed back again, smashing into Edward's nose, filling the air with burning pepper and hot iron.

Sodding. Bloody. Son of a bitch.

He threw a punch of his own, clouting Harlaw on the ear.

A fist flew, catching Edward on the chin, and he lunged forward. Grappling. Snarling. Trying to land a kick as Harlaw grabbed his wrists and just missed with a headbutt.

They battered into a chest of drawers, tipping the thing over to crash into a coffee table in a crescendo of splintered wood.

Edward wriggled free, yanked his knee up and pistoned his heel into Harlaw's stomach, knocking him over backwards.

Right.

He turned and scrabbled across the floor in a half-crawl,

reaching for the vanity unit – only for his knees to disappear out from under him as Harlaw grabbed his ankles and pulled.

His body hit the concrete with a *whump*, the point of his chin getting a more serious clattering than the punch had managed. But not enough to stop him heaving forwards, right arm at full stretch, fingers questing in the leaping shadows beneath the vanity unit for the glittering canister.

A weight thumped down on his back and a fist smacked into his exposed ribs. Only single-padded with high-vis kapok this time, so shards of burning gravel slashed out across his side.

Almost there . . .

Another blow landed in the same sodding spot, forcing a guttural groan from his mouth that stirred up a cloud of dust to dance in the headtorch's beam.

His fingers brushed the smooth metal surface.

Come on, you *utter* slippery little bastard . . .

A hand dug into the hair at the back of Edward's head, hauled it up, then slammed his face into the floor.

Thunk.

The damn pepper spray was *just* out of reach.

Please, for God's sake . . .

Thunk.

His forehead bounced off the concrete again, bringing with it the ringing of a million old-fashioned phones, wrapped up in a wave of searing black-and-yellow dots.

Forget trying to grab the thing, you moron: flick it away instead.

He curled his hand into a fist, then sprang the fingers outwards – the tips smacking into the canister and sending it flying off to *clang* against the wall and bounce back. Wasn't quite in the palm of his hand, but close enough to—

Thunk.

The ringing doubled in volume, and so did the dots, bringing with them a stabbing pain that danced through his skull on ice skates and sharpened crampons.

But his fingers *finally* closed around the pepper spray.

He flattened his other hand against the ground and shoved,

heaving with his knees and feet, but Harlaw's weight just shifted. It was enough to get Edward over onto his side though, glaring up at the bastard from the corner of one eye.

Edward jabbed the pepper spray into Harlaw's face and jammed his thumb down on the trigger.

Nothing happened.

No great plume of droplets, no screaming, no bright-red puffy eyes streaming with tears as the industrial-strength capsicum worked its horrible, nerve-searing magic.

He pressed the trigger again.

Nothing happened *again*.

'Sorry.' Harlaw smiled down at him. 'Did you really think we'd give you a loaded one? When the plan was to take you out and get rid of you? Nah, mate, you're—'

Edward used it as a knuckleduster instead, crashing his fist into that smug face hard enough to send Harlaw rearing backwards.

Edward fought his way to his feet, new high-vis half unzipped, bloody, and torn.

Sod this.

Run.

He got three steps towards the exit before a hand wrapped around his ankle, tripping him up, sending him battering headfirst into a dining-room chair. He went straight through the thing, leaving a splintered mess of wooden staves behind.

Edward rolled, thumped into the table the chair belonged to, then scrambled to his feet just before Harlaw arrived in what looked like the run-up to a free kick.

The foot lashed out, heading for Edward's balls. Somehow managed to bounce off his thigh instead.

He threw a punch, so did Harlaw, the pair of them battering off each other, scrambling to grab hold, the lapels of Edward's Armani ripping in Harlaw's grip. Jostling each other. Fists and elbows.

Harlaw let go with one hand, coiling it back to hurl another blow, but Edward rushed forward before he could swing, shoving him off balance, sending him staggering backwards.

Making just enough space for Edward to rip the oval mirror off that vanity unit and crash it down on Harlaw's head.

It shattered, each shard shining in the headtorch's glow, shooting out reflected beams of their own as they tumbled to smash on the floor.

Harlaw wasn't far behind them. He collapsed onto his knees, then keeled over sideways. *Clunk.*

Oh, thank Christ and all the Hairy Apostles . . .

Every breath was a struggle – gasped in and whoomped out of Edward's burning lungs; blood, *lub-whump-lub-whump-lub-whump*ing in his ears and skull; sweat trickling down his spine.

He pulled out his handcuffs and slapped one end on Harlaw's right wrist, dragged him across to a heavy, cast-iron bedframe, shoved the cuffed arm through a gap in the bars and fastened the other end around Harlaw's left ankle.

Get out of that, you wee shite.

Then he helped himself to Harlaw's handcuffs, keys, extendable baton, and pepper spray.

Edward stood, wheezing and panting. Wiped the blood from his top lip, mouth, and chin.

'You hear . . . hear that, Sarge? . . . It's . . . one against one . . . now.'

The sound of feet scraping on the concrete came from somewhere over by the far wall, getting further away, turning into the *clump-clump-clump* of someone trying to sprint in wellington boots. Then pale grey light oozed into the room as the alley door flew open. Sergeant Farrow had legged it.

'Sod . . .'

Edward lumbered his way to a hobble, then a jog, nearly managing a run as he burst out into the snow again. Stumbling, almost colliding with the other side of the narrow lane.

Righting himself and checking up and down the gloomy—

There!

Sergeant Farrow – loping towards the police station, following the beam of her headtorch. As soon as she hit the end of the lane the wind slammed into her, buffeting her sideways, slowing her down as she disappeared around the corner.

Come on – not done yet.

He forced one leg in front of the other, working his way back up to something almost resembling a run again. Breath rattling in his throat; heart pummelling his chest. 'THERE'S NOWHERE TO GO! WE'RE SNOWED IN!'

He barrelled out of the lane and into the blizzard, skittering to a halt as the wind smashed against him – trying to shove him off his feet, setting the open front of his high-vis snapping and whipping. Snow swirling past him at speed, crackling into the back of his jacket as he turned away from it and lurched after Sergeant Farrow.

She was following the groove they'd carved through the drifts on the way here, but it was still much deeper than it'd been in Dunbrae Lane, that screaming wind already causing the snow to blow into the hip-deep, single-file canyon.

Sergeant Farrow probably wasn't *that* far ahead, but the blizzard stole her figure for long moments at a time, before returning it again: pale and grainy in the middle distance. Moving a lot faster than he was. But then no one had just tried to kill her in a furniture exchange.

She passed the dark silent bulk of the Glenfarach House Hotel and waded out into Market Square, elbows up, staggering as the wind did its best to scoop her off her feet every eight or nine paces.

And Edward struggled along in her wake. Getting slower as the adrenaline rush faded, letting the aches and pains and sheer bloody weariness of the last three days seep into his bones. 'COME ON, SARGE! DON'T BE AN IDIOT! IT'S OVER!'

She shouted something back at him, but the wind ripped it away.

The police station loomed on the other side of the square, a couple of upstairs lights shining out into the horrific afternoon. Burning through that generator diesel. But at least they made it easier to see Sergeant Farrow wade her way over to the Big Car.

She was digging her keys out as Edward limped past the clock tower/monument – at not much more than walking pace.

Sergeant Farrow clambered into the driver's side and the engine's guttural growl ripped free. The headlights clacked on, then the roof-mounted spotlights stabbed their beams through the hurling snow, the blue-and-whites flickering.

He'd almost reached the last cordon of trees when the Big Car's wheels spun, going nowhere – spitting out clouds of flakes to glow blood red in the running lights – as she floored it. Then the snow chains dug in and the Land Rover surged forward.

Accelerating.

Straight towards Edward.

He stumbled to a halt. 'Oh, buggering . . .'

The Big Car charged at him through the snow, moving fast enough to do some serious damage, and getting quicker with every passing second.

No doubt about it: she was actively *trying* to run him over.

With a dirty-great-big Land Rover.

WELL, DON'T JUST STAND THERE!

He leapt to the side, and the Big Car roared through the place he'd been standing a moment before.

Sergeant Farrow clearly wasn't happy that she'd missed, because the brake lights flared – the nose dipping as she hauled the wheel around for another go. Only problem was, those chains were good for everyday sensible driving in wintery conditions, *not* rallying in heavy snow.

The back end kicked out and the Big Car spun, still moving in the same direction, pirouetting as it battered through the drifts, and only stopping when its bonnet slammed into the clock tower – bringing everything to a sudden jarring halt.

That grumbling diesel engine died, but the lights stayed on.

If this was TV, the horn would've been blaring, instead of which the whole scene was silent. Just the wind and the crackling impact of yet more snow to break the lack of artistic drama.

Edward staggered over to the driver's side, peching and heeching all the way. He opened the door and peered inside.

Sergeant Farrow was slumped sideways in her seat, a gash snaking across her forehead. Leaking dark red to drip on the Land Rover's upholstery.

That didn't look promising.

He climbed up onto the running board, the wind shoving and grabbing at his shoulders, trying to claw its way into the Big Car as he reached in and felt for a pulse . . .

Thank God for that.

Still alive.

She was going to have a *monster* headache when she regained consciousness, though.

He sagged forwards, eyes closed, getting his breath back as snow swirled in through the open door.

'OK.'

Edward levered her upright and pushed one of Sergeant Farrow's hands between the spokes of the steering wheel, before pulling out the handcuffs he'd pinched from Harlaw and fastening both her wrists together. Then liberated her keys, *her* cuffs, and her tiger's-head walkie-talkie.

He climbed down onto the snowy road, rocking as another gust jostled his high-vis, then slammed the driver's door shut.

And, just for old times' sake, he stuck two fingers up at Sergeant Farrow through the window.

Icy white flakes whipped past as he turned to face the blizzard again, one hand up to shield his eyes – squinting in the general direction of Mr Bishop's house.

They'd probably killed the DI already – especially if they'd heard Sergeant Farrow's *'I know what you did'* call on the walkie-talkie. And as Mr Richards had Edward's teddy bear now, and the things transmitted to every handset, there was zero reason to believe they hadn't. So she was almost certainly dead.

Yeah . . .

But 'almost certainly' wasn't the same as 'definitely', was it.

And it didn't mean he shouldn't *try* to save her.

Edward pulled his shoulders back, chin up, facing down the storm.

Mind you . . .

How the hell was he supposed to mount a one-man rescue

mission, with nothing but an extendable baton and a pilfered canister of pepper spray, in the middle of the worst winter for *at least* a decade?

What he needed was an edge, some sort of secret weapon, an ace in the hole to stop this turning into: Operation Edward And Bigtoria Get Murdered By A Vicious Pair Of Old Bastards.

He frowned.

Then turned away from the angry wind and its millions of frozen daggers to stare off down West Main Street instead.

A smile spread its way across his stinging face.

'Now *there's* an idea.'

Thirty-Six

A paraffin lamp hissed out its warm white glow from the mantelpiece, making long dark shadows up the blood-red walls. Its light was bolstered by a handful of candles, flickering away in storm lanterns, giving the impression that the three of them had gathered around a campfire in a prehistoric cave, as the snow howled outside like a hungry wolf. Wondering if the sun would ever rise again.

Someone had re-covered the carpet with fresh plastic sheeting, awaiting the walls' next coat of colon-coloured paint.

Marky Bishop was hunched in his wheelchair, face grey and lined as crumpled newsprint, sucking on his oxygen mask as if it were the only thing keeping him upright. A tartan blanket thrown over his pale-cream chinos, hiding those bony knees. Razors paced the floor in front of the fireplace, blocking out the lamp as he passed it, slippers squeaking on the plastic sheeting. Leaving Victoria to claim the corner of the room where she'd 'killed' DC Reekie, now home to the stepladder and a small stack of paint pots. Doing her best to radiate menace, because that seemed to be the atmosphere everyone else was aiming for.

She folded her arms. 'And how do I know you won't screw me out of my share?'

Marky's voice wheezed out from behind the oxygen mask. 'You're not . . . not very trusting . . . for a detective . . . inspector.'

A snarl from the pacing Razors. 'Nothing but a buggering whinge.'

'You'll get . . . your cut . . . when *we* . . . get out of this dump.' A grunt made those skeletal shoulders twitch. 'If the snow . . . ever stops.'

'I'm not—' That ridiculous circus theme song burst into its faux-cheery bleeping, deep inside her high-vis's pocket.

A similarly awful rendition of 'Teddy Bears' Picnic' jingled away to itself in Razors' cardigan.

She pointed at him and shook her head, before pulling out the clown walkie-talkie.

Farrow's voice crackled from both speakers: *'Golf Foxtrot Four to Alpha Charlie One, safe to talk?'*

She raised a hand, forestalling any crap from Marky or Razors. 'Safe to talk.'

'I know what you did.' Damn it. *'And you are so going to fudging pay for it.'*

Victoria jabbed her thumb down on the clown's nose and held it there – putting the walkie-talkie into transmit mode. Stopping anything else coming in. Blocking Farrow before she could say something stupid. Or dangerous.

Which raised the horrible question: what did she know? And how on earth did she find out?

Razors' pointy chin came up, a crooked finger pointing at the clown's head. 'What she mean, "what you did"?' Every word dripping with suspicion. 'What you done, hen?'

'Oh, go screw yourself with a dishcloth, Cleaning Boy.'

Marky sagged in his chair. 'Not this . . . again.'

'Naw, man, she's up to something.' His eyes narrowed, dentures bared as he scowled at her. 'What – did – you – do?'

'Maybe Sergeant Farrow found out I killed DC Reekie.' She squared up, chest out, shoulders back, and gave him a scowl of her own. 'How would she do that, I wonder?'

'You calling me a *clype*?' Leaning on that last word as if it were the most offensive one in the dictionary.

Marky surfaced from his mask. 'Just . . . shut up . . . the pair . . . of you.' Then clamped it into place again – his breath amplified and echoing, making sounds like a deep-sea diver struggling at the bottom of the ocean. 'Please . . .'

'No' this time.' Razors stomped across the plastic sheeting and loomed over the wheelchair. 'You can't see what's right in front of your wheezy, buggering face, can you?' That crooked finger jabbed in Victoria's direction. 'She's bad news. Can't be trusted. Never could. And you're too blind to see it!' Flecks of spittle sparkled in the candlelight. 'Wouldn't even *be* here if I hadn't shoved that old bitch down the stairs! All the bastards I tortured and killed. *For you.* And what: you're gonnae take *her* word?'

Razors wiped a hand across his mouth, then pulled out his cut-throat. 'Naw, I'm putting this one out her misery before she screws us.' He unfolded the blade and stepped towards her, a grin stretching his wrinkled face. 'Gonnae enjoy this.'

Victoria bent her knees, getting ready. Turning sideways to make a smaller target. 'You're nothing but an OAP Weegie arsehole, "Paul".' She pulled her extendable baton from her inside pocket and clacked it out to full length. Which evened the odds a bit. Yes: the blade was sharp, but the baton had reach. 'I'm going to tear you apart.'

That was the ticket – confidence.

He advanced, the cut-throat dancing back and forth in a glittering figure of eight. 'Been wanting to do this for ages, but.'

Marky shot out a hand. 'Razors, no!'

The old git didn't take his eyes off Victoria as the cut-throat curled through the air, like a snake. 'I'm done taking orders, Big Man. She dies right here, right now.'

Another three steps and he'd be in baton range.

Go for the wrist first – man that age, the bones would be brittle as dried twigs. Break the wrist and his blade could be as sharp as it liked; didn't matter if it was lying on the floor.

Razors' grin widened. 'Look on the bright side, Marky, this means one less bugger to share it all with.'

The lines deepened across Marky's forehead. 'When you put it . . . that way . . . Aye.' He nodded. Then stood – not the creaky levering of bones he usually needed to get out of a seat or the wheelchair, but a smooth, fluid motion, standing up straighter than she'd ever seen him do.

He produced a snub-nosed matt-black semi-automatic pistol from somewhere, aimed. A deafening bark rang out, rattling around the living room, reverberating off the bare walls. Blood sprayed out of Razors' chest, glittering and dark red. Pattering down on the plastic sheeting, warm wet flecks freckling Victoria's face.

Then Razors crumpled to the floor, his eyes wide, mouth moving. But no words came out, just a scarlet froth. He curled onto his side, staring at Marky, reaching out for him with both hands.

Marky rolled his neck in a circle, stretched his back. The oxygen mask still muffled his voice, but he sounded like a man half his age. ' "One less bugger to share it all with." ' The gun drifted down to point at his friend's head. 'Thanks, Razors.'

The second bark was even louder than the first, punching a hole through Razors' forehead, sending his skull bouncing up from the plastic sheeting as red and pink and grey exploded out the other side. Then his head *splatch*ed down again, much flatter at the back now. Mouth hanging open, a look of betrayal on his empty face.

Marky took off his oxygen mask and dropped it on the floor with a sigh. 'That's *better*.' He rubbed at the grooves it had left in his skin. 'I imagine that must be how it feels to get your bra off at the end of a busy day.'

Victoria didn't move, keeping her eyes on Marky Bishop, trying not to stare at the gun. 'You were never ill at all.'

'It's amazing what you can do with a bit of leverage. Bit of bribery and corruption. The odd threat or two delivered by a large associate on the outside.' He nudged Razors' body with his shoe. 'Next thing you know you've got a faked blood test and an X-ray of some poor bastard's shadow-filled lungs.'

'He was your *friend*! And you killed him.'

'Well, he was beginning to grate a bit. Don't get me wrong, I loved the guy like a brother, but Christ, he didn't half go on.' Marky looked down at his gun, as if seeing it for the first time. 'Besides, he was right about only having to split it three ways.' The pistol turned from side to side, matt-black and horrifying. 'So now it's just you, me, and the nice man who's going to set us up like royalty in the Seychelles.' A smile slashed across that skeletal face. 'But maybe I should keep *your* share too?' The barrel raised until it pointed straight at Victoria's chest. 'I want to thank you for all your help, Detective Inspector Montgomery-Porter. Couldn't have done it without—'

She threw the stepladder at him, not hanging around to see if it hit or not as she bolted from the room. Battering out into the pitch-dark hallway, bouncing off the stairlift, staggering to where the snow's spectral light oozed in through the glazing on either side of the front door.

Victoria wrenched the door open and stumbled out into the blizzard.

She didn't look back.

Running would've been easier if she wasn't stuck in a pair of borrowed wellington boots, but sometimes you just had to make the best of what you had. She launched into a wobbly sprint, speeding down the cleared ramp, then crunching through the knee-deep snow that covered the pavement. Heading for—

The gun barked again.

Victoria's left leg collapsed, and she crashed into the drifts, tumbling through them, gouts of white spiralling out. Coming to a halt, flat on her back, blinking up at the screeching wind.

What on earth was—

And that's when the pain kicked in – radiating out in pulsing scarlet waves, making her thigh glow with the sheer throbbing agony of it.

'Jesus . . .' Gritting her teeth tight, both hands clamped around her leg as dark blood oozed out in the ghost light. The sodding exit wound was the size of a Tunnock's tea cake, fringed with torn fabric and stinging as though a million burning wasps were rampaging their way through her skin. Breath hissing in and out, in and out, in and out.

Tourniquet. She needed a tourniquet. Something to stop the bleeding before it was too late.

She let go of the leg and blood pulsed out again; her trembling, stained fingers fumbling with her belt. Yanking it off and wrapping it around her thigh, a couple of inches above the wound. Buckling it, then grabbing the loose end in her left fist and hauling it *tight*. Grunting as the pressure set off a whole new swarm of wasps.

'*OOPS!*'

Victoria dragged her eyes away from the hole in her leg.

Marky stood in the doorway to Bishop House, waving at her, like someone on his way out for a pleasant afternoon stroll. As if putting a bullet in her from that distance was nothing to him. And he could do it again any time he liked.

Thirty-Seven

Victoria struggled onto her front, pushed herself upright and fought her way across the road, dragging her injured leg through the wind-sculpted drifts to the rusty churchyard gates. At least the sodding things weren't locked. She dropped her shoulder and shoved, forcing one side open as far as it would go before the mass of snow stopped it, and squeezed into the cemetery.

The headstones were partially buried under a thick shroud of white: ancient lichen-crusted stone crumbling away beneath the winter's blanket; Celtic crosses and weeping angels wearing bonnets of ice; box tombs topped with two feet of the stuff. And still more snow hammered down from the sky, whirling around the darkened church, as if the Devil had come to claim his own.

She forged a path through the hip-deep drifts, left arm trembling with the effort of holding that tourniquet tight. Limping and staggering between the gravestones. There was no way to hide – if it hadn't been snowing, maybe, but she was leaving a great gouged trail behind her, smeared with ink-dark blood.

Then what was the point of running?

Not getting shot again, *that's* what.

Marky Bishop's voice roared out through the blizzard. *'DON'T WORRY: IT'LL ONLY HURT FOR A LITTLE BIT.'*

No thanks.

She kept going, shoving between the jumbled ranks of headstones. Thankfully, many were almost as tall as she was, offering some protection from the next bullet to come her way.

Hopefully.

Every step was getting more difficult, her injured leg screaming out in protest each time she tried to put any weight on it. Slowing her down even more.

He was going to catch her, and he was going to kill her.

Only one thing left to try.

Victoria sheltered in the lee of a big stone slab with a skull-and-crossbones carved into it, and pulled out her walkie-talkie. Jabbing her thumb down on the clown's nose. 'MAYDAY, MAYDAY! THIS IS ALPHA CHARLIE ONE: I'M IN THE GRAVEYARD. MARKY BISHOP IS TRYING TO KILL ME!' She let go of the button, but there was no reply. 'REPEAT: I NEED URGENT ASSISTANCE, OVER!'

She slumped back against the gravestone. Teeth gritted. Biting down on the pain.

'YOU'RE WASTING YOUR TIME, BIGTORIA, NO ONE'S COMING TO SAVE YOU.'

Maybe if she could get inside the church, there'd be a place to hide? Or somewhere to ambush the old bastard? Find a makeshift weapon and bash his brains out.

Of course, it would've helped if she'd still had that bloody extendable baton, but it went flying when he shot her. And she was *not* going back for it.

The church would have some sort of side door, wouldn't it? So the priest, or minister, or whatever denomination this was, could sneak in and out without the congregation seeing. That would be much easier than breaking in through the main doors. Less visible too.

Deep breath. 'THEY'RE ON THEIR WAY, MARKY; YOUR LITTLE SCHEME'S DEAD AND BURIED! MIGHT AS WELL PUT THE GUN DOWN.' Then she bent nearly double, hobbling along, keeping below the tops of the gravestones, making for the dark bulk of Glenfarach Church. Putting as much distance as possible between herself and where she'd been when she'd shouted.

Because hopefully Marky would be heading there, giving her a couple of minutes to reach safety.

His voice ripped through the howling wind. *'THINK I WON'T PUT A BULLET IN THEM TOO? DUMP ALL YOUR BODIES IN THAT HORRIBLE WEE HOUSE AND BURN THE BASTARD DOWN!'* A laugh rang out. *'BY THE TIME ANYONE FINDS OUT, I'LL BE ON A WHITE SANDY BEACH, UP TO MY OXTERS IN COCKTAILS, WOMEN, AND CASH.'*

She kept moving, limping her way through the snow, getting closer to the church with every barbed-wire step.

Less than twenty feet to go.

But her left leg gave up before she was even halfway there, crumpling like a piece of wet tissue paper. Leaving her sprawled face down in the deep, deep snow. And no amount of gritting her teeth, grunting, or pulling on the tourniquet would make it work again.

So that's it? Going to give up and just lie there, waiting for him to come and blow the back of your skull off?

MOVE.

Victoria hauled herself through the blizzard, hand over hand, good leg shoving her forward. Crawling along as snow tumbled down on top of her.

Not far now. Only five, maybe six feet and . . .

'THERE WE GO.' Marky stepped out from behind a large carved angel, the gun by his side. Cardigan flapping in the wind. Holding onto the angel's plinth as another gust hurled icy flakes across the graveyard. 'HAVE TO ADMIT YOU'RE A LOT TOUGHER THAN I EXPECTED. BIG COPPERS TEND TO BE ALL STEROIDS AND NO BALLS. BUT YOU'VE GOT A PAIR THE SIZE OF STONEHAVEN!'

Don't stop.

Don't give in.

Don't give the bastard the satisfaction.

He leaned against the angel to watch Victoria crawling past. 'I'M GOING TO MISS SCOTLAND, I SUPPOSE. NOT ENOUGH TO MAKE ME LEAVE MY TROPICAL ISLAND PARADISE, BUT THERE'S BOUND TO BE A WEE TUG AT THE HEARTSTRINGS.'

Marky waded after her, taking his time, matching her slow, painful pace. 'MIGHT EVEN BE A TEAR IN MY EYE AS I SINK THE ODD

PIÑA COLADA OR MOJITO, AND THINK OF THE COLD AND FROSTY WINTER'S DAY I SAID GOODBYE TO THE LEGENDARY DI MONTGOMERY-PORTER.'

Her fingertips brushed the wall of the church.

If you're going to die, die on your feet.

She let go of the tourniquet and dragged herself up a black-metal downpipe with frozen fingers. She'd been aiming for the side of the building, but had ended up at the front corner, just around from the main doors.

As good a place to take her last curtain call as any. At least it would have a sense of theatre about it.

Propping herself up with her right hand against the stonework, she limp-staggered through the thigh-deep snow.

'THERE'S MY BRAVE GIRL. YOU GO FOR IT.'

The wind came to an abrupt halt the moment she hobbled around the corner, blocked by the church's granite bulk. It should've made things easier, but she was struggling now. Every step taking more energy than she had.

But still she kept going.

Kept fighting.

All the way to the big double doors.

Victoria slumped back against them, breathing hard.

At least *one* thing was in her favour – maybe it was loss of blood, or maybe it was the cold, but her left leg didn't hurt any more. Didn't feel anything at all.

Victoria bared her teeth, raising her chin as Marky lurched over to the foot of the steps. 'You won't . . . get away . . . with this.'

He spread his arms as if he was about to bless the congregation. 'Are you kidding? With what's in those safety-deposit boxes? There isn't a single police force in the country that would *dare* go after me.'

A flickering orange glow grew behind him, turning the falling snow into flakes of gold and copper. Someone had set fire to another building. Come tomorrow morning, Glenfarach would probably be like something out of *Mad Max*.

Just as well she wouldn't be here to witness it.

The whole place could burn.

Good riddance to it.

Marky raised the gun. 'Any last words?'

She spat, but it fell short. 'I'll see you in Hell.'

'Save me a pitchfork.' He gave her a smile and a wink. 'Bye, Bigtoria.'

The flickering orange was brighter now, bringing with it a deep dark grumbling howl that slashed through the blizzard's roar. Maybe Hell was coming to them, instead of the other way around?

38

OK, here we go . . .

Edward tightened his grip on the steering wheel, hauling it left as the snowplough thundered down Church Row.

The ancient truck bounced over something, then smashed into the churchyard gates with a spectacular *CRASH*, sending them flying open – spinning off their hinges in crumpled snakes of wrought iron as the plough battering-rammed its way into the cemetery.

There can't have been a straight driveway up to the church itself, because rows of headstones stood between the gates and the main doors, a clear stretch of unbroken snow twisting in a sweeping curve from here to there. Probably very pretty in normal circumstances, but not so great when you were strapped into ten or twelve tonnes of hurtling snowplough.

The first headstone hit the huge metal blade mounted to the front of the truck with an almighty clang, and went flying, swiftly followed by the next and the next and the next as he literally ploughed his way through the graves, heading straight for a pair of figures by the church doors – caught in the glare of the snowplough's headlights.

Was that Mr Bishop?

It *was*. Only he wasn't in his wheelchair, or hunched over like a little auld mannie any more: he was standing tall with a gun in his hand. Mouth hanging open, eyes wide as he stared at the oncoming behemoth and its flickering hazard beacon.

Then the gun arm snapped up.

Oh *shite*.

Edward ducked sideways, keeping hold of the wheel as a hot-white flash sparked off the snowplough's blade. Then another and another and another. Pinging and ricocheting. Three shots cracked through the windscreen, spiderwebbing it – punching holes out through the back of the cab.

And the church was getting really, really close . . .

He stomped on the brakes as two more rounds clanged into the big metal blade, the steering wheel jerking as a Celtic cross whirled up to batter off the snowplough's roof, stoving it in about eight inches.

'AAAAAAAAAAAAAAAAAAARGH!'

The brake pedal shuddered and thrummed beneath his foot, the whole truck rocking forwards as they bit, tyres skidding across the snow, grinding their way through what sounded like gravel as the engine stalled and the plough *finally* came to a halt.

Edward stayed low, shifting just enough to peer over the top of the dashboard and the edge of the blade.

Marky was standing there, inches away from that wall of scarred metal, eyes wide as dinner plates, mouth hanging open, arm still outstretched – the slide on his semi-automatic pistol locked in the back position. Out of ammunition. Then a dark stain spread across the crotch of his pale trousers.

Looked like that prostate of his had got over its performance anxiety. Bit undignified, though.

Behind him, Bigtoria slumped against the church doors. Her left leg glistened with blood – from the nasty hole in her mid-thigh all the way down, past her wellies, and into the snow at her feet. A thick, dark trail of it was smeared along the wall, disappearing around the corner.

Ah . . .

That wasn't good.

She pushed off the doors, though, and limped forwards – left knee locked, thumping down the stairs on her heel. Hobbling towards Mr Bishop with her teeth bared. 'HOY, MARKY!'

Mr Bishop turned to face her, just in time for Bigtoria's fist to smash right into his nose.

And down he went. Like a sack of tatties.

Edward opened the driver's door and waved at her. 'Need a lift?'

She sagged forwards, forearms on top of the plough's blade – holding herself up, head hanging, eyes closed, puffing and panting and clearly in a *massive* amount of pain. 'You're *late*.'

'Yeah.' He grinned. 'I get that a lot.'

—enter the cavalry—

(better late than never)

39

Amazing the difference a bit of sunshine made. The sky was a brilliant shade of Saltire blue; the birds were tweeting in the trees; and best of all, it hadn't snowed in three whole days.

Hallelujah, pass the communion wine and a bag of cheese and onion, it's party time.

Edward stepped out of the station's side door onto a soggy pavement – damp with meltwater and gritty with salt and sand – pausing for a moment to shut his eyes and turn his face to the glorious sun, soaking up those lovely warm rays.

Mmmmm . . .

Then a nice sip of hot chocolate.

Then a happy sigh.

A collection of patrol cars and unmarked vehicles and Black Marias – which weren't actually black these days, but never mind – and white Transit vans full of scene-examination kit, was parked outside the station, lining the road on both sides. An ambulance had recently joined the fun: sitting directly opposite the side door, its swirling lights giving the place a festive flair.

No sign of the tow truck yet, though, so the Big Car remained where Sergeant Farrow had left it – the front end all buckled around the memorial clock tower. Which didn't seem to be working any more – the hands were stuck at twenty past two and the red curfew line had fallen off. Other than that, it was fine.

The snow hadn't completely disappeared. Drifts of the stuff

lay piled up at the side of the road, their pristine white tainted a dirty shade of grey, but you could actually see tarmac in places now.

The plough rumbled down the street towards him; PC Phil 'Shammy' Samson behind the wheel with a gauze bandage wrapped around his head and a great-big smile on his face as he wound down the driver's window, honked the horn, and bellowed out a cheery 'EDWAAAAAAAAAAAAAAAAAAARD!' on the way past.

Nice to be appreciated.

Edward gave him a wee wave – halfway between a salute and doffing an imaginary cap.

Had another sip of sweet, chocolatey goodness.

Happy sigh.

The station door clunked open and out came Sergeant Farrow and Constable Harlaw, squinting in the sunlight, hands cuffed behind their backs, paisley-pattern bruises mottling their angry faces. They glared at him as uniformed constables marched them across the road to a pair of waiting patrol cars.

He toasted them with his hot chocolate. 'Lovely day!'

Got nothing but glowers in return.

Some people were just rude.

They were still giving him the evil eye as the patrol cars pulled away from the kerb, taking them off to Aberdeen for a trip to the Sheriff Court and, hopefully, a nice long stay in a cosy prison somewhere.

Couldn't happen to a nicer pair of arseholes.

He watched them dwindle into the distance.

When he turned back, there was Jenna Kirkdale, sashaying along the pavement. She wasn't wearing the high-vis-and-beanie-hat ensemble she'd worn when fixing the station's Airwaves, swapping IT chic for jeans and a shirt and a nice jacket. The greying hair had gone too, swapped for an out-of-the-packet, rich auburn-brown, styled and curling around her shoulders.

Scrubbed up well.

She crossed the road and stopped right in front of Edward. Just a *little bit* too close for comfort. Sending a wave of heat spiralling up his neck and cheeks. 'Hey, handsome.' Looking up at him with those big doe eyes. 'My poor battered hero.'

He swallowed. 'Ms Kirkdale.'

'Come on, Eddie, you can call me Jenna.' Biting her bottom lip. 'Or "Sexypants", if you're feeling frisky.' She inched even closer. 'You're not leaving us, are you?' Putting on a Cupid's bow pout. 'We've only just met.'

Edward backed away, but the station wall blocked off his only line of escape. 'Yes . . . Ermm . . .' He cleared his throat. 'I've got . . . you know . . . with all the arrests?'

She closed the gap again, pressing right up against him, sand-wiching him between her breasts and the cladding. Gazing at him through her eyelashes as she fingered his shirt buttons. 'I'm going to *miss* you, Eddie. You will come back and visit me sometime, won't you?' Her pink tongue slid along those shiny cherry lips, slow and suggestive. 'We could have a *lot* – of *very – naughty – fun*.'

Eeek . . .

His eyes went wide as she stood on her tiptoes, grabbed both sides of his head, and dragged him into a massive snogging kiss. Holding him there.

A voice cut through the ringing in his ears. *'Ahem!'*

It didn't stop Ms Kirkdale, though.

'Am I interrupting *something?'* Bigtoria.

Ms Kirkdale released her grip on Edward, reached round and had a quick grope of his bum. 'Don't be a stranger, Eddie.' A wink, and she was off, whistling a jaunty tune and putting a *lot* of wiggle in her walk.

'Anything you'd like to tell me, Detective Constable Reekie?' Big-toria's face was creased, her eyes narrow mouth pinched. Clearly, whatever Doc Griffiths had prescribed, it wasn't strong enough. She was propped up on a thick wooden walking stick, a loose pair of jogging bottoms swollen out around her left thigh where all the bandages must've been.

Still, at least the bruises she'd got arresting Siobhan Wilkins were starting to fade. *His* were in full bloom.

Edward straightened his hair, heat radiating from his face like a three-bar electric fire. 'Thanks for rescuing me, Guv.' A shudder wriggled its way between his shoulder blades. 'No idea why she finds me so . . . you know: irresistible.'

Bigtoria snorted, shifted her weight, winced. 'Hate to burst your bubble, *Casanova*, but imagine you're a single woman living here, and the only available men are paedophiles, rapists, killers, or violent bastards. Even a lanky streak of pish like you is a catch, compared to that.'

Wow. Way to give his ego a boost.

Time to change the subject to something a little less cripplingly embarrassing.

Edward pointed at the ambulance. 'This your ride home?'

'Not quite.'

Right on cue, the station door clattered open and a pair of paramedics trundled Mr Bishop out in that squeaky old wheelchair of his. He was all hunched into himself, trembling away beneath the NHS blanket they'd wrapped around his shoulders. A second one covering his skeletal knees. Yet another oxygen mask on his bruised face. Not quite big enough to hide the *massive* shiner Bigtoria had given him.

Edward sucked air through his teeth. Kept his voice down. 'Cheeky bastard.'

Mr Bishop raised a shaky arthritic claw and pointed it at Bigtoria. Doing his best impersonation of a proper wobbly OAP. 'She hit me! . . . I didn't do anything . . . I'm a poor, sick . . . *dying* old man . . . and she hit me.'

Bigtoria tried a lopsided loom. 'YOU'RE NOT FOOLING ANYONE, YOU LYING GIT!'

The paramedics frowned at her, clearly shocked at the lack of compassion on display from the big lady with the pronounced limp. They fussed Mr Bishop's wheelchair into the back of the ambulance, and off it went too.

Glenfarach was a busy little town today.

Wasn't over yet, though, because a figure in the full Police Scotland uniform emerged from the station: all proud chin and steely blue eyes as she watched the ambulance disappear down East Main

Street. She pulled her bowler hat on – complete with a band of black-and-white Sillitoe tartan, oversized crest, bar, and oak leaves – matching the crown and pip on her epaulettes. Then turned her gaze on Bigtoria, raised an eyebrow, and drawled out a public-school accent with more than a hint of Glaswegian hiding underneath. 'Hardly *professional*, Detective Inspector.'

'Sorry, Boss.' Not sounding sorry in the slightest. 'Must be the painkillers from when Marky Bishop *shot* me.'

'Hmph . . .' Chief Superintendent Pine looked Edward up and down. 'And I understand you were instrumental in saving the DI here, capturing Mr Bishop, breaking up a drug ring, arresting two corrupt police officers, and rescuing a social worker from a rape gang.'

Edward wiped a hand across his mouth – in case Ms Kirkdale had left any lipstick or lip-gloss behind – and stood up nice and straight. 'Yes, Boss. Thank you, Boss.'

'Well done.' The Chief Superintendent patted him on the shoulder. Then straightened her hat. 'Now, if you'll excuse me, I have to go figure out what we're going to do with this whole clusterfuck of a situation.' A nod, and she headed back inside, leaving them to the sunshine.

'Wasn't that nice?' Edward took a sip of hot chocolate. 'One thing I don't understand, Guv – you can't have *planned* to get snowed in, so what was the—'

'Guthrie and I would've had car trouble and been stuck in town. Next morning the Duty Inspector calls in sick and asks me to sub for him. Leaving *me* free to work on Marky Bishop.' She sniffed and looked off down the street. 'Instead, I had to make the best of what I was lumbered with.'

Wait a sodding minute.

'Lumbered? You heard the Chief Super.' He poked himself in the chest with his thumb. 'Hero of the hour, here.'

Bigtoria cleared her throat. 'Yes. Well.' She cricked her neck from side to side. Shuffled her weight on the walking stick. Looked off down the street again. 'Thank you for . . . saving my life. I'll be recommending you for a promotion.'

That was more like it.

He grinned. 'I think we make a pretty good team, don't you?'

Her eyes narrowed.

'Seriously, Guv, we should do this more often.'

'Don't push it.' She limped away towards Market Square, where their manky Vauxhall chariot awaited.

He was definitely growing on her – you could tell from the warmth and bonhomie oozing out of her like frozen rice pudding.

It was a start anyway.

Edward took another swig of hot chocolate. Maybe now would be a good time to—

Bigtoria's voice barked out through the clear sunny air. 'Are you coming or not?'

Grin.

See?

And last, but not least, Stuart says thank you . . .

This book, like all the others I've written, wouldn't have been possible without the help of some very clever people. And it would be rude of me to get to the end of this story and not say thank you to them for all the effort they've put into keeping me on the straight and narrow.

So, here's a great-big 'thank you' to my indispensable font of all things policey, Inspector Bruce Crawford; my excellent editor, Frankie Gray; Imogen Nelson, Sarah Adams, Bill Scott-Kerr, Kate Samano, Richenda Todd, Josh Benn, Jessica Read, Jason Ward, Tom Chicken, Laura Garrod, Emily Harvey, Laura Ricchetti, Natasha Photiou, Louise Blakemore, Julia Teece, Louis Patel, Leon Dufour, Marie Goodwin, Emma Matthews, Lucy Middleton, Phil Evans, Richard Ogle, Sarah Scarlett, Lucy Beresford-Knox, Larry Finlay; top-notch Stuart wrangler, Tom Hill; and everyone else who makes Transworld tick; the pocket-rocket force of nature that is Phil Patterson, Guy Herbert, Leah Middleton, Sandra Sawicka, and the team at Marjacq Scripts; and m'good friend and colleague, Mr Allan Buchan, AKA: Allan Guthrie, whose keen eye and input are very much appreciated.

And let's not forget all the booksellers and librarians out there who do so much to keep civilization from crumbling into A Swamp Of Stupid™. Then there's you. Yes: you – the person reading this book! Mankind seems to get collectively thicker by the day, but THANK YOU for fighting the tide!

As ever, I couldn't have done any of this without Fiona, but let's also give an honourable mention to Onion, Beetroot, and Gherkin. Who haven't actually *helped*, but at least they haven't interfered too much (except for Beetroot).

Stuart MacBride is the *Sunday Times* No.1 bestselling author of the Logan McRae and Ash Henderson novels. He's also published standalones, novellas, and short stories, as well as a slightly twisted children's picture book for slightly twisted children.

Stuart lives in the wilds of north-east Scotland with his wife Fiona; cats Gherkin, Onion, and Beetroot; some hens; some horses; and an impressive collection of assorted weeds.

For more information visit:
StuartMacBride.com
Facebook.com/StuartMacBrideBooks
@StuartMacBride

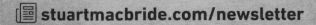

Read the instant *Sunday Times* bestseller

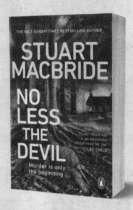

'We are each our own devil,
and we make this world our hell.'

It's been seventeen months since the Bloodsmith butchered his first victim and Operation Maypole is still no nearer to catching him. The media is whipping up a storm, the top brass are demanding results, but the investigation is sinking fast.

Now isn't the time to get distracted with other cases, but Detective Sergeant Lucy McVeigh doesn't have much choice. When Benedict Strachan was just eleven, he hunted down and killed a homeless man. No one's ever figured out why Benedict did it, but now, after sixteen years, he's back on the streets again — battered, frightened, convinced a shadowy 'They' are out to get him, and begging Lucy for help.

It sounds like paranoia, but what if he's right? What if he really is caught up in something bigger and darker than Lucy's ever dealt with before? What if the Bloodsmith isn't the only monster out there? And what's going to happen when Lucy goes after them?

OUT NOW IN PAPERBACK, EBOOK AND AUDIO

dead
good

Looking for more gripping must-reads?

Head over to Dead Good —
the home of killer crime books,
TV and film.

Whether you're on the hunt for an intriguing
mystery, an action-packed thriller
or a creepy psychological drama,
we're here to keep you in the loop.

Get recommendations and reviews from
crime fans, grab discounted books at bargain
prices and enter exclusive giveaways
for the chance to read brand-new releases
before they hit the shelves.

Sign up for the free newsletter:
www.deadgoodbooks.co.uk/newsletter